PAULA DANZIGER

DEAN

Everyone Else's Parents Said Yes first published in Great Britain 1989
Make Like A Tree And Leave first published in Great Britain 1990
Earth To Matthew first published in Great Britain 1991
Not For A Billion Gazillion Dollars first published in Great Britain 1992
All by William Heinemann Ltd

This special omnibus edition first published 1994 by Dean
an imprint of Reed Consumer Books Limited
Michelin House, 81 Fulham Road, London SW3 6RB
and Auckland, Melbourne, Singapore and Toronto

Published by arrangement with Dell Publishing Co., Inc.,
New York, New York, U.S.A.

Map in *Earth To Matthew* courtesy of The Franklin Institute Science Museum,
Philadelphia, Pa. Although there really is a Califon, N.J., the incidents and characters are
fictional. The schedule and activities at Camp-In are constantly changing and growing,
so the ones depicted in this book may no longer be in practice or they may be fictional.

ISBN 0 603 55371 0

A CIP catalogue record for this title is available from the British Library

Printed in Great Britain by The Bath Press

Everyone Else's Parents
Said Yes

To Fran and Jules Davids,
with a lifetime of love

ACKNOWLEDGMENTS

Patricia Reilly Giff: for support and "noodging"
The Danzigers: Barry, Annette, Sam, Carrie, Ben and Josh
The Stantons: Frank, David, Paul and Brian
The Children All Over The Country Who Have Shared Their Ideas, Experiences And Suggestions

CHAPTER 1

'Mom. You know there are only five more days, fifteen hours and thirty-two minutes until my birthday party.' Matthew enters the kitchen holding a computer printout.

Matthew Martin can be very organised and accurate when he wants to be, and he wants to be. Since he's the youngest person in his sixth grade class, birthdays really count.

'I know, honey.One hour ago, you came in here and told me that there were only five more days, *sixteen* hours and thirty-two minutes until your birthday party.' Mrs Martin can also be very organised and accurate, even while she is busy following the recipe for zucchini carob chip bread.

'Listen to him. You'd think that no one ever had an eleventh birthday before.' Amanda Martin applies polish to her very bitten down nails and wrinkles her nose at her brother. 'I didn't make a big fuss about it two years ago when I had my eleventh birthday. You're such a big baby.'

'Two years ago, you *did* make a big fuss about it.'

Mrs Martin grins, reminding her. 'Nothing would do but to take twelve girls to *ADORNABLE YOU*, the store where you make things to decorate yourself.'

Matthew offers, 'I'll get the picture out of the scrapbook to prove it. You and those goofy girls wearing . . .' Pausing, he puts his hand on his hip and acts like a model. 'All those silly feather things and ugly sparkly jewellery. Goofy, goofy girls. Yuck.'

'Shut up, runt.' Amanda glares at him.

'I'm not a runt. Just a little short for my age. Daddy says he was like that too, and now look at how tall he is!' Matthew shouts at her. 'And look at you, runt chest, who do you think you are?'

Mrs Martin sighs. 'Amanda, stop calling your brother a runt and Matthew, don't refer to your sister's chest as a runt chest. In fact, don't refer to your sister's chest at all.'   Amanda and Matthew can tell that their mother is trying not to grin.

Amanda stands up and yells, 'It's not funny! He's disgusting. I hate him. And you make it worse by laughing at what he says. Why did he ever have to be born? Why did I?'

'She always acts like the big shot she isn't.' Matthew sticks his tongue out at her.

Amanda stomps out of the room.

Mrs Martin puts her hand on her head, leaving batter on her forehead. 'Children. I should have got goldfish as pets instead.'

'Then you could have had a pool party for the

goldfishes' birthday.' Matthew licks the cake beaters.

Wiping the batter off her forehead, Mrs Martin says, 'Very funny. Now Matthew, I want you to stop teasing your sister so much. She's just entering adolescence, actually stomping her way into it, and it's not going to be an easy time for her. Not for her . . . not for me . . . not for any of us, I have a feeling.'

'I was born to drive her nuts,' Matthew informs her. 'And we both know that's not going to be a long trip.'

'Matthew.' His mother has a way of saying the name so that it takes forever and means stop being a wise guy.

'Oh, okay, Mom.' Matthew puts down the cake beaters. 'Now, about the party: you said I should think about it. Well, I've decided. I want a sleep-over in the garden.'

'Okay. Remember, your father and I work hard and we need your help with the party.' Mrs Martin smiles.

'Right.' Matthew shows her the computer print-out in his hands. 'Don't worry. I've got everything under control. Here are the lists.'

Mrs Martin pours the batter into a pan, puts the pan into the oven, sets the timer, washes and dries her hands, and finally sits down to look over Matthew's lists.

THE KIDS

BILLY KELLERMAN
TYLER WHITE
JOSHUA JACKSON
BRIAN BRUNO
DAVID COHEN
PATRICK RYAN
MARK ELLISON
PABLO MARTINEZ

THE FOOD

HOT DOGS

HAMBURGERS

POTATO CHIPS

SODA

CAKE

ICE CREAM

ALL THE JUNK FOOD
IN THE WORLD

8

THINGS TO DO

GET PRESENTS

OPEN PRESENTS

HAVE COMPUTER NINTENDO TOURNAMENTS

GIVE OUT PRIZES TO TOURNAMENT WINNERS

EAT

ALL OF US MAKE FUN OF AMANDA AT ONCE

TELL JOKES

GIVE OUT PRIZES FOR BEST JOKES

GO TO SLEEP

WAKE UP

EAT

ALL OF US MAKE FUN OF HOW AMANDA
LOOKS IN THE MORNING

EVERYONE GOES HOME

PLAY WITH MY PRESENTS

'I think that you are going to have to re-examine your lists.' Matthew's mother smiles. 'The guest list is fine but there are a few items in the other lists that will have to go.'

'Okay, so we won't go to sleep.' Matthew grins at her.

'That's not it, kiddo.' She pats him on the head. 'You will leave your sister out of this.'

'That's all I ever want to do: leave my sister out of everything, my life, the house . . .' Matthew sticks his fingers into the left over zucchini batter and then licks them.

'Matthew.'

'Oh, okay. I'll take all of the stuff about her off the lists. Then will everything else be okay?'

Another 'Matthew.'

'Yes.' He grins, knowing what she's going to say.

'I really feel that you should reconsider all that awful junk food on your list and make some healthy substitutions — carob candy, fruit bars, things like that.'

'Come on, Mom. Everyone else's parents let them eat junk food.'

Mrs Martin sighs. 'Matthew Martin. How many times must I tell you that we're not everyone else's parents. If everyone else's parents let them jump off the roof, should we let *you* jump off the roof?'

'It's just a little junk food, not nuclear destruction,' Matthew pleads.

'I'm not sure that there's much difference between eating junk food and nuclear destruction.'

Mrs Martin shakes her head.

Matthew sometimes wishes that his mother were more like his best friend Joshua Jackson's mother, who says things like, 'Isn't Granola a Latin American country?' and 'Tofu, isn't that the crud under your toenails?'

'Mom, please. Look, the guys will hate me if we serve the stuff you like. They call *that* stuff junk food, and even Dad likes junk food . . . and anyway, everyone else's . . .' Matthew stops himself from repeating his favourite phrase.

Mrs Martin sighs again. 'This is against my better judgement, but all right. You may have *some* junk food at your party. It's a losing battle with you sometimes, but I'm telling you right now. I'm going to make a very healthy cake.'

'Oh, okay.' Matthew tries to look sad, like he's giving in, but deep down inside he feels like he's won the Super Bowl prize for Handling Mothers. He's actually got his mother to agree to some junk food!

It was going to be a great party, no doubt about it.

CHAPTER 2

'Hey, want to swap desserts?' Matthew stares at the contents of Joshua Jackson's lunch box.

'Are you kidding? Your mom makes you eat healthy junk.'

Joshua takes out a packet of three cupcakes, which are filled with cream and covered with marshmallow and coconut icing.

'Please, I'll be your best friend if you share those with me.' Matthew holds back a drool.

'You already are my best friend.' Joshua starts taking the cellophane off the cupcakes.

'Ummm. Look at this.' Matthew holds up his dessert.

'What is it?' Joshua makes a face.

'Wholewheat fruit slices. Yummy. I'd be willing to give up four of them, all four of them, for just one of your three cupcakes. What a deal!' Matthew holds up the packet as if he's holding up a trophy.

'No deal.' Joshua licks the top of one of the cupcakes and then takes a bite out of it.

'I'll be your best *best* friend,' Matthew pleads.

'You said that last week. What was that mess I swapped a cupcake for?'

'Cottage Cheese Yoghurt Cake,' Matthew reminds him. 'Oh, Joshua. This is better. Come on. Please. I can't help it if my mother makes me eat this stuff.'

Joshua looks at his remaining two cupcakes and then at his best friend. 'Here's the deal. I give you the cupcake. You don't give me the fruit slices.'

'Fair deal.' Matthew reaches for a cupcake.

'Not yet.' Joshua stops Matthew's hand in mid-grab. 'You have to help me learn how to play Defender Dragons better.'

Defender Dragons. Matthew's best computer game, the one where he racks up the highest scores of anyone in the class, of anyone in the entire school.

Matthew looks at his friend, then at the cupcake, and back to his friend. The cupcake. The friend. 'All right, not all of my manoeuvres, but enough to get you to the next level. How about that?'

'It's a deal.' Joshua hands over a cupcake and thinks that with the kind of stuff Matthew's mother cooks, he's going to be able to learn how to get to all of the levels.

As Matthew puts the cupcake into his mouth, he tries to eat it slowly, tasting every little bit, licking the icing, eating the cake, saving the cream centre until the end.

It's too late. Something in Matthew acts like a

vacuum cleaner, sucking up the cupcake in what seems like seconds.

Looking down at the wholewheat fruit slices, Matthew thinks of how his parents are always telling him not to waste food, to think of the poor starving people in the world.

Mr Farley, the head lunchroom monitor, goes up to the microphone, taps it and yells into it. *'All right, you kids!* It's time to go out to the playground. Don't forget the rules. Make sure all litter is put in the bins, go out quietly, no pushing or shoving and if anyone has spilled milk or food, notify us immediately so that no one gets hurt.'

Mr Farley has been very worried about spilling since the time he rushed over to stop a fight between two sixth grade boys and he slipped on milk and banana.

He broke his foot and used crutches for a long time to walk and once to separate the same two sixth grade boys who were fighting again.

Everyone rushes out.

Mr Farley steps back.

Matthew gets into line to throw out his rubbish.

Lizzie Doran is in front of him.

Stepping on the back of her sneakers, he says, 'Ooops, so sorry.'

She turns round. 'I know you're not sorry. Matthew Martin, you are so immature.'

'Thank you.' Matthew loves to annoy Lizzie.

'You're not welcome.' She turns her back and ignores him.

Matthew smiles.

School gets boring sometimes, he thinks. It's fun to do stuff like this.

Matthew throws out his rubbish, holding on to his dessert which he places under a tree outside thinking that maybe some poor starving birds would like to eat it.

As he looks down at the wholewheat fruit slices, he thinks that the birds won't like it either, that they would prefer worms, that he would probably prefer worms if he were a bird.

'Keepaway! Sixth grade boys over here to play Keepaway,' Brian Bruno is yelling.

Joshua and Matthew run over to where Brian is standing with the ball and start running from it as fast as they can.

Matthew is beaned by Tyler White.

As Matthew stands on the sidelines and watches, he is glad that Tyler White is no good at Defender Dragons.

Looking round the playground, Matthew checks on what everyone is doing. The six graders are hogging all the best spaces, like they always do. At Elizabeth Englebert Elementary, where the cheer 'Go E.E.E.' sounds like pigs squealing, the sixth graders get dibs on practically everything.

Matthew has waited a long time for his class to reach the sixth grade. The next big event for him will be becoming a teenager.

Matthew thinks about his approaching birthday and how he's getting closer.

Looking at the sixth grade girls who are also playing Keepaway but at the other side of the playground, Matthew thinks about how it was back in the old days at E.E.E. when they all played together, not just in gym class.

Something had changed and now it was all different.

Matthew remembers how he spent the first few weeks getting used to the school's new computer graphics program and teaching all the boys how to make fancy signs for their doors that said ALL GIRLS, KEEP OUT. THIS MEANS YOU.

It amazed Matthew that not all of the boys were interested in making that sign, that some of them even wanted to make others — especially Patrick Ryan, who made one that said ALL GIRLS, ENTER. THIS MEANS YOU.

Mark Ellison is out next, yelling, 'Not fair!'

Mark Ellison always thinks it isn't fair when he loses.

Then Patrick Ryan is out. He walks away making jokes as if he doesn't care, but he does. Patrick Ryan plays to win.

Soon it is down to Joshua against Tyler White.

Tyler throws the ball at Joshua's head, but Joshua ducks, grabs the ball and throws it at Tyler, hitting him on the rear end.

Everyone cheers and gives high fives to Joshua.

Heads you lose, tails you win, thinks Matthew as the bell rings, signalling back-to-class time.

Usually Matthew hates that bell, but not today.

Today he's going to ask Mrs Stanton for time to do his party invitations using the new computer graphics program.

He can hardly wait.

CHAPTER 3

'We sent out two gorillas in tutus, one six-foot tall pink singing chicken, four tap dancing birthday cakes, a teddy bear on roller skates and a grand-mother who delivers chicken soup.' Mrs Martin hands the plate of broccoli to Mr Martin. 'And that was just the early part of today.'

Mr Martin is interested in his wife's new job at the place that sends out people in costumes to deliver singing telegrams, gifts, balloonograms and other surprises for special occasions. 'What about later in the day?'

'It was a disaster. There were only two major jobs — a birthday party for a six-year-old and a fiftieth wedding anniversary. Mickey Mouse and Minnie Mouse were supposed to tap dance a birthday song to the kid and a man in a tuxedo was supposed to deliver a dozen roses to the couple. Did that happen? No. It did not.'

Waiting for a minute to build up the suspense, Mrs Martin shrugs.

Matthew, trying to find a good place to hide the

18

broccoli, asks, 'What happened?'

'Mrs Grimbell, the owner, made a mistake and confused the orders. She seems a little distracted. Anyway, the guy in the tuxedo delivered the roses to the boy who kept saying, 'Where are my helium balloons? I wanted us to inhale them and make our voices change,' and the couple could not quite believe that there, in their own living room, were Mickey and Minnie tap dancing "Happy Anniversary to You," and throwing confetti all over the place.'

'What did the old folks say?' Mathew chops up his broccoli and puts it under the rim of his plate.

'The woman kept saying, "Look at this mess. Are you planning to vacuum it up?" and the husband said, "Helium balloons. Great. We can inhale them and listen to our voices."' Mrs Martin laughs.

'It sounds much more exciting than my day,' Mr Martin says. 'Want to swap? I'll take your job and you can be a lawyer.'

'Nope.' Mrs Martin shakes her head. 'I like what I'm doing. However, maybe you can help out. There's a chance that tomorrow I will be one person short. Would you be willing to put on a gorilla suit and go to an engagement party, wearing a sign that says, *Melvin Goes Ape Over Gina*?'

'I'd love to.' Mr Martin nods. 'And then I can wear the gorilla suit in court. That way the people who believe that there's a lot of *monkey business* going on in court will think that they have proof.'

'Daddy. Don't. I'd die if anyone saw you dressed

19

as a gorilla,' Amanda whines. 'And Mom, why can't you get a normal job like other mothers? You do this just to embarrass me. Everyone's asking if you do strip grams.'

'Not me personally.' Mrs Martin acts horrified. 'And Amanda, your father and I are just kidding around. He's not going to get dressed in costumes.'

'Shucks.' Mr Martin looks sad. 'You have all the fun. You can dress up in all these costumes.'

'Only if it's an emergency. That's not my regular job,' Mrs Martin reminds them.

'Mom. Promise you won't wear costumes. I would die!' Amanda begs and threatens.

Mrs Martin shrugs. 'A woman's got to do what a woman's got to do.'

Deciding to change the subject, Mrs Martin holds up the plate.

'Anyone want seconds of the tuna tofu casserole?'

'No thanks.' Matthew shakes his head, waves the plate away and wonders what Joshua is eating tonight.

'No thanks, honey.' Mr Martin looks down at his half full plate and remembers the great meal he had at lunch. 'So, kids, how was your day?'

'Great.'

'Terrible.'

Both responses come out at the same time.

'Which of you would like to go first?' Mr Martin asks.

'He might as well, since his day was so wonderful

and mine wasn't.' Amanda bites her nails.

'Honey, stop biting your nails.' Mrs Martin reaches for Amanda's hand.

Amanda pulls her hand away.

Matthew decides to ignore Amanda and speak. 'Mrs Stanton gave me permission to work on my party invitations using the new program, and I've decided what to put in the goody bag, and everyone I'm inviting is going to be able to come to the sleepover.'

'What do you need the invitations for, then?' Amanda asks.

Matthew continues to ignore Amanda. 'And I've got a great idea for the design of the invitation and the graphics and the colours.'

'I really should upgrade our machine.' Mr Martin thinks out loud.

Amanda jabs at her tuna tofu. 'Doesn't anyone care about my day? All he's talking about is making up invitations for the party to send to people who already know about it and have already said that they're coming. How dumb can you get?'

'Amanda.' Mrs Martin makes the name sound five times as long.

'Well, it's true. And here I sit with my life in a shambles, and it's all your fault.' Amanda's lower lip moves forward.

'Why is it our fault?' Mr Martin asks.

'Today, Bobby Fenton called me *four eyes*.'

Well, she is, Matthew thinks, annoyed at being interrupted. The four F's: — Four Eyed, Flat, Funny

Looking, and Fingernail-Stubbed.

He bites his lip to keep from saying it out loud. No reason to take a chance on getting grounded just before his party.

Amanda starts to cry. 'It's all your fault. If only you'd let me get contact lenses. . .'

'No. We've been through this already. Dr Sugarman says to wait a little bit longer. By next year, you can get them.'

'Next year,' Amanda sighs. 'Everyone else's parents let them get contact lenses this year.'

Not true, Matthew thinks, knowing at least six of her classmates who wear glasses.

'We're not everyone else's parents.' Her mother says. 'We're your parents and we say that you must wait for the lenses until the doctor thinks it's right.'

'A year.' Amanda makes a face. 'Well, at least let me have plastic surgery, then.'

'What!' Her parents yell at the same time.

'For my ears. One is lower than the other and my glasses are crooked. If my ears were even, the glasses wouldn't be tilted.'

Everyone looks at Amanda's face.

Everyone thinks her glasses look perfectly fine.

Mr and Mrs Martin think her face looks perfectly fine.

Matthew thinks she should have plastic surgery on her entire face.

'Amanda. Be reasonable. Dr Sugarman said that there was a slight difference in your ears, that many people have that problem and that all it takes is to adjust the glasses a little. He did that. There's no problem. You are very pretty.' her father says.

'You're my father. You have to say that.' A tear rolls down Amanda's face.

Matthew cannot understand what she's making such a big deal about and hopes that he doesn't turn weird when he becomes a teenager.

He also thinks about how long it will be before she goes away to college and he has the house and his parents to himself. Too long. Not soon enough.

Tomorrow wouldn't be soon enough, let alone five years.

While Amanda continues, Matthew tunes out and thinks about the contents of the goody bag that each person at the party will get — M&Ms, a box of raisins, Sweet Tarts, wax teeth with fangs, a packet of baseball cards with bubble gum, and one of those liquorice rolls with a sweet centre. He's happy with the choices — junk food with one healthy thing, the raisins, to make his mother a little happier. To make himself a little happier, he would have added about eight other kinds of sweets, but his parents and the budget that they gave him wouldn't allow it.

He tunes back in to what's happening.

Amanda is still talking. 'And it's all your fault that I have to wear glasses. If you two didn't have bad eyes, I wouldn't.'

Matthew thinks, maybe she should blame it on their grandparents. They had to wear glasses, too. Maybe she should blame it on the dinosaurs. They probably caused cavemen to squint from looking up at them. Then the cavemen needed glasses and it was passed on to future generations.

Amanda doesn't give up. 'And it's not fair. Look at that little twerp. He doesn't have to wear glasses.'

'That's because they like me better than they like you,' Matthew teases. 'And my ears aren't even lop-sided.'

Matthew has trouble stopping once he starts. 'And I'm not ugly, and dumb, and acting like a turkey.'

Amanda stands up. 'You repulsive little runt.'

'Enough!' Mrs Martin yells.

'To your rooms. Both of you,' Mr Martin orders.

'It's not my fault!' Amanda and Matthew yell at the same time.

'Well, it's definitely not our fault,' their father says. 'I want you to go to your rooms and think about what you've done.'

Both kids go off to their rooms, mumbling, 'It's not fair. It's not my fault.'

Matthew goes to his room and thinks about what he's done. Nothing.

It's Amanda's fault.

It always is.

Someday, he thinks, *some* day, I'm going to get even.

CHAPTER 4

I I I I = 4 EYES

= FOUR EYES

$$\frac{2 GOOFY}{2 BE} \; 4 \; GIVEN$$

AMANDA MARTIN

Roses are red,
Violets are perkle.
Amanda Martin is a four-eyed jerkle.

'Matthew. That's not very nice.' Mrs Stanton looks over his shoulder. 'And I don't think that you've really followed the assignment.'

'Why not?' Matthew, with an ink mark on his nose, looks up at her. 'You said that we should make up a greeting card using words and numbers. Well, I did.'

'That's not a very nice greeting,' Mrs Stanton tells him.

'It's for my sister. She's not a very nice person so she doesn't deserve a very nice greeting card. The only greeting she ever gives me is, "Get out of my way, nerd face."'

'Matthew. When your sister was in my class, she was very nice. I know that brothers and sisters don't always get along.' Mrs Stanton speaks softly. 'But your sister is really very nice. Some day, I'm sure you will realise it.'

Matthew says, 'I'm never going to like my sister. She's turned into a monster. We're never going to get along, ever. Not now. Not when we're ninety.'

'Well, I hope that you aren't always going to feel that way, and Matthew, you really shouldn't call people names. It's not right to call someone four-eyes.'

Matthew realises that Mrs Stanton is wearing glasses.

He's not sure what to say.

She continues, 'And you shouldn't call her a jerk.'

He knows what to say about that. 'I didn't. I

called her a jerkle. That's a word that I made up. It means "dear, sweet, wonderful sister."'

He can tell by the look on Mrs Stanton's face that she doesn't believe him.

He wouldn't believe himself either if he were the teacher.

Mrs Stanton sighs. 'Start again, Matthew. Throw that card away and start over.'

Matthew pleads, 'Do I have to?'

'Yes.' Mrs Stanton means business.

'I'll do a card to my mother and I'll throw this one away later.' He promises, knowing that there is no way that he wants to throw out the card to Amanda.

'It's your choice, Matthew. Throw that card away now and be able to use the computer later for your invitations or hold on to the card and not be able to use the computer later for your invitations.'

'Ah.' Matthew knows when he's beaten. 'I'll throw the card out now.'

'Good boy.' Mrs Stanton says.

Matthew goes up to the waste paper basket, puts the card in and thinks about how he's going to make another card when he gets home.

Jill Hudson calls out 'Oh. Oh. Oh!' She keeps waving her hand.

Jill Hudson finds it impossible to just hold up her hand and wait until she gets called on by a teacher. She has had this habit since kindergarten.

'Yes, Jill.' Mrs Stanton calls on her.

'Can I make an announcement to the class? Oh, Oh, Oh. It's very important.' Jill is practically jumping out of her chair.

'Very important?' Mrs Stanton doesn't sound so sure.

'Oh. Oh. *IT IS! IT IS!*'

'All right.' Mrs Stanton looks like she's not too sure that she's making the right decision.

Jill announces, 'I've decided that my name is very boring.'

'So are you!' Brian calls out and then pretends to yawn.

All of the boys start pretending to yawn.

Jill ignores them. 'Everyone else has nice names, like Cathy, who can also be called Cath, or Catherine. Lizzie can be Liz or Elizabeth. Ryma, whose mother promised to name her after her grandmother Mary, but made the name nice and different. Lisa Levine, whose names go well together. Vanessa, Jessica, Zoe and Chloe, who have beautiful names if people don't make them sound like they rhyme with toe.' Jill stands up at her desk. 'You know, if they make them rhyme with Joey —'

'Jill, please get to the point.' Mrs Stanton is grinning and shaking her head.

'I am. I am. Katie can be Kate or Katherine or Kath, and Sarah's name is just so pretty.'

'The point, Jill. You've named all of the girls in the class so get to the point.'

Mrs Stanton looks up at the clock on the wall. 'It's almost time for break.'

Jill gets to the point.

Jill is not the kind of person who likes to be late for break.

'I've decided to make my name more exciting. I can't change it to Jilly because the dumb boys will make it rhyme with Silly.'

'And Pilly and Dilly,' Tyler calls out.

'Billy and Jilly sitting in a tree.
K — I — S — S — I — N — G.'

'Shut up, Tyler!' Billy Kellerman yells out. 'I'm going to get you for that.'

'Children.' Mrs Stanton uses her 'very teacher' tone.

Jill ignores all the fuss. 'So I've decided that from now on my name will be spelt Jil!, with an explanation point at the end to make it more exciting.'

'Ex*clam*ation point,' Mrs Stanton grins.

'Whatever.' Jill, now Jil!, goes on, 'And when you say my name make it very dramatic, because that's what the explanat — because that's what that mark means.'

'Oh! Oh! Oh!' Pablo waves his hand, doing a Jil! imitation.

'Mrs Stanton, I think that it should be Jil? with a question mark instead. To show that it isn't easy to understand how Jil? got so weird.'

The bell rings for break.

Mrs Stanton excuses the class.

The students, except for Matthew, rush outside.

Matthew sits down at the computer, prepares a new disc, and begins.

It's going to be the best invitation ever.

29

CHAPTER 5

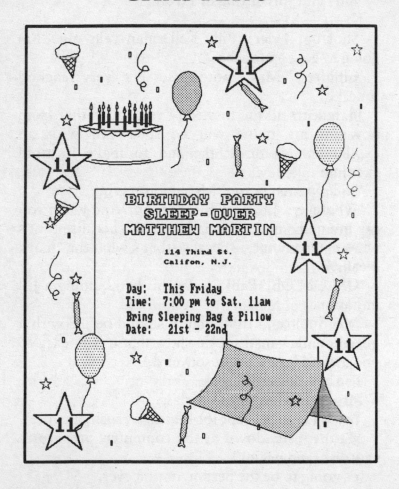

Computers.

Cakes.

Stars with elevens in them.

A tent.

All the important information.

It had taken Matthew the entire break and lunch period to finish, but it was worth it.

Everyone would know that Matthew Martin was the best in computer design.

He did the work himself.

No program for him.

He was the best.

No one could beat him at computer.

David Cohen was better at remembering the planets and elements.

Katie Delaney always won the spelling bees. In fact, practically everyone in the class was a better speller than Matthew.

Joshua and Tyler were great athletes.

Brian Bruno was already a brown belt in karate.

Best artist was Mark Ellison.

All the girls thought that Patrick Ryan was 'the cutest'.

Matthew doesn't care about cute. He doesn't think much about what he looks like. He knows that he has straight brown hair that never looks combed even when it is, because Amanda is always saying things like 'Doofus. You should use hair conditioner on that mess.' Amanda also says, 'Your eyes look like they could use a pooper scooper.' It's not the brown eyes that bother Matthew, but the freckles drive him nuts. His grandmother always pinches his cheeks and says, 'My darling little freckle face.' Matthew knows that he doesn't look like Frankenstein, Dracula or Freddy from Nightmare on Elm Street. What he doesn't know is what makes a girl think that someone's cute and actually he doesn't care that he doesn't know.

What he does care about is computers and no one could ever say that Matthew Martin wasn't the best at computer, especially after they see the invitations.

Matthew continues work on the invitations, adding little details, while the rest of the class comes running in.

'Hey, Matthew. You missed it. I got six baskets.' Joshua pretends to still be dribbling the ball.

'Great.' Matthew doesn't look up.

'Matthew. It was really fantastic. You should have been there.' Joshua tries to get his friend's attention.

Matthew still doesn't look up.

'That's it.' Joshua is getting annoyed. 'Stop with that stupid machine already. *Or else.*'

Looking up, Matthew sees that Joshua is holding on to the computer cord.

'Don't fool around with that!' Matthew yells.

In the background, he can hear Tyler singing 'Billy and Jilly sitting in a tree.'

'Stop that!' Billy yells, 'or you're going to be sorry — very sorry.'

Before Joshua can put down the computer cord, Billy pushes Tyler, who bumps into Joshua, who accidentally pulls the plug out of the extension.

It's all over for the invitation, which Matthew had not yet stored.

Matthew stares at the now darkened computer monitor.

Joshua comes over and looks at the screen. 'I'm sorry. I didn't mean to. It was an accident.'

The rest of the class comes into the room.

Mrs Stanton, who comes in last, takes one look at the room and rushes up to pull Billy off Tyler, who is lying face down on the floor.

'It was an accident. I slipped.' Billy tries to look innocent.

'Sit down.' Mrs Stanton points to a chair.

'Are you all right?' She helps Tyler get up and hands him a tissue for his bloody nose.

'Gross.' Chloe looks at the blood coming down Tyler's face.

Matthew continues to stare at the darkened monitor.

'Everyone sit down while I take care of this,' Mrs Stanton says.

'I'm sorry,' Joshua repeats, tugging on Matthew's sweatshirt. 'Come on. Say something.'

Matthew looks at the screen where four minutes earlier had been something that he had been planning for weeks and had worked on for most of the day, the free time part of the day.

It was all gone.

'Joshua. Go to your seat.' Mrs Stanton calls out. 'Now.'

'Say something,' Joshua says, before heading for his seat. 'Say something.'

Matthew glares at him and whispers, 'I hate you. I don't want you to come to my party. I don't want you to be my friend.'

'Well, if you feel that way about it, who cares. You act so dumb sometimes.' Joshua turns and goes to his seat.

'Matthew. Back to your seat too. You can finish that invitation later.' Mrs Stanton walks with Tyler to the door. 'Tyler, go to the nurse and then I want you to go to the principal's office and explain what happened.'

Billy Kellerman is smiling because Tyler has to go to the principal.

'You may go there right now, William Kellerman,' Mrs Stanton says.

Billy Kellerman stops smiling and gets up.

Matthew Martin is sitting at his desk and feeling rotten.

CHAPTER 6

Today has to be one of the worst days of Matthew's life.

Three whole days without speaking to Joshua . . . and today Joshua was really disgusting.

Joshua Jackson, his best friend — no, his ex-best friend — brought in bags and boxes of junk food for everyone, everyone except his best friend, his ex-best friend, Matthew Martin.

It must have cost him two months' allowance. There were jujubes, sugar babies, gum drops, chocolate necco wafers, cheetos, sour cream and onion ruffle potato crisps, circus peanuts, snickers, gummy bears, worms and dinosaurs, Reeses peanut butter cups and M&Ms, plain and peanut. It was torture.

Passing the junk out at lunch to all of the sixth graders, except for his ex-best friend, Joshua ignored Matthew except to say, 'Enjoying your rice cakes with sugar-free jam, turkey?'

'If you want more,' Joshua informed everyone, 'you better not give any to Matthew.'

It was terrible.

Lizzie Doran refused to take any because it was mean, what Joshua was doing to Matthew, even though it was true that Matthew sometimes drove her nuts.

Matthew decided that Lizzie Doran was okay and that he would never again do things to bug her.

Brian Bruno sneaked one brown M&M to Matthew.

Then at Keepaway, Matthew was not only the first person out, but he was out because he got slammed by Joshua.

Before, Joshua had never aimed for Matthew. It was always someone else who had got him out.

In school, Matthew noticed that Joshua was having trouble with one of the computer programs.

When Joshua said, 'Could someone give me a hand with this?' Matthew pretended to be engrossed in a maths problem.

After school, the time when the two boys usually hung out together, both went home alone, even though they lived down the street from each other.

Both acted as if it didn't matter, as if they were invisible to each other.

Now Matthew was home and there was more trouble.

'Kids. Your mother has to work late and I don't want to miss bowling tonight. It's the first round of the tournament,' Mr Martin tells his children.

Matthew is rummaging through the refrigerator, hoping that one of the carrot sticks has magically turned into a lemon meringue pie.

Amanda is in the kitchen only because she has been called downstairs for this discussion.

Most of the time, she stays in her room, pouting about being contact lens-less, about not being able to have plastic surgery on her ears and about not being able to have a private phone in her room.

Mr Martin continues, 'Now, listen. I've tried to get a baby sitter.'

'I don't need one,' Amanda informs him. 'Kids my age are baby sitting already.'

'That's what I want to talk to you about,' Mr Martin says. 'I want you to babysit for us today.'

'I'm not a baby. I don't need a sitter!' Matthew yells. 'And definitely not *her*.'

'Are you going to pay me?' Amanda is thinking about the possibility of saving up to have her own private phone installed.

'Are you going to pay *me*?' Matthew is thinking about how he deserves combat pay for putting up with his sister.

Mr Martin shakes his head. 'You two are impossible. You should be happy to help out, to be part of the family. The only reason for a babysitter is that your mother and I won't be home until very late and that we don't think it's safe to leave the two of you at home alone, without a referee. However, we can't seem to locate one for tonight. They are probably all officiating at wrestling matches and hockey games instead of realising that we would need them to watch our children.'

'That's because you won't leave junk food for

them, the babysitters, I mean. They're all sick of the stuff in our refrigerator,' Amanda informs them.

Matthew is not surprised by this piece of information.

However, his father is. 'Honey, that's not true. We've always tipped very well and no one has ever complained.'

'It's in the unwritten babysitters' code not to complain to the parents. But it is true. I know it is. There's a kid in my class, Sharlene, and her older sister, Darlene, babysits a lot. Darlene told Sharlene that there's a list that babysitters share with each other grading all of their jobs. In the food category, we got a G.'

'What's a G?' Mr Martin is getting a headache.

'It's like the school grades, where we get A, B, C, D, or F. We didn't even rate an F. We were below Failure.' Amanda sighs. 'It's so hard being part of this family.'

Standing up, Mr Martin holds up his hands to signal *stop*. 'I've got to get going. Now I want you to be in charge, Amanda. I will pay you.'

'Not fair.' Matthew yells. 'I'm in sixth grade. You treat me like such a baby. No one else's parents get a baby sitter.'

'Be good and I'll pay you too.' Mr Martin offers. 'I can't believe it. I'm offering my children bribes to act like human beings. It's against everything I believe in and I'm doing it anyway.'

'I'm in charge, right?' Amanda asks her father.

'Right. Don't abuse the authority.' Mr Martin

picks up his bowling ball and heads out the door.

Amanda grins evilly at her younger brother.

Matthew's day keeps getting worse and worse.

It's not even fun thinking about his upcoming birthday party any more.

Amanda goes to the phone.

For the next two hours, she is on the phone talking to her girlfriends.

Stupid girlfriends, Matthew thinks. Stupid Amanda.

It's not fair. She's going to get paid to be on the phone all night, which is something she's not allowed to do when their parents are home.

Matthew sits in his room, thinking that if he and Joshua were still friends he could have gone over to the Jackson house and not had stupid Amanda in charge. Or Joshua could come to the Martin house and they could have ganged up on Amanda by making rude noises into the extension while she was talking to her stupid friends. That it was harder to do stuff like that alone. It was more fun to gang up on her together with Joshua. She had more trouble trying to catch both of them at once.

This being mad at Joshua was no fun.

But Joshua deserved it.

Matthew only hoped that Joshua was just as miserable.

CHAPTER 7

'Open the door, nerd face. I want to talk to you.' Amanda pounds on the door.

Matthew yells, 'Stay away, baboon breath!'

Amanda is silent for a minute and then knocks on the door again.

'Go away.' Matthew is in a bad enough mood already without having his sister come in and play boss.

'Honey baby, I really have to talk to you.' Amanda pleads.

Matthew can't believe that she's calling him 'Honey baby.' She hasn't done that since they were little and he actually believed that she was going to be nice to him. He was too smart for that now.

'Honey baby.' Amanda opens the door and sticks her head in the door.

Matthew pretends that she is invisible.

In the old days, it was never safe when she said 'Honey baby' so nicely. Once she did it when she was eight and he was six and she decided to give him a 'new look.' She cut his hair all spiky, with the pinking shears, and then sprayed it bright pink. It took months for it to grow back and he was the only kid in the first grade whose mother had to dye his hair every couple of weeks. And then there was the time in second grade when she conned him out of every cent in his Fred Flintstone dino-bank so that she could get her ears pierced after their parents had told her she couldn't. They made the holes close up by not letting her put earrings in. She never repaid him and when he complained to their parents, they said it was his fault for loaning her money for something that she wasn't supposed to do.

When Matthew was little, he was very gullible when it came to his sister. Now he knew better.

'Honey baby.' Amanda comes into his room and stands by his bed, looking so sweet.

'No.' Matthew says. 'No. No. No. Absolutely not.'

'But I haven't even asked you for anything yet. How do you know that I want anything?'

'NO. NO. NO.' Matthew sticks his fingers in his ears.

Amanda tries a different method of getting to her brother. 'Listen, Pea Brain. I want you to help me.'

Now Matthew feels better. They are on familiar ground. He's used to dealing with his sister this way. He doesn't feel as defenceless with name calling as he does when she's doing her 'Honey baby' routine.

'It's going to cost you.' Matthew stares at her. 'You're going to have to give me part of the money you're going to get for babysitting me.'

Amanda says, 'That's not fair. You're getting paid too.'

'Fair? You're my sister. Who says I have to be fair to you? You never are to me.' Matthew isn't sure what they are fighting about but it doesn't matter.

'Please.' Amanda pleads, looking so sad that Matthew feels sorry for her.

'Oh, okay. I'll listen. But don't expect me to say yes.'

Amanda sits down on the edge of his bed and then jumps up because she has just sat on his Invaders of the Universe rocket ship. 'Matthew, can't you ever be neat?'

'It's my room,' he reminds her.

This time she checks before she sits down.

'Matthew, I want you to do me a favour. Could you please watch yourself for about a half an hour?'

'You want me to stand in front of a mirror and look at myself for half an hour?' Matthew grins at her. 'I don't know, Amanda, that could be very tiring.'

'You goofbrain,' Amanda says, forgetting for a second that she's trying to get him to do something for her.

'Goofbrains don't do favours for sisters.' Matthew is having fun for the first time all day.

'Honey baby, please.' Amanda really begins to beg. 'I just want to go over to Cindy's house for half an hour. It's very important.'

Cindy is Joshua's older sister. Cindy's house . . . that's Joshua's house, too.

Matthew thinks, maybe I should say yes, it's okay. And then I should wire Amanda with a bomb that will go off when she gets over there. That would solve a lot of my problems . . .

Matthew thinks about it for a minute and knows that that is too awful and disgusting a thing to do, even to Amanda and Joshua.

'Please,' Amanda begs.

'Why?' Matthew wants the details.

'Because,' Amanda tells him.

'Tell me.' Matthew knows he's got his sister exactly where he wants her.

'Oh, okay.' She relents. 'I'll tell you. But you've got to promise not to tease me or anything.'

'I promise.' Matthew is not sure if he will keep the promise; after all it is only to his sister.

'You'd better.' Amanda glares at him, forgetting for a second that she really wants something from him. 'This Friday is very special.'

'I know. It's my birthday party,' Matthew says.

'No,' she says. 'Really special. You have a birthday every year. That's not so special.'

Matthew gets ready to tell her why it's very special, but she doesn't give him the chance.

'*Really* special. There's a school dance . . . and Danny Cohen asked me to go with him.'

Danny Cohen: that's David's step-brother . . . David, who is in my class, Matthew thinks. I hear

43

that Danny's really a nice guy. Why does he want to go out with my sister? I wonder if insanity runs in his family. I'd better ask David tomorrow.

'And I have to go over to Cindy's house to try on some clothes so I have something to wear on Friday. I have nothing to wear!'

'Nothing to wear.' Matthew picks up the rocket ship and pretends to be dive bombing at her head. 'Nothing to wear! You have so many clothes that they don't fit into your wardrobe. You have to use the hall cupboard too.'

'I have nothing *new* to wear. Nothing special. I'm going to wear something of Cindy's and she's going to wear something of mine. That way it'll be like we've each got new clothes.' Amanda sighs. 'I don't know why I'm trying to explain this to you. You don't even care about clothes. You're the kid who went away to camp and never changed your underwear for an entire week.'

'That was a long time ago,' Matthew tells her.

'Yeah. Last summer.' Amanda pushes her glasses back on the bridge of her nose.

'You can go over to Cindy's house,' Matthew tells her. 'It's going to cost you, though. Half of whatever you make tonight babysitting.'

'A quarter,' Amanda bargains. 'I've decided to spend it on a new pair of shoes. Real high heels. And I won't have enough money if I have to give half of it to you.'

'Half. Take it or leave it.'

Amanda looks at her watch and realises that the

longer it takes to compromise the less time she'll have at the Jacksons'. 'Okay, okay,' she relents. 'And you promise not to tell the parents.'

'Promise.' Matthew thinks about how he can use the babysitting money to buy more stuff for the goody bags . . . that he'll use it to buy Almond Joys, Joshua's favourites. Then he remembers that he and Joshua are no longer friends.

'Thanks, Matthew. I really appreciate this.' Amanda sounds like a normal person. 'And Matthew, one more thing . . . '

Matthew grins. Another favour. It's going to cost her.

'Matthew.' Amanda continues. 'Cindy and I were talking —'

'I know. That's all you two ever do,' Matthew teases her. 'Yak. Yak. Yak.'

'Shut up and listen for a minute. Cindy and I were talking about you and Joshua and the fight. She said that Joshua is really unhappy about it, and I can tell that you are, too.'

'Am not.' Matthew shakes his head and folds his arms across his chest.

'You are, too. I can tell.' Amanda pushes her glasses up again. 'Cindy told me what happened. It really did sound like an accident. You and Joshua have been friends for too long to act like this to each other. I remember when Cindy and I had a fight in sixth grade. It was really dumb. Look, I'm older than you are. I have more experience in stuff like this. Listen to me. It was only a dumb invitation.'

'I'd worked on it for hours. It was the best invitation ever.'

'Matthew. I know that computers are important to you, and how good you are on them. You're better than almost anyone I know. But it's also important to have friends. You can't play ball outside with a computer, or have a real-friends type of talk with a computer. A computer can't share junk food with you.' Amanda looks at her watch. 'I've got to go. Think about what I said. Your dumb birthday party is important to you. Are you going to ruin it by not having your best friend there? That'll turn this whole thing into a big deal.'

'Why are you telling me this?'

'You're my brother,' she shrugs. 'Sometimes, weird as it seems, I even like you. Look, I've got to go. Promise that if our parents get back you'll call and warn me.'

'I promise.' Matthew nods.

'Bye.' Amanda jumps off the bed and rushes off.

'One more thing, turkey!' Matthew calls out.

'Yes?' Amanda stops.

'Keep all of the stupid babysitting money. You can buy your stupid high heels. Even though you'll probably break your stupid neck wearing them.' Matthew can hardly believe that he is saying this.

Amanda comes back, gives him a kiss on the forehead, and then rushes out.

Matthew wipes the kiss off his forehead and wonders if he's been possessed by a devil who is making him so generous.

Then he thinks about what Amanda said.

Maybe she's right.

Maybe she isn't.

Maybe he will talk to Joshua tomorrow.

Maybe he won't.

Whoever said that being a kid was easy never had a best friend, or a sister and would never be invited to Matthew's birthday party, not ever.

CHAPTER 8

'That breakfast is really gross.' Amanda looks down at her brother's plate. 'How *can* you eat granola with ketchup?'

'Easy.' Matthew grins. 'With a spoon.'

'Ha, ha.' Amanda looks up at her brother. 'You wouldn't be able to do that if Mom and Dad were here.'

'But they aren't. You know that they both had to go to work early. And Mom made me promise to eat the granola. I really hate it. I really like ketchup. I'd rather mix it with vanilla ice cream and chocolate syrup but since we can only have that stuff on special occasions, I put ketchup on it.' Matthew puts some in his mouth. 'Friday, I will actually be able to have some ice cream, syrup and cake *because* —'

'I know. I know. *Because* it's going to be your birthday.' Amanda makes herself some wholewheat toast. 'Really, Matthew. I can't understand why you're making such a big deal out of your birthday. After all, everybody has them.'

Matthew swirls the granola-ketchup mixture with his spoon. 'It's important. It's the one day a year when people really make a fuss over a kid. When everyone has to be nice to you, and you get a lot of presents that you could never buy for yourself. And in this family, it's one of the few times we can have junk food. When you're a kid, it's practically the biggest day of the year, except for Christmas, maybe. Did you buy me a present, Amanda?'

She looks at him. 'You are so greedy.'

'Yes.' He grins. 'So what did you get me?'

'I'm not telling.' She puts grape jelly on her toast.

'So you did buy me a present.' Matthew claps his hands. 'Tell me what it is.'

'Matthew. Stop it.' Amanda pulls her brother's hair. 'Stop being a pest. And hurry up, you're going to be late for school. Mom made me promise that I'd be sure to get you out of here on time.'

Matthew stares down at the breakfast that he has hardly eaten.

'Get going. And thanks for not squealing on me. I owe you one.' Amanda puts the toast into her mouth.

'Good.' Matthew tries to get her to pay up immediately. 'If you owe me one, would you please eat my breakfast for me?'

Amanda looks down at the granola-ketchup mixture and says, 'Not a chance. I'd be sick.'

Matthew picks up the bowl. 'I have an idea.'

'Just don't be late for school or you're going to be

49

dead meat.' Amanda shakes her finger at him. 'I've got to go to school now. Cindy and I are getting to school early. We have to talk.'

Matthew thinks about all of the talking they did yesterday, first on the phone and then in person, and thinks about how much girls gab. He was sure that Danny Cohen and whatever sucker was taking Cindy to the dance were not spending all this time talking about what they were going to wear and junk like that.

Amanda leaves.

Matthew looks down at his breakfast and knows that when his mother comes home, she's going to check the dustbin to see if he ate the granola.

He thinks of flushing it down the toilet, but knows that he can't. The last time he tried that, the five grain eggplant souffle blocked up the toilet. So no toilet stuffing allowed.

Putting the breakfast in a polythene bag, he takes it and his books and lunch outside. He grabs a shovel out of the garage and buries the breakfast bag under a bush in the front garden.

He debates burying his spelling book too, but realises that's not a good idea.

Matthew is so intent on burying the evidence that he doesn't realise that Joshua is standing behind him, watching the whole thing.

'Ashes to ashes. Dust to dust.' Matthew remembers what he saw on television once. 'The next thing I'll bury is wholewheat crust.'

'That is so lame.' Joshua starts to laugh.

50

Matthew looks at his friend and stands up. 'Hi,' he says quietly.

Both boys just look at each other and then both say, 'I'm sorry,' at the same time.

Then Joshua punches Matthew on his arm, not a fight punch but a friend punch.

Matthew does the same to Joshua.

The fight is over.

'We'd better get to school,' Matthew says, grabbing his books and lunch. 'We don't want detention. We have to plan for the party.'

'Okay. Race you.' Joshua starts to run.

I'll never keep up, Matthew thinks, but Joshua doesn't run as fast as he can, so the two boys run side by side.

'I brought an extra pack of cupcakes today.' Joshua holds up his lunch bag. 'You can have them unless your Mom packed you something better.'

The thought of the cupcakes makes Matthew sprint even faster. 'She packed tofu sunflower seed brownies. Even though it's going to be a sacrifice, I'll give them up for the cupcakes.'

As they near the school playground, Matthew thinks about something they'd learned in school, about how Indians used to pass the peace pipe when they wanted a war to end.

With Matthew and Joshua, it was peace cupcakes instead.

Matthew was glad the fight was over . . . with or without the cupcakes.

Planning the party was going to be fun again.

CHAPTER 9

'I'm in deep trouble, deep deep trouble,' Brian Bruno informs the guys. 'I'm not sure that I'm ever going to be allowed out of my house again, except for school and church.'

'What did you do?' Mark asks.

Brian starts to grin. 'You know my little sister, Fritzie the Pain?'

Everyone knew Fritzie. Before she learned to talk, she learned to bite. Each boy had at least one scar on his leg to remind him of Fritzie. Four years younger, Fritzie was a real pain . . . in a real way.

Brian continues. 'You know how she's always following us around, butting in?'

Everyone nods.

'Well, I decided to get even. So I trained her,' Brian tells them.

'Trained her not to bite? Trained her to give herself a rabies injection?' says Patrick Ryan, looking down at his ankle where there is still a Fritzie scar.

'No such luck,' Brian shakes his head. 'No, I trained her to do something else. Every time I said, "Who am I?" She would have to say, "King Brian, the terrific." And then I would say, "Who are you?" and she would say, "Fang Face, pig Brain, Fritzie."'

'Great,' says Mark. 'I'll have to teach that to my little sister.'

'No way.' Brian shakes his head. 'My parents heard us and they got mad, told me that I was the oldest and should know better, that I was being mean and had to be punished.'

'Oh, no. You can't come to my party,' says Matthew, who knows how Fritzie must feel being the youngest, but still sides with Brian.

'I begged them. I got down on my knees and pleaded with them to let me go,' Brian says. 'I promised them if I could go, I'd give Fritzie my goodie bag, that I'd take her to the movies two times without complaining, that I would never call her Fang Face again.'

'What happened next?' Matthew needs to know.

'I apologised to the little snaggletoothed creep in front of my parents and they said that I could go to the party, that my punishment wouldn't start until after the sleepover and then the punishment would start. So no one have a party for the next month, okay?'

Matthew thinks about how hard it is for brothers and sisters to get along; about the time he dropped water balloons on Amanda's head and she screamed, 'I will not use force on you. I will use verbal!' Sisters sure are strange.

Mrs Stanton walks into the room. 'Class, everyone sit down quietly.'

Trouble, Matthew thinks. I have a feeling that there is something I have not done.

Once everyone is seated, Mrs Stanton says, 'Who would like to hand out the paper?'

'Oh. Oh. Oh.' Jil! is practically jumping over the top of her desk, frantically waving her hand.

'Ryma. Please pass out the papers.' Mrs Stanton turns to the quietest child in the class.

Once the papers are on everyone's desk, Mrs Stanton says, 'Number from one to twenty.'

The spelling test! Matthew remembers, but he remembers too late to do anything about it.

Ten minutes later, everyone puts his or her pencil down on the desk.

Matthew's paper is a mess. It's so erased that there are holes in the paper. There are crossouts. Smudge marks. It looks like it's been in the hands of a dirty demento.

'Exchange papers with the person to the right of you,' Mrs Stanton tells them.

Matthew groans. He has to give his to Vanessa Singer. She hasn't liked him since the time he put the class gerbil in her Barbie lunchbox. It's not that he expects her to cheat for him. He just hopes that she doesn't scream out his grade. Maybe she'll be nice.

No such luck.

'Has anyone else got fifteen wrong . . . or has

Matthew won the Spelling Booby Prize again?' she yells out.

'Vanessa. That isn't very nice.' Mrs Stanton looks at her. 'How would you feel if someone did that to you?'

Vanessa sticks her nose up in the air, and shakes her curly red hair. 'There's no way that could happen to me. I would never get that many spelling words wrong. *Never*.'

Matthew wants to murder her.

He also wants to die of embarrassment.

It's not fair.

Why is spelling so important?

His computer program beeps and changes wrong spellings, so why are they bothering with these stupid spelling tests anyway?

Finally, the agony ends and the class has independent reading time.

Matthew pretends to read but actually thinks of ways to get even with Vanessa.

He can feel something start to rumble inside his body.

He debates asking for a cloakroom pass but decides against it.

Instead, he sits at his desk and expells the gas in Vanessa's direction, one of those SBDs, Silent But Deadly. Then he immediately holds his nose and calls out, 'Oh, yuck. Vanessa. How could you do that? You're so disgusting.'

Everyone in the class turns around and looks at Vanessa.

'I didn't do anything. You did, you disgusting pig.' Vanessa is blushing.

Matthew puts on his most innocent look, his most hurt look. 'Me? Why don't you just confess? I'm sure it was an accident. Don't be so ashamed.'

Everyone near them starts moaning and holding their noses.

Vanessa gets redder and redder.

Matthew is having a great time.

Vanessa looks like she's going to cry.

Matthew feels a little bit guilty until he remembers how she told everyone what a dope he was in spelling.

This will teach her.

Matthew may not be the world's best speller but he has just made everyone think that Vanessa is the world's worst smeller.

Next time Vanessa will think twice before she messes with me, Matthew thinks.

Little does he know that Vanessa is already plotting her revenge.

CHAPTER 10

Amanda Martin Cohen
Amanda Cohen
Mrs. Amanda Cohen
Mrs. Danny Cohen
Ms. Amanda Martin
Mandy Cohen
Mrs. Amanda Martin-Cohen
Mandy Martin
Mandy Martin Cohen
Amanda M. Cohen
A. Martin Cohen
Mrs. Daniel Cohen
Mr. and Mrs. Danny Cohen
Mr. and Mrs. Daniel Cohen
Mrs. and Mr. Dan Cohen

Matthew feels like he's struck gold. He's got the blackmail evidence of the century!

Going through Amanda's school notebook to get some paper, he has found the list.

Mrs Stanton said that he had to write each mis-spelled word ten times.

Ten times fifteen words. That's going to take a lot of paper.

Mrs Stanton had warned him.

He is not to do it using his computer, writing it once and having the computer repeat it fourteen more times.

He did that last time.

This time she says that if he does it again, he's going to have to handwrite each word twenty-five times.

Twenty-five times fifteen is more than Matthew cares to compute.

So he was prepared to write it out, using cursive.

However, he's left his notebook at school.

Going into the kitchen to look for paper, he has found Amanda's notebook.

It's like striking gold.

He can really blackmail her with this.

He's sure that she'd be willing to write fifteen spelling words ten times each rather than have anyone see what she's been doing.

Matthew is sure that all he is going to have to do is threaten her with giving the paper to David Cohen, who will then give it to his step-brother, Danny.

Amanda walks into the room, just as he begins to pull the page out of the notebook.

'What are you doing, you little runt?'

Matthew holds up the page.

'Wait until Danny sees this!'

Amanda rushes towards Matthew, backing him against the refrigerator.

He ducks under her arm.

Sometimes being a runt has its advantages.

However, he ducks right into his father, who is behind Amanda.

Getting his son into a headlock, Mr Martin says, 'Hi, boy. What's going on?'

'Nothing,' Matthew says. 'How about letting me go, Dad? I have some spelling homework to do.'

'Kill him!' Amanda screams. 'Break his stupid little runt neck! He's stolen something very important of mine.'

Mr Martin, who does not believe in physical violence, shakes his head.

The hold on Matthew is not strong but Matthew knows better than to try to break away.

'Drop it.' Amanda sounds ready to do serious harm.

Matthew grins at her. 'Mrs —'

'Shut up.' She pulls his hair.

'Let go,' Mr Martin says. 'Matthew. You let go of your sister's paper. Amanda. You let go of your brother's hair.' Matthew lets go of the paper.

Amanda lets go of his hair.

Mr Martin lets go of Matthew.

'Now what's going on here?' Mr Martin wants to know.

Matthew knows that if Amanda squeals, he's going to be in trouble. He also knows that if

Amanda squeals, he's going to have to tell about her leaving the house the other night while she was supposed to be babysitting.

Amanda knows that if she squeals on Matthew, he's going to squeal on her.

'It's all right, Dad. I'm not going to press charges.' Amanda has been watching People's Court.

'Are you sure?' Mr Martin asks.

'I'm sure.' Amanda sighs.

Mr Martin looks down at his son. 'Matthew. I'm not sure what you were up to but I have a feeling that you were up to no good. Watch your step, son.'

Matthew knows that he's going to need his father's help in setting up the tent for the sleepover, so he uses his most innocent look and says, 'Yes, sir.'

Mr Martin, remembering how he and his sister always used to fight when they were little, looks at his two children. He only hopes that some day they will learn to get on together, just the way he and his sister, their Aunt Nancy, now get along.

Matthew looks at Amanda.

It doesn't look like she's too happy with him.

However, he decides to press his luck.

'Can I borrow some paper from you? I need it to do my homework.' Matthew asks.

Amanda debates stepping on his head but then looks at her father who senses that she wants to step on Matthew's head and is going to make sure that doesn't happen.

'Oh, okay. What do you need?' She opens her notebook, careful that only empty pages are showing.

'Five pages,' he tells her.

'Spelling words again.' She shoves the paper at him. 'Next time, ask first.'

'Okay.' Matthew takes the paper and leaves.

Amanda looks at her father. 'He's such a child.'

Mr Martin remembers that it was only a week ago that his daughter said, 'It's not fair. I'm only a kid,' when she was asked to help clean up the house.

Amanda sits down on the kitchen stool. 'Daddy, can't you help me convince Mom that I need contact lenses?'

'No way.' Her father shakes his head.

'Plastic surgery?' she persists.

He shakes his head again.

'For my date with Danny, can I have him meet me at Cindy's house? It's going to be awful having him meet me here with that stupid party going on. Matthew is going to do something terrible to embarrass me. I know he will. Please, Daddy? Oh, please.' Amanda puts her head down on the kitchen table.

'Get up, honey.' Mr Martin runs his hand over the back of her head.

'Not until you help me with this problem.' Amanda is hard to hear because she is talking into the table.

Mr Martin thinks for a minute and then says,

61

'Your mother and I want Danny to come here. You can't deprive us of seeing you go out on your first date. However, I do know that there is a chance that Matthew may try to do something embarrassing.'

Mr Martin is remembering his sister's first date and how he rigged up the stereo system so that as they walked out of the door, 'Here Comes the Bride' played loudly enough for the whole neighbourhood to hear it.

'I'll talk to him, warn him, I promise,' Mr Martin tells her.

Amanda raises her head. 'Thanks, Dad.'

Getting up, she gives her father a hug.

As she leaves the room, she says, 'Tell him if he's not good, we're going to give all his presents away. That should do it.'

Mr Martin says, 'I'll take care of it.'

Amanda walks upstairs and heads directly to Matthew's room. 'Listen, you little brat, if you ever tell anyone about that page, you are dead meat.'

Matthew smiles at her.

'I'm not kidding.' She stares at him. 'If you do anything when Danny picks me up, I'm going to tell everyone how, when you're upset, you still sleep with your Babar stuffed elephant, the one you got when you were a baby.'

'I don't and you know it.' Matthew stands up.

'You know that and I know that but no one else will. They'll believe me and think you are a nerd to the Nth degree.' Amanda grins evilly.

Amanda knows she's got Matthew, that the kids will tease him even if it's not true. She also knows that she'd really never do that to him but he doesn't know that.

As Amanda leaves the room, Matthew sits down again.

What a day.

One hundred and fifty spelling words to write.

Amanda's threatening to turn him into the Class Geek.

And somewhere out there, Vanessa Singer is planning her revenge.

CHAPTER 11

We, the girls of Grade Six of E.E.E., do hereby form an organisation called GET HIM, which is short for Girls Eager To Halt Immature Matthew.

We plan to do everything possible to make Matthew Martin's life as miserable as he has made ours.

SO MATTHEW MARTIN, WATCH OUT!!!!!!!!!!!!!!!!!!!!!!!!!!!!!!!

THE GET HIM EXPLANATION:

Just so people don't think that we are being unfair ganging up on Matthew Martin, fink of Califon, fink of New Jersey, fink of the United States. North America. Earth. The Universe Matthew Martin, slimeball of all eternity, we do hereby list just a few of the sneaky, disgusting, and rotten things that he has done to us!

1. Putting ketchup and mayonnaise in his mouth, puffing up his cheeks, smacking them to make the goop come out of his face onto Cathy Atwood's brand—new dress, and screaming, "I'm a zit! I'm a zit!"

2. Always making fun of Jessica Weeks's last name, saying dumb things like "Jessica Weeks makes many daze." And whenever he sees her with her parents and little sister, yelling out, "Look! It's the Month family——Four Weeks equals one month." Enough is enough!

3. Rolling up rubber cement into tiny balls, labelling them "snot balls," and putting them into Lisa Levine's pencil box.

4. Ever since preschool, kicking the bottom of the chair of the person who is unlucky enough to be seated in front of him.

5. Whenever anyone taller stands up in front of him, yelling, "I can't see through you. What do you think, that your father's a glazier?" We can't help it if practically everyone in the class is taller than Matthew. It's especially mean when he does it to Katie Delaney. She can't help it if she's the tallest person in the class.

6. Putting a "Sushi for Sale" sign in the class aquarium.

7. Teasing any boy who wants to talk to one of the girls, acting as if it were the crime of the century. Just wait until Matthew gets old enough and acts more mature (if that ever happens, especially since he is the baby of the class) and wants to ask some girl out on a date. No one in this class is ever ever going to go out with him. We've made a solemn promise as part of GET HIM. He's going to have to ask out some girl who is presently in preschool or not even born yet because we have also made a solemn promise to inform every girl in the world to WATCH OUT!

8. During the Spring Concert quietly singing the theme song from that ancient TV show <u>Mr Ed</u> while everyone else was trying to sing the correct songs.

9. Putting Bubble Yum in Zoe Alexander's very very long blonde hair, so that her mother had to spend four hours rubbing ice cubes on it, and then, when told about what a pain it was, said, "I guess that helped you cool off, you hot—head."

65

10. On last year's class trip to the Bronx Zoo, going up to the attendants, pointing to all the girls, and saying that they had escaped from the monkey cages.

11. Bothering all the girls at lunchtime to make them swap their meals for the sprouty stuff he always brings.

12. Always acting like such a bigshot about computer stuff, never helping out any girl who needs help, and acting like Chloe Fulton doesn't exist because she's almost as good as he is at it and could be even better if she didn't have so many other interests. SO THERE!

13. For the Valentine Box, giving the girls envelopes filled with night crawlers. Even though it was anonymous, we all know who did it. Even if Mrs Stanton said we couldn't prove it, we know it was Matthew because most of the names were spelled wrong. So was the handwritten message, LET ME WERM MY WAY INTO YOUR HART.

We, the eleven members of GET HIM, could go on forever listing all the stuff he's done to us, but we've decided to list just thirteen things. The unlucky number, thirteen, is only the beginning.

From now on Matthew Martin is going to have to watch out. We're going to make his life as miserable as he has made ours. He's never going to know when something is going to happen.

WE ARE SERIOUS!!!
WE ARE ANGRY!!
WE AREN'T GOING TO TAKE IT ANY MORE!!!!!!!!!!!!!!!!!!!!!!!!!!

SIGNED,
VANESSA SINGER, President

KATIE DELANEY, Vice President

JIL! HUDSON, Secretary

LIZZIE DORAN, Treasurer

MEMBERS: Cathy Atwood, Lisa Levine, Jessica Weeks, Zoe Alexander, Chloe Fulton, Ryma Browne, and Sarah Montgomery

✰VANESSA SINGER✰

Katie Delaney

Jill Hudson

LiZZIE DORAN

Cathy Atwood   LISA LEVINE

Sarah Montgomery   Jessica Weeks

68

Ryma Browne

Zoe Alexander

69

CHAPTER 12

'You're in for it,' Joshua says, when the boys discover the GET HIM declaration on Matthew's desk. 'I'm glad that I'm not you.'

'Me too,' says Tyler White. 'But then I'm always glad that I'm not you. I'm glad I'm not you when we're playing Keepaway. I'm glad I'm not you when we're opening up our lunches. I'm glad —'

'Shut up,' Matthew says.

Tyler continues, 'And I'm really glad that I'm not you today. When all the girls gang up on someone, it's awful.'

Matthew looks at the Declaration that has been stuck to his desk with plastic imitation 'dog do' and then he looks up at Tyler again. 'Shut up.'

'Really original.' Tyler smiles at him.

'You only wish you were me when we're playing with the computer or Nintendo.' Matthew stares at him.

Tyler stares back, but he's the first one to blink and look away.

Matthew smiles for the first time since he's got

into the classroom and seen what's on his desk.

All the boys in the class are crowding around his desk.

All the girls are standing by the aquarium, talking to each other and looking his way.

Some of the girls are giggling.

Others are glaring.

Vanessa Singer looks very proud of herself.

Matthew looks round the classroom and tries to figure out what to do next.

The girls keep glaring and giggling.

Matthew is in deep trouble and he knows it.

He's not going to let anyone else know that he knows it.

Mrs Stanton walks into the room and looks round.

Everyone tries to look very innocent. They immediately head for their desks, very quietly.

Mrs Stanton looks round, trying to figure out what's going on without making too big a deal of it.

She looks at Matthew, who she figures has probably done something.

He is putting away the incriminating evidence, the plastic dog do and the declaration.

It's going right into his backpack.

There's no way that he's going to be a squealer.

That just isn't done in the sixth grade at E.E.E.

It's okay to tell on a brother or sister at home but not to tell on a classmate at school, as long as it's not a serious thing, the kind of thing that kids really should tell grownups.

This is not a serious thing. It's serious, but not SERIOUS, like drugs or abuse or something dangerous.

There's no way that he's going to act like a baby and have Mrs Stanton take care of it by talking to the girls. That would only make things worse, and Matthew Martin has a feeling that things are going to be bad enough as it is.

Vanessa Singer keeps sneaking looks at him and snickering.

'Would you like to share the joke with us, Vanessa dear?' Mrs Stanton says stuff like that a lot when she wants kids to stop fooling around.

It works.

Vanessa takes her notebook out of her desk and looks at the next spelling list.

So does everyone else.

There is a lot of giggling going around.

Not just the girls, but the boys, too.

All of the boys except Matthew, who is beginning to wonder if he's finally going to be paid back for all the things he has done to other people.

Matthew goes into his desk to take out his spelling list.

Someone has put cling film wrap over all the stuff in his desk and covered the wrap with lime jelly. It keeps wiggling back and forth.

It looks so gross.

Matthew wishes he had thought of doing it . . . to someone else, probably to Vanessa Singer. But he would have added little pieces of his mother's tofu, which would have made it look really gross.

But he didn't think of it. Someone else had, and now it was in Matthew's desk, looking like the Slime That Ate Califon.

Green jelly was the only flavour he hated. Someone who knew his habits was out to get him.

Looking round the room, he realised that there were eleven someones who were out to get him.

This wasn't fair to do to someone with a birthday coming up, someone who was going to be very busy getting ready for his party, someone who didn't want to waste his time thinking about what a bunch of dumb girls were going to do to him.

Maybe this will be it, Matthew thinks. Maybe the dumb girls have had their dumb fun and they'll leave me alone.

Three minutes later, Matthew feels someone kicking the bottom of his chair.

He turns around to check it out.

It's Lizzie Doran . . . and she's smiling.

CHAPTER 13

'Matthew. Something seems to be bothering you lately.' Mr Martin looks up from the book he is reading.

'It's nothing.' Matthew shakes his head and continues to doodle all over his maths homework.

'Are you sure?' Mr Martin stares at his son. 'You know you can tell me anything. And now is a good time with your mother and your sister out shopping for an outfit for the dance.'

Matthew draws a skull and crossbones on the paper and labels it POIZON: FOR SIXTH GRADE GIRLS. 'No. No trouble at all.'

He looks down at the paper and thinks about how rotten everything has been lately; how all the girls are making his life absolutely miserable, how most of the other boys don't want to start an anti-girl club, how even Joshua won't do it, and how Joshua had said, 'The girls aren't against all of us, just you. And Matthew, you've got to admit it, they do have their reasons to be mad at you.'

Matthew thinks about all the stuff he's done to

the girls, but he also thinks about how he's done stuff to everyone. It's not that he's especially against the girls, it's just that school gets so boring sometimes that he's got to do something to liven it up. He thinks about how all of the girls have been against him for three days now, kicking his seat, putting signs on his back saying things like 'SO DUMB HE SPELLS IT DUM' and 'G.E.T. H.I.M. wants you to KICK HIM.' He thinks about how someone's putting messages into the computer saying things like 'MATTHEW MARTIN IS NOT USER FRIENDLY' and 'WATCH OUT . . . WE'RE GOING TO PUT A MAGNET NEXT TO ALL YOUR DISCS AND WIPE THEM OUT', and how Jil! Hudson has been doing really terrible things like telling everyone that they are engaged and that he is secretly going steady with her, then making these disgusting barfing noises and all of the girls giggle.

'Son. Are you sure you're all right? You haven't mentioned your party once today. Your mother and I are getting a little concerned.' Mr Martin puts down his book.

Shaking his head, Matthew says, 'It's all right, Pop. Honest.'

All Right, Matthew thinks, Ha! All Right. There are eleven people picking on me. It's not fair. So, it's true. Sometimes I do things to other people, but I don't mean to be really mean. I don't gang up on anyone, and I have eleven people against me all at once. But what's the use of telling anyone?

'Matthew.' Mr Martin stands up. 'I've been

thinking. As one of your birthday presents, your mother and I were going to give you a bubble-making set, with instructions for making huge bubbles, for doing lots of tricks. Why don't you and I take that present out now and try some stuff out so that you can use it at your birthday party?'

Matthew smiles. Finally.

Mr Martin says, 'I'll go get the bubbles. Don't follow me. I don't want you to know where the secret hiding place is.'

As his father leaves, Matthew smiles again.

He knows where the secret hiding place is, where all the secret hiding places are.

After all, when a person has spent his entire life living in one house, it's easy to figure out stuff like that unless, of course, you are a prince or princess and live in a huge castle. There are probably millions of places in a castle to hide things but most people, Matthew is sure, live in places where anyone can figure out the hiding places after almost eleven years of life. And Matthew has figured them out.

Sometimes stuff is hidden in the old trunk in the attic. Sometimes, if it's small enough, it's in his mother's drawer where she keeps her nightgowns. Sometimes it's in the garage, hidden behind the rakes and stuff, where the parents are sure no kid is going to look. Once, at Christmas, they even hid stuff in boxes in the freezer. Since his mother had labelled it LIVER, Matthew never found it.

Matthew is sure that the bubble stuff is on the top

shelf of his father's wardrobe, behind the scarves.

He sneaks into his parents' bedroom and spies on his father who is taking the present out of the clothes hamper in the bathroom.

Wrong, Matthew thinks, but at least I know another hiding place.

Matthew quietly rushes back into the living room, jumping on the couch and landing in a horizontal position. He stares up at the ceiling as if he's been lying there for hours.

Carrying the package into the living room, Mr Martin says, 'We'd better do this outside. Your mother's going to have a cow if we get soap all over the furniture.'

As they head outside, Matthew thinks about some of the weird stuff his parents say.

His father is always saying, 'Your mother's going to have a cow if . . . ' When Matthew was little he used to wonder where they were going to put the cow if his mother actually had it. He always hoped that it would go into Amanda's room, where it would sleep in her bed and keep her awake all night mooing. But his mother never did have a cow, even if she did get pretty angry sometimes.

In the front yard, Matthew and his father pour the bubble mixture into a large aluminium baking pan and then make large wands, using coat hangers with string wrapped around them.

The bubbles are huge.

Matthew only wishes he could make them big enough to put a dumb sixth grade girl inside each one and float them all up to Mars, or at least over Budd Lake so that some bird could peck the bubbles and the girls would plop into the water.

Just as Matthew starts to say something, one of Mr Martin's bubbles travels across the lawn and lands on Matthew, breaking right on his face.

'*Yug.*' The taste of the bubbles is not wonderful nor is the sticky feeling all over his face.

Mr Martin starts to laugh and moves closer, blowing more bubbles at Matthew, using a smaller wand.

This is war.

Matthew runs over to the box, takes out another small wand and starts blowing bubbles into his father's face.

His father is winning until Matthew gets a lot of liquid into the wand and blows so hard that there's no bubble, just liquid glob all over his father's face.

This is more than war. It's annihilation.

Mr Martin grabs his son's foot, pulls him to the ground and sits on him.

Then he takes the wand and keeps blowing bubbles all over Matthew's face.

Matthew can't stop laughing.

He also can't manage to get the wand away from his father.

'Boys.' Mrs Martin arrives on the scene.

Amanda is right behind her. 'You two are so gross.'

Mr Martin blows bubbles towards her. 'I am not gross. I am your father.'

'Mother. Make them stop. Everyone can see them. What if one of my friends comes by?' Amanda sighs. 'It's bad enough that my brother is so immature . . . '

'Young lady. You'd better stop before you say anything else.' Mr Martin continues to blow bubbles at her and then starts blowing them at his wife. He is still sitting on his son.

'Stop. You're getting me all sticky.' Mrs Martin is laughing.

'You ain't seen nothing yet.' Mr Martin gets off his son and starts moving towards his wife. He's picked up the very large wand.

Mrs Martin moves towards the tap where the garden hose is attached.

'I'm getting out of here.' Amanda clutches the packages containing her new clothes and runs into the house. 'You are all nuts!'

'Nuts?' We're your parents, not nuts,' Mr Martin tells his daughter and then turns back to Mrs Martin. 'Come here, my little cashew.'

Matthew watches as his mother holds up the hose and says, 'Michael Martin. I'm warning you. I've known you since second grade and there are days I don't think you've changed all that much since then. If you blow bubbles at me once more, you're going to be sorry. Very sorry.'

'I dare you.' Mr Martin grins, moves closer and blows bubbles at her.

She aims the hose at her husband and turns the water on.

Soaked, he drops the bubbles and runs over to try to capture the hose.

Amanda sticks her head out the window. 'Would you all stop? Please, you are so embarrassing.'

Matthew watches as his mother continues to spray his father until his father captures the hose and sprays his mother.

Amanda, in the background, is pleading for her parents to stop.

Soaked, Mr and Mrs Martin look at each other and laugh.

Then they hug each other, kiss and then whisper something to each other.

Matthew is standing there, watching the whole thing.

After they whisper, his father hands the hose to Mrs Martin and starts walking over to Matthew.

Both parents are grinning.

Matthew can tell he's going to get it.

As he tries to run, his father catches up and pulls him down to the ground again.

His mother rushes over with the hose, sprays Matthew and then sprays Mr Martin again.

The three of them are laughing.

Mrs Martin looks down at the two very wet men in her family and says, 'Maybe you guys should go take a nap right now and say a little prayer, like, "Now I spray me down to sleep." '

Mr Martin groans at the pun.

Matthew says, 'I think we should buy a water bed.'

Mr Martin stands and reaches his hand down to help his son get up.

Mrs Martin turns off the hose.

Matthew gets up.

His mother hugs him.

He hugs her back.

He's beginning to feel like the old Matthew, before the girls ganged up on him.

Amanda sticks her head out of the window again. 'Would you all come into the house? Please.'

'Join us.' Mr Martin uses a funny teasing voice.

Looking at her family as if she thinks they should all check into a roach motel, Amanda shakes her head and vanishes into the house.

Mrs Martin says, 'Inside, before we catch pneumonia.'

As they squish their way back inside, Matthew thinks about how this has been the best day in a very long time, how those dumb girls have driven him nuts long enough, how the old Matthew is back again.

Those dumb girls better watch out.

Instead of G.E.T. H.I.M., it's going to be G.E.T. T.H.E.M.:

GIRLS EASY TO TORMENT HOPES EVIL MATTHEW.

CHAPTER 14

WAYS TO GET EVEN
By Matthew Martin

1.

Put Silly Putty in Cathy Atwood's baloney sandwich.

2.

Next time Lizzie Doran kicks the back of my chair,
grab her foot and not let go of it. Also, pretend
to be looking under my chair for something and tie
her laces together so that when she stands up, she
won't be able to walk.

3.

Take the large science magnet and see if it can
attach to all the girls who wear braces.

4.

Put a whoopie cushion on Vanessa Singer's chair.

5.

Make puking noises in Lisa Levine's ear. It always makes her sick.

6.

Since Sarah Montgomery has a horse, act like she smells like one. Say things like "Howdy, NEIGHbour." Sniff when I am near her, saying, "Hay. What did you step in?"

7.

Next time Jill Hudson says that we are going to get married, tell her that the only one dum enough to marry her would be King Kong because he's a big ape just like she is.

8.

Tell Jimmy Sutherland, the fifth-grader that Chloe has a crush on, that she has the creeping crud.

9.

Stand behind Zoe Alexander and ask, "What goes one hundred miles an hour backwards?" and then blow my snot back up my nose. That always gets her.

10.

Pretend to take my eyeball out of my face and into my mouth and wash it. That grosses out all the girls.

11.

Put a sign on Vanessa Singer's desk. YOU CAN PICK YOUR FRIENDS . . . YOU CAN PICK YOUR NOSE . . . BUT VANESSA SINGER PICKS HER FRIEND'S NOSE.

12.

When Katie Delaney is in front of the class giving
a book report, make faces at her, like trying to touch
my nose with my tongue, pulling my lower eyelids as
low as they can go, wiggling my ears. Katie busts a
gut when stuff like that happens. Do all of that
without getting caught by Mrs Stanton.

13.

Collect belly-button lint and toe crud from all of the
boys and put it in Vanessa Singer's desk.

Matthew grins as he finishes printing up the list.

It may not be perfect. There may be more tortures
to think of doing but it's a start.

And there are thirteen on the list. Just like there
were on the dumb girls' list.

Matthew is sure that the girls are going to regret
the day that he started this war.

Leaving the computer on because he plans to get
back to it once he's got himself a little snack,
Matthew puts the printout next to the computer,
and heads for the kitchen.

Amanda and his mother are already there, doing
something at the table.

Going over to see what's going on, Matthew
looks at his mother putting artificial nails on top of
Amanda's bitten-down fingernails.

The make believe nails are bright red and
Amanda keeps grinning.

'These look so wonderful,' she gushes. 'I'm going

to look so grownup for the dance.'

She looks up at Matthew and says, 'What are you staring at, nerdface?'

Matthew does not like being called nerdface, especially when he has done nothing to deserve it.

He pretends to study Amanda's face. 'How grownup can you look when you have that giant ugly gross pimple on your chin? It looks like a volcano.'

Quickly covering her chin with her hand, Amanda's whole mood changes. 'Oh, no. What am I going to do? There are only two more days until the dance. I can't go. Mom, you have to call Danny and tell him that I have appendicitis.'

'It's only a disgusting looking pimple.' Matthew smiles at her. 'Maybe he gets turned on by pus.'

'Matthew Martin. I want you to stop teasing your sister immediately.' Mrs Martin shakes her fist at him and then turns to her daughter. 'Amanda. There is no pimple on your face. You have to stop letting your brother torment you like this.'

Amanda rushes out of the kitchen to look in a mirror.

Matthew goes over to the refrigerator, opens the door and asks, 'Anything good to eat?'

Mrs Martin says, 'Matthew. This fighting has got to stop. I'm sick and tired of the way that you tease your sister all the time.'

'Nerdface. She called me nerdface,' Matthew reminds her. 'I didn't even do anything and she called me nerdface. Do you think that was right?'

Mrs Martin sighs and sits down at the table.

Amanda rushes back into the room. 'You little nerdface. There was nothing on my face.'

'Yes, there is.' Matthew grins at her. 'There *is* something on your face. Lopsided glasses.'

'Matthew.' Mrs Martin stands up again. 'Enough — and stop calling your brother nerdface, Amanda.'

Amanda smiles.

That is not the response that Matthew expects.

She also holds up the computer printout that Matthew has left in the study.

That is definitely not something that Matthew expected either.

'Mom. I just found something you really should look at.' Amanda is trying hard to look concerned, not incredibly happy at getting back at her brother. 'This could get dear little Matthew into big trouble at school. I would never show it to you if I weren't so worried.'

Ha, Matthew thinks. Worried is not the right word.

Amanda continues, faking a very grownup voice. 'As I said, I'm only showing this to you because I don't want Matthew to do these things at school and maybe turn into a juvenile delinquent and maybe someday turn to a life of crime. It's for his own good and I only hope that he doesn't use this opportunity to make up stories about things that he wants to make you believe that I've done.'

Mrs Martin stares at her children, not positive

about the best way to handle the situation.

She wants to respect her children's privacy.

She also wants to protect them from harm.

She remembers all the times her own mother said, 'Just wait until you have children of your own.'

Amanda waves the list in front of her. 'I'm serious. This could cause a lot of trouble and torture.'

Mrs Martin sighs again. 'Amanda. Give me the paper and then go to your room. I will finish helping you with your nails later.'

Amanda smirks as she leaves the room.

Matthew watches as his mother reads the list.

Mrs Martin turns away from him so that he can't see her face.

Matthew wonders if he can convince his mother that he is just doing homework that Mrs Stanton assigned.

It's doubtful.

Mrs Martin turns back and looks at her son.

Matthew can tell by her face that even though she's trying very hard not to smile, she's not going to accept any kidding around about this, that he's going to have to explain what's really going on.

Matthew sits down to, as his father says, face the music.

He only hopes that when everything is over, his parents won't cancel the sleepover, and that the only music that he will have to face is the guys singing, 'Happy Birthday To You.'

CHAPTER 15

WHY I WILL NOT TRY TO GET EVEN BY MATTHEW MARTIN

I will not get even for many reasons.
The first one is that my parents say that if I do
I can't have my birthday party. That is really the
biggest reason that I won't try to get even.

I will also not try to get even because my parents
will make me write another composition just like this
one. I personally don't think it's a good idea to make
a kid like me write something that's not for school, just
for his parents. It's especially not grate (great) when the
kid is not a good speller and they have said that everything
should be spelled correctly. I personally believe that
there should be a seperation (separation) between home and
school.

My mother told me why I should not get even so I will
use some of her reasons so that this paper is long enough.
She said that even though some of the things seemed harm-
less, someone could get hurt with some of them, if not
fisically (phisically, physically), their feelings could
get hurt. She also said that swallowing Silly Putty could
be danjerus (dangerous), that braces are expensive to repair,
and that I seem to have an abnormel (abnormil, abnormal)
interest in snot.

I could tell that she wasn't <u>so</u> mad, because there were times when she almost laughed out loud. But then she said how I should try to work things out more directly, maybe apologize for some of the things that had made the girls mad in the first place, and not ever do them again.

I tried to explain why that wasn't going to work (my mother doesn't realize what a crudball Vanessa Singer really is and how stubborn she can be). But I did agree to write this paper about how I won't do any of the things that I said I would do on my list.

So now that I have written this, I can have my party, right?

Signed,

Matthew Martin

'Matthew, I'm willing to accept this essay as proof of your intention to not wage war with the Girls of G.E.T. H.I.M.' Mr Martin keeps smiling, even though he is trying to look very strict. 'You will, as I understand it, give up all thoughts of G.E.T. T.H.E.M. Correct?'

'Yeah.' Matthew looks at the floor.

'Yeah?' Mr Martin lifts his son's chin. 'Yeah? Is that the way to talk while you are trying to convince your old man of the sincerity of your words? Look at me and tell me that you mean what you say.'

'Yes, sir,' Matthew sighs and looks his father in the eyes.

His father is smiling and remembering some of the things that he, himself, did when he was a kid. He is also remembering how his parents made him promise to do things that he really didn't want to do and only hopes that Matthew will really do what he has said he would do. Disciplining his children is not one of Mr Martin's favourite things about being a father.

Mr Martin ruffles his son's hair. 'Okay, your mother and I spoke to Mrs Stanton this afternoon and she has promised to talk to the girls.'

'Aw, Pop. You know I didn't want you to do that. Now everyone is going to think I'm a nerd, a complete and total nerd. Now the girls will really torture me and you've made me promise to do nothing. I'm a dead duck.'

'It'll be all right,' Mr Martin says, hoping that it will be, but not sure.

Fat chance, Matthew thinks. Mrs Stanton will tell the dumb girls that they will get detention if they do something at school but she can't control what they do off school grounds.

Matthew is sure that he is in deep, deep, deep, deep trouble. And there is nothing he can do about it since he's promised not to fight with the girls and to do nothing to Amanda for squealing on him.

Life sure isn't fair, Matthew thinks.

He's just glad that Amanda is out shopping with their mother so that she can't gloat about his problems.

He hopes that Danny Cohen regains his sanity and un-asks her to the dance and that Amanda turns into a social reject.

He tries to figure out what he can do to get back at all the girls who are making his life miserable, but it's no use. His parents have warned him, if he breaks his promises, he will have *no* more birthday parties, not ever, no allowance and two pounds of alfalfa sprouts and tofu a day. (The threat of alfalfa sprouts and tofu came from his father. His mother said, 'Your father is just kidding about that. We don't use food as a reward or punishment.') Matthew heard his father mumble that sprouts weren't just punishment, they were torture.

Torture, Matthew knows, is what the girls are going to do to him when they realise that he can't fight back.

'Matthew. Where are you? Are you daydreaming?' his father asks.

Matthew looks up. 'It's more of a nightmare.'

'How about putting the tent up? That way if there are any problems with it, we'll know about them now, instead of tomorrow, when everyone is here for the party. And it'll get your mind off your troubles.'

'Great idea,' Matthew says. 'Also, I should probably fill the goody bags tonight and sample the sweets to make sure that we aren't giving away any stale old sweets. We wouldn't want anyone to get sick and sue us for a million-billion dollars.'

Putting his hand on his son's shoulder, Mr Martin says, 'I think it's my responsibility as your father to help you test those sweets — especially the M&Ms and the liquorice, which are my personal all-time favourites.'

'It's a deal.' Matthew smiles, glad that his father is not as nutty about health food as his mother.

'Race you to the garage.' His father starts running. 'People over thirty get a head start.'

Matthew and his father race to the garage to get the tent and to pig out on sweets. It's Matthew's last day as a ten-year-old and he intends to live it up.

CHAPTER 16

'Mom. Do you promise that you aren't going to have one of those goofy people from work come over here and embarrass me? All of the guys are going to think it's so corny to have people in costumes singing and dancing and acting like goof balls.' Matthew moves his finger around the mixing bowl and picks up left over icing.

'I promise.' Mrs Martin looks up from the cake that she's decorating. 'It costs too much, even with my discount and anyway, everyone is booked this weekend. Also, I promised your sister not to do it since she is afraid that she too will die of embarrassment. I wonder when I turned into such an embarrassment for my children. Back in the old days, you used to think that I was always right, always wonderful. Look, I promise. I'm not sending anything . . . scouts' honour—'

'You're not a girl scout,' Matthew reminds her.

'Okay: mother's honour . . . wife's honour . . .

working woman's honour.'

'Mom!' Amanda calls out from her room.

'I'll be right there, honey.' Mrs Martin puts down the cake decorating tube.

'Mom.' Matthew looks at her. 'This isn't fair. You keep going into Amanda's room to help her instead of getting ready for *my* party, which is definitely much more important. The guys are going to be here any minute, *any minute* — and my cake only says Happy B. It's not fair. Amanda has been getting dressed for her stupid date for the last five hours. She keeps changing her clothes. She keeps trying on new make-up. She keeps practising trying to walk without her glasses. She keeps tripping over things and looking squinty. She's really a mess. And you keep going in to help her.'

'You only have a first date once.' Mrs Martin smiles. 'Matthew, some day you will go out on your first date and you'll care about how you look, too.'

Matthew picks up the cake decorating tube, holds it over his face and squeezes some icing into his mouth. Some of it spills on to his cheek. He wipes it off, streaking it across his face.

'On second thoughts, maybe you won't ever care.' Mrs Martin kisses him on the forehead.

'No licking it off my face.' Matthew grins.

Mrs Martin sighs. 'Matthew.'

'Mom!' Amanda yells. 'It's an emergency. I can't decide which earrings to wear.'

'Coming, honey.' Mrs Martin heads upstairs.

'Coming, honey.' Matthew softly mimics his

94

mother. 'Coming, honey. Of course, your stupid first date is very important, more important than my only son's birthday because . . . because you are such a dweeble that no one is ever going to ask you out again.'

Matthew looks down at the cake, then up at the clock — and thinks that the guys could arrive any time now. No one waits until the exact second the invitation says to show up. What if the guys show up and look at the cake and see only HAPPY B? They'll know that everyone in the family thinks that dumb Amanda is more important than he is.

Matthew points the decorating tube at the cake and thinks, here goes. I can do this myself.

On the cake appear the words, HAPPY BERTHDAY.

Matthew is very proud of himself for taking care of things himself.

He looks at the cake.

Something does not look right.

Matthew looks at it for a few minutes, but he isn't sure.

Amanda rushes into the kitchen, goes to the refrigerator and pulls out a can of diet soda. 'I'm never going to be ready on time.'

'You've been getting ready for weeks. I don't understand what your problem is. Anyway, I've got problems of my own.' Matthew points to the cake.

Amanda looks at it. 'Let me guess. You wrote out HAPPY BERTHDAY yourself.'

'Mom did half of it, and then she had to go and

help you.' Matthew makes a face.

Amanda debates leaving the cake the way that it is, but then thinks about how rotten Matthew is going to feel if everyone sees how 'Birthday' is mis-spelled. 'It's I, not E. Look is there any more icing left, besides what is on your face?'

Matthew hands her the mixing bowl.

Amanda looks at the clock on the wall, thinks about how she should be getting her nails on and looks back at Matthew.

It is not going to be much fun for him if all his friends tease him on his birthday.

Taking a knife out of the drawer, Amanda scrapes the E off the cake, fills in the hole with brown carob icing, and inserts the I.

'All better now.' Amanda grins at her brother. 'Happy Birthday, Creepling. Now I've got to go.'

She rushes out of the kitchen and back to her bedroom, where her mother is putting clothes back on hangers and placing them back in the wardrobe.

Matthew looks at his cake and smiles.

Amanda did a pretty good job.

Nobody is going to be reminded what a lousy speller he is.

Amanda was actually nice for a change.

There is a good chance that this party is going to be great, especially if everyone brings terrific presents, Matthew thinks.

The doorbell rings.

It's Joshua, carrying a sleeping bag and a present.

The present looks very flat, not like a toy or game or computer disk or anything good at all.

Joshua hands the present to him. 'It's a dumb shirt. My mother made me bring it. I wanted to get you a Destroyers of the Earth zap gun, but my mother said your mother wouldn't allow it in the house.'

'I wish you had brought it. I could have used it on the girls of G.E.T. H.I.M.' Matthew holds up the present and pretends that it is a zap gun.

In walks Mr Martin, carrying a large bag. 'Hi, guys. Ice cream delivery.'

'What flavour did you get? Did you get my favourite one — Bubble Gum Ripple?' Joshua asks.

Shaking his head, Mr Martin says, 'No. That was the last flavour of the month. I got double fudge with butterscotch, blueberry cheesecake . . .'

'Yuk,' say both of the boys at the same time.

'More of it for me.' Mr Martin rubs his stomach. 'It's not often that we get real ice cream into this house. So when we do I try to make the most of it. We also have Peanut Brickle, Pistachio, Chocolate Mint and Banana Royale.'

'That's enough for an army.' Joshua licks his lips.

Mrs Martin comes back into the kitchen and looks at all the ice cream that Mr Martin is showing the boys.

'All that sugar.' She sighs. 'We're going to have a group of boys spending the night with us who are all sugared up. I thought that you were going to get one flavour, maybe two.'

Mr Martin tries to look sorry for what he has done but it's obvious that he's not. 'They didn't have Granola Grape or Sprout Sundae as this month's flavour of the month.'

Mrs Martin shakes her head. 'I married you for better or for worse. Your food preferences are definitely not among your better qualities.'

As Mr Martin puts the ice cream into the refrigerator, the doorbell rings.

Billy Kellerman and Pablo Martinez arrive.

Mrs Martin goes outside to talk to Mrs Kellerman.

Earlier in the week, Mrs Martin had Matthew give all the boys a paper to take home. A parent was to fill out the form, saying whether the boy was allergic to anything, who to call in case of emergency, and if a boy got homesick was he to go home or stay anyway.

Mrs Martin believes in organisation.

Billy Kellerman never takes papers home.

Tyler White and Mark Ellison show up on their bikes, doing wheelies.

Brian Bruno, Patrick Ryan and David Cohen march up to the front door, with their sleeping bags on their heads, singing 'I Love A Parade'.

'Let the wild rumpus begin!' yells Joshua, using a saying from one of his favourite books from when he was a little kid, *Where the Wild Things Are*.

Everyone goes into the den.

Matthew opens the presents.

There are more baseball cards for his collection

and a new Nintendo cartridge, a couple of tapes, a magic set, a squirting calculator, the shirt that Joshua's mother picked out, a Transformer that turns into a working camera (a present sent by Matthew's grandmother in Florida), The Oozone Layer, a game that gets slime all over everyone, and more clothes, picked out by more mothers.

'Awesome!' 'Rad,' and 'Excellent,' are some of the responses as Matthew opens the package from Mark Ellison and Patrick Ryan.

In the package are suction cup bullet holes, to be put on someone's skin. Also included are capsules of make-believe blood, to be broken over the skin where the bullet holes are placed.

Matthew looks over at his mother as he unwraps some more of the items in the box.

She definitely looks underwhelmed by the presents.

Matthew only hopes that she will let him keep these gifts.

There are also some make-believe tattoos and one of those baseballs that look like a monster's eyes.

'Wow. Thanks.' Matthew puts the eye ball in front of his own eyeball.

His mother is shaking her head.

His father is laughing.

'I can use this all for my next book report.' Matthew thinks fast. 'Mrs Stanton said we should do a mystery. This stuff will come in handy for the oral report.'

'I'm sure.' Mrs Martin sounds a little sarcastic.

'Really.' Matthew puts on his most angelic look and decides to change the subject and not to pull out the last item, a skull and crossbones bike sticker. 'What's in that big box over there?'

Mr and Mrs Martin hand Matthew a large package.

Matthew rips off the wrapping paper as his mother yells, 'Save the bow. We can use it again.'

Matthew forgets and demolishes the bow, opening the package to discover a remote control car.

'Luck-y,' say several of the guys at the same time.

'Let me see that.' Tyler holds out his hands.

'Me first.' Matthew takes the car out of the box and he and his father set it up.

'This is from your sister.' Mrs Martin shows Matthew a certificate that says that Matthew now has a subscription to *Radio Control Car Action*.

'Luck-y.'

'I get first dibs on borrowing it after you're done,' Joshua says.

Mr and Mrs Martin go out of the room and some of the guys start playing with the car.

Two tournaments begin. Nintendo and Computer.

Four people play.

The rest cheer or boo.

Soon everyone goes over to the bowl of gummy worms and puts a gummy worm above his lips, pretending to be the principal, Mr Curtis, who has just started to grow a moustache.

The doorbell rings.

'I thought everyone was here already,' Matthew says, eating the tail of the gummy worm — or maybe it's the head. He's not sure.

'I think it's my brother, my step brother,' David says.

'The date,' Joshua says. 'Let's do something to get them all embarrassed.'

'My brother said he would kill me if we did anything.' David shakes his head. 'Let's not, and say we did. That way I'll still be alive to have my own birthday party in two months.'

Matthew is glad that David has said not to do anything, that he isn't the one who had to do it.

He's thinking about how, even though Amanda is a real pain sometimes, she did help him with the birthday cake and she really doesn't deserve to have her first date messed up, even though it would, in some ways, be a lot of fun to do something to her.

'You guys promise to stay in here, and I'll ask my Mom if we can have the cake and ice cream now.'

'A bribe. I'll take it,' Brian Bruno says.

Mark Ellison, who has ten gummy worms coming out of his mouth, is walking around shaking his head at everyone so that the worms look like they are alive.

Matthew goes out of the room and sees Amanda standing in the hallway. She's trying to keep her balance on her new high heels, biting her press-on nails and attempting to see without her glasses.

She's a wreck.

Matthew tries to make Amanda feel better. 'For a

goofy girl, you don't look half bad.'

Amanda smiles, a little. 'Thank you . . . I think.'

They walk into the living room.

Mr and Mrs Martin are standing there, talking to Danny, who looks a little nervous, too.

Mr Martin takes out a camera and says, 'I hope that you two don't mind, but I'd love to take a picture.'

'Oh Daddy, that's so embarrassing.' Amanda looks like she's going to die.

Danny says, 'If you're going to take a picture of anything, sir, I think you might want to take a picture of what's happening on your pavement.'

'What's happening?' Mr and Mrs Martin go immediately to the front door.

So does Amanda, who says, 'This is so gross.' She starts to giggle.

Matthew goes up to the door and looks out.

It's the girls of G.E.T. H.I.M. and they are marching back and forth, carrying picket signs and wearing t-shirts that they have decorated themselves.

The t-shirts say:

The girls of G.E.T. H.I.M. Strike Again!

CHAPTER 17

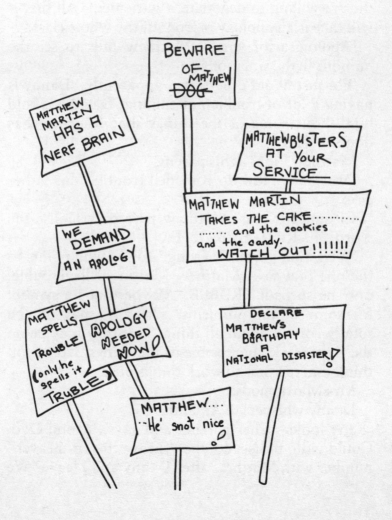

'Oh, gross. This is so gross,' Amanda is laughing.

'They asked me to bring in a message.' Danny is laughing too, although he's also feeling a little embarrassed that there are so many people around to watch him pick up his date. 'They said that they're willing to negotiate a settlement. All that it will take is an apology in front of the whole class.'

'Apologise for what?' Matthew fails to see the humour in the situation.

'For just about everything, apparently.' Danny is having a lot of trouble not smiling. David has told him about some of the things that Matthew has done in class.

Matthew looks at his parents.

'Matthew. How do you spell trouble?' his father asks.

Closing his eyes, Matthew tries to visualise the word. 'T - R - U - B - B - L - E.'

'Well, that poster is wrong.' Mr Martin points to the one that says, Matthew Martin spells Trouble, only he spells it TRUBLE. 'Maybe that's a symbol for some of the problems. The girls may not be totally correct about all things, but they may be on the right track about some of the things. Don't you think that it's time to work things out?'

Mrs Martin nods.

Danny whispers to Amanda.

She looks at her parents and says, 'Mom. Dad. Could you please do the "Leave It To Beaver" number with Matthew after Danny and I leave? We have to go over to the Jackson's house and get our ride to the dance there.'

'Okay, Wally. We'll talk to the Beav after you go.' Mr Martin is laughing and pretending to be Mr Cleaver.

'Leave It To Beaver' is the old television show that the Martins always watch together, and at the end Mr Martin always says, 'Why can't our family be more like that? Why can't all families be more like that?'

Mrs Martin gets into the act too. 'Now, I want you to make sure that you children are careful, get home on time, and Just Say No to all the things that you know that you are to say No to. And if you see Eddie Haskell be sure to give him my regards.'

Mrs Martin always hisses when Eddie Haskell comes on the show.

Amanda looks at Danny. 'I can't help it. My family is weird. I warned you.'

'That's all right. Ever since my mother's remarriage, my family tries to be the Brady Bunch.' Danny reaches out and holds Amanda's hand. 'It could be worse. They could try to be The Munsters.'

As Amanda and Danny go out the door, the girls all start yelling things like, 'MATTHEW MARTIN, COME OUT RIGHT NOW! WE DEMAND AN APOLOGY. APOLOGISE. APOLOGISE. APOLOGISE.'

Amanda turns around and looks at Matthew.

'Thank you so much for causing all this commotion when all I want to do is have a happy memory of this.'

'It's not my fault.' Matthew goes to the door.

'It's always your fault.' Amanda trips on her high heels.

Danny catches her.

The girls catch sight of Matthew at the door. 'APOLOGISE. APOLOGISE. APOLOGISE. APOLOGISE.'

'What are you going to do?' Joshua walks into the living room.

The rest of the boys follow.

Tyler White waves to Zoe Alexander, who is his girl friend.

Cupping his hands, he calls out, 'I thought you were going over to Vanessa's to have a pyjama party!'

She calls back, 'We are, but first this.'

Vanessa Singer looks very proud of herself.

Matthew wishes that a tornado would come and take all of the girls to Kansas.

The tornado doesn't materialise.

'I think you should talk to them before the neighbours begin to complain about the noise,' Mr Martin says.

'Let them complain.' Matthew shakes his head. 'Then they'll call the cops and have the girls arrested.'

'I think that there is a better solution.' Mrs

Martin puts her hand on her son's shoulder.

'Call the F.B.I. in?' Matthew feels that would be the better solution.

'Matthew.' Mrs Martin says.

'I think you should apologise and let the girls have ice cream and cake with us,' Joshua suggests.

'No way.' Matthew shakes his head.

Pablo Martinez says, 'Come on, Matthew. The girls aren't so bad. You know that you like some of them, that you used to be friends with them.'

Matthew thinks about how hard it is to always be the youngest one in his class, how he always feels like he's playing Catch-up, how it seems like everyone is always a little ahead of him. Can he help it that he's always the youngest — in his family — and in his class?

He wishes that some new younger kid would move into town and be put in the sixth grade class.

He wishes that his parents would have another kid: a younger one, obviously.

He wonders if it's too late to ask for one, instead of the remote control car.

He wonders if he can have both, the baby brother and the remote control car.

'Matthew, you've got to do something.' Billy Kellerman points to the girls, who are now sitting on the lawn with their arms linked, singing an old peace song that Mrs Stanton taught them in history class called 'We Shall Overcome.'

Matthew looks out at the girls and then turns

back and says, 'Let's just ignore them.'

'Ignoring the problem won't make it go away,' Mrs Martin says.

'My mother always says that, too.' Mark Ellison nods.

'My parents, too,' say a couple of the other kids.

'Everyone else's parents would let them ignore the girls.' Matthew is feeling desperate.

'Matthew. Let me list all the possible responses to that.' Mr Martin is smiling. 'Would we let you jump off the roof if everyone else's parents did? We're not everyone else's parents. As long as you are living under our roof, it doesn't matter what other people's parents say and, that old standby, No way José. Now did I miss any?'

'My father always says, "I brought you into this world. I can take you out",' Billy Kellerman offers.

Mr Martin says, 'So you see, Matthew, my son, you are going to have to deal with this problem. Think of your friends waiting for their ice cream and cake. Think of your dad waiting for his ice cream and cake. Think of how much better you're going to feel once you resolve this problem.'

Looking at the boys, then at his parents and then out the window at the girls, Matthew realises there's only one thing to do; actually, two, if you count moving to Disneyland, which his parents probably would not let him do. So there really is only one thing to do. Talk to the girls and work out some kind of truce.'

'Okay, I'll talk to them,' Matthew says softly.

'Terrific. I'll get a pillowcase, tie it to a stick and go out to the enemy camp to work out the arrangements. That's what they always do in movies and books.' Mr Martin heads out of the room.

'Honey. I don't think that's necessary.' Mrs Martin calls after him.

'It'll be fun,' he calls back.

Mrs Martin looks at Matthew and smiles. 'Your father. I married him because of his high sense of play. He sometimes drives me nuts with his high sense of play — and you take after him.'

Everyone watches as Mr Martin heads out of the door.

Everyone watches as Mr Martin goes over to the group of singing girls, sits down with them and talks.

The talk goes on for several minutes.

Finally, Mr Martin returns and says to Matthew, 'Here's the deal. You are very lucky, young man, that you have a lawyer for a father. This is what I have negotiated. The girls will come inside. You will apologise for all the things that you did that led to the formation of G.E.T. H.I.M., and I want that apology to sound sincere.'

'Okay.' Matthew stares at the floor.

'And,' Mr Martin continues, 'the girls have agreed, if your apology sounds sincere, to apologise for all the things that led to the formation of G.E.T. T.H.E.M.'

'Okay.' That word sounds a lot happier this time when Matthew says it.

'And,' Mr Martin says, 'the last part of the negotiations involved the kind of cake to be served. One of the demands is that there be no carob icing, just mocha, and that the cake be filled with butterscotch custard. That was their final demand. I gave in to it in the cause of furthering trust and understanding.'

'Huh.' Mrs Martin puts her hands on her hips. 'There's something fishy going on here. *That* is your favourite cake.'

'Not fishy — cakey.' Mr Matthew puts his hand on his son's head. 'What say we wrap up the apology session and I'll make the supreme sacrifice and run over to the supermarket and get the cake.'

Matthew smiles at his father, realising that his trouble is almost over. 'It's a deal.'

CHAPTER 18

'First you had to eat crow, then you got to eat cake.' Mr Martin pats his son's back.

'Huh?' Matthew looks up at his father.

'Eating crow is a phrase that means you had to say you were sorry in such a way that it seemed like a major punishment.' Sounding like a teacher, Mr Martin reaches for his third piece of cake.

'It would have been easier to eat a crow than to look at Vanessa acting like such a big shot winner.' Matthew runs his finger around the paper at the edge of the cake to get the icing.

The male Martins are in the kitchen alone, while the party is going on in the living room.

Mrs Martin is hiding out in her bedroom reading a book and worrying about the health of her family.

'Actually, things turned out all right,' Mr Martin says. 'The girls did apologise too. Although I do think that Vanessa saying, "I'm sorry that it was necessary to do all those things to you," was not the best apology in the world. But look at the bright side, there's a truce and you are the host of the first sixth grade girl-boy party. And you are a year older.'

'And I got lots of great presents.' Matthew grins.

Mr Martin grins back. 'You really did. Do you think I could borrow the suction cup bullet holes and one of the capsules of make believe blood? I'd like to wear them to work on Monday.'

'Absolutely.' Matthew nods.

'Thanks, kid.' Mr Martin wipes his face off. 'Are all the crumbs gone? I don't want any evidence when I go back to the room. Otherwise your mom is going to say . . .'

Both male Martins, in unison, say, 'Lips that touch sugar won't touch mine.'

Matthew heads into the living room.

The compact disc player is on, loud.

Most of the girls are standing on one side of the room. The boys on the other.

Walking up to Matthew, Vanessa Singer points at him and whispers, 'Listen, doofball. No more silly stuff or the girls of GET HIM will activate Plan B.'

Matthew debates doing something really gross, like another SBD or belching out a chorus of 'Happy Birthday.' Instead, he clutches his heart and pretends to writhe in pain. 'Oh, no. Not Plan B. Anything but Plan B.'

Sticking his tongue out, he crosses his eyes and sinks to the floor, muttering, 'Help. She's picking on me. What's Plan B?'

Vanessa looks down at him. Then she looks at everyone else looking at them and realizes that they know that she is the one who started it this time.

She sticks her nose up in the air and, after stepping over Matthew, says loudly, 'Just remember, a truce is a truce.'

Matthew jumps up and calls out, 'And a moose is a moose!'

Everyone laughs, except Vanessa.

Then Matthew goes over to Joshua and says, 'I guess there's no chance for the tournaments to finish.'

'I don't see why not.' Joshua cups his hands and calls out, 'Nintendo and Computer Tournaments are back on. Who else wants to join up?'

'Also we can drive the remote control car,' Tyler says, turning to Zoe, and smiles. 'Want to go for a ride with me?'

'But you don't have your licence,' Zoe frowns.

'It's a miniature car,' Lisa Levine tells her.

'And it's remote,' says Jil! Hudson, who thinks that Zoe is a little remote, too.

'Anywhere you want to go, I want to go too, Tyler,' says Zoe, sounding like syrup.

Ryma Browne pretends to stick her fingers in her mouth and makes little retching noises.

'Some day, when you two are more mature, you will understand what it's like to have a boyfriend.' Zoe makes a face at Jil! and Ryma.

'Trust me. I will never act the way you do around boys.' Ryma makes a face.

'My mother told me how to act, and she must be right. I have the boyfriend, not you.' Zoe looks like she owns the world.

Jil! debates asking if Zoe's mother knows so much about men, how come she has had four husbands, but Jil! decides not to.

Tyler looks a little embarrassed, but he also looks like he enjoys the attention. With four older brothers, he thinks he knows a lot about dating.

The tournaments begin.

Billy Kellerman wins at Nintendo.

His prize is a hand held game called Parachute.

Matthew wins at computer but, since it's his party, the prize goes to the second prize winner, Chloe Fulton.

'Good game,' Matthew says, glad that he had practised for a week before the party and extra glad that Chloe didn't know which game would be used in the tournament.

Chloe gets a set of science fiction books, which is terrific since she loves to read everything, especially science fiction.

'Can I borrow them when you're done?' Pablo Martinez asks.

'Absolutely.'

By the time the boy-girl part of the party is almost over, everyone is talking to everyone else. No one is fighting. Nobody is making a big deal out of it being a boy-girl party, except for Zoe, who keeps blowing into Tyler's ear because she heard that was a sexy thing to do. He keeps wiping the spit off, finally begging, 'Say it. Don't spray it.'

Jil! Hudson comes up to Matthew when he is standing alone by the bowl of gummy worms. 'I'm really sorry that I teased you so much about being boyfriend and girlfriend. I was just joking around.'

Matthew looks at Jil!, who is nervously chewing on the end of her hair.

He thinks about how much fun she can be when she isn't picking on him, how she's always thinking of fun things to do, how she's always so creative. He also thinks about Zoe's comment about how Jil! isn't mature enough to have a boyfriend.

'That's okay,' he grins. 'Some day when you're more grown up, maybe then we can be boyfriend and girlfriend. And if you really play your cards right, maybe we could be just like the Cleavers and live happily ever after.'

Then he picks up a gummy worm and puts it above his lip to form a moustache.

CHAPTER 19

Sunday.

All the boys have finally left after the sleepover.

Two were sick.

All of them watched as Danny and Amanda came back from their date.

All of them made kissing sounds with their lips on their hands when Danny started to kiss Amanda on the porch.

Amanda threatened to put all of them in the microwave, piece by piece and then she begged to be sent away to boarding school or to have Matthew sent to Reform School.

Matthew said it was not his fault.

Amanda disagreed.

The boys, at breakfast, ate ninety-four pancakes, spilled the syrup all over the flour, devoured three packets of vegetarian sausage without realising that it wasn't the real thing, drank two containers of orange juice and then held a belching contest.

Mrs Martin refused to award a prize to the winner of that competition.

'Thank goodness for paper plates,' Mr Martin says, throwing a bunch of them into the dustbin.

Trying to fit just one more glass into the dishwasher, Mrs Martin says, 'I didn't get any sleep last night with all of the laughing, did you?'

Mr Martin shakes his head.

'What did the boys want to talk to you about this morning? What was so private?' she asks, starting the dishwasher.

'They wanted me to judge the joke telling competition.' Mr Martin looks in the freezer to see if there is any ice cream left over for breakfast.

He can't find any.

'Who won?' Mrs Martin closes the freezer door before he can find out that she has hidden the ice cream container in the empty frozen spinach box. 'And what was the joke?'

'Patrick Ryan. And you don't want to know.' Mr Martin sits down at the table.

Matthew enters the kitchen very quietly, whispering, 'Is the coast clear? Did Amanda go over to Cindy's or is she hiding behind the refrigerator waiting for the chance to kill me?'

'She left an hour ago.' Mr Martin shakes his head. 'You know, you and the guys should not have used the computer to make up that sign, "Amanda Martin makes a Spectacle(s) out of herself." That wasn't very nice, and anyway, how did you know that glasses used to be called spectacles?'

'We studied Ben Franklin.' Matthew is glad that

117

he can show his parents that he actually remembers something from school.

There's silence at the table for a few minutes while Matthew waits to see if his parents are going to say anything else about how he's always tormenting Amanda.

Mr and Mrs Martin say nothing. They are so glad that there is peace and quiet again in their house.

'Mom.' Matthew breaks the silence. 'Dad. Do you realise that there are only three hundred and sixty-four days, eight hours and twenty-eight minutes until my next birthday?'

Mr and Mrs Martin look at each other as if they have been put in front of a firing squad.

Mrs Martin is the first to speak. 'Matthew Martin. Everyone else's children said they wouldn't bother their parents this morning. What do you have to say about that?'

Matthew grins. 'I'm not everyone else's child.'

'True.' Mr Martin looks at his son and realises that Matthew has the suction cup bullet holes on his arms. 'Very true.'

The looks that the parents give each other are unmistakable.

What will Matthew do next?

Make Like A Tree And Leave

To Susan Haven and
Pamela Curtis Swallow

ACKNOWLEDGMENTS

The Danzigers of Califon
Dr Steven Sugarman
Dr Mark Sherman
The Woodstock Conservancy

Chapter 1

'The suspense builds.' Mathew, holding up a baseball cap, looks at the three classmates who are sitting on his bedroom floor. 'Inside this very hat are four small, blank, folded pieces of paper. The fifth has an X on it. One of us and only one will get that X. Who, I ask you, who will get that paper?'

'If you'd cut out the drama and let us pick, we could answer that question very quickly.' Brian Bruno looks as if he's ready to grab the cap out of Matthew's hands.

Holding the cap behind his back, Matthew says, 'How can the suspense build if we pick right away?'

'I don't want suspense. I want to find out now,' Billy Kellerman says. 'Why do you always have to turn everything into a major production?'

'Because it's more fun that way.' Matthew grins. 'Anyway, Mrs Stanton made me the chairman of the Mummy Committee, so I get to do it my way.'

'Baloney,' Billy says. 'I overheard Mrs Stanton tell Ms Wagner that she only made you the chairman of the Mummy Committee because she's "trying to get you to use your leadership qualities in a more positive way".'

'Baloney to you . . . I don't believe it.' Matthew glares.

'It's true. I was in the toilet in the nurse's office and the nurse had gone out for a minute, and the two of them came in and didn't know I was there. I also found out that Ms Wagner is going out with Mr King. You can learn a lot hanging out in the nurse's office.' Billy grins. 'And Ms Wagner told her about the time she made you the chairman of the fourth-grade Volcano Committee.'

'That explosion was NOT my fault!' Matthew protests.

'We only have two weeks to finish . . . We'd better get started,' Joshua Jackson reminds them. 'Come on, Matthew. Let's not start fighting and instead of letting the suspense build, let's build the mummy.'

'Oh, okay.' Matthew relents, holding out the baseball cap. 'Hurry up and pick, then. See if I care.'

Joshua closes his eyes and selects a piece of paper.

Billy Kellerman keeps his open and stares at the papers, wishing that he had X-ray vision, and then he chooses.

Brian Bruno crosses his fingers and then picks a piece of paper.

The paper falls to the ground because Brian Bruno is not good at holding on to paper with crossed fingers.

Matthew takes the last one out of the cap, puts the cap back on his head with the visor facing backwards, and says, 'At the count of three,

122

everyone open his paper . . . One . . . two . . . three . . . go.'

Matthew looks down at his paper. There is no *X*.

He's not sure whether he's sad or happy . . . or relieved.

There's no question that Joshua is happy. He's waving his paper and yelling, 'No *X*. No *X*.'

For a minute Matthew thinks that he should have put an *L* on the paper instead of an *X* so that Joshua could have yelled out 'No *L*. No *L*,' since he's acting like it's Christmas even though it's only October.

Then he looks around.

Billy's smiling.

Brian says, 'How about if we make it the first person who gets two *X*'s? Isn't that a great idea?'

'Come on. It'll be fun. All we have to do is turn you into a mummy like the Egyptians used to do,' Matthew reminds him. 'It'll be easy. Billy got all the stuff to do it from his father's supply cabinet. It took the Egyptians seventy days to prepare a body. We'll be done today.'

'The Egyptians only did it to dead people,' Brian reminds him.

'Dead animals too.' Joshua has been doing a lot of research.

'I'm still alive.' Brian gets up and starts pacing around. 'I'm not a dead person. I'm not a dead animal. I'm not sure that this is a good idea.'

'You thought it was a great idea until you got the *X*.' Matthew gets up too. 'It'll be fun. We'll use the plaster gauze stuff that Dr Kellerman uses all the time on his patients. Remember, we used that stuff in third grade to make face masks.'

'That was just our faces. You're going to do it to my whole body. What if I get claustrophobia?' Brian looks less than overjoyed.

'Claustrophobia.' Matthew grins. 'Isn't that fear of a little old fat man in a red suit who shows up at Christmas?'

'That's so funny I forgot to laugh.' Brian scowls. 'You know that means fear of being closed in.'

'Look.' Billy starts taking out the boxes of plaster gauze that they've been storing at the bottom of Matthew's already messy closet. 'I'm planning to be an orthopaedist just like my dad and I've watched him work before. It'll be a breeze . . . and the plaster dries very quickly and then we'll cut it off of you. Nothing to it. Nothing at all.'

'And I'll teach you how to win at Super Gonzorga, that new computer game. You'll be able to beat everyone but me,' Matthew says.

'Everyone but you and Chloe Fulton,' Billy reminds him. 'You know she's almost as good as you are . . . sometimes she even beats you.'

Matthew chooses to ignore Billy. 'And Brian, I'll do the hieroglyphics poster with you. We'll do a poster about a guy named Hy Roglifics, who invents the Egyptian alphabet.'

'Let's not and say we did.' Brian shakes his head.

Joshua puts his hand on Brian's shoulder to stop him from pacing. 'I'll ask my father to make you the peanut butter cookies that you like so much.'

'It's a deal.' Brian smiles for the first time since

he's picked the X.

The boys hear a door slam downstairs as Amanda Martin enters the house.

'Matthew? Are you home, you little creepling?'

They also hear her yell again. 'Are you there, Barf Brain?'

Matthew helps Billy take out more boxes of plaster.

'Aren't you going to answer her?' Billy asks.

'Not when she calls me names. I bet that one of her dumb friends is with her. She always acts like a big shot when that happens.' Matthew makes a face. 'Maybe we should tie her up and put this stuff around her, but not leave the mouth, eye, and nose openings for her, and put her in the bottom of my closet for seventy days and use her for our school project.'

'Sisters.' Joshua says, knowing what it feels like to have an older sister, since he has one who is Amanda's best friend.

There's a pounding on Matthew's door, and Amanda flings the door open.

She's wearing a Hard Rock Café sweatshirt and a pair of old blue jeans. Blonde-haired, with blue eyes, Amanda squints as she glares at the boys, since she has given up wearing her glasses, except for when she absolutely needs to see. She is wearing at least one ring on each of her fingers, dozens of silver bangle bracelets on her right arm, and earrings. The one on the right side has stars and moons on it. The earring on her left earlobe is a heart that is engraved 'Amanda and Danny Forever.'

'Privacy!' Matthew yells, thinking that every time he looks at his sister, she seems to be getting much older . . . and much meaner.

'You didn't answer. I needed to know if you were here, since Mom and Dad said that I have to check on you. It's not my fault that they both work and I have to check.' She looks around the room at all the boxes. 'What are you guys planning to do . . . make face masks like they do in third grade? You'd better do it downstairs, on the back porch, so it doesn't make a mess. You know that our parents will kill you if you ruin the new wall-to-wall carpeting.'

Matthew realizes she's right but still doesn't answer.

Amanda stares at him. 'Cindy's with me and we're going to be upstairs in my room discussing private stuff. So don't bother me.'

Matthew is getting sick of the way that she acts towards him in front of his friends but knows that if he says something, it will get worse.

It's not fair that one kid gets to be older and the boss all the time.

Amanda leaves.

Matthew looks at his friends and says, 'Let's go downstairs and get as far away from that dweeb as possible.'

'And as close to the refrigerator as possible.' Joshua is getting hungry until he remembers how Mrs Martin believes in health food. 'Is there anything good in there . . . anything edible?'

Matthew grins widely, showing his dimples. 'My dad and I made a deal with her. We can have one box of stuff in the freezer and one thing in the refrigerator that she isn't allowed to complain about. We have a large bottle of soda and a box of frozen Milky Ways.'

'Great. Let's get these boxes downstairs and then do some serious snacking before we get to work,' Joshua suggests.

As the boys head down the steps carrying the plaster gauze, Matthew thinks about how this is going to be the best sixth-grade project ever. Mrs Stanton is NOT going to be sorry that she picked him to be chairman.

Chapter 2

Brian Bruno stands on the porch wondering why he didn't join the Pyramid Committee instead.

A giant dustbin bag with a hole in the middle for his head has been placed over his body so that only his feet, neck, and head show.

A bathing cap covers his ears and red hair.

Vaseline is smeared over his freckled face.

Joshua Jackson is holding a Milky Way bar to his mouth so that he can nibble on it.

'We're going to have to stop feeding you soon,' Matthew informs him. 'We're almost up to your chest area and what if you start to choke? We won't be able to do the Heimlich manoeuvre on you because you'll be all covered up with plaster.'

Matthew is trying to be the most responsible chairman of a Mummy Committee ever.

Continuing to wind the bandages around, while Billy wets the gauze so that it turns almost instantly into a plaster cast, Matthew says, 'Brian, how about letting us do some of the real stuff that the Egyptians used to do? We can cut a slit in the left side of your body and take out your liver, lungs, stomach, and intestines.'

'Forget it,' Brian mumbles, his mouth full of Milky Way.

Matthew does not care to forget it. 'Then we can embalm them and place them in a jar.'

'Cut it out.' Brian is getting very unamused.

'That's what I was just suggesting.' Matthew smiles and continues. 'Did you know that the Eyptians used to remove the brain through the nostrils, using metal hooks? That would be a cinch. I'd just have to look up in the attic for one of the hooks we used to use when we made pot holders. Don't you think that's a great idea?'

Brian looks like he does not think it's a great idea. He thinks that Matthew may not be the best head of the Mummy Committee of all time.

The other guys look at each other and think that it's time to change the subject.

Billy looks at the mummy/Brian and says, 'We should use the three-inch tape for his face, not the four-, five-, or six-.'

'Let's do another layer or two first on the rest of the body,' Matthew says. 'We have to make sure that it'll be strong enough not to break after we cut it off Brian, put the two sides back together, and plaster it together.'

'Fair deal.' Billy is really enjoying pretending to be a doctor.

As they work, Joshua holds up a glass of soda and a straw so that Brian can sip.

He keeps talking to Brian to help him keep his mind off what's happening. 'It's a shame that

Amanda and Cindy are so rotten that they'd never give us any old jewellery even if we asked them. Did you know that there should be magic amulets tucked between the wrappings? That would make it more accurate.'

Brian doesn't want a history lesson. 'Would you guys please hurry up? I'm beginning to have trouble standing here. This is getting heavy . . . and I think I'm going to have to go to the toilet soon.'

Joshua immediately puts the soda away.

'We're almost done.' Matthew starts putting the gauze on Brian's face, careful to leave large holes for his eyes, nose, and mouth. 'Billy, stop working on the body. Help me with Brian's face.'

As Billy starts working on the face, Joshua helps to prop up Brian.

Matthew goes for his mother's biggest pair of scissors.

He returns just as Billy is finishing.

It looks great.

'Get me out of here, you guys.' Brian's voice sounds a little muffled.

Checking, Matthew sees that Brian is getting enough air.

Looking, he can see how Brian just might be getting a little tired.

'No sweat,' Matthew says, to reassure him.

'Easy for you to say. You're not covered by a plastic dustbin bag and a ton of cement.' Brian does not sound happy.

Matthew sits down on the floor, ready to cut Brian out of the mummy cast.

It doesn't take him very long to realize that the scissors are not going to cut through the cast.

'Why don't *you* try this, Billy?' He hands the scissors over, trying to look and feel calm.

It takes Billy an equally short period to discover the limitations of the scissors. 'This always worked in third grade.'

'I don't think we had as many layers,' Matthew says softly, knowing that he is in deep trouble, deep deep deep trouble.

'What's going on out there?' Brian begins to sound panicky.

Matthew goes up to his mummy/friend and says, 'I don't know how to tell you this, but we've run into a minor problem.'

'My father's going to kill me if he finds out,' Billy says. 'I asked if I could take just a few rolls. He thought that we were making masks again.'

Joshua says, 'Someone give me a hand supporting this. He's getting heavy.'

Matthew makes a decision, one that he doesn't like but knows is necessary. 'I'll be right back. I'm going up to get Amanda.'

'Hurry,' everyone else says at once.

Rushing out of the room and racing up the steps, Matthew realizes that while Brian Bruno is in heavy-duty plaster, he, Matthew Martin, is in heavy-duty trouble.

And it's not going to be easy to get either of them out.

Chapter 3

Matthew knocks at the bedroom door, yelling, 'Amanda! Amanda! Open up.'

'What do you want? I told you not to bother me.' Her voice comes out loud and clear through the closed door.

Matthew opens it anyway.

Amanda and Cindy are sitting on the bed, using the machine that Amanda got for her birthday . . . the Crimper.

Their hair looks like it's been caught in a waffle iron. Cindy's is totally wrinkly. Amanda's is half-finished.

'I told you —' Amanda starts to scream.

'Emergency. It's an emergency. You've got to come immediately.' Matthew is almost out of breath. 'And you can't tell on me, promise.'

Amanda and Cindy jump off the bed.

As they run downstairs, Cindy remembers that the Crimper is still on and runs back up the stairs.

Matthew explains to Amanda as they rush into the kitchen.

Amanda looks at Joshua and Billy, who are

holding up the mummy and looking very scared.

The mummy doesn't look like it has much emotion, but it's obvious that Brian does.

He's yelling, 'Get me out of here. I want to go home.'

Amanda tries the scissors.

Cindy walks in and says, 'We've got an electric carving knife at home, but that would be too dangerous, right?'

'Right.' Amanda nods, knowing that she is going to have to be in charge of this situation and wishing this time that she were not the oldest.

'I'm calling Mom.' She picks up the phone and dials.

Asking for her mother, she listens for a minute and then says, 'Please have her call the second she gets back. Tell her it's an emergency ... No ... Everything is all right ... sort of ... but please have her call.'

Amanda informs everyone: 'One of the gorillas called in sick. Mom had to put on the costume and go deliver the message.'

Picking up the phone again and mumbling, 'I've begged her ... absolutely begged her to get a normal job ... but did she listen? ... no ... and she's even bought the company and has to spend more time there.'

'Hurry,' Matthew pleads. 'Do something.'

'I'm thirsty,' Brian says softly.

Rushing over to get the glass, Matthew realizes that the problem could get even worse ... if that was possible to imagine.

Going back to Brian, he says, 'Which is worse? Thirst — or having to go to the toilet? Because if I give this to you . . . you know what's going to have to happen sooner or later. You're going to have to go.'

Amanda is on the phone explaining the situation to her father. 'And hurry, Dad, hurry.'

Amanda hangs up and looks at Cindy as if to say, 'Do you believe this?'

Then she looks at Matthew.

'Don't say "I told you so," because you didn't,' he says. 'When's Dad coming home?'

'He's on his way immediately . . . and he's going to call Dr Kellerman from the car phone to find out what we should do,' Amanda explains.

The boys look terrified.

All they wanted to do was make the best project.

'I can't stand up any more.' Brian sounds like he's going to cry. 'And I want to talk to my parents and I can't because they've gone away on a holiday and my grandmother's looking after us and she's going to have a heart attack if she finds out about this.'

Amanda walks over and pats the cast. 'Brian. It'll be all right. I promise you . . . Just hang in there.'

'Where else am I going to go?' Brian asks and for some reason finds what she's said very funny and starts to laugh . . . and laugh . . . and laugh.

'Hysteria,' Amanda, who has been reading psychology magazines, thinks. What should I do? . . . Should I do what they always do in the pictures? . . . slap him and say, 'Get a hold of yourself'? But how can that help? . . . I'd only be hitting the cast . . . and breaking one of my nails . . . and how *can* he get a hold of himself? . . . He's in a full-length body cast.

Amanda is beginning to feel a little hysterical herself.

Mr Martin rushes into the house and looks at the situation. 'Okay. Everyone stay calm. I've talked with Dr Kellerman and here are the possibilities.'

'I want to go home.' Brian has stopped laughing and is very upset. 'I want to get out of here.'

'Okay. I promise that we will get you out of there as quickly as possible, in the best way possible.' Mr Martin looks over at the scissors and quickly realizes that they are not going to work. 'Dr Kellerman says that we can put you in a warm tub of water and the cast will become soft enough to take off in about half an hour.'

'He won't fit into the bathtub. He's too tall and standing too straight.' Amanda is calming down, now that she is not the oldest person in the room.

'Then we're going to have to get you over to Dr Kellerman's right away,' Mr Martin decides. 'But he won't fit into my car. . . . We just may have to call an ambulance.'

Brian starts to cry.

Actually no one in the room is feeling very good either.

There's a moment of silence, and then as Mr Martin picks up the phone to call the emergency number, Mrs Martin rushes in, wearing the gorilla costume.

'I just stopped by on my way back to work to see

if you needed anything and . . .' She looks at everyone. 'What's going on?'

Quickly Mr Martin explains.

Mrs Martin says, 'Amanda. Cindy. Come with me. I want you to help me empty out the station wagon. Amanda. First, though, I want you to put your glasses back on. You know that you must wear them.'

As the females rush out, Mr Martin says, 'Brian. Everything's going to be all right. I'll be back in a minute. I'm going to get something out of the garage.'

'Don't leave us alone.' Billy is afraid that he's getting too tired to help keep Brian from falling.

'Just for a minute.' Mr Martin rushes out, returning in a few minutes with a piece of equipment that is used to move heavy things. 'I just remembered this dolly. We haven't used it in years.'

Mrs Martin and the girls return.

Mr Martin continues, 'Honey. I want you to help the boys support Brian while he hops onto this dolly.'

It takes a few minutes but finally Brian is on the dolly, and Mrs Martin and the kids make sure that he stays on while Mr Martin wheels the dolly over to the car.

Mrs Martin works her way into the front of the back section of the station wagon. It is not an easy task for a person wearing a gorilla suit, but there is no time to change.

Everyone helps lift and slide Brian into the back section of the car.

'I want someone to hold my hand,' he cries out.

'I'll get in and pat on the cast.' Amanda crawls into the back, her hated glasses back on her face. 'Cindy, could you wait here until we get back? If Danny calls, don't tell him about this. I want to . . . later.'

'Okay.' Cindy nods.

'I'll drive this car,' Mrs Martin says. 'Honey, you take your car.'

'I want to go. Please,' Matthew pleads. 'I want to help.'

Mrs Martin quickly says, 'Billy. Matthew. You come with me. Joshua and Cindy, would you please put this stuff in the garage?'

She points to some of the things that are used by her message-delivery company . . . a chicken suit, boxes of balloons, Mouse outfits, confetti, and heart-shaped boxes.

'Sure.' The Jacksons immediately get to work.

Mrs Martin talks quickly. 'Just let your mother know what's going on. And we'll call Brian's family as soon as we get to the doctor's.'

While they're driving along, Matthew looks at his mother, who has taken the gorilla head off but is still wearing the gorilla body. 'Mom, I'm sorry. We didn't mean to do anything wrong. I promise. Is Brian going to be all right?'

Mrs Martin nods. 'I think so. Just stay calm. We'll discuss this later. The important thing right now is to get him out of there and never do anything like this again.'

'I promise.' Matthew sits quietly for the rest of

the drive.

Amanda also sits quietly, hoping that no one she knows sees them. A mother in a gorilla suit and her own half-crimped hair are just too embarrassing for words.

Billy Kellerman sits in the back seat wondering what his father is going to do. He knows what he's going to do to *Brian* . . . help him. . . . He's not so sure what his father is going to do to him, his son.

Everyone gets to the office at the same time. Dr Kellerman is waiting at the door with a stretcher. He and his nurses and the Martins, as well as some of the relatives of waiting patients, lift Brian onto the stretcher and get him into the office.

Once Brian is on the examining table, everyone except the medical staff and Mr and Mrs Martin goes back into the waiting room.

Matthew and Billy explain to everyone how it was all a mistake, how they were just trying to do the best sixth-grade project, that they had no idea that it would all end like this, that they hope that Brian is going to be okay.

'He'll be fine, boys. Don't worry.' An older woman tries to comfort them. 'Dr Kellerman is a wonderful doctor.'

Her husband looks at Amanda and says, 'Is she also part of your Egypt unit, or did she just stick her hand in an electric socket?'

Amanda puts one hand up to her half-crimped hair, puts her other hand over her face, and tries to think of the best way to get back at Matthew.

'Don't listen to him,' the old woman says. 'My

husband is quite a kidder. He just likes to joke around.'

Amanda is all ready to say, 'Yeah. He's about as funny as a rubber crutch,' until she remembers where she is, in an orthopaedic doctor's office. She says nothing.

The old man continues, 'I guess your little mummy friend is all wrapped up in his problems. . . . But don't worry . . . there's really no gauze for concern. . . . Get it? No *gauze* for concern.'

'Melvin, that's enough.' His wife pats him on the hand. 'Remember, there is a little boy in the office who needs help. This is not the time for your corny jokes.'

Everyone in the office quietens down and thinks about Brian, who is at that moment being talked to by Dr Kellerman.

'Brian, there is nothing to worry about. In a little while we will have you out of there.' Dr Kellerman speaks softly, calming down not only Brian but also Mr and Mrs Martin, who are standing nearby.

In a very muffled voice, Brian says something.

Leaning over, Dr Kellerman asks him to repeat it and then tells the Martins, 'Brian says that as long as it's gone this far, I should try to save the cast so that they can still use it for the mummy project.'

'What a guy.' Mr Martin pats the cast. 'Brian, don't worry. We'll do whatever is best for YOU.'

'What is best?' he asks the doctor.

Dr Kellerman smiles. 'We can do both. Get him out quickly and save the cast.'

Leaning over, he explains. 'Okay, Brian. I'm going to use the cast cutter. Don't worry. I know that it looks like a pizza cutter and sounds like a buzz saw . . . but it's not. It'll be a little noisy because attached to the saw is a vacuum cleaner, which sucks up the dust from the cut cast. Brian, don't worry. The saw doesn't even turn round and round. It vibrates quickly. First I'm going to take the face mask off to give you more breathing room and then I'll take off the rest.'

The Martins stand there and watch the doctor work.

Dr Kellerman cuts through the plaster around Brian's face, uses a cast spreader, and then lifts off the face mask.

Everyone looks down at Brian's face, which is all scrunched up and covered with dust.

As Dr Kellerman brushes off the dust, he says, 'See, I told you it would get better. How are you feeling?'

Brian nods. 'Better. But I need a pee . . . soon.'

Dr Kellerman continues working.

Mrs Martin strokes Brian's face and talks to him.

Dr Kellerman and his nurse lift the front of the cast off.

Taking it, Mr Martin leans it against the wall.

The doctor asks the nurse for a pair of scissors.

'No.' Brian yells. 'Don't cut me. You promised.'

'I'm going to cut the garbage bag off,' Dr Kellerman explains. 'It's not good for you to be in it, and it's covered with plaster.'

'But I only have underpants on under this.' Brian

looks up at everyone.

'I'll loan you one of my doctor jackets,' Dr Kellerman says. 'Now, let's get you up and out of there.'

Mr Martin and Dr Kellerman help Brian sit up.

Brian looks at Mrs Martin. 'You're dressed like a gorilla.' And then he starts laughing.

Everyone begins to laugh.

Dr Kellerman and Mr Martin help Brian get out of the plastic bag.

The nurse and Mrs Martin look the other way, since that was the only way that Brian would agree to get out of the garbage bag.

Then Mr Martin helps Brian to rush to the toilet.

When they come back, Dr Kellerman gives Brian an examination to make sure that everything is okay.

It is, and Brian stands up to get a hug from Mrs Martin.

Brian, dressed in a doctor's coat that is about five times too large for him, gets a hug from Mrs Martin, dressed in her gorilla suit.

Dr Kellerman takes a Polaroid picture and then looks at Mr Martin. 'I believe that there are several young men in my waiting room, one related to you, one related to me. Something tells me that these young men should have a talking to.'

'I agree,' Mr Martin nods.

'I'll take Brian to his house and meet you at home soon,' Mrs Martin says and leads Brian out into the waiting room, where all the waiting patients, their families, their friends, and Amanda applaud the release of Brian from his plaster prison.

The two people cheering the most are extremely happy, even though they know that they are due for the lecture of their young lifetimes.

Nurse Payne sticks her head out the door. 'William. Matthew. Please come in. The doctor and Mr Martin will see you now.'

Chapter 4

'Timber!' Matthew yells as the plaster mummy almost falls to the classroom floor.

Mrs Stanton helps to prop it up against the back wall and says, 'Boys, be careful. You worked very hard on this project and I would hate anything to happen to this mummy.'

Pablo Martinez says, 'Yeah. Especially since Brian was so *into* the project.'

'I understand that after his performance as Mummy Dearest, when Brian got out . . . there was a cast party.' Tyler White starts to laugh.

The Mummy Committee pretends to ignore all the kidding.

Mrs Stanton makes sure that the mummy will stand on its own and says, 'Enough joking around. This is an excellent project. Now, everyone get ready. In a few minutes Egyptian Feast day is going to begin.'

Everyone starts rushing. Some of the students finish setting up projects. Others are getting costumed.

Visitors start to arrive: parents, Mrs Morgan, the

principal . . . Mr Peters, the vice principal, the media specialist, Ms Klein, who is carrying a video camera and is ready to immortalize the day on film, Mrs May Nichols, who is the seventy-eight-year-old who lives on the farm right next to the school.

Matthew comes running up to her. 'Hi, Mrs Nichols. Long time no see. Did you have fun on your trip? Did you bring me anything? Got any of those great chocolate chip cookies on you?'

Mrs Nichols smiles at Matthew, who is one of her all-time favourite people. 'Yes, I had fun on my trip. I brought back some wonderful stories about some of the great places I visited . . . and oh, yes . . . I know how you all feel about my cookies, and since it's been almost a year since I've been here, I baked a huge batch of them.'

She goes into her knapsack and pulls out a huge tin of cookies. 'I don't think that this is Egyptian, but I know how much you all like these.'

Everyone rushes over.

Matthew, who is there first, stuffs two cookies into his mouth at once and pockets three more.

'Piggard.' Vanessa Singer turns up her nose at him.

Matthew acts like he's whistling and sprays some cookie crumbs on Vanessa.

Mrs Nichols wipes the crumbs off Vanessa and softly says, 'Matthew, I think that you owe Vanessa an apology.'

Matthew remembers the time Vanessa started a club called G.E.T.H.I.M., Girls Eager to Halt Immature Matthew, and how everyone made him give in when the group picketed his birthday party. An apology is not what he wants to give Vanessa. Cow chip cookies is what he would like to give her.

'Matthew,' Mrs Nichols repeats, 'you got cookie crumbs all over Vanessa.'

Grinning at her, Matthew smiles and shows his dimples.

'Dweeble.' Vanessa glares at him.

'Matthew. An apology is in order, and Vanessa, dear, no name-calling.' Mrs Nichols thinks about how much she has missed seeing the sixth-graders, for whom she has been classroom volunteer since they were in kindergarten.

Matthew wants to please Mrs Nichols, so he shrugs, crosses his fingers behind his back, and looks at Vanessa.

'I'm sorry.' Matthew wants to add, 'I'm sorry that you exist in non-bug-like form.'

'Vanessa, aren't you going to accept his apology?' Mrs Nichols tests her luck.

'Oh, okay.' Vanessa wants to make Mrs Nichols happy too. 'Matthew, I forgive you . . . this time.'

Walking away, she thinks, But I'm not sure that I can ever forgive your mother for giving birth to you.

Mrs Nichols smiles at the children and wonders what her own child would have been like if he hadn't died of polio when he was three. Even though it happened over fifty-five years ago, she still thinks about it sometimes.

Matthew grins at her. 'You going to go sledging with us this winter again?'

Mrs Nichols remembers last time she went with Matthew and how they ended up in a huge snowdrift and she laughs. Somehow things are always fun when Matthew is around. She also remembers how much her 'old bones' hurt after that and she says, 'Maybe. But even if I don't, you can still sledge on my property, and I promise to make hot chocolate and cookies for all of you.'

'And you can always come to our parties.' Mrs Stanton pats her on her shoulder. 'You are the best classroom volunteer I've ever had.'

Matthew waves to Mrs Nichols, pockets two more cookies, and goes over to the area where some of the students are still setting up their projects.

There's the Egyptian house made by Chloe Fulton.

Matthew looks closely at the figures and yells, 'I didn't know that Barbie and Ken lived in early Egypt.'

The girls choose to ignore Matthew and continue with their own conversation.

'Egyptian Feast Day . . . It's finally here and it's going to be "so fun!" ' Jil! Hudson jumps up and down in the classroom. 'Everyone is all dressed up . . . well, actually just all the girls . . . not the boys, since they refused to wear kilts . . . But we girls look great . . . and so do the projects . . . and the food . . . and it's just so terrific.'

Jil!, who changed the second *l* in her first name to an exclamation mark because she wanted more excitement in her life, loves it when Mrs Stanton has a learning celebration at the end of a unit.

146

All the girls are putting the finishing touches on their costumes . . . the jewellery, the make-up.

'Mellow out a little, Jil!' Vanessa Singer says, as she looks in the mirror and applies a lot of eyeliner around her green eyes.

Since Vanessa's parents say she is too young to wear make-up every day, Vanessa loves to use it when it's 'legal' at school on costume days.

'How do I look?' Chloe asks. 'I couldn't find my sandals this morning. Do you think Egyptians wore Reebocks?'

Lisa Levine says, 'It's an anachronism.'

Chloe, who has no idea that *anachronism* means 'anything out of its proper historical time,' says, 'I prefer to think of it as a fashion statement myself. Sort of Style on the Nile . . . Chloepatra, queen of the Nile.'

Everyone groans and then Cathy Atwood sighs and fingers the wig on her head, which is from an old Raggedy Ann costume. 'Don't worry. You look terrific. I, however, look like a first-class jerk. The rest of you all have hair that was long enough to bead.'

Ryma Browne vigorously shakes her head from side to side, causing the rows of beaded hair to hit the back of her head and then the front of her face. 'Bead lash . . . Listen, you're so lucky, Cathy. You saw what it was like at last night's pyjama party. It took hours to plait and then bead our hair . . . and then some of us had trouble sleeping on it.'

Jessica Weeks laughs. 'I told you to wear tights on your head. That would keep it in place while you slept. But some of you wouldn't listen. I should know. My African ancestors used to cornrow and bead their hair all the time. And so did my mother when she was younger. So I know.'

Cathy giggles, remembering the scene at the party. 'You did look pretty silly with tights on your heads. Especially you, Sarah.'

'Well, no one told me to cut off the legs first.' Sarah Montgomery blushes.

Lisa Levine, who loves to study, speaks. 'Actually Cathy is more historically accurate than we are. Egyptian grown-ups wore wigs of flax. They shaved their real hair and polished their heads.'

All the girls say 'Yuck' at once.

Lisa continues, 'If we wanted to be even more historically accurate, we would put cones of scented fat on our heads, and then as the feast goes on, the scented grease would melt and run down our faces. That's what they used to do to stay cool.'

There is another chorus of 'Yuck.'

On the other side of the room Ms Klein is filming Pablo Martinez, who is holding onto his pet snakes, Boa'dwithSchool and Vindshield Viper, and explaining how the Egyptians used reptiles to get rid of vermin.

Matthew is standing in the background, making faces and hoping to get into the picture.

'Enough, Matthew.' Ms Klein lowers the video camera. 'I already took a picture of the Mummy Committee and their project.'

Trying his best to look innocent, Matthew says, 'I was just standing guard to make sure that the snakes didn't eat the class gerbils.'

'Enough, Matthew,' Ms Klein repeats.

Matthew grins. 'You know that in Egypt some of the snakes were called asps. In fact one of them bit Cleopatra and she died. I'm just hanging around here to make sure that Pablo doesn't spend so much time with his snakes that he turns into one himself. I wouldn't want him to make an asp out of himself.'

'That's more than enough, Matthew Martin.' Ms Klein is never sure what to do when Matthew is around, whether to laugh or give him detention.

Mrs Stanton claps her hands. 'All right. Everyone settle down. We're getting ready to play some games . . . Get ready for $100,000 Pyramid, Name that Sphinx, Pharaoh Feud, and Scribeble.'

Everyone quietens down.

Matthew looks across the room.

Mrs Morgan is writing down Mrs Nichols's chocolate chip cookie recipe.

Mrs Nichols is dictating the recipe and at the same time helping to adjust Jil! Hudson's sheet/dress, which is in danger of falling off.

Pablo is trying to get Mr Peters, the vice principal, to kiss a snake.

Matthew looks across at the mummy and thinks about how much Mrs Stanton likes it.

Looking at Vanessa Singer, he thinks about what kinds of things he can do to torment her.

Matthew is happy that the work part of the unit is over and the party is about to begin.

He wonders what the next major class project will be.

Chapter 5

'Popcorn time.' Mr Martin sticks his head into Matthew's bedroom. 'I'm taking a little break. Why don't you?'

Sitting on the floor of his bedroom wardrobe, Matthew feels like he's been saved, at least temporarily, from a fate worse than death — the dreaded closet clean-up.

Before his mother left to take Amanda to the eye doctor, she threatened to call the Board of Health and have his wardrobe quarantined if he didn't straighten it up and throw things out. More important, she threatened to take away television viewing for a week for every day that the job wasn't done.

The work has begun . . . and it's not a pretty sight. Things have been scattered all over the floor as Matthew throws them out of the wardrobe, not sure of where to put everything. There is his baseball card collection . . . four nerf balls . . . his remote-control car . . . a Yahtzee game with two dice missing . . . with three pieces gone . . . a broken ant farm with no ants . . . reams of wrinkled computer paper . . . a pair of Superman pyjamas with an attached cape that Matthew hasn't worn since he was five but doesn't want to throw away . . . and his collection of forty-two baseball caps, with slogans on them.

Matthew looks at the junk in his wardrobe that he hasn't even got to yet, and then he looks at the rubbish bin, where he is supposed to throw away a lot of things. So far the only things in there are notes from last year's teacher that he never gave to his parents, a used-up tube of Slime bubble gum, wrappers from junk food that he didn't want his mother to know about, two paper clips, and a used plaster.

It's definitely time for a break, he thinks. If his father can take a break from important law work he, too, can take a break from dumb old wardrobe cleaning.

'I'm coming.' Matthew stands up, hits his head on a wire hanger, and wonders if that's punishment for not finishing off first.

He also wonders if a wire hanger concussion would be just cause for getting out of cleaning a wardrobe.

He decides not to push his luck and mention it.

Joining his father, they go down the steps and head into the kitchen.

'It's terrific to have some time to spend together.' Mr Martin smiles, as he takes out the new Stir Crazy popcorn maker. 'Being a lawyer is not always easy. I've had to spend a lot of time on one of the cases, but I promise that it'll be over soon, and then we'll have some "quality time." '

Matthew grins, because he knows what fun he has when he is with his father, how his father can sometimes act like a kid.

Mr Martin takes out the oil and the jar of popcorn. 'I can't seem to find the directions. The only time we used it, your mother made it. Oh well, it can't be too hard to figure out. I'm going to put in two tablespoons of oil. Do you remember how much popcorn your mother used?'

Scrunching up his face, Matthew tries to concentrate on visualizing his mother at the popcorn maker. 'I think she used two cups.'

'Two cups it is, then.' Mr Martin fills the bottom of the machine, puts the plastic yellow dome on, and plugs it in.

They watch as the stirring rod pushes the kernels around. In a few minutes the dome beings to steam up and the popcorn starts to pop and jump up.

Just then the front-door bell rings and Matthew and his father go to check who is there.

It's the postman and he needs a signature in exchange for a large envelope.

Mr Martin signs, sees that it is business information, and says, 'I can hear that the machine is still popping. We shouldn't leave it unattended. Let's get back.'

They reach the kitchen at the same time and both stare at the popper in amazement.

The dome is practically up to the kitchen cabinet. Popcorn is exploding all over the place, coming out the sides.

'How come this didn't happen when Mom did it?' Matthew shakes his head and then starts to laugh.

Mr Martin also begins to laugh and quickly pulls out the plug.

He stares at the machine and tries to figure out how to turn the bowl over without spilling the popcorn that is above the Stir Crazy base and below the yellow dome bowl. There's obviously no way this is going to work.

Mr Martin attempts it anyway, snapping the yellow plastic cup over the bottom of the dome, being careful of escaping steam, and laughing as he turns over the bowl.

The bowl is filled with popcorn.

So are the worktops and the floor.

It looks as if the Martin kitchen has been bombarded with a popcorn blizzard.

There are crunching sounds as Mr Martin and Matthew walk across the room.

Matthew sticks his hand into the yellow bowl, grabs a handful of popcorn, and puts it in his mouth. 'It's a little dry, Dad.'

Looking at the floor, Mr Martin says, 'It's a little messy, Matthew. I think it's Broom Time.'

Matthew decides that this is probably not the perfect moment to ask his father why he forgot to melt the butter and instead gets a broom, which he hands to his father.

Sweeping, Mr Martin wonders how this happened, how he could manage to graduate from college with high honours, get through law school easily, pass the law boards with no problems, and not be able to make popcorn, at least not the correct way.

Matthew watches, continuing to eat the popcorn.

'Get the dustpan.' Mr Martin is beginning to think this is not as funny as he originally thought it was, because there is still popcorn all over the place.

'Hi, pop,' Matthew says, picking up a piece of the popcorn.

Mr Martin looks at the mess. 'Sometimes this family gets pretty corny.'

As they look at each other and laugh, in walk Mrs Martin and Amanda, who crunch on some of the popcorn.

'I'm afraid to ask.' Mrs Martin shakes her head.

'I don't suppose that you would consider taking over sweeping this up, would you?' Mr Martin asks, hopefully.

'No.' Mrs Martin sits down at the kitchen table. 'I don't think so.'

It was worth a try, Mr Martin thinks.

'This looks so gross. Let me guess.' Amanda takes a handful of popcorn. 'This is the work of my only brother . . . the incredible Matthew Martin.'

Matthew makes a face at his sister, folding his upper eyelids up, flaring his nostrils, and sticking his tongue out.

He figures it's safe to do, since she doesn't have her glasses on and she'll never see it.

'Mom, tell Matthew to stop making that disgusting face, that he'll be sorry . . . that one of these days his face is going to freeze like that.'

Amanda puts her hand on her hip.

It's a miracle, Matthew thinks. My sister has twenty-twenty vision, to go with the rest of her measurements, which are twenty-twenty-twenty.

Mrs Martin says, 'Would someone please explain what happened?'

'I just wanted some popcorn,' Mr Martin says.

'Well, you got your wish,' Mrs Martin teases.

'Here's the story.' Mr Martin gestures. 'I put in two tablespoons of vegetable oil.'

'Good start,' Mrs Martin tells him.

Nodding, Mr Martin continues. 'Then I couldn't find the directions.'

'They're in the silverware drawer,' Mrs Martin informs him.

'Oh, of course.' Mr Martin grins. 'I should have known . . . the silverware drawer . . . the perfect place . . . Anyway, Matthew and I tried to figure out what was the correct amount of popcorn to put in . . . He seemed to remember that you used two cups.'

Mrs Martin starts to laugh. 'He did see me put in two cups . . . but I used a one-third cup measuring cup. I used two of them to have two thirds . . . One tablespoon of oil takes one-third of a cup. Double it and it's two-thirds of a cup — not two cups. The popper is designed to make six quarts of popcorn. You made twelve quarts, using half the recommended amount of oil.'

Everyone starts to laugh, except for Amanda.

'Isn't anyone going to notice that I am NOT wearing glasses? That I FINALLY got my contact lenses.' Amanda, who had been pleading for the lenses, wants everyone to tell her how wonderful she looks.

Her father does.

Matthew says, 'This popcorn really is too dry. Can we melt some butter, please?'

Amanda ignores him. 'I'm so excited. Dr Sugarman says that this is a new type of lenses that will work for me.'

She looks so happy.

Mrs Martin says, 'I remember my first pair of contact lenses. I got them when I was older than you are, Amanda . . . and you'll never guess what happened.'

She looks a little embarrassed. 'Maybe I shouldn't tell this story.'

'Tell us, tell us,' everyone begs.

She debates it for a minute and then says, 'Oh, okay. I guess I'll tell you. One day, about a week after I got the lenses, I was making out with my boyfriend and he swallowed one of the lenses.'

'Oh, Mom. That's so gross.' Amanda makes a face.

'What did the contact lens taste like, Dad?' Matthew wants to know.

Mr Martin looks up as he empties the popcorn into the waste can. 'It wasn't me. I didn't know her then.'

Amanda and Matthew both look at their mother, who grins at them.

'It's really gross to think of your own mother making out with someone who isn't your father. It's gross enough to think of your parents making out with each other.' Amanda looks shocked. 'I think we should change the subject. Preferably back to me.'

Matthew says, 'I want to know who the other guy was so I can call him up and ask him what the contact lens tasted like.'

'I haven't seen him in years,' Mrs Martin tells him.

Just then the phone rings.

Mrs Martin gets up to answer it.

Matthew hopes it is his mother's long-gone boyfriend so that he can ask him about the lens.

Amanda hopes that it is her boyfriend, Danny.

Mr Martin, who hates talking on the phone, hopes it is for anyone else or that it's a wrong number.

It's obviously for Mrs Martin, since she calls no one else over to the phone.

It's a serious call. Everyone can tell by the expression on her face and the things that she is saying like 'Oh, no . . . When did it happen? Is she going to be all right? What can we do to help?'

She listens for a few minutes and then says, 'Let me know what's happening . . . what can we do.'

Hanging up, she turns to her family, who are sitting there very quietly.

'That was Dr Kellerman,' she informs them. 'He wants us to know that there's been an accident. Mrs Nichols has got hurt.'

Chapter 6

Mrs Stanton explains to the class, 'Over the weekend, on Saturday, Mrs Nichols got up on a ladder to change a light bulb and she fell off.'

Matthew thinks, I wish I'd gone over to her house to say hello. I could have changed the bulb and then she'd be okay.

Continuing, Mrs Stanton says, 'She broke her hip and couldn't get up. Luckily she has a neighbour who calls every day at a certain time, and when there was no answer, the neighbour came over, found her, and called an ambulance.'

'I was in an ambulance once,' Mark Ellison says. 'Did they use the siren?'

Everyone has heard a million times about how Mark's aunt works for the rescue squad and how she let him sit in the ambulance once and turn on the siren.

Billy Kellerman volunteers the information that he knows. 'The neighbour, Mrs Enright, called my dad. And he examined her . . . and she's got a broken hip . . . and he's going to fix it. At least he's going to try to fix it. He said it's not so easy when it's a seventy-eight-year-old hip. But he's going to try. And my dad is real good. So I guess it's going to be all right.'

Matthew informs everyone, 'And then they called my mother because she and Mrs Nichols have known each other for a long time and Mrs Nichols was going to work for my mother.'

'What was she going to do . . . dress up in a chicken suit or something?' Tyler White asks, laughing.

'That's a really old chicken,' Mark Ellison says.

'Stop it,' Chloe yells out. 'You both are being really gross and disgusting. Mrs Nichols is really nice.'

The boys know that, but all they can think of is Mrs Nichols dressing up as a chicken or a gorilla and delivering messages for Mrs Martin's company.

Matthew explains. 'One of the things my mother's company does is deliver get-well messages and presents to sick people. Mrs Nichols was going to be a grandmother who brought over chicken soup and stuff.'

'In a chicken suit.' Mark can't stop laughing.

'Enough, Mark.' Mrs Stanton is not pleased.

'Did your mother send over another old lady with chicken soup to Mrs Nichols?' Zoe Alexander asks.

'No.' Matthew shakes his head. 'She and my dad went over to the hospital yesterday and brought her the soup, some get-well balloons, and my dad brought her candy and my mother brought her some granola bars.'

'Ugh.' The students have all tasted Mrs Martin's

granola bars.

Matthew does not mention that, when they went over, his father was wearing a dog costume and carrying a sign that said 'Hope things aren't too Ruff for you,', and his mother was dressed in the chicken suit.

Matthew also doesn't mention that he didn't go with them because he gets real nervous around hospitals and that Amanda refused to go because being with parents dressed that way was just 'too embarrassing for words.'

Mrs Stanton continues, 'It's not always easy when you get older. But I'm sure that everything that can possibly be done for Mrs Nichols will be done. You know, I think it would be very nice of all of you to write a note to her. She's been a wonderful class-room volunteer, and I know how much she likes all of you.'

David Cohen, who hates to write, says, 'Can't we just call her?'

Patrick Ryan, who doesn't like to write or to be on the phone, says, 'Can't we just ask Ms Klein to videotape us saying something?'

Ryma Browne, who hates to look at herself on videotape, says, 'Let's just write notes.'

Mrs Stanton says, 'It's not a good idea to call too much . . . and there are no videotape machines at the hospital . . . so I think that the best thing is cards . . . or you can use the tape recorder, too.'

David Cohen raises his hand. 'Is it okay if some of us work together?'

Nodding, Mrs Stanton says, 'Yes.'

David, Mark Ellison, and Patrick Ryan call out, 'All right!'

Cathy is sent to the media centre to pick up a tape recorder and tape.

Mrs Stanton hands out the supplies — paper, glue, markers, pens, pastels, and crayons.

There is some disagreement on what to say on the tape recording.

The boys want to make animal sounds into the tape recorder to 'entertain' Mrs Nichols.

Mark suggests holding a belching contest into the recorder and letting Mrs Nichols be the judge.

The girls like neither of those ideas.

Nor does Mrs Stanton.

Finally the recording group settles down and speaks into the tape recorder, saying hello, that they hope that she gets better.

Mark yells 'Hip, hip, hooray' into the recorder.

It's erased because everyone else thinks that's a mean thing to say to someone who has just broken her hip.

Everyone puts the finished letters on Mrs Stanton's desk and it's back to schoolwork.

Chapter 7

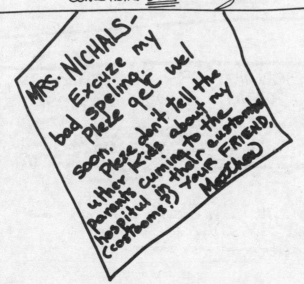

GET WELL SOON

I went over to your barn to feed Prince.
(He's still the most _wonderful_ horse in the world!
Everyday I think about how great you were
to sell him to me and let me keep him at
the farm.) I told him about your accident.
He looked _so_ sad. So am I.
 Come home _soon_. LOVE,
 Sarah

MRS. NICHALS'
Excuze my
bad speling.
Pleze get wel
soon.
 Pleze don't tell the
uther kids about my
parents cuming to the
hospital (in their custombr
cooftooms?) YOUR FRIEND,
 Matthew

FOR OUR FRIEND, MRS. NICHOLS,

What's the best time of the year......
Is it Jan? Feb? March? or April?
No!!!! It's **MAY**.
What's the best money.......
Is it quarters, pennies or dimes?
No!!!! IT'S **NICHOLS**.

MAY NICHOLS - SHE MAKES SENSE.

(cents- nickles, get it?)

GET
WELL
SOON

Ryma Cathy
Katie

PERSONAL · PERSONAL · PERSONAL ·
FOR MRS. NICHOL'S EYES ONLY

PLEASE, OH PLEASE, OH PLEASE, GET BETTER SOON.
I MISS YOU SO MUCH EVEN THOUGH IT'S ONLY A FEW DAYS.
YOU HELP ME SO MUCH EVEN WHEN I FEEL REALLY BAD....
.... LIKE THE TIMES WE TALKED WHEN MY PARENTS GOT DIVORCED....
......WHEN MY DAD MOVED TO MONTANA .... WHEN MY GRANDMA DIED
AND YOU SAID YOU'D BE MY ADOPTED GRANDMA.......
PLEASE DON'T LET ANYTHING BAD HAPPEN AGAIN.
I LOVE YOU.

LIZZIE

I wrote small so that no one else would
see this. I am sending this letter with a
magnifying glass. ♡♡♡♡♡

ROSES ARE RED
VIOLETS ARE BLUE.
MAYBE THEY CAN FIX YOUR HIP
with CRAZY GLUE!
HA. HA. JUST KIDDING.
signed. Your F.
Ruddo David

Dear Mrs. Nichols —
Sorry about how you broke
your hip.
Are you going to have
to wear a cast?
I ~~didn't~~ feel sorry for
you because ~~I~~ personally
~~know~~ know what it's like
to wear one.
WARNING: Don't let the
mummy committee near you.
Brian Bruno

Get
We!!
Soon
Ji!!

Dear May,

Here are the kids' notes — also a tape. I haven't censored or corrected anything. I know how much you love the kids and I hope that this cheers you up.

Try not to worry.

I've been thinking about yesterday's phone call.

I know it's scary having something happen and having no family. Don't forget, though, that there are a lot of people in this town who really care about you — the kids you've helped (many who are now grownups) your friends, everyone at church.

Don't panic. Don't think the worst. See you tomorrow

Suzanne
Stanton

Chapter 8

'Mom, dad.' Amanda bounds down the steps, yelling. 'You've got to give me permission to kill Matthew.'

Mr and Mrs Martin are sitting at the kitchen table.

'No. Permission denied.' Mrs Martin sips her herbal tea. 'And why are you dressed all in black?'

Amanda, who has on black shorts, a black tee-shirt, black tights, and black shoes, starts pacing back and forth. 'I have decided to try out different fashion looks, to find the "real me." But please don't change the subject. I want to know if I can rip Matthew into tiny little shreds and stuff the pieces down the toilet.'

'Absolutely not.' Mr Martin picks up his coffee cup. 'Plumbers are too expensive. I am, however, curious about what your brother has done this time to merit your homicidal rage.'

Amanda continues to pace back and forth.

'Everything. . . . If I tell you all of them, I'll be eighty years old before I'm done. He listens in on my phone conversations. . . . He imitates me. . . .

167

He's always threatening to blackmail me for something that I've never even done. . . . He "captures" the TV remote control and keeps changing MY shows to his stupid wrestling ones. He put washing-up detergent in my mouthwash. He told Danny that I have a very rare and highly communicable lip fungus. . . . And now today he's done the final thing. It's just the final straw, and he does it all the time.'

'If it's the final straw, how can he do it all the time?' Mr Martin looks at his daughter.

Amanda sighs. 'Don't try that lawyer logic on me. I know I'm right about this. That little creep never puts in a new roll of toilet paper when he's used up the old one . . . and then when I need it, absolutely need it, there's none there.'

Matthew, who has been outside the room, listening, walks in. 'That's right. Blame me. It's always my fault. How do you know I did it? Maybe it wasn't me. Boys don't always need toilet paper, you know.'

'Matthew. We really don't need a lesson in biology.' Mr Martin smiles and shakes his head.

Not finished with her rage, Amanda continues, 'Why do I have to share a bathroom with that creep?'

'I share a bathroom with your mother,' Mr Martin says. 'You don't hear us fighting.'

Actually Mr and Mrs Martin do argue about toilet paper. They just do it more quietly. Mrs Martin always puts it on the roller so that the paper rolls out from the bottom. Mr Martin always switches it around so that it rolls from the top. In fact he switches it around at houses where he is just visiting and at public lavatories too. Sometimes when the Martin parents disagree about something else, Mrs Martin reverses the paper just to get back at her husband. They do not, however, mention this squabble to their children, preferring to be good examples.

Amanda's pacing becomes even faster. 'I know he's responsible for not putting the toilet paper out. He never does . . . and he leaves the toothpaste spit in the sink . . . and he never puts the toilet seat down.'

'And she never leaves the toilet seat up. Also, she leaves all her dumb make-up all over the top and she spends hours hogging the bathroom.'

'Three bathrooms in the house and there's still all this fighting.' Mr Martin shakes his head. 'When I was a child, there was only one bathroom for four people. Of course the cat did have its own kitty litter pan.'

'Oh, Dad. Would you please take this more seriously? You never take my problems seriously.' Amanda begins a serious pout.

Matthew puts waffles into the toaster. 'The downstairs bathroom doesn't have a shower . . . and anyway, why do I have to be the one to run downstairs all the time? It isn't fair.'

Mrs Martin looks at her husband. 'Is this the way you want to be spending our day off? Listening to our children fight?'

He shakes his head. 'Enough. I want you kids to

stop this bickering. Whoever finishes the roll, put out another one. That's it.'

'And not just leave half a piece of paper on the roll so that you don't have to change the stupid roll.' Amanda glares at Matthew, who is busy filling each little square of his waffle with a drop of syrup.

Mr Martin shakes his head. 'Matthew, don't leave half a piece of paper on the stupid roll.'

Grinning, Matthew looks at his father. 'Tell her not to leave her stupid make-up all over the place.'

Mr Martin smiles at his daughter. 'Amanda, don't leave your stupid make-up all over the place.'

Amanda does not return the smile.

She turns to Matthew, who gives her his widest grin, then crosses his eyes, puts his finger up his nose, and sticks out his tongue.

Amanda sneers at him. 'Why don't you go to boarding school . . . or better yet, reform school. In fact why don't you do us all a big favour . . . MAKE LIKE A TREE AND LEAVE.'

Stomping off, she mumbles about how no one in the house understands her, how Matthew is such a big baby.

Matthew looks up at his parents and says, 'I guess she just made like a banana and split.'

Mr Martin laughs.

Mrs Martin just sighs and says, 'Matthew.'

Matthew sits down at the table and speaks in his most adult voice, one that he has been practising in the privacy of his own room. 'She really has turned into quite a pain, hasn't she? I just don't know what we are going to do with that child.'

His parents' mouths start to move into a smile, but they both stop before the smiles begin.

Matthew continues, 'Her attitude is rather awful, isn't it. Stamping around, talking to herself, hogging the telephone, putting on all that make-up, acting like such a big shot, treating a younger child so badly, accusing him of misuse of paper supplies. I do think that some form of punishment is in order. What do you think? . . . Taking away her telephone privileges, not letting her use eye make-up gunk for at least a week, sending her to reform school? . . . I ask you.'

Mr Martin looks at his son, who has just stuffed almost a whole waffle into his mouth and who has syrup running down his chin. 'Matthew. I want you to remember what Martin Luther King said: "We must live together as brothers or perish as fools."'

Nodding, Matthew tries to look wise and mature. 'I would be ever so happy to, Dad, but Amanda is my sister, not my brother.'

Mrs Martin sighs.

Mr Martin gets up to make himself some waffles.

Mrs Martin sighs again and wishes that they would eat what she is having, yogurt with granola.

Finishing the waffle, Matthew wipes up the left-over syrup with his finger.

'Matthew, stop that,' his mother says. 'So what are you planning to do today?'

'I'm meeting Joshua.'

'Where are you going?' Mrs Martin is one of those mothers who is most comfortable when she knows, at all times, where her kids are.

171

'Over to the clubhouse,' he tells her, referring to an area on Mrs Nichols's property, an old play house on her property that she has let the boys use since second grade.

Matthew's parents look at each other, and then his mother says, 'Enjoy it while you can. There's a rumour that Mrs Nichols is going to have to sell the property.'

Matthew can feel the waffles at the bottom of his stomach.

'And,' his father informs him, 'the contractor who wants to buy it is planning to put a housing development there, as well as a small shopping centre.'

Matthew feels like the waffles are going to make a return trip up and out.

Chapter 9

'We have to do something.' Vanessa Singer puts her hands on her hips. 'I've never heard of anything so disgusting in my entire life.'

For once Matthew and Vanessa agree on something.

Usually, when Vanessa uses the word *disgusting*, she is referring to Matthew.

This time, though, she is talking about the possibility that Mrs Nichols's property is going to be turned into a housing development and shopping mall.

'Maybe it won't be so bad. Maybe there will be some really great stores there. You know that there's no place around here to shop,' Zoe says.

Lisa Levine sighs. 'Zoe, sometimes you are so shallow . . . like a ditch.'

Zoe, who is standing next to her boyfriend, Tyler, and has her hand in his back pocket to show that they are a couple, says, 'Don't use language like that to me, Lisa Levine. We may not always agree, but I'd never call you a name like that.'

'D . . . ITCH . . . she said *Ditch*.' Jil! explains.

'Look, let's not fight with each other. Shake hands and make up. We've got to spend our time on more important things, like what we can do to save Mrs Nichols's property so that we have nature nearby, a place to go skating and sledging, a place that's really pretty. So, come on, you two, shake and make up.'

Matthew interrupts and begins to twitch. 'Shake. Shake. Shake.' And then he pretends to put on lipstick. 'Make-up. Make-up. Make-up.'

Vanessa glares at him and says, 'Disgusting,' and is not talking about the possible loss of property.

Lisa ignores Matthew, looks at Zoe, and smiles. 'Oh, okay.'

Zoe tries to take her hand out of Tyler's pocket but has a problem. Since she is wearing a large cubic zirconia ring on her left hand, it gets caught in Tyler's pocket, and when she turns her hand around, attempting to remove it, the ring scratches Tyler.

Finally her hand is freed.

She shakes Lisa's hand, while Tyler stands there wondering how badly his rear end has been scratched.

Vanessa continues. 'My parents said that some of the grownups are starting something called a conservancy to buy the land and save it for everyone's use . . . and that it's going to take a lot of fund-raising . . . that everyone is going to have to pitch in and help.'

Matthew pantomimes being a baseball player and says, 'Pitch. Pitch. Pitch. . . . And don't worry,

Zoe, I'm not referring to you.'

Even though Matthew really cares about saving the property, he can't seem to stop fooling around, especially when Vanessa is getting a lot of attention.

Vanessa tries to pretend that he is invisible. 'I think we should all do something to help earn the money . . . like a bake sale or a car wash.'

'Boring.' Matthew pretends to yawn. 'Boring.'

Vanessa no longer pretends he is invisible. 'Listen, twerp. My ideas are not boring. You are what is boring. You and the way you act. . . . You know how we could make a lot of money? We could charge you a nickel for every word that you misspell, a dime for every time you get detention. That way we could buy the land very fast. . . . We would probably have enough money left over to buy China, and I'm not talking about dishes.'

People laugh.

They think several things are funny. Matthew's spelling is one — *werm, sertain, nickle, alwaze, acetera*. Another funny thing is how Matthew can always get Vanessa angry, and then what happens next.

Matthew stares at Vanessa.

He does not like it when she mentions his bad spelling.

'Come up with something better.' Vanessa sneers at him.

'We could have a school fair and have a kissing booth and people would pay a lot of money not to have to kiss you,' he sneers back.

'We could have a Dunk The Doofus game and

you could be the Doofus.' She glares. 'Be serious, Matthew. Come up with something real. Or shut up.'

Now Matthew is really annoyed.

'I'm waiting.' Vanessa smirks.

A brainstorm hits Matthew.

So does a paper airplane thrown by his best friend, Joshua Jackson.

Matthew lobs the plane back to Joshua and speaks. 'Teams. We set up teams. You're the captain of one. I'm the captain of the other. Whoever raises the most money for the conservancy wins. You with your boring ideas. Me with my great ones. Deal?'

Vanessa looks at Matthew and then looks at the class.

She thinks, This is a good time to reassemble G.E.T.H.I.M., Girls Eager to Halt Immature Matthew, and says, 'It's a deal. G.E.T.H.I.M. against your team.'

Matthew thinks about the group that he wanted to start when the girls started their group and realizes that now is the time for G.E.T.T.H.E.M., Girls Easy to Torment Hopes Eager Matthew. Only this time the Second *T* won't be for Tormenting, but for TOTAL, as in *total* up more money, turn them into total wrecks.

Mrs Stanton walks into the classroom.

Joshua debates swallowing his paper aeroplane so that there is no evidence but instead quickly hides it in his back pocket.

Everyone in the classroom looks guilty, except

for Mrs Stanton, who looks a little annoyed.

She clutches her heart. 'Is this really *my* class of sixth-graders, the people who I told to take out books and read independently *at their desks*, while I answered a very important phone call? Can this really be my class, or have I stepped into an alternative time zone and found a class that looks like mine but is totally lacking in the ability or inclination to follow directions? Has an alien life-form invaded this room?'

Mrs Stanton's independent reading includes a lot of science fiction.

'Pay no attention to that woman behind the curtain,' Matthew says, thinking of the line from *The Wizard of Oz*.

'Detention, Mr Martin.' Mrs Stanton shakes her head at Matthew, who makes her laugh but also drives her nuts sometimes.

Matthew grins. Detention with Mrs Stanton will be much more fun than going home and having Amanda in charge.

'We're just talking about what it's going to be like if the woods by the school become a housing development and a shopping centre,' Lisa explains. 'Mrs Stanton — can't you do something to help us?'

'It's current events.' Pablo Martinez is sitting on top of his desk and swinging his legs back and forth. 'Aren't you always talking about how we should know what's going on in the world? How we should take stands on things?'

Mrs Stanton looks at her students. 'Everyone sit down. We will take some time to talk about this, but I have to make something perfectly clear. This situation is becoming a very big political issue in town, and as a teacher, I have to be fair and present both sides.'

'I bet you want more places to shop, too.' Zoe says.

Smiling, Mrs Stanton nods. 'It wouldn't be bad . . . not having to travel a half an hour away to buy clothes for my family. I'm just not sure that the Nichols property is the best place. There doesn't seem to be an easy solution.'

'What about all the animals?' Sarah sits down at her desk. 'What are they going to do . . . go to a store named Woods Are Us?'

'My mom says that the reason we moved here from the city was to get away from crime, to have fresh air, to be in a small town. A housing development is going to bring in more people, more cars, more pollution. That's what my mom says.' Mark Ellison shakes his head.

'Well, my dad says that it'll bring in more money for taxes to pay for more services and that it will provide more jobs for people . . . that you can't stand in the way of progress . . . that change isn't always such a bad thing,' Cathy Atwood calls out. 'I'm sick and tired of listening to everyone say bad things about the houses and the malls. My dad is the contractor.'

'Yuck.' Ryma Browne makes a face. 'How can your father even think of ruining that property, the place where we've all played since we were babies? I'm glad that my father doesn't have anything to do with trying to wreck everything. If my father did, I'd hate it. I'd rather have Freddy Kruger as my father, the *Nightmare on Elm Street* guy.'

Cathy looks like she's going to cry. She loves the property, too, but she also loves her father and knows that he's really a nice person.

'That really was not appropriate, Ryma.' Mrs Stanton shakes her head. 'Look, there are many sides to this issue, many things to consider. Mrs Nichols and her property have been part of my life since I was a little girl, so I understand how you feel. I can also see Mr Atwood's reasons for feeling the way that he does.'

'You were a little girl?' Matthew asks, grinning.

Mrs Stanton chooses to ignore his comment. 'I want each of you to think about why this is important to you and I want you all to consider both sides.'

'I don't care either way.' Patrick Ryan raises his hand. 'Because of my parents' divorce, my mom and I are going to move at the end of the school year anyway, so what's the difference to me?'

'That is an important point. There are obviously a lot of different reactions to this situation.' Mrs Stanton thinks for a minute. 'Instead of beginning our Greek civilization unit next, let's do our own Califon, New Jersey, unit. You will be part of it. I want you to go home and talk to your parents... or parent... or guardian... about your own roots, where your families come from... then I want you to do a family tree... tell about how your families came to Califon... and how you feel

179

about the Nichols property and about what may happen to it. You can all take out a piece of paper and write down some of the questions you will ask your family. Any questions?'

'How long does this have to be?' Lizzie Doran asks.

'As long as it takes to be finished,' is the answer.

'Does spelling count?' Matthew wants to know.

Mrs Stanton nods.

Vanessa makes a little snorting sound.

Matthew continues, 'And you want us to ask our parents where we came from?'

Again Mrs Stanton nods.

Matthew grins. 'Last time I asked where I came from, they gave me a lecture about the birds and the bees.'

The glass giggles, all except for Vanessa Singer, who whispers, 'How immature' under her breath, and Mark Ellison, who practically falls off the chair laughing.

'Matthew.' Mrs Stanton uses her soft teacher voice. 'Enough already . . . I want everyone to get to work on this project right now.'

David Cohen raises his hand. 'Can we work together?'

Mrs Stanton shakes her head. 'It's a family tree. How can you work together unless you both come from the same family?'

'Someday,' Zoe announces, 'someday Tyler and I will be in the same family . . . and you'll all be invited to our wedding.'

Tyler blushes, and somewhere in the room

someone makes a retching noise.

'Get to work.' Mrs Stanton uses her stern teacher voice.

As the students take out their notebooks, their teacher smiles and thinks about how exciting this unit is going to be.

Matthew sits at his desk and thinks about how he would like to leave Amanda off the family tree and whether Vanessa is going to be drawing her family tree with a lot of apes swinging on it.

Chapter 10

'A pet wash. That sounds like a great idea.' Mr Martin looks up from writing a cheque to the conservancy. It is the first of three that they have pledged over a period of three years. 'I hope that you make a lot of money for the conservancy. It is a cause that your mother and I really believe in and it's wonderful that you and your classmates are helping.'

Matthew feels proud, but has one very important question about something that has been bothering him. 'Dad, what exactly is a conservancy?'

Mr Martin explains. 'You know that Mrs Nichols needs money and has to sell the land. You also know that a lot of people want to preserve the land and see that it's not commercially developed. In order for that to happen, all of the people who feel that way about the land have to donate money or come up with ways to get money.'

'Like an animal wash.' Matthew grins.

'Yes.' His father continues, 'If the money can be raised, the land will be preserved and watched over by the conservancy, which is a nonprofit group dedicated to saving places of special beauty and/or importance.'

Matthew wonders if the conservancy will ever want to save his house because it may some day be of historical importance because it's where he's grown up.

Mrs Martin walks over behind her husband and puts her hands on his shoulders. 'I just wish that Mrs Nichols was not in a position where she has to sell her land to take care of herself. That's a very sorry position to be in. She loves the place so much. When I visited her yesterday, she said that she wished that she were rich so that she could just stay there and eventually leave the land to the town.'

'That would be wonderful.' Mr Martin looks very thoughtful, the way that he often does when he's doing legal work. 'That really would be terrific. Mrs Nichols is so nice. How is she feeling?'

'Better.' Mrs Martin sits down at the table and puts unsweetened marmalade on her bran muffin. 'It's so sad. Remember how Mrs Nichols took that long trip last year and did all of the things that she always wanted to do . . . white-water rafting . . . a balloon ride . . . a mule caravan along the Grand Canyon . . . and she never got hurt? And then she comes back and falls off a stepladder in her own kitchen. How unlucky.'

Matthew looks down at his bran muffin and thinks how unlucky Mrs Nichols continues to be, that his mother brought a dozen bran muffins over to her at the hospital.

From upstairs comes the sound of Amanda

yelling. 'Don't anyone pick up the phone when it rings. It's for me.'

'Don't stay on too long,' Matthew yells back. 'I'm expecting a call from Brian about our animal wash.'

Mr Martin looks at his wife and son. 'Wasn't there a time when we actually saw Amanda's face ... when there weren't just shrill orders coming out of her room? Tell me, Matthew, are you going to be like this when you become an adolescent?'

'No way, José.' Matthew grins, glad that for once he is not the bad one.

The telephone rings ... and rings ... and rings ... and rings ... and rings.

Matthew waits for Amanda to pick up the phone, hoping that it's really for him or there's a good chance that the line will be busy for hours, maybe even weeks.

'Enough. How do we know that it's not for one of us? How do we know that Amanda has not picked this moment to begin one of her endless bathroom marathons, doing who knows what to her hair?' Mr Martin picks up the phone. 'Hello. This is the Martin Home for the Chronically Bonzo. Head warden speaking.'

'Honey,' Mrs Martin sighs. 'What if that is someone from work? What if there is an emergency and someone needs to talk to me about a delivery? What if it is one of your clients?'

'It's not.' Mr Martin smiles and yells, 'Amanda. It's for you.'

Amanda rushes into the kitchen, sighing. 'Dad, I said not to answer it. Please. Doesn't anybody ever listen to me?'

'It rang eighteen times.' Mr Martin hands the phone to her.

'I can't find the receiver for my new cordless phone.' Amanda informs them. 'Cindy's just calling so that I can listen to the sound of the ring and locate the phone. I was getting really close to finding it and then *you* picked up the phone.'

Mr Martin hands her the phone.

'Cindy. Call me right back.' Amanda speaks into the receiver.

Mr Martin says, 'Make that five minutes. I want to talk to you.'

Sighing, Amanda says, 'Five minutes. . . . HE wants to talk to me.'

'*He*.' Mr Martin shrugs his shoulders. 'Now I'm *he*. Whatever happened to the good old days when I was Daddy? The daddy who could do no wrong, the *best daddy* in the whole wide world?'

'That changed just about the time I became *she*,' Mrs Martin informs him. 'I think it was about the time that "I hate my parents" hormone developed. In the psychology books I think it's called adolescence onset.'

Matthew adds, 'I think *he* and *she* is better than what she calls me: "Pukeface." '

Amanda puts down the phone. 'I don't think it's fair that you think this is all so funny. You act like it's a crime that I'm growing up, trying out new things . . . not being a dumb little kid who thinks her parents are perfect . . . and don't worry, Matthew, I never did think that you were perfect.'

Matthew pulls an imaginary knife out of his heart.

'We're just kidding around,' Mr Martin says, trying to be reasonable. 'Why are you so serious about everything? So sensitive. Can't you take a joke? And can't you stop tying up the telephone lines, the *family* telephone lines?'

Matthew thinks about how sometimes, especially in the old days, Amanda could be so nice and now that she's in eighth grade, she's so different. Maybe he should write a book about it and illustrate it. The book title could be *I Didn't Ask for Her to Be Born*, subtitled *She Couldn't Be Stopped*.

'It's not as if I didn't ask you not to pick up the phone. I did ask and you picked it up anyway.' Amanda feels justified in her annoyance.

'If it were more organized in there, you'd be able to find it.' Mrs Martin gives her daily commercial for neatness.

The phone rings again.

Amanda looks at her parents. 'Please. Let me go upstairs and find the receiver. It should only take a few seconds.'

They nod.

As Amanda rushes upstairs, Matthew speaks, using the grown-up voice. 'I really do think that you let that child get away with murder. I know that she bought the cordless with her own money, but don't you think that you should encourage her sense of sharing? Especially with her younger brother, who is often inconvenienced by not being able to get his own phone calls because she is always on the phone.'

The aforementioned phone stops ringing.

Amanda yells down the stairs, 'It's for you, Pukeface.'

'I'm going up to talk to her,' Mrs Martin says.

Mr Martin nods.

Matthew says, 'Talk is cheap. How about torture?'

His father picks up the receiver and hands it to Matthew.

It's Brian, asking him to come over to the house a few minutes early to help set up.

'I'm not sure if I can.' Matthew thinks about how messy it's going to be.

Brian says, 'My mother's making double-fudge brownies and said that if you get here soon, we can lick the bowl and the mixing spoon.'

'I'll be there in three minutes,' Matthew decides. 'Tell her that she doesn't even have to bother baking them, that the batter is best.'

As Matthew rushes out of the house, he hopes that the boys of G.E.T.T.H.E.M. make more money today than the girls of G.E.T.H.I.M.

He also hopes that Mrs Bruno is making a very large batch of double-fudge brownies.

What can go wrong on a day with brownies only a few minutes away?

Chapter 11

'Wash basins. Hose. Soap. Perfume. Mouthwash.' Brian points out the things that are ready.

'Perfume. Mouthwash.' Matthew's mouth is filled with brownies. 'What do we need those for?'

'To make the animals smell good . . . doggy breath . . . C.O. . . . D.O. . . . stuff like that.' Brian shoves a brownie into his mouth.

'C.O.? D.O.?' Matthew picks up another brownie.

'It's like B.O., but it's cat odour . . . dog odour. . . .' Brian grins. 'I made it up.'

Brian's seven year-old sister, Fritzie, comes out. Matthew backs up, remembering how when Fritzie was little, she used to bite everyone. Even though she no longer does, everyone is still very careful around her.

'When will the animals get here? I want to watch.' Fritzie, who thinks she's very funny, purrs and then barks.

Brian, clearly embarrassed by his little sister but sure that his parents will not lock her in the cupboard as he requested, says, 'Don't worry. Her bark is *now* worse than her bite.'

Matthew is relieved, but continues to back up.

Fritzie takes a brownie.

Matthew moves forward and takes another brownie, thinking that he's more worried about a Fritzie bite than about getting bitten by one of the dogs or cats that the boys are planning to wash.

Joshua Jackson arrives with a huge board. 'My father cut this out for us and he gave us the spray paint to do the sign. I'll do the writing part, so that the spelling is correct, and Matthew, you can do the drawing.'

While the two best friends work on the sign, the rest of the boys arrive.

'Where's Tyler?' Patrick looks around.

'He helped put up the posters all over town,' Billy informs them. 'And now he's at his house.'

'Didn't Zoe let him off his leash?' Matthew looks up from the picture he is painting.

'He's allergic,' Billy says. 'Whenever he gets around dogs and cats, he sneezes and wheezes.'

'Sneezes and wheezes.' Matthew laughs. 'I wonder how he can go out with Zoe. She's the only kid I know with a mink coat.'

'A mink coat!' Fritzie gasps. 'That's like wearing a pet on your body. That's gross.'

'Go away, Fritzie.' Brian glares at her.

Putting her hand on her hip, she says, 'Make me. I'll tell Mommy that you're being mean to me.'

Brian continues to glare at her but he does nothing. His parents have already warned him that he is to 'let her have fun too . . . not be mean . . .

she's only a little girl.' Brian feels like there is no way to win with Fritzie, that maybe some day he'll get lucky and a huge tornado will lift her and take her to Juneau, Alaska, where the tornado will drop her in the middle of a very cold glacier. Until then Brian knows he's stuck with her.

'A mink coat,' Fritzie repeats. 'Did she give it a name like Spot?'

'She got it from her father. It was a "guilt gift,"' Patrick says. 'When her parents got a divorce, he gave it to her because he left the family . . . At least she gets something . . . My parents, when they split, didn't feel guilty and give me stuff . . . They said it was the best thing for everyone . . . I think I should have got a Porsche.'

'Does Zoe wear the coat to school?' Fritzie licks brownie off her fingers. 'And what do you want a porch for?'

'Fritzie. Please. Would you just go play in traffic.' Brian scowls at his sister.

'She wears it for special occasions,' Patrick says. 'Look, Fritzie. What if we bribe you to go away?'

Fritzie grins at Patrick, who is her favourite of all her brother's friends, even though she once bit him so badly that his ankle still has a scar.

She shakes her head.

'Okay. Everyone just ignore her. Pretend that she's not there,' Brian instructs.

'How does the sign look?' Matthew holds it up. It says, 'Paws for the Animal Wash.'

'Great.' Fritzie dances in front of it.

Everyone pretends she's not there.

While the sign is placed in front of the house, a station wagon pulls up, and out comes a woman, who takes out a German shepherd.

Not just any German shepherd, but a very smelly one.

'Skunk time.' Fritzie holds her nose. '*Adiós, amigos.*'

As she goes into the house, she takes the plate of brownies.

The woman says, 'We heard something in our garage and let Puppy go outside to see what it was.'

'Puppy!' Billy shakes his head. 'That dog must weigh two hundred pounds.'

'Two hundred very smelly pounds.' Matthew holds his nose.

The woman nods. 'I know. Not only was our dog sprayed. So was our car. I was so glad that my husband remembered seeing your sign on the telephone post by our house.'

Everyone wishes that Tyler had missed going to the lady's block.

She starts pulling cans of tomato juice out of the back of the car.

'Washing the dog in this will help get rid of the smell.' She smiles at the boys, who don't smile back. 'Look, boys, I know that the money that you earn is going to the conservancy. My husband and I were going to make a donation to it anyway. We'll give you the cheque and it can be part of what you earned . . . And we'll get Puppy cleaned. It's actually a good deal for everyone.'

The dog walks over to Matthew and licks his

191

hand.

Puppy's owner hands him the cheque.

Looking at it, Matthew sees the amount.

'That's what we were planning on giving,' she says. 'So how about it?'

'It's one hundred bucks, guys.' Matthew tells everyone. 'Think about how many cars the girls are going to have to wash today to get that much, and this is just our first job of the day.' Joshua whistles. 'One hundred dollars.'

'The conservancy is a good cause. When our children were little, they used to sledge on that land,' the woman says.

The boys look at each other.

One hundred dollars is a great start for G.E.T.T.H.E.M.

Matthew nods. 'We'll do it.'

'Great.' She smiles. 'Now if only I can get the smell out of my car. I don't suppose that you would be interested in doing that, would you?'

Matthew gets a brainstorm. 'You would just pay the regular price to get your car done, right?'

She nods. 'That cheque is really all that we can afford.'

Matthew grins as he thinks about how bad the car smells.

'Some of the other kids in our class are doing a car wash. You should just pay them the regular price that they are asking to wash cars. Here's the address of where to go.' Matthew writes Vanessa's address on a piece of paper, since that's where the girls are having their car wash. 'By the time you get your car clean, we'll have Puppy here smelling as good as new.'

'Do you promise to take good care of my dog while I'm gone?' The woman looks at the boys.

Brian steps forward. 'I promise. My parents are inside, and once we get this dog cleaned up, I'll put it in my sister's room for safe keeping. I promise.'

As the woman drives off, the boys smile as they think of the girls having to clean that car and getting very little money for it.

And then they hold their noses and get to work.

Chapter 12

'You dweeble. You double dweeble. You dirty double-crossing double dweeble.' Jil! Hudson stands in front of Matthew's locker, grinning at him. 'Someday I'll pay you back for what you did. Do you have any idea how smelly that station wagon you sent over was?'

Matthew nods. 'You should have smelled the dog.'

'Our team was trying to figure out how to get even. We were hoping that someone brought the skunk or a boy-eating piranha to be washed.' Jil! shakes her head. 'Vanessa's mom contributed two cans of air freshener to the cause.'

'We put perfume on the dog. When the lady picked him up, she said that he smelled like Eau de Bow Wow, or something like that,' Matthew says. 'How many cars did you wash?'

'All of our parents' cars and about eight others. Your mother brought her station wagon over. Boy, does she have a lot of fun stuff in there for her business. I asked her if I could have a job as soon as I'm old enough. I'd love to deliver balloons dressed as a chicken, or we could both deliver balloons. I could be Dweebledee and you could be Tweebledum.' Jil! imagines what they would look like in those costumes and who they would be delivering balloons and a message to, dressed like that.

Matthew has several thoughts. One is how come his mother helped the girls earn money when she knows the two teams are competing. He is glad that he didn't have to wash the car. And he wonders why he likes talking to Jil! so much and when she got cute and when he started to notice that she was so cute. This last thought is a very puzzling development to Matthew Martin.

'How many animals did you wash? Enquiring minds want to know.' Jil! asks.

Matthew counts on his fingers. 'We had seven dogs, two cats . . . boy, do they scratch . . . and some lady brought her two-year-old kid who refuses to take a bath. Even she called him El Stinko.'

Jil! giggles. 'What did you do with El Stinko?'

'We told him that he was going to be able to play with "the big boys" and that we were playing "water wrestle with the halloween football," which we made up but which worked. Then we ran after him, watered him down with the hose, soaped him up, rinsed him off, and dried him with Mrs Bruno's hair dryer. He loved it. His mother asked us if we'd do it every night.'

'Tyler told Zoe how much money you made, how much the smelly dog and car lady paid you.' Jil!

makes a face. 'I guess you beat us. But we would have made more if someone hadn't pulled down some of our posters.'

Matthew is surprised. He didn't know about that happening.

Jil! continues, 'You didn't do that, did you? Vanessa said it was probably you, but I said I didn't think you would do anything like that.'

Matthew shakes his head no.

He wouldn't do anything like that, although he and the other boys did ask their parents not to take their cars over to the girls' car wash. He did that after he heard that the girls asked their parents not to take pets to the animal wash.

Matthew is kind of glad that his mother didn't listen, because something about what is going on doesn't seem right to him.

Even though he wants to win, he wants to make money for the conservancy more. Something definitely doesn't seem right.

Vanessa walks over and looks at Jil!. 'Traitor. You're talking to the enemy.'

Jil! looks first at Vanessa, then at Matthew, then over at Cathy Atwood, who isn't in any group, because her father is also trying to buy the land and Cathy didn't think she should work against him. Cathy is standing alone by her locker, looking very unhappy.

Jil! looks at Vanessa. 'I'll talk to anybody I want to.'

Vanessa says the one thing she thinks is going to make Matthew feel bad: 'Aren't you two getting lovey-dovey? I guess you're going to be the next class couple.'

Matthew looks at Jil!, who is blushing a little but looking at Vanessa as if she's slug slime.

He can feel that he is also turning a little red too. 'That's impossible, because I heard that you and King Kong are going to be the next class couple.'

Vanessa opens her mouth to say something else that is nasty.

Before she has a chance, Matthew says, 'I've had it, no more. This is dumb. We're supposed to be working to buy the land. We all would have made more money this weekend if we didn't tell people not to go to the other group. I didn't tear down your dumb posters, but if one of our guys did, that was wrong. I know you don't like me. Well, I don't like you either. But I think everyone should work together. Vanessa, we'll just work together apart.'

Vanessa says, 'You can't make us all work together. You're just trying to break up G.E.T.H.I.M.'

Matthew says something that is always said to him, that he never expected to be saying to anyone else. 'You are *so* immature.'

Jil! adds, 'And I have a feeling that we're not the only people who think we should all work together.'

Vanessa, who is not sure of what to say, says the one thing that she can think of. 'Well, I hope that the two of you are very happy together.' And stomps off.

'Quadruple dweeble.' Jil! looks at her and then

turns to Matthew. 'Look, just because she said all of that stuff doesn't mean that you have to rush out and buy me an engagement ring or anything.'

'What a relief,' Matthew kids.

'That doesn't mean that you can't call me sometimes.' Jil! is feeling very bold.

'What should I call you?' Matthew teases.

Jil! feels a little weird because she was so bold and that Matthew is probably never going to want to talk to her again, at least not without teasing her.

Matthew wonders for a minute if this is what his mother would call 'adolescence onset' and looks at Jil! 'Actually, I'd kind of like to call you and stuff.'

The bell rings.

They smile at each other.

As they walk to class, Matthew says, 'Let's talk to the two groups and plan a project together.'

Jil! nods. 'And let's figure out what we can do so that Cathy doesn't feel so bad about not being included.'

Matthew thinks, Maybe 'adolescence onset' is not going to be such a terrible thing.

Then he has an awful thought.

What if he starts acting like Amanda?

Nah!

Chapter 13

'Show time.' Mrs Stanton claps her hands. 'Let's get this show on the road.'

Mrs Stanton always says that when the class is going to start something that she considers exciting.

However, she never says that before a spelling, maths, or grammar test.

Mrs Stanton smiles at the class. 'You know that because of what's been happening with the property next door to the school, I've decided that we should study our own history, to understand why people feel the way they do about land . . . why some people want to preserve it and why others want to see the town grow and change. This will help you to make your own decisions. Now, who has some interesting facts about Califon? You may use your notes.'

Notebooks are taken out and hands are raised.

'Ow. Ow. Ow.' Jil! always makes that noise when she wants to be called on.

Mrs Stanton nods.

Jil! takes a very deep breath and begins. 'Califon is just a little more than two square miles. . . . It's in

Hunterton County, New Jersey, and in 1850 it was originally named California.'

She pauses to take a breath.

Mrs Stanton immediately says, 'Does anyone know why it was named California?'

'My turn,' Jessica calls out.

Once Jil! starts, it's hard for anyone else to get in a word, so everyone tries to act quickly.

Mrs Stanton nods. 'Go on.'

'It was named California because some guy named Jacob Neighbor was important in town, and that's where he came from,' Jessica says. 'It's funny. If he had come from Arizona, maybe we'd be living in a place called Arizon or something.'

'My turn,' Billy Kellerman says. 'Once there was an area called Peggy's Puddle. . . . And speaking of water, sometime in the early 1930s there was a chance that a dam was going to be built and there would be no more Califon.'

'That would be a dam shame,' Matthew says.

Jil! grins at him.

Vanessa scowls.

Mrs Stanton says, 'Matthew.'

'I didn't say anything wrong.' He grins.

'Three facts, please,' his teacher says.

Vanessa hopes that he can't think of three facts and that everyone will think he's a doofus.

Matthew thinks about his research and the facts that he liked best. Actually the dam one was his favourite, but he is sure that he can come up with others.

'I'm waiting,' Mrs Stanton says.

Matthew nods. 'Three facts. In 1903 indoor plumbing began. Everyone was very happy about that. In 1918 Califon Electric Light and Power Company brought electricity to the town.'

'How did they use their hair dryers before that?' Chloe shows concern for the early Califon residents.

Matthew continues, 'The first telephones, nine of them, came in 1903. They had to use switchboards. That means that all calls went to somewhere else first and then to the house. And everyone had party lines.'

'Party,' Mark yells out.

Mrs Stanton says, 'Party lines means that you have to share them and that each house has a specific sound of ringing.'

'And other people can listen in?' Zoe looks at Tyler.

Mrs Stanton says, 'They weren't supposed to.'

'What fun,' Ryma, who loves gossip, says.

'Back in the old days, did you have party lines?' Sarah asks.

'Yes.' Mrs Stanton remembers. 'When I was little, there was a changeover to dial.'

'Wow. Ancient history,' Chloe gasps.

'Not exactly as far back as Cleopatra,' Mrs Stanton reminds them. 'I'm not that old.'

Pablo Martinez, who is mathematically inclined, calculates that Mrs Stanton is about four times as old as they are, not all of them together but each of them. He also figures that in dog years Mrs Stanton would be about three hundred and eight years old.

To him that seems like ancient history for children and animals. He does not, however, choose to mention this to Mrs Stanton.

Somewhere in the back of Mrs Stanton's head she is trying to remember what she thought was old age when she was eleven or twelve.

The thought is depressing her just a little.

Matthew, however, is feeling great that he was able to give three facts.

He looks over at Jil!, who grins and mouths the words, 'My hero.'

He does not look over at Vanessa, who is annoyed because he used the facts that she remembered.

'Anything else you want to share?' Mrs Stanton asks.

Lizzie calls out, 'I have a great true story. My parents told it to us at dinner last night. It's about "The Great Califon Duck Roundup." What happened was that shortly after one of the mayors got into office, he decided that there were too many ducks in Califon River and that they were going to starve to death. So he decided that as a good deed, he would have "The Great Califon Duck Roundup." He had the chief of police take him out on the river in a rowing boat. Then he threw bread out of the boat so that the ducks would follow him. Then he was going to beach the boat and throw some bread into a caged-in area. The ducks were expected to follow and get captured. Then the ducks would be sent off to other places. The ducks followed him but they wouldn't go into the cage.

They went back into the water.'

Cathy Atwood adds, 'My mother says that her family had a favourite duck so they put food colouring on that duck so that if it got captured, they could come get it.'

'My dad told me that the mayor said that if it didn't work, he would become a lame duck mayor,' Lizzie says. 'My mom laughed, but I don't get it.'

'It's not nice to make fun of ducks with orthopaedic problems.' Sarah makes a face.

Mrs Stanton explains that *lame duck* in government means that the official will not be serving the next term.

Sarah feels much better.

Everyone continues to talk about the town and how some of them have always lived there and how some have just been living there for a short time.

Then they all begin to talk about where all of their families came from and how they feel about Mrs Nichols's land.

Everyone is beginning to realize about how history isn't just something to study, that they all have their own histories of who they are and where their families have lived.

'Okay,' Mrs Stanton claps her hands. 'We've got the show on the road.'

Everyone is feeling very pleased.

'Homework tonight,' she informs them.

Everyone is not so pleased.

'I want everyone to write a paper entitled "What Califon Means to me."' Mrs Stanton assigns the work. 'You may take out your notebooks and start now.'

'How long does it have to be?'

'Does spelling count?'

Mrs Stanton ignores the questions.

As everyone begins, Matthew thinks about all the things that always have been important to him and about the things that are becoming important to him now. It's as if now he's old enough to begin writing 'The Matthew Martin Story.'

He looks at Jil! and thinks that maybe he would like to be at least a chapter in any book she'd write. He looks at Vanessa and figures any book that she would write would sit in a library and collect mould. He looks around the room and realizes that there are a lot of people in the room whose story he would really like to read.

WHAT CALIFON MEANS TO ME

by Matthew Martin

I'm just a kid and normally I don't think a lot about this subject. (Except when my teacher makes me - just kidding).

I like living in Califon.

For one thing it's an easy place to spell. I would be in deep trouble if I lived in a place like Albakirkee, New Mexico, or Metuchen, New Jersey. (My parents' friends live there and personally I think it should be spelled Mitt-Touch-In.) Another town that I would have trouble living in is Piscataway, New Jersey. (I'm not even going to tell you how I think that town should be spelled.)

Another thing I like is that you get to know people in your class. (That's good except for one person and I'm not going to mention her name because to quote my teacher, you, Mrs Stanton, 'If you can't say something nice about someone, you shouldn't say anything at all.' So I won't even mention the V.S.'s name.) It's not like in some places, where there are so many kids, you never know who they are. I bet I can tell you the name of every kid in the whole school, even the kindergarten babies.

I also like that everything I need is easy to get to by bike, sweet shops, a bagel place, a sub shop, not where you go to get replacements for sick teachers but really good sandwiches, not the kind that my mother makes. There's not one sprout in any sandwich they sell.

Another good thing is that you can ride a bike just about anywhere. Someday I hope to be riding a Porsche or a Lamborgeknee, but for now Califon is a good place to ride a bike. The busiest street is Main Street and the most you ever have to wait there is two minutes and that's during rush hour. (Maybe they should call it rush minute, or something.) Also, if you get tired of riding a bike and want to sit and rest, there are a lot of trees with a lot of shade. And most people don't chase you away.

A person who really never chases you away is Mrs Nichols. I never used to think about it much because she was always just there (except for when she took her big trip, but I always knew that she was coming back). Anyway, going to visit her has always been fun - the sledging, the skating, the things she gives us to eat. Anyway, I hope that Mrs Nichols and her property are not going to be 'Past History,' that they will still be 'Current events.' My parents and I were talking about all of this last night and they say that it's important not just to conserve the land but to help keep old people as part of our lives. I hope that they can do something. Mrs Nichols has always been a part of my life. There's another thing about her. At Halloween she gives out the best sweets, not the dinky little candy bars made especially for trick-or-treating but the regular ones that you can buy all year round. I don't want you to think I just like her because of the junk food. I really do like her for a lot of reasons, but

I don't want to sound too mushy.

Speaking of Halloween, it's a good time in Califon. Lots of sweets are given out, and the only real danger is having to bob for apples and knowing that Vanessa Singer drools into the water.

Any small crime in Califon is a headline story, so it's really a pretty safe place to live.

My older sister, Amanda, is always saying that she'd like to live somewhere bigger with more stuff to do. Personally I hope that she moves to somewhere bigger too. Alone.

I just thought of something else. Since the school goes from kindergarten to eighth grade, I really know my way around and don't worry about getting lost.

My parents say that they like living here for lots of grown-up reasons. (My mother grew up here and then went away to college and met my father, who grew up in New York City. They lived in New York for a while and then moved here and, as my father says, 'had kids and crabgrass.') I could tell you what they say, but then the homework assignment would have been 'What Califon Means to My Parents.' Maybe on 'Back-to-School Night' you could make them right. Don't worry. They can spell.

To sum all this, I like living here.

THE END

P.S. I spell-checked this on my computer, so my spelling should be better.

P.P.S. I hope that I've written enough for this homework assignment.

Chapter 15

'Matthew, we're here to collect the money.' Lizzie holds out her hand. 'Cough it up.'

There's no way to escape.

Lizzie has Matthew backed up to the wall by the water fountain. Sarah Montgomery and Chloe Fulton are on either side of him.

'Let's make a deal,' Matthew bargains. 'Tomorrow I'll pay double.'

'No dice, Matt.' Lizzie shakes her head.

'Matthew. Not Matt. I like to be called Matthew.' He tries to change the subject. 'Just because you like to have a nickname doesn't mean I do.'

Lizzie shakes her head. 'I know that you like to be called Matthew. That's why I called you Matt. I'm going to do it every time you don't pay up.'

'Just leave me money for one chocolate bar a week,' Matthew pleads. 'I know that we all promised to give up what we spend on sweets each week to the conservancy, but the rest of you have parents who let you have sweets at home. You know that my mom doesn't, and even my dad is pledging the money he usually spends on junk food to the conservancy.'

'That's tough.' Sarah sounds sympathetic. 'Even my horse gets a sugar cube sometimes. I'll bring you something from home tomorrow.'

'Fork it over, or they'll be dragging Califon River for your carcass.' Lizzie has been watching a lot of old gangster movies in order to perfect her collection techniques. 'I haven't got all day. I have to get the money from the rest of the kids.'

Matthew reaches into his pocket, pulls out the money and thinks, Good-bye, M & M's.

He also thinks about how he's been managing to survive without the sweets, that the time that he's been spending with Jil! and his other friends working on the project has kept him really busy and not craving so much junk food.

Still, a couple of M's for old time's sake would not be a bad idea, Matthew thinks.

Lizzie puts the money in an old Garfield lunch box, that she stopped using in the third grade.

The box is filled with change.

'What happens if the conservancy can't raise all the money?' Matthew wonders.

Lizzie has the answer. 'If the conservancy doesn't make enough money to buy the property, the cheques will be returned. The cash that we've all collected from the walkathons, the readathons, the bake sales, auction, and sweets give-up . . . that will go into starting a fund to build a new playground.'

The end-of-school bell rings.

'Drats. We're running late.' Lizzie rushes off to collect more money.

As Chloe leaves, she says, 'Don't forget. We have to get the computer illustrations ready for the cookbook.'

Matthew nods, remembering that the cookbook meeting is going to be held at his house tonight since the computer being used is there.

The cookbook is the sixth grade's special project to earn money for the conservancy.

Matthew rushes to his locker, opens it, and throws his stuff on the bottom.

Actually his stuff goes on top of what is already on the bottom of his locker; more school books, four overdue library books, a nerf ball, a New York Yankees baseball cap, two sweatshirts, a broken pair of sunglasses, and two non-matching gloves.

It's a good thing that his mother never sees his locker or she'd again threaten to call the Board of Health.

The dreaded after-school hunger pangs strike, and Matthew searches the top shelf for any junk food that might have been left there.

No luck.

All he can find is old granola bars, shrivelled-up cinnamon-apple chunks, and carob balls with fluff on them.

There is definitely 'a fungus among us,' thinks Matthew as he debates throwing the food out or putting it in Vanessa Singer's lunch some day.

While he is debating, he hears a sound that is a little like an answering machine.

It's coming from a locker, which Matthew finds a

little strange, since he didn't think that the phone company had started installing phones in lockers.

Matthew looks to his right. The only person there is a fourth-grader who has decided to see if he can fit into his locker.

He looks to the left.

The sound is coming from Zoe's locker.

Zoe and Chloe are standing by the locker, looking at a piece of equipment that Zoe has placed on the inside of the door.

Matthew eavesdrops as Zoe explains.

'My mother gave this to me. See, this is a machine that you hook up inside the locker. It comes with three whistles, which you give out to three friends. They come up to the locker and whistle. That activates the tape recorder and they leave a message for me, not more than twenty seconds' worth, and then I can hear the message when I come back to the locker.'

This information explains why Matthew had seen Tyler blowing kisses into her locker earlier in the day.

Matthew is relieved to know that Tyler has not developed a sudden attraction for lockers.

Zoe continues, 'Three whistles are not really enough. I ordered six more.'

Matthew wants to go over and ask Zoe why she bothers having the machine when anyone who wants to leave her a message can just tell her in class.

He decides not to go over, because then they'll

213

know that he's eavesdropping.

Pretending to search the bottom of his locker, he tries to figure out how to invent something that will sound like one of her whistles so that he can leave her messages that will make her think that her locker has been haunted.

Joshua comes over. 'We have that dumb cookbook meeting. How did we get involved in doing that so we can't go over to my house and play Nintendo tonight?'

He dribbles an imaginary basketball, which he then throws to Brian.

Matthew holds his arms together as Brian dribbles the imaginary ball up to him, dunks it in, and yells, 'Two points.'

Joshua repeats, 'So how did we get involved in this stupid cookbook thing?'

'Because we get to eat the samples that people send over,' Matthew reminds him. 'And I get to do some of the computer stuff. You know I like doing that.'

'And Jil! is the editor, and you know how Matthew feels about that,' Brian teases.

Joshua crosses his arms in front of himself and turns his back to the boys.

From the back it looks like Joshua is kissing someone, especially since he keeps moving his arms up and down and saying, 'Oh, Matthew. . . . Oh, Jil!'

Brian starts making kissing sounds on the back of his hand.

Matthew remembers the 'good old days,' when he used to act immature like that.

He forgets that the good old days were less than a month ago.

Chapter 16

Amanda rushes into the rec room.

Her hand covers her left eye. 'I need your help. I really need your help.'

'If it's something medical, you'd better get Mom or Dad. They're in the dining room holding a conservancy meeting,' Matthew says nervously.

'No. I don't want them to know. I dropped one of my contact lenses on my bedroom floor and I need help finding it.' Amanda is almost breathless. 'Honey, baby. Please help.'

'Everyone's coming here for the cookbook meeting.' Matthew continues doing a computer illustration. 'I don't have time. How come you always say stuff like "Make like a tree and leave" and then, when you want something, it's "honey baby"?'

Amanda knows that he is right.

She also knows that her parents are going to be *very* angry if she's lost another lens.

After the third one went down the sink, they told her that they wouldn't claim another one on the insurance or they might lose the policy and that she would have to buy the next one herself.

Joshua walks into the recreation room, sits down, and listens.

Amanda begs again. 'Please, Matthew. I dropped the lens when I rubbed my eye, and now it's somewhere on the carpet and I can't find it. And now I'm getting dizzy from using just one eye.'

'Getting dizzy!' Matthew looks up from the picture he is doing of Mrs Stanton's spaghetti recipe. 'You normally are dizzy.'

Amanda gets ready to yell, until she remembers that she wants something from Matthew. 'Please. Look. This is going to cost me a lot of money and I don't have a lot right now. I took what I've been saving and contributed it to the conservancy.'

Matthew stares at her. 'You're not just saying that?'

'Honest.' Amanda raises her hand, the one that is not covering her eye, and swears, 'I promise.'

Pushing the keys to make sure to save the computer illustration, Matthew says, 'Oh, okay. But just remember . . . this tree is not planning on leaving any time soon, and I don't want to be told to go any more. I have just as much right to be here as you do.'

Amanda has no choice but to nod.

'When the rest of the kids get here, you can feed them some of the junk in the refrigerator. My dad and I went shopping, so don't worry,' Matthew tells Joshua. 'I'll help Cyclops, the one-eyed monster, and then be back.'

As Amanda and Matthew head out of the room,

Matthew says, 'Remember the other day when I was sick and got to stay home from school?'

Amanda remembers.

She definitely remembers.

That was the day she came home from school, opened her private diary, which she kept hidden under her mattress, and found out that Matthew had written comments in the margins.

So Amanda does remember but decides that now is not the time to start screaming again.

Matthew continues. 'Well, there was this television show that had this helpful-hints person on . . . and the helpful hint for that day was how to find contact lenses, the hard kind, on rugs.'

'How come you didn't tell me about it?' Amanda asks.

'You were too busy trying to kill me.' Matthew is sure that his sister was most upset because on the page in her diary where she gave grades to the rear ends of the boys in her class, he wrote, 'BUTT BRAIN.'

Amanda is careful not to start yelling again, concentrating instead on how happy she will be if they can find the contact lens.

'Take off your shoes,' she warns him. 'You might break the lens if you step on it with your shoe. I'll try using the torch again to look, to see if the light shows where it is and you tell me about the helpful hint.'

Matthew says, 'Get the vacuum cleaner.'

'You're crazy.' Amanda gasps.

Matthew glares.

'Sorry.' Amanda speaks softly.

'And a pair of tights.' Matthew can hear a car pull up in the driveway and wonders if everyone is downstairs waiting for him, and whether they are eating up all the junk food before he returns.

She races to get the vacuum cleaner and then hands him the tights.

'Gross,' he says holding them. 'Don't you feel like you've been tied in rubber bands when you wear this?'

'They're Mom's support tights. Don't tell her I took them.' Amanda giggles. 'I'm down to my last pair of regular stockings and didn't want to take a chance on ripping them.'

Matthew takes the tights, sticks the vacuum cleaner hose on the inside part of the leg and turns on the vacuum.

'We put this on the rug where you think that you dropped the lens and it'll pick it up without breaking the lens. The tights act like a screen.' Matthew is very proud of himself. He knew that watching that part of the show would come in handy some day, especially with 'lose-a-lens-a-day Amanda' as sister.

Matthew carefully puts the vacuum/tights nozzle near the carpet where Amanda is pointing.

'I think we caught a spider.' Matthew looks at what he has picked up.

'Yuck,' Amanda makes a face and then grins. 'That's my missing false eyelash.'

It's Matthew's turn to go 'Yuck.'

Matthew points the nozzle down again and then

looks at what he has picked up. 'BINGO. One contact lens found.'

Amanda checks and makes sure that it is in good shape. 'Oh, thank you. Thank you. Thank you.'

She goes over to the cleaning solution to get all the carpet fuzz off the lens.

Just as she says, 'Thank you,' Matthew goes 'Faster than a speeding bullet, more powerful than a locomotive, able to leap tall buildings in a single bound, Supermatthew saves the day and returns to the waiting company.'

As he heads out of the room pretending to fly, Amanda admits to herself that there are moments when she actually likes her younger brother.

Then she looks down at her marked-up diary and admits to herself that there are many moments when she doesn't.

Chapter 17

Matthew rushes down the steps and flies into the recreation room.

Everyone is there already and Jil! is leading the meeting. She grins at Matthew and then says, 'Attention, everyone. It's time for the reports. Let's do those quickly so that we can get on to the important stuff, the after-the-reports party.'

Katie raises her hand. 'We have sent out one hundred letters to famous people and are waiting to hear from them.'

'I asked all of the actors for their favourite recipes, and if they were in a television series, I asked them to let me know if there was a part for me. I included my picture,' Jessica informs them.

Mark wishes he had thought of asking the Knicks for an autographed basketball instead of just dumb recipes.

'Cathy. How about your report?' Jil! asks her assistant editor.

Some of the kids think it's a little weird for Cathy to be working on the committee since it is her father who is competing to buy the land, but almost everyone knows how awful she felt not being a part of everything.

Her father was the one who really knew how rotten she felt, so he said that she should find something to do that would benefit everyone, that he would just appreciate it if she didn't say bad things about his work.

Cathy reports, 'We have Mrs Nichols's chocolate chip cookie recipe and she also sent over her recipes for ginger snaps, lasagne, and pudding cake.'

Someone's stomach starts to growl.

Matthew looks around the room, pretending that it's not his. He grabs a strawberry Twizzler.

Cathy continues, 'Matthew's mother gave us her recipe for granola bars.'

Everyone groans, except for Matthew, who starts to make retching sounds.

'Shh. She might hear you,' Jil! whispers. 'We don't want to hurt her feelings.'

Matthew informs her, 'They can't hear from the dining room to here. I've tried to listen when Amanda and Danny are down here making out and I can't hear anything.'

Joshua does his kissing imitation again.

Jessica throws a pretzel at him.

Jil! ignores him and sounds editorial. 'We have to include the recipe. It's not poison, and some people actually like it.'

'Name two,' Matthew wants to know.

'Your mother and my dog.' Joshua starts to laugh.

So does Matthew.

'Speaking of mothers, Joshua, yours gave us a recipe,' Cathy informs him.

Everyone is amazed because Mrs Jackson is a living legend in Califon. She is referred to as the Queen of the Frozen Food Section, the person who hates to cook. Mr Jackson is the great cook in the family. He's already sent over his legendary recipe for Chicken Bombay.

'My mother? A recipe? What did she do? Tear off the directions from a beef pot pie?' Joshua can't believe it.

'No,' Cathy informs him. 'It's a recipe for microwave popcorn. It says, 'Put the bag in the oven and nuke it.'

Everybody laughs and then David Cohen says, 'My mother is really weird about the microwave. When she turns it on, she makes everybody leave the room. She thinks that we're going to get zapped by radioactive rays.'

'Why does she use it, then?' Ryma likes things to be logical.

'It's faster.' David shrugs.

'Parents. They're just so weird sometimes.' Jil! giggles, thinking about her own parents, who sometimes like to pretend that they are old-time movie stars Fred Astaire and Ginger Rogers and dance around the middle of streets. 'And sometimes they're not just weird. They're embarrassing.'

Cathy thinks about what she's been going through lately and says, hoping that there will be no comments, 'My dad sent over a recipe for chilli.'

'Chilli. Is he trying to buy that land too? Is the

recipe called Chilli Con Shopping Centre?' Vanessa laughs.

Jil! gasps. 'You are so mean sometimes.'

Vanessa shrugs. 'I just say what I feel.'

'I think that you should say that you feel stupid, then, because you just said something very stupid.' Matthew turns his back on her.

Everyone sits quietly for a minute, not sure of what to say next.

Challenging Vanessa is not always easy, because then she says rotten things to the person who challenges her.

Matthew doesn't care.

He's had to deal with her before, and this time he's not giving in.

He's also going to try very hard not to act like she acts, so he uses the grown-up voice that he has only used when he's kidding around with his parents. 'Psychologists say that people who are mean to other people have major problems and are going to suffer for it the rest of their lives. Probable outcomes of meanness are body parts falling off, oozing sores, and eventually being put in a rubber room. Nine out of ten health care professionals believe this to be true.'

He grins at Vanessa.

Jil! decides to take control of the situation. 'Chloe. Matthew. Why don't you show everyone the computer drawings that you've done for the cookbook.'

While Chloe and Matthew show everyone their artwork, Vanessa sits at her desk looking angry.

Anyone who looks at her would think that she's angry at someone, but the one she is really angry at is herself. She can't figure out why she's always doing things like this and she can't figure out how to stop.

'And this is the illustration for devilled eggs.' Chloe is holding up a piece of paper. 'I figure that it should look like a regular devilled egg with the outside holding the fixed-up yolk. Matthew, however, thinks we should do a devilled egg with horns and a tail, saying "Ha, ha. The yolk is on you."'

A vote is held and Matthew's drawing is selected.

Then someone asks whose recipe it is, and Cathy looks it up. 'It's the minister's wife.'

'Repeat vote.' Jil! calls out.

A vote is reheld, and Matthew's drawing is not selected.

There's a knock on the door.

Everyone looks out.

There's a six-foot-tall pink chicken.

'Come in.' Jil! calls out and starts to giggle.

Matthew knows who it is immediately.

As he tries to sink into the floor, he thinks, How can she do this to me? My own mother.

The six-foot-tall pink chicken is followed by Mickey and Minnie Mouse, Batman, and someone dressed as a Califon duck. The gorilla is also present.

Joshua is laughing hysterically until he notices a ballerina, dressed in a pink tutu with a moustache. It's his father, who is supposed to be home at this very moment writing the Great American Novel.

Joshua's mother is dressed in a chef's costume.

Everyone in costumes is carrying helium balloons.

They start sprinkling confetti around the room.

The sixth-grades have no idea what is going on.

Finally the Califon duck takes off her mask. It's Mrs Stanton.

Mr Jackson takes off his pink mask, which is decorated with feathers. He leaves on the moustache, which is growing on his face.

Batman leaves his mask on because he likes it so much. He speaks first.

Matthew recognizes his father's voice.

Why aren't all of these people out in the grown-up world doing what they are supposed to be doing? Matthew thinks. They're supposed to be upstairs, doing conservancy stuff.

His father explains. 'We've just finished holding the meeting. We've worked out some very important things and wanted to come down here and tell you about it, when we noticed all of these things lying around that my wife uses in her balloon-message delivering business.'

All the kids look at Matthew, who is beginning to think that this is a lot of fun. After all, a lot of fathers dress in three-piece suits. His dad's just happens to include a cape and a mask.

Mr Martin continues, 'We want everyone to know that the conservancy has enough money to buy the land. Part of it is already collected, part is pledged, and then we have estimated how much money we will get from projects like your cookbook. So we can buy the land.'

All the kids start to cheer and applaud, even Cathy, who hopes that her father doesn't find out about her reaction.

Sarah, Ryma, and Patrick do the whistle that they have been practising . . . the one that they are going to use to get cabs when they all grow up and move to New York City.

'Settle down for a minute. I have more good news.' Mr Martin takes a moment to adjust his mask. 'Mrs Nichols is feeling much better. We just used the speaker phone to talk to her.'

Everyone applauds again.

'I'm really going to miss her,' Jil! sighs.

Mr Martin holds up his hands for emphasis. 'There is even more good news. Dr Kellerman is going to be able to do a hip replacement on her and thinks that eventually she will be able to walk again and hopefully be self-sufficient. In any case, with the money coming in, Mrs Nichols will be able to have home care. And this is the best news: For as long as she is able to, she will be able to continue to live in her own home.'

More applause.

Mr Martin decides not to explain all the things that have been worked out, how Mrs Nichols wants to will everything to the town for the children's use when she dies, how, since she had no family, he has promised to be her guardian if she ever gets very old and frail and can't take care of herself. He just wants everyone to know the really wonderful news for now.

The land is saved.

Mrs Nichols has a home.

Everyone runs around the room giving high fives.

Joshua looks at his father and thinks about how ridiculous it is for an overweight middle-aged man in a pink tutu and a moustache to be jumping up and down giving high fives.

Matthew looks over at his father and listens to what Mr Martin is saying to his mother. 'Life's not always easy . . . or fair . . . and it certainly doesn't always end with "and they lived happily ever after." I'm glad that this time things turned out so well.'

And then Matthew watches Batman kiss the six-foot-tall pink chicken.

He watches as Mrs Stanton, dressed as the Califon duck, stands over Zoe and Tyler, who will use any excuse to kiss.

Mrs Stanton taps them on their shoulders and says, 'Cool it, kids.'

Matthew wonders if Mrs Stanton will do the same thing to his parents.

Then he turns to Jil!

'We did it! We all did it.' She reaches out and hugs him.

Soon everyone is hugging everyone else.

Finally, when everything settles down, Matthew looks at everyone and says, 'So when do we start working on getting the playground built?'

And so it ends and begins again.

Earth To Matthew

To Samuel Anthony Danziger,
Terrific Nephew and a great Consultant

ACKNOWLEDGMENTS

To Pam Swallow and Sue Haven – for listening
daily, over the phone, to the manuscript
To Ann M. Martin, Martin, Martin for the
echo-system, system, system
To Everyone at Franklin Institute, especially
Marty Hoban and Elaine Wilner, and to the
fantastic staff and volunteers who make
Camp-In a wonderful, wonderful programme

Chapter 1

'Ready for blast-off?' Mr Martin turns to his son, who is sitting next to him in the car, eating a slice of pizza.

Matthew nods, pizza sauce dripping down his chin.

Mr Martin pays the carwash attendant and pushes the button that rolls up the car window.

Matthew pretends to be the co-pilot. 'Car in neutral.'

'Check.' Mr Martin moves the stick shift to N.

'Foot off the brake,' Matthew continues.

'Check.'

'Pizza in mouth.' Matthew hands his father a slice.

'Check.' Mr Martin folds the piece and starts eating it.

Outside, the attendant is hosing down the car and putting soap on it.

It's a family tradition at the Martin household. Every Saturday morning Matthew and his father take the sports car or the estate car to be cleaned.

Boy-Bonding Time is what Mr Martin calls it.

Yuckoid is what Matthew's thirteen-year-old sister, Amanda, calls it.

'I don't want to Girl-Bond any more. I prefer to think of myself as an only-child orphan,' is what Amanda says.

Mr Martin has made Matthew promise that in two more years, when Matthew becomes a teenager, he will not rebel . . . at least not against Boy-Bonding Time. Matthew's made the same deal with his mother for Matthew-Mom Bonding.

Sometimes Matthew thinks his parents are more like kids than the sixth-graders in his class.

The hosing ends and the car moves forward.

Brushes move against the side of the car.

'That tickles.' Matthew jokes and laughs, even though he has made that statement every time the car has been washed since the tradition began five years ago.

'Martian asteroid monsters attacking overhead,' Mr Martin yells as the huge rubber strips go over the top of the car.

Matthew makes a sound like a machine gun and points the pizza slice at the strips.

As the car slides forward, leaving the strips behind, Mr Martin breathes a make-believe sigh of relief. 'Good work, partner. You've saved us once again.'

A white light flashes, signalling that the underside of the car is getting washed.

Then the car gets polished and waxed and rust inhibitor is put on.

'Trouble up ahead,' Matthew yells, as something looking like a pool raft approaches the car.

'Duck,' yells Mr Martin as the machine blows the car dry. 'Otherwise it's going to capture us and take us to its planet for scientific study. You have been chosen because they are planning special experiments to discover what causes some earthlings to have red hair and freckles. I will be kidnapped to act as their lawyer at intergalactic court if they ever get caught and put on trial for their dastardly deeds. I will refuse to defend them, of course, and they will send me into hyper-space, never to see my family again . . . never to eat your mother's tofu tuna casserole. Not eating the casserole is the good news. The bad news' – Mr Martin ducks, pretending to avoid the machine – 'is that never seeing my family again would be truly terrible, and I can't imagine Martian food. That just might be even worse than tofu and bean sprouts.'

Matthew ducks. The car moves out of the building, the attendants give it a final drying off, and the men of the Martin family stop ducking.

'Another successful mission. . . . We're back from outer space and the NASA technicians are cleaning off the radiation particles.' Matthew sips his soda. 'Once that is done, you can put the car

233

antenna back up so that we can hear the latest earth music, the kind I like, not the old-fashioned junk that you listen to.'

Mr Martin acts upset. 'How dare you call those masterpieces of music junk? Those, young man, are "oldies but goldies".'

'"Oldies but mouldies" is more like it.' Matthew grins.

As they drive off, Matthew says, 'Next week let's pretend we're surfers who wipe out and are rescued by a submarine that immediately has to go under the ocean.'

Mr Martin nods. 'And now, young man, let's meet the rest of our family at the school. It's almost time for the big event . . . the dedication of the brand-new playground.'

Matthew helped build the giant wooden-horse slide. He looks down at his thumb, which is still black and blue from missing the metal nail with the hammer and hitting the Matthew Martin one instead, and decides that the pain was worth it.

He thinks about how much fun the dedication is going to be, a real party with all his friends there and lots of sweets, cake and fizzy drinks.

Matthew hopes that his mother has not got all dressed up for this occasion. Lots of mothers get dressed up, but not many mothers own a company that hires people to dress up in costumes to deliver messages. When Matthew's mother dresses up, it doesn't always mean a dress and heels. It sometimes means she puts on a gorilla or chicken suit or something like that.

The radio comes on.

'Now *this* is music.' Mr Martin grins and begins to sing along.

Matthew makes puking sounds in time to the music.

Mr Martin takes the hint and turns off the radio.

Matthew stops making noises.

'Would you mind telling me what all the noise was about this morning?' Mr Martin glances over at his son. 'What were you and your sister fighting about? Why did you have to act like an alarm clock on one of the few mornings that your mother and I could sleep late?'

'It wasn't my fault.' Matthew pretends that he is in a courtroom and that his father, the lawyer, is questioning him. 'I'm innocent until proven guilty, and even then, I'm innocent.'

'This isn't a court of law.' Mr Martin shakes his head. 'I asked a simple question. I want a simple answer.'

Raising his right hand, Matthew vows, 'I promise to tell the truth, the whole truth, and nothing but the truth. I was in the vicinity of the kitchen on the morning in question and had just poured milk on my breakfast cereal and was in the process of putting bananas on top.'

Mr Martin tries not to grin. 'Get to the point or I'm going to hold you in contempt of . . .'

He's not sure of what to hold him in contempt
– court, car, parenthood?

Matthew continues. 'The suspect entered the
room.'

'Are you referring to your sister?'

Matthew nods. 'I said a simple hello and she
yelled, "Drop dead. You left the toilet seat up
again." In simple self-defence I had to throw the
banana peel at her. No court in this country would
convict me for doing that. If I get punished, I'm
going to have to a-peel against it.'

Matthew laughs at his own pun.

So does Mr Martin, who is trying not to.

'I rest my case,' Matthew says.

'You may rest your case, but the noise kept your
mother and me from resting ourselves . . . and the
way you and your sister act sometimes is a clear
case of a-rested development.' Mr Martin laughs
at his own pun.

Matthew doesn't get it but laughs anyway so
that his father stays in a good mood.

'In any case,' Mr Martin says, 'if your sister
shows up at the dedication, I want you to pretend
that you like each other and stop this constant
bickering.'

Matthew protests. 'She's the one who always
starts it and now she's getting even worse. She
doesn't even have to start because she never stops.
No matter what I do, she picks on me . . . and not
just on me, on everyone. She yelled at Joshua the

other day and he's not even her brother. He's my friend. And she and Mom are always fighting.'

His father sighs. 'I know.'

'Why couldn't you have waited and just had me?' Matthew slurps some soda and then gargles it.

'Matthew . . . we love you . . . and we love your sister. I don't want you to think we don't. And *you* are not perfect either. Just remember all of the times you have done things that were less than perfect. You're no angel either.'

Matthew decides to pretend that he's on the witness stand again. 'I *object*. Not fair badgering the witness. I've done nothing wrong. She has . . . and you're picking on me.'

Mr Martin calls out, 'Order in the court. Order in the court.'

'I'll have two more slices of pizza and another can of soda and a couple of Mallomars and eleven Strawberry Twizzlers,' Matthew says.

'What are you talking about?' Mr Martin looks over at his son.

'You said, "Order in the court," so I'm ordering.'

Shaking his head, Mr Martin laughs. 'Look, let's have a great time. This is a special day with a lot to celebrate. A new adventure playground built on land that we managed to save for the town . . . Mrs Nichols can not only stay on that land but the playground is being named for her.'

Matthew nods and decides not to worry about anything. So what if his sister exists? So what if his mother may be there dressed as a chicken?

His friends will be there.

So will a lot of junk food.

Nothing's going to ruin the fun.

Chapter 2

'Over the teeth and over the gums, look out, stomach, here it comes.' Matthew wolfs down his fourth cupcake and takes a swig of his soda.

There's marshmallow icing across his upper lip.

Joshua Jackson, his best friend, reaches for a handful of chocolate chip cookies. 'I can't believe that you aren't eating more of these. Mrs Nichols made them. You know they are the best, the absolute best. I can't believe that you aren't eating these.'

Holding open his backpack, Matthew shows that he has taken about a dozen of them.

Mrs Martin approaches her son.

Matthew quickly zips shut his backpack.

His mother gets closer.

Matthew hopes that she doesn't notice how close he is to the junk food table. He also hopes that none of his friends realize that it is his mother, since she is dressed as a guinea pig.

Matthew hates having a parent who looks like a hairball, and wishes that she had dressed like everyone else instead of getting into a costume to hand out helium balloons to all the little kids.

Standing directly in front of her son, Mrs Martin points at him with one of her paws. 'Young man, are you eating a lot of sugar? You know how I feel about that.'

Shaking his head no, Matthew hopes that she doesn't do a breath check and then check his backpack, his pockets, and underneath the hat on his head.

She looks at his upper lip covered with marshmallow frosting, licks her paw, and reaches out to wipe off the marshmallow.

'Mom.' Matthew backs off. 'That's gross.'

His father, who changed into a guinea pig costume when he got to the playground, comes up and says, 'It could be worse. Rodent moms lick faces.'

'Gross.' Matthew and his mother say at the same time.

Mr Martin reaches for a doughnut.

Mrs Martin takes it out of her husband's hand, puts it back on the table, and removes the can of soda from her son's grasp.

'I just want my family to be healthy. Please, honey, no more soda. There's fruit juice too.'

Matthew wipes off some of the fur from the costume that has mixed with the marshmallow on his face. *'Mom.'*

'Don't "Mom" me,' she says.

Matthew looks at his mother. 'Guinea pig.'

'Don't "guinea pig" me either.' She laughs.

A little boy interrupts, tugging at her leg. 'Can I have a balloon?'

The little boy's mother says, 'Did I hear a please?'

Matthew thinks of all the times his own mother has said that to him. He is willing to bet that the little kid's mother also uses her own spit to wipe off the kid's messy face.

Mrs Martin hands the boy a balloon, pats him on the head, and turns back to Matthew. 'Just remember, the dedication will begin in a few minutes. Why don't you stop eating and congratulate Mrs Nichols for having the park named after her?'

'All right, Mom.' Matthew picks up his soda again, and then gargles it.

Mr Martin says, 'Look, there are a whole bunch of kids who haven't got balloons yet. Honey, why don't you go over to the ones by the equipment and I'll go over to the other side.'

'Okay. See you later.' She takes Matthew's soda out of his hand. She empties it this time and puts it in the correct garbage can.

After she leaves, Mr Martin leans over to his son, wiggles his whiskers, and whispers, 'I've been watching you store away junk food.'

Matthew looks down at the ground.

Mr Martin continues, 'Save some for me,' and

then he leaves to hand out balloons.

Glancing around to make sure that his mother is not looking, Matthew grabs another cupcake and rushes over to talk to Mrs Nichols.

On the way he sees Amanda, who turns away from him and pretends he doesn't exist.

She and her friend laugh, meanly.

Matthew debates going over and doing something to embarrass her, like asking if she shops at Flat Chests R Us, but remembers that he promised his father not to fight with her. He thinks about how he's got to stop making promises and then he decides to keep going.

Rushing away, pretending that he never heard Amanda, he runs into Vanessa Singer, his worst enemy. Matthew *literally* runs into Vanessa, cupcake first.

Her brand-new T-shirt, which said 'Born to Shop' now says 'Born to hop' because marshmallow is covering part of it.

Chapter 3

Vanessa looks like she's going to hit the roof or, in this case, the sky . . . or Matthew.

Matthew is not sure what to do. He knows 'I'm sorry' is not going to work. This is the Vanessa Singer who once started a group called G.E.T.H.I.M. – Girls Eager to Halt Immature Matthew. This is the Vanessa Singer who would like to see Matthew's name on the Ten Most Wanted List, to see him hunted down and put in solitary confinement so that she will never have to spend another day in school with him, not ever again. The Vanessa Singer who wants him to graduate from high school and then college while he is in jail so that his diploma reads 'P.U. – Prison University.'

A crowd of sixth-graders starts to gather around them.

Matthew decides to try apologizing, even though he realizes that probably won't do any good.

After all, it really was an accident.

'I'm sorry,' he says.

Vanessa puts her hand on her hip. '"I'm sorry" isn't good enough, bozo.'

She thinks about all he has done to her and starts to list things. 'Should I start with the gerbil in my Barbie lunchbox in second grade, or the note on my back in third grade that said "Cootie Motel", or the other eighty zillion things that you've done to me?'

She stamps her foot, which lands on Matthew's foot.

He hops up and down, yelling 'Ow' and pretending she's broken it.

'Now look who's "Born to hop" . . . and what are you going to do about the mess you've made of my new shirt?' She ignores his supposed pain.

'Why don't you offer to wipe it off her?' Mark Ellison jokes.

Matthew looks at where the icing has landed and can feel himself start to blush.

Vanessa yells at Matthew, 'Try it and I'll knock your block off.'

Matthew says, 'I didn't say I was going to do that. I wouldn't want to touch you anyway, not with a ten-foot pole. Look, it was an accident. What do you want me to do? I'll buy you another stupid shirt. I've already said I'm sorry, that it was an accident.'

One of their classmates, Ryma Browne, moves a little closer and softly says, 'Come on, Vanessa.

Why don't you turn the other cheek, let it go. It really was an accident.'

Vanessa sneers, 'Why should I turn the other cheek? This goofball would probably hit it with a pie.'

Ryma backs off.

Vanessa, who cannot calm down once she gets angry at Matthew, yells, 'You are such a pain.'

Matthew stares at her.

He just doesn't know what to do.

He knows what he would like to do but he's not sure where he could find a rocket that would shoot Vanessa to Mars.

Mrs Stanton, their teacher, walks up to them. 'Vanessa, I saw what happened. Matthew didn't do it intentionally. . . . Although he really should have been watching more carefully. He's offered to buy you a new shirt . . . although I do believe it will all wash out. So what else do you want?'

What Vanessa really wants is for the whole thing to be over, for everyone not to be staring at them, for the icing to not be on her chest. But she doesn't know how to get out of this situation without seeming like she's backing down.

So she says, 'I want Matthew to get detention for a month.'

Mrs Stanton sighs. 'Vanessa. It's Saturday. Technically this is not school business. I just thought I could reason with you and try to work this out. I can't give anyone detention. And I really don't think this situation merits it.'

Mrs Stanton stares at her two students and wonders why she let herself get in the middle.

'I have an idea.' Jil! Hudson, who changed the second *l* in her name to give herself more excitement and who loves getting people involved in doing things, comes forward. 'I volunteered to help clean up at the end of the dedication. Maybe Matthew can help, to atone for his deed.'

Matthew wonders what *atone* means, if it has something to do with music or body building, and then he remembers how Mrs Stanton said that if you don't know a word, try to figure it out by the rest of the sentence or by the situation. He figures that he's really going to have to pay for this one . . . or die.

Vanessa frowns. She knows that Jil! and Matthew kind of like each other, so it's not going to be absolute torture. Still, the thought of Matthew having to deal with rubbish appeals to her since she thinks that 'Matthew Martin' is another way of saying 'garbage'.

'Oh, okay.' She gives in. 'But if I can't get this clean, he's going to have to get me another one.'

She walks away, feeling a little uncomfortable that she's turned everything into such a big deal but glad that Matthew is going to be stuck on the garbage detail.

'ATTENTION.' A voice blares over the loudspeaker. 'It's time for the ceremony to begin.'

Everyone gathers around at the front of the playground area. There's a large crowd because building the adventure playground was a real community effort. The design was done with the help of one of the parents who is an architect. The students helped to plan what was going into the playground.

Money was raised. Supplies were donated or bought at cost from community stores.

And then it was the spring holiday. And everyone who could, worked on the playground. Some built. Some watched the little kids of people who had other playground jobs. Some people served the food, which had been made by parents or donated by local restaurants and supermarkets. There were lots of jobs to do, and people worked day and night.

The mayor starts to speak, thanking all the people who helped, listing all the businesses, going on for a very long time.

Matthew puts his head on Jil!'s shoulder and pretends to snore.

It is the first time he has really done anything like that and he hopes that she doesn't think this means that they are engaged or something.

She giggles and then raps him lightly on his forehead with her knuckles. 'Earth to Matthew. Wake up. Mrs Nichols is going to speak.'

Matthew looks up immediately.

Mrs Nichols, the seventy-eight-year-old person

the playground is being named after, is one of the people that Matthew likes best in the world. Not only is she a lot of fun, not only has she been a part of his family's life since he was born, not only does she make the best chocolate chip cookies in the world . . . but she is also an adult who really talks to kids and listens to them, not just asks dumb questions like 'How old are you?' and 'What grade are you in?'

Mrs Nichols uses a cane to go up to the microphone. She smiles and then speaks. 'I have so much to be thankful for today. It's such an honour to have this wonderful playground named after me, and I can hardly wait until my hip is better and I can go down the slide and use the swings.'

Many people laugh, thinking that she's joking.

Matthew, however, remembers how much she used to like going sledging with him and his friends and knows that she is serious.

She continues, 'I am thankful that so many people have helped me.'

Matthew remembers how, after she broke her hip, she almost had to sell her land to someone who wanted to turn it into a shopping centre. He is thankful, too, that so many people helped her so that she didn't have to go away.

Mrs Nichols concludes, 'I am so proud to be part of a community that cares. Again, I thank you.'

Matthew looks around.

Several people are crying, remembering how Mrs Nichols has always helped, always volunteered at the school and church, always shared food from the farm with people who needed it, always offered good advice.

Everyone applauds when Mrs Nichols finishes speaking.

After Mrs Nichols is done, Mrs Morgan, the principal, gets up to explain how the playground is for school use during the day and for community use after school and over the summer.

Then someone else explains how the next project will be to build a community recreation centre on the property.

Matthew is beginning to think that the speeches are going to take longer than it took to get the playground built. He also remembers how much fun it was to plan and build the playground.

He thinks about how, by the time the speeches are done, the little kids are going to be adults.

Tuning out, Matthew looks around.

Ms Klein, the media specialist, is rushing round filming everything.

As she points the camera in his direction, he crosses his eyes and puts his hands on both sides of his mouth and makes 'fish lips.'

Ms Klein turns the camera away from him, so he looks to where his sister is standing with her boyfriend, Danny Cohen, and makes fish lips at her.

Amanda ignores him.

He notices that Vanessa is standing off by herself, pouting. The icing has come off and her T-shirt is wet. 'Born to Shop' is back, although Matthew thought 'Born to hop' was more appropriate and that 'Born to Crab' would be even more appropriate.

He spots his parents, who are still in the guinea pig outfits. They have their arms around each other. In third grade there used to be guinea pigs in the classroom and they used to have babies practically every three minutes. Matthew hopes wearing those costumes does not give his parents ideas, since he thinks one sister is more than enough.

Putting his head back on Jil!'s shoulder, he starts to snore again. Getting bored with that sound, he starts to snort.

Jil! sighs and says, 'How come it's never like this in the movies?' She then answers her own question. 'That's probably because the movies are hardly ever about sixth-graders.'

Matthew starts making chirping sounds and wonders if there are any cupcakes left at the refreshment table.

Finally the speeches are done and the little kids rush to use the playground, which looks like a magic wonderland.

Wood, ropes, and tyres have been combined to form castles, pyramids, Viking ships, jungle mazes, and animal forms.

Matthew wonders what's going to happen next, now that the playground is completed.

'Clean up time,' Jil! reminds him.

Matthew pretends that he doesn't hear Jil!, that he is intently watching some second-graders go through the tube slide.

Jil! raps him on the head with her knuckles, a method she has found that works with him, and says, 'Earth to Matthew. Pay attention.'

He pretends to pick up a microphone on a spaceship communicator. 'I'm up here in the clouds.'

'I know. Your head is often up in the clouds.' She pretends to pick up the earth space-station communicator and says, 'It is mission control's responsibility to make sure that even though you're up there, you can still come down to deal with the stuff on our planet. It's a tough job, but someone's got to do it. And anyway, if you don't, I have a feeling that this place is going to be littered with more than just this garbage . . . if Vanessa finds out that you got out of doing what you promised.'

Matthew says, 'I'm not afraid of Born-to-Hop Vanessa Singer, but I *did* promise, so I guess I'll land this vehicle.' He continues pretending that he really is an astronaut. 'Ground control. Get ready. I'm coming in for a landing. Ten . . . nine . . . eight . . . seven . . .'

251

He pretends to land.

Jil! hands him a biodegradable rubbish bag. 'Your assignment, sir, is to collect specimens of trash for further study and investigation.'

Matthew looks at the bag and then at Jil! 'Couldn't my assignment be to check out the snack-eating habits of earthlings? Don't you need that information for your study?'

Jil! looks around the brand-new playground at all the litter and shakes her head. 'Your assignment as a humanoid is to help clean up the playground. Can't you hear it calling out to you? Earth to Matthew, Earth to Matthew.'

Matthew puts his hands by his ear and bends down to the ground. 'I think I can hear it. It's saying, "Earth to Matthew, Earth to Matthew, how about some some cupcakes . . . a frozen yogurt with M&M's on top, a banana split?"'

'Matthew.' Jil! puts her hand on her hip.

'Jil!' Matthew puts his hand on his hip, imitating her. 'If that's what the earth is calling out to me, to clean up garbage, my line is busy.'

'Matthew, please.' Jil! looks very unhappy.

Matthew feels a little confused. Back in the old days, at the beginning of sixth grade, he wouldn't have cared what Jil! thought, and he probably would have been one of the kids messing up the playground.

It's different now, somehow.

He wishes that earth had a computer so that he

252

could send it a message. 'Matthew to earth, Matthew to earth . . . What in the world is going on?'

Chapter 4

'Let's get this show on the road.' Mrs Stanton claps her hands, signalling that everyone in class should be seated. 'We're getting ready to start a brand new unit.'

After everyone sits down, Matthew raises his hand. 'Mrs Stanton, I have a scientific question to ask you. It's about the animal kingdom.'

'About your relatives, the apes?' Vanessa sniggers.

'Vanessa.' Mrs Stanton uses the teacher voice that means, 'Go one step farther and you're in detention for two days.'

Matthew makes monkey sounds at Vanessa – '*Chee-chee*' – and then scratches himself and pretends that he is picking fleas off his body and flicking them at Vanessa.

'Matthew.' Mrs Stanton uses the teacher voice that says, 'And you're going to be joining her.'

Matthew stops acting like a monkey and looks directly at Mrs Stanton, giving her his best student look, the one that says, 'I'm not a bad kid. I'm just trying to get through school in the only way I can, by joking around a little. But don't forget that I still get good grades, so don't get too angry at me.'

Mrs Stanton smiles. 'Ask your question, Mr Martin.'

Matthew grins back. 'You know how you're always saying that we should learn all we can about nature and how it works?'

Mrs Stanton nods.

'Well,' Matthew continues, 'I have a question about chickens.'

Mrs Stanton thinks, Perhaps he has read about the recent outbreak of salmonella in eggs . . . or perhaps it's one of those stupid chicken jokes he likes so much. Either way, she thinks, I'll let him go for it.

Matthew grins again, showing his dimple. 'Why did the chicken cross the new playground?'

Shaking her head, Mrs Stanton thinks about how hard the class has been working and about how a few minutes of joking is all right. 'Mr Martin, tell us. Why did the chicken cross the new playground?'

'To get to the other slide,' is the answer.

Some people groan.

Some laugh.

Vanessa Singer mumbles, 'That's so funny, I forgot to laugh.'

Jil! calls out, 'That was a fowl joke.'

Mrs Stanton, who loves puns and encourages

them in her classroom says, 'The delivery of that joke wasn't exactly poultry in motion.'

Raising his hand, Joshua Jackson looks at her. 'Eggsactly what did you mean by that? I thought that was an excellent yoke.'

'An eggshellent joke. It broke me up.' Lizzie Doran giggles.

'I don't want to be hard-boiled about this, but dozen everyone think it's time to get back to our regular class.' Mrs Stanton calls the class to attention. 'Now, let's get serious.'

Matthew debates asking her who Serious is and why does she want to get him, but decides not to do it.

'Today we are going to begin a major study of the ecosystem,' she informs them.

Matthew can't stop himself. Making it sound like he's calling out from a mountaintop, he says, 'Today we are going to begin a major study of the echo-system . . . system . . . system.'

'Enough.' Mrs Stanton grins, but uses the teacher voice that says, 'Enough is enough is enough.'

Everyone tries not to giggle.

She says nothing for a few minutes and then begins again. 'The ecosystem, or the ecology system, is about how things in a specific area relate to each other and their environment. If something in nature changes or is disturbed, it affects every other part. If something harms the environment, such as a flood, that affects the people who live there, their health, their economy. It also concerns the people who may not live there but who help them. It may cost them money, they may use their own resources. Another example is oil. If the oil supply in the Middle East is threatened because of politics, it affects every other part of the world. Prices go up. People may have to ration. Businesses that use oil and petrol will raise their prices, even though they don't directly sell those products. So you see, there is a lot that is interdependent. Life, economy, politics.'

Matthew thinks about how science used to be so much easier to understand, how it was just one subject to study, and now it involves history, geography, maths, and lots of other things.

Mrs Stanton looks at everyone. 'Who would like to give some other examples of how one thing environmentally affects something else?'

Vanessa is waving her hand wildly. 'Me. Me. Me.'

Like if Vanessa's parents got transferred to a different state, it would make me very happy, Matthew thinks.

'Like if someone, who will remain nameless, was absent from school, that would make me very happy, and then I would be in a good mood, and that would make Mrs Stanton very happy, and then she might even decide to give the entire class A's for the day, except for that nameless absent person, and then everyone would be very happy. Isn't that what it would be like?' Vanessa smiles at her own explanation.

Matthew calls out, 'Like if someone, who will remain nameless, was outside one day and a giant vulture swooped down, captured her, took her back to its nest, and the baby vultures ate her. Then the barfing baby birds fell out of the nest into the water and died, polluting the water with the disgustingness of the nameless person. Then the fish who got sick from the pollution got scooped up into a net and sold to the company that sells stuff to the school cafeteria. Then we all got sick from the polluted fish cakes. That's how it works, right?'

'I've warned everyone before, there is to be no making fun of anyone else in this class, no meanness toward each other, no name-calling,' Mrs Stanton says.

'I said "the person who will remain nameless".' Matthew and Vanessa say at the same time.

'You heard me.' Mrs Stanton takes out a piece of chalk. 'Now, enough. To get back to the subject, you are both right: Ecosystems deal with how one thing affects another thing and then that affects something else. And it can continue.'

'Ow, ow, ow,' Jil! waves her hand. 'I want to say something.'

Matthew watches as Jil! practically jumps out of her seat.

He really likes the way she always gets so excited by things and wants to be involved.

Jil! says, 'My mom is going to have a baby and she's decided to use a nappy service, not disposable nappies, unless absolutely necessary, because she did some research and found out that a baby can use eight to ten thousand nappies before it becomes fully toilet trained.'

'Wow, that's a lot of you-know-what.' Patrick Ryan holds his nose.

Jil! continues, 'She found out that it takes the pulp from one tree to make five hundred nappies. So that comes to about twenty trees for each baby. Multiply that by the number of babies that use disposable nappies and we're wasting a lot of forests, and forests are important for a lot of reasons.'

'My mom says that she loves disposable nappies, that in the old days it was a real mess.' Ryma Browne makes a face.

'Do we have to talk about this gross stuff?' Zoe Alexander looks over at her boyfriend, Tyler White, whom she plans to marry and have two perfectly wonderful children with. She worries that if he listens to all of this, he may change his mind and take back the cubic zirconia ring he has given her. Since Zoe's mother has been married a lot and so has her father, she wants to get her own life settled as soon as possible.

Tyler is sitting at his desk pretending to look

interested in the class conversation, but really thinking about how hungry he is and wondering what the cafeteria is serving today. He hopes it is not polluted fish cakes.

'I'm not done yet.' Jil! jumps up and down. 'And when my mother called the nappy company, she made sure that they don't use lots of chemicals to get the nappies really white. You know, stuff like chlorine bleach.'

'That's expensive,' Katie Delaney says. 'Nappy services are expensive.'

'So are disposable nappies. People can do the wash themselves.'

'Yug.' David Cohen looks at Mrs Stanton. 'Is this important? Do we have to talk about this? It has nothing to do with me. My mom says that there is no way that she's going to have any more babies, that there are enough children and stepchildren in our family.'

'It does have something to do with you, with all of us,' Lisa Levine tells David. 'That's what the ecosystem is all about.'

All about . . . about . . . about, thinks Matthew.

Mrs Stanton explains, 'I realize that we've used a lot of time to talk about nappies, but I think it's important. It's something that affects people worldwide.'

'Yeah. It's something that everyone does.' Brian Bruno laughs.

'Put a cork in it.' Vanessa snarls at him. 'You all

act so immature sometimes.'

'Maybe that's the answer.' Brian laughs. 'Someone should sell corks instead of nappies.'

'Ugh.'

Mrs Stanton continues, 'Part of every day, for the rest of the school year, will be spent working on this project. I'm going to break you up into groups and appoint a chairperson.'

'Not Matthew,' Brian calls out without thinking.

Everyone in class chuckles when they remember how Matthew as chairperson of the Mummy Committee got Brian encased in plaster and how Dr Kellerman had to free him. Actually everyone but Brian is laughing. Everyone but Brian and Matthew.

They also remember the explosion when he was chairman of the Volcano Committee.

'I've chosen people who have not been chairperson yet, so that by the end of the year you will have all had the opportunity to exhibit your leadership qualities.'

Katie Delaney squirms in her seat, knowing that she is going to be made chairman of a committee and not wanting to do it. She would rather just sit quietly and exercise her 'followship qualities.'

Mrs Stanton passes out pieces of paper. 'Here are the committee assignments. You will do group research on your topics and then work individually on your own project. Come up with some suggestions for changes that could be made worldwide and that we can do here in Califon, in your homes, at school. Suggestions that you can make to your parents and friends. You will also find out whether any of this is controversial, whether there are differences of opinion about anything.'

Matthew looks down at the paper. Under 'Recycling,' he sees his name.

Katie Delaney is chairperson.

Tyler White is on the committee. So is Jil!

Zoe frantically waves her hand. 'Can we swap with someone? Please. Oh, please. You've put me on the Conserving Energy At Home Committee and what I'm really interested in is recycling.'

What you're really interested in is Tyler, Matthew thinks.

Mrs Stanton shakes her head. 'The assignments are made. No changes will be made. Zoe, I'm sure that you will be a valuable asset to your committee and learn a lot.'

Zoe pouts.

The only energy conservation at home that she cares about is not having her parents spend so much time marrying, divorcing, and dating.

Mrs Stanton claps her hands. 'To celebrate all of the work that you will be doing on this unit, when we are finished, at the end of the year, at the end of the sixth grade, there will be a very special surprise trip for all of you who do your work.

Remember, you must do your work or you won't be able to go.'

Matthew and Joshua look at each other, remembering the adventure-book-report assignment.

Given permission to work together, they had played Nintendo instead of reading.

Panicking the night before the assignment was due, they decided to fake a book report. Matthew remembered a book that his mother talked about a lot because she thought Mr Martin was like the main character. From memory Matthew made up the story about this guy named Don, who acted a lot like a knight in shining armour. Matthew and Joshua turned in a report about a book called *Don Coyote*, written by Sir Vantays.

Mrs Stanton informed them that the book was *Don Quixote* by Cervantes. She also informed them that they couldn't go on the class trip to McCarter Theatre.

They had to spend the entire day in the third-grade classroom while the rest of their class went to Princeton, New Jersey.

Mrs Stanton also warned them that their next project had to be extra good if they wanted to go on the next trip.

And they want to go on the next trip.

'Where is the trip?' Pablo Martinez raises his hand.

'It wouldn't be a surprise if I told you. Trust me. You are all going to love it.' Mrs Stanton gathers up some papers on her desk. 'Now, I want you all to separate into your groups and get started. Talk about your subject. Brainstorm. Then we'll go to the library and do some research.'

There's a lot of noise as people start to move desks around.

Finally everyone is seated.

Matthew's group has gathered in the corner of the room, next to the shelves of books that are available during free reading time.

Jil! passes a note to Matthew.

Hi!!! Lisa is having a party. Not this Saturday, but next Saturday night. Want to go together?
It doesn't have to be a real date, not if you don't want it to be.
But it could be if you want it to be. Or we could go separately. Or you could take Vanessa (just kidding). Or maybe you're busy.
Let me know during lunch. I'll be the one eating the peanut butter and banana sandwich.

Matthew looks at the note and then at Jil!, who seems to be a little embarrassed but also smiling.

He remembers how at the beginning of the school year he hated girls and wonders what has happened to change that. Except for Vanessa. And of course Amanda.

Katie says, 'Well, I guess we should get started.'

Matthew thinks she is referring to Jil!'s note and then realizes that she is talking about the recycling project.

Tyler starts talking about how he wants his project to be about how things should be recycled so that the space in landfills doesn't run out. He says, 'My project will be called "Down in the Dumps".'

Matthew sits quietly for a change, wondering what he's going to tell Jil! at lunch.

Chapter 5

'This will be just like old times.' Mr Martin pulls into a parking space at the circus fairgrounds.

'Boring.' Amanda folds her arms and makes a face. 'I can't believe that you made me come to this stupid thing when I could be at the mall with my friends.'

Matthew sits in the back seat next to her and can't believe that they made her come either.

He also can't believe that he and his father didn't get to go to the carwash this morning because of this trip. He had really wanted to talk to his father about how he was going to Lisa's party with Jil!. There were a lot of questions he wanted to ask boy-to-man, and the next Boy-Bonding wouldn't be until the day of the party.

Tomorrow, Matthew thinks, I'll talk to him tomorrow or later tonight, if we get the chance to be alone.

'Boring,' Amanda repeats.

'We're a family.' Mr Martin turns off the key in the ignition and turns round. 'And we're going to act like a family. Now, let's get out of the car and have fun.'

Amanda sighs and doesn't move.

Making his fish face at her, Matthew wonders why she has to ruin everything all the time, why she has to be an ecosystem disaster.

Turning round, Mrs Martin says, 'Come on. Give it a chance, Amanda. You know how much your father likes circuses, how much fun we used to have at them. This is what your father wanted for his birthday, so the least you can do is be gracious about it.'

'I gave him a tie,' Amanda sneers. 'Isn't that enough? It's not fair that I can't get my allowance unless I do this.'

Matthew steps on her foot as he gets out of the car. 'Oops. Sorry about that.'

'You did that intentionally.' Amanda whines. 'You didn't even have to be on my side of the car for any reason.'

'Amanda. Out of the car . . . now.' Mrs Martin gets out of the car and opens Amanda's door. 'And I mean now. Be reasonable. I hate it when you make me yell at you.'

'So don't yell at me. Just let me lead my own life.' Amanda gets out of the car and faces her mother.

Mr Martin comes over. 'Please. It's my birthday.'

Amanda just stands there.

Matthew looks over at his parents, who look very upset.

He looks at Amanda, who also looks upset.

He can't figure out what's happening to his family. Sure, Amanda always acts like a pain, but not as bad as she's been acting lately. Before, everyone kind of got along. Sure there were problems: his mother's fixation on health food, Amanda's being the oldest and getting to boss him around. But it was never Amanda who did stuff, it was usually Matthew 'Trouble Is My Middle Name' Martin who did things. Like the time in first grade when he started a snot scrapbook, collected some from his friends, put it in the book, and labelled it, giving special sticker prizes to things like the longest one, the greenest, and the gooshiest. Or the time when Mrs Stanton called home because he was spending all of his free time playing Super Mario and not doing his homework.

'Let's just have a good time.' Mr Martin reaches forward to rumple his daughter's hair, the way he always did when she was little.

'Don't touch my hair.' Amanda backs away. 'I really don't want to be here.'

'You can either come with us or sit in the hot car,' Mrs Martin says.

'I'll sit in the car.' Amanda gets into the car and closes the door.

'She could roast to death in there.' Mr Martin sounds worried.

'Only if we're lucky,' Matthew says. 'Come on. Let's go.'

The three of them start to walk away.

The sun is very hot.

'I'm not sure that this is a good idea,' Mrs Martin says softly to her husband. 'I'm not sure what we should do.'

He puts his arm around her waist as they walk along. 'I don't know either. Kids should be born with instruction manuals attached.'

Walking alongside of them, Matthew says, 'Did we come with warranties? Remember when my bike broke and the company had to fix it because the warranty wasn't up? Is there a warranty on Amanda? You could trade her in for another model.'

'Stop talking about me.' Amanda is walking right behind them. 'It was too hot in the car. So I'm going to this stupid circus. Just don't expect me to have fun.'

Matthew looks at her. He doesn't expect her to have fun. He *does* expect people to mistake her for one of the clowns the way she is dressed – wearing all black. Her trousers are ripped and held together with safety pins. On her long black shirt she is wearing chains of skulls and bones, and her earrings are flourescent green skulls. She is wearing make-up, a lot of make-up.

'Cotton candy.' Mr Martin pays for the tickets, spots the wagon selling junk food, and turns to his wife. 'Remember, it's my birthday. The deal is no complaints about what we eat. Cotton candy . . . corn dogs . . . a cherry snow cone.'

Matthew continues. 'Popcorn . . . french fries . . . candy apples.'

'I'm not holding anybody's head,' Mrs Martin informs them. 'If you guys eat all of that and throw up, you're on your own.'

Matthew knows that isn't true. He knows he can always count on her, remembering when he made a brownie mix and ate all of the dough without even baking it. She stayed up with him all night that time.

'Here you go, kid. Cotton candy.' Mr Martin hands his son a paper cone covered by the spun sugar.

'If any of my friends see me here, I'm just going to die,' Amanda whines.

'If any of your friends see you here, Doofus, it's because they are here too.' Matthew makes a moustache out of the cotton candy and places it on his lip. 'Now, look, I'm getting sick of this. From now on the only sister I'm going to deal with is the one right here.'

He points to the empty space right next to them. 'This is my imaginary sister, Samanda. She's happy to be at the circus and to be part of this family. And from now on, until you turn human again, she's the only sister I have.'

As the Martins enter the tent, Matthew is

talking to the space next to him. 'So, Samanda . . . how about a piece of cotton candy? Who do you think's going to win the World Series this year? Nice clothes you're wearing. I've always thought you looked good in pink. Did you hear the joke about the bed? . . . No? . . . Well, it hasn't been made yet.'

When the Martins take their seats, Matthew makes sure that a place is left for Samanda.

'He's just doing this to embarrass me,' Amanda informs everyone.

The lights dim.

And the circus begins.

Chapter 6

Matthew is sitting between Amanda and Samanda.

Amanda is sitting on his left, Samanda on his right, and his parents 'next to' Samanda.

Mr Martin is trying very hard not to sit on Samanda.

Matthew is trying very hard to ignore Amanda, who is sighing nonstop.

'There's not even a band at this bogus circus,' Amanda observes. 'Look at that. There's just one guy playing a drum set and the rest is coming from a computer. This is so bogus. And so dinky. A circle of five rows of bleachers and they're not even totally filled up.'

'Samanda. Isn't it nice that we're here at this nice little circus where it's not so big that there are bad seats? And that it's not too crowded on such a warm day?' Matthew pretends to talk to his 'new sister'.

The ringmaster introduces the first act. There are four birds that go up and down a small set of slides.

'Boring.' Amanda yawns.

Matthew agrees but will not let her know that.

Mr Martin informs them, 'This is just a small family-run circus. Don't be too hard on it. It's fun, just not that big.'

Someone comes on and foot-juggles things like kegs, logs, and flaming batons.

'I could be at the mall having a good time.' Amanda makes a face and mumbles.

'You could be at the mall giving grades to boys' butts. I see where you gave the new kid, Ned, a ninety-nine.' Matthew grins at her.

'You've been reading my diary again! You little creep. You bird brain!' Amanda punches his arm.

Matthew turns to Samanda. 'It's so nice that *you* are not a mall mole, that you spend your time reading, doing volunteer work, starting a group called SPCYB. Society for the Prevention of Cruelty to Younger Brothers. No *if*s, *and*s, or *butt*s about you.'

'Twerp.'

'And now, ladies and gentlemen and children of all ages,' the ringmaster announces, 'we must ask you to be absolutely quiet for our next act, brought to you from Paris, France . . . the Amazing Antoine, who will perform daring feats on the tight wire.'

'That wire is no higher than a balance beam,' Amanda observes.

Matthew disagrees. 'It's about twice as high as that.'

'Real daring.' Amanda giggles. 'If he falls off, he might break a toenail.'

They watch as the guy jumps back and forth on the wire.

'Did the ringmaster say that the tightrope walker was going to do a daring feat or that he had daring feet, feet that dared him to do something?' Matthew puts his hand in Amanda's popcorn box.

She smiles and says, 'Take some more if you want to.'

Matthew looks at her and wonders if this is really his sister or if Amanda and Samanda have changed seats. He thinks of the old days when it really was fun to be with her and wonders how long her good mood will last.

There's a little applause when the act ends.

The clowns arrive, pretending to trip over things, squirting each other with make-believe flowers, and riding around in small cars.

Some of them run into the audience and start doing things to the people who are in the bleachers.

One of them with a big red nose, a squirting flower, polka-dotted pants, a striped shirt, and huge red shoes comes running up to where the Martin family is and discovers Amanda. He pantomimes putting his hand on his heart, as if he is falling in love with her. He bends his knee and acts as if he is proposing to her.

'Bug off,' Amanda whispers.

He pulls paper flowers out of his sleeve and offers them to her.

Amanda is getting redder and redder as everyone looks at them and laughs.

'You quit that clowning around,' she yells.

People around them start to laugh louder.

The clown puts his hands on his heart again.

Matthew hears Amanda whisper, 'The only good clown is a dead clown.'

Finally the clown leaves, pantomiming a broken heart.

Amanda sits there with her arms folded in front of her body looking as if she's going to explode.

Matthew turns to her. 'You should have accepted. Then you could have little clownettes.'

'Shut up.'

Matthew can't stop. 'And if it didn't work out, people could say things to you like "I told you not to marry that clown."'

Mr and Mrs Martin start to laugh.

Amanda does explode. 'It's not fair. You always think he's so funny. You don't even care about how embarrassing that was to me.'

'Honey, calm down,' Mr Martin says. 'Someday you'll look back on this and think it's very funny.'

'Never.' She stares straight ahead.

'Well, Samanda.' Matthew looks to his right.

'You liked the clowns, didn't you?'

He pretends to listen intently. 'Oh, you love everything about the circus but you're getting a little hungry? What would you like? A hotdog, you say? And a soda? I'm sure that Dad would be glad to get it from that guy who is selling food.'

'Haven't you had enough, honey?' Mrs Martin asks her son.

'It's for Samanda.'

Mr Martin signals to the guy, who comes over to the side of the row and hands them the food, accidentally stepping on Amanda's feet as he passes the food over.

'Ouch,' she yells.

'If you'd passed it to us, instead of sitting there with your arms folded, you wouldn't have got hurt.' Matthew informs her.

'Shut up,' she says once more.

During the interval Mr Martin tries to act as if everything is going wonderfully.

He turns to Amanda and says, 'Honey, I love clowns, but I can see why you might have got a little upset by that mime.'

Amanda says, 'I'm going to find the ladies' room.'

'I didn't know it was missing.' Matthew looks at her.

'Does this family have to turn everything into a joke?' Amanda sneers.

'I'll go with you.' Mrs Martin stands up.

'Oh, okay.' Amanda sighs. 'If you must.'

As they leave, Mr Martin looks at them and says, 'I have a theory about why the queues at the ladies' rooms are much longer than the ones at the men's rooms. I think that it's because women often decide to accompany the other one, probably to talk about us.'

Matthew looks at the empty space next to him. 'Even Samanda went with them.'

The ringmaster introduces 'Antonio, the daring young man on the flying trapeze, from Rome, Italy.'

Looking carefully, Matthew sees that Antonio from Italy is the same guy who was Antoine from France. The only difference is that he is wearing a new costume and a phony moustache.

Even his assistant is the same one, only now she's wearing a blonde wig.

She looks like the person who was selling balloons at the interval.

Matthew wonders if later they are going to bring back another act, Anthony from Albany, who will be the same guy, but a juggler, with a beard.

No wonder Mr Martin says that it's a family circus.

Family circuses are something that Matthew is beginning to understand.

With the way things are going, he's beginning to think that he lives in one.

Chapter 7

'My mother's going to have a cow when I tell her that balloons can be bad for the environment.' Matthew shakes his head. 'A cow? She's going to have a herd when she hears it. Part of her business is sending people out in costumes to deliver balloons to people.'

'You've got to tell her.' Jil! is adamant. 'I read that the balloons that fly away sometimes break up and end up in the water. Then fish, whales, and dolphins see it floating, think it's food, and swallow it. Then it can make them choke and die.'

Matthew says, 'The balloon industry says that's not true.'

Jil! shrugs. 'What else are they going to say, "Buy a balloon, kill a creature?" Look, Matthew, we did a lot of research. There are two sides to just about every story, or at least manufacturers want you to think there are. I just think that you've got to tell your mother and have her make a decision.'

Matthew thinks about how hard his mother has worked to build up her business, how she has finally started to make a profit. He also thinks about dead beached whales who have been found with plastic inside them. That also makes him think about how water creatures sometimes get caught in the rings that hold together six-packs, how they die. He's glad that his mother's business doesn't have to worry about that and thinks about how he's going to go home and remind his parents to cut the rings up before throwing them out.

'Life was much easier before we started studying all of this stuff.' Matthew looks up from the book he is using for research of his subject: *Precycle Before You Have to Recycle.*

Katie Delaney holds up her notebook. 'Look at all of the uses I've found for old tights: tie it with a rubber band to an indoor vent pipe at the rear of the dryer and use it as a fluff catcher. You can use the old tights to store the new tights, being sure to colour-code it so that your pink holds pink and . . .'

Tyler and Matthew look at each other and start to laugh.

'I'll have to remember to do that to all of my tights.' Tyler is laughing so hard that he has to hold his stomach.

'That's probably what bank robbers do with the panty hose that they use as masks when they rob banks. They colour-code them so that they can say, "Today I'll wear my grey mask to go with my sweat suit."' Matthew is also holding his stomach.

Jil! says, 'Katie, just ignore these bozos.'

Katie continues, 'You can cover a broom with tights and dust walls and ceilings with it.'

'Right. With the feet on it, the broom will walk around the room by itself.' Matthew shakes his head.

'There's more.' Katie shakes her finger at the boys. 'Now keep quiet. In the garden you can tie up bushes to fences. It'll blend in if you use the brown panty hose.'

'It gives a whole new meaning to garden hose.' Matthew is laughing so hard that there are tears in his eyes.

'Cloth animals for kids to play with can be stuffed with old tights. You can cut up the legs into rings and use them as loops for weaving potholders . . . after you dye them.' Katie holds up her wrist. 'And I made this bracelet out of those loops, to show how it can be done.'

'That's really nice.' Jil! looks at it.

'I made one for you, too.' Katie holds it up shyly.

Jil! grins, takes it, and puts it on.

Matthew picks up a pair of tights that Katie has brought in for her presentation.

Looking at it for a few minutes, he says, 'Once I used a pair of these to find my sister, Amanda the Hun's, contact lens. Attach one of these suckers to a vacuum hose and it'll help find the lens without doing anything to ruin it.'

'That's very helpful.' Jil! smiles at him. 'We really are a good group.'

Matthew puts the tights on his head so that the legs hang down over the sides of his face. 'And you can do a rabbit imitation with them.'

'Have those been used?' Tyler makes a face.

'By my mother. But they've been washed,' Katie says.

Matthew pulls the tights off his head.

'And remember the Egypt unit,' Jil! says, 'how the girls corn-rowed our hair and put the tights over our heads to keep our hair neat while we slept.'

'Enough about tights for now,' Matthew says. 'Let's talk about the important stuff. What kind of food is Lisa going to have at her party?'

'Matthew.' Katie, as chairperson of the committee, is trying to keep control. 'We have to concentrate on our project.'

'Am I going to have to gag your mouth with tights?' Jil! puts her hand over his mouth.

He lightly bites her hand.

Jil! checks for teeth marks.

'Are we going to play Pin the Panty Hose on the Donkey?' Matthew starts to laugh.

Katie starts to put away the two pairs of tights that she is planning to plait and turn into a dog leash.

'Wait. Give it to me for a minute.' Matthew puts a pair in each hand. 'The pair in my right hand is

Hose A. The one in my left hand is Hose B.'

'Look.' He holds up the pair in his left hand. 'Hose B is much better than the other one – NO WAY HOSE A.'

Everyone groans and Katie wonders how she's going to get the group's report to be good enough so that everyone can go on the surprise trip that Mrs Stanton is planning.

Chapter 8

'Matthew, you look very spiffy.' Mrs Martin looks proudly at her son.

'Oh, Mom.' Matthew stares down at his high tops, which he's tied in honour of his first date.

'Very spiffy,' Mrs Martin repeats.

Wearing new jeans and a blue-and-white-striped polo shirt, Matthew stands in the living room, not feeling totally comfortable.

'I'll be glad to drive you to Jil!'s to pick her up and then drive you to the party. I'll even borrow the chauffeur costume from Mom's company.' Mr Martin grins.

'No. Please. Oh, no. Not the chauffeur's costume. Not a gorilla costume. Not a chicken costume. Nothing. I just want to walk over to Jil!'s, pick her up, and go to Lisa's,' Matthew pleads. 'It's too babyish to have your parents drive you. And it's too weird to have parents in costumes when it's not even Halloween.'

Mr Martin looks at Mrs Martin. 'Drats. I was really looking forward to putting on that costume.'

'Why don't you put it on anyway? I'll get dressed up in the princess costume and you can chauffeur me for pizza.' Mrs Martin grins. 'I'll even put on my rhinestone tiara.'

'You're going to do take-out, aren't you? Oh, please.' Matthew is terrified that someone he knows will see them.

Mrs Martin nods.

Amanda walks into the living room and says, in a challenging voice, 'Like the way I've done my hair?'

Everyone stares at her.

Her hair has been coloured black, with plum-coloured highlights. One side is cut short. The other side is long. The back of her hair has been pulled into a ponytail.

'Well, I guess I'd better get going.' Matthew doesn't want to hear his parents explode.

His mother is making little clicking noises in the back of her throat.

Matthew's not sure but he thinks he can hear his father start counting . . . one, two, three, four, five, six, seven, eight, nine. . . .

Amanda smiles.

There's silence from both parents.

Matthew repeats, 'Well, I'd better get going.'

Mrs Martin looks at her daughter and then at her husband.

Mr Martin makes a motion that seems to say, 'Stay calm. Don't give her the reaction she's looking for.'

Mrs Martin turns to Matthew. 'Honey, have a wonderful time. Please call us when you're ready to leave. We really don't want you and Jil! to be walking home in the dark, late at night.'

'Okay.' Matthew nods, careful not to look at Amanda or to say anything to her.

Mrs Martin looks like she's trying not to explode. She takes a deep breath and says, 'Matthew, by the way, I want to let you know that I thought about what you said about the balloons being bad for the environment. I've decided to give them up and create gift baskets to present instead. They'll contain things like books and little items that have to do with the occasions being celebrated. Thanks for being so considerate and letting me know about that.'

Matthew is going to remind her that she's already told him all about that and then he realizes that she's talking about it to stay calm and to mention how good he is being, in contrast to Amanda.

As Matthew leaves, he thinks about what a creep Amanda is and wonders if she's going to try out for a part in a horror film or if she's just trying to turn their house into a horror film.

He wishes he could hear what's going on in his house right now and is also very glad that he's not there to hear it.

Walking away quickly, he starts to think about

Jil! and how this is going to be his first date. What is it going to be like? How should he act when he picks her up? Should he kiss her good night at the end of the evening? What should he do in between those two events, the beginning and the end?

He only hopes that things go all right at Jil!'s house and that nothing embarrassing happens at the party.

Matthew thinks about it.

The bad news is that this is his very first date and he has no idea what to do.

The good news is that this is his very first date and he's never going to have another very first date again.

Chapter 9

'Okay, Matthew. Look this way and smile.' Mr Hudson points the video camera at Matthew and Jil!

'This is humiliating, absolutely humiliating. Totally and completely and absolutely humiliating.' Jil! blushes and covers her face with her hands. 'Matthew, I am soooooooooo sorry. He always does this. I can't stop him.'

'Some day you're going to appreciate this.' Mr Hudson jumps up on a chair. 'Now, look up here and smile. Jil!, take your hands away from your face.'

Mrs Hudson hands them a piece of cardboard, on which is printed:

FIRST DATE: JIL! AND MATTHEW MARTIN
SIXTH GRADE

'Okay, kids. Each of you hold on to the sign and look happy.' Mr Hudson films them.

'Dad. Please. That's enough.' Jil! looks like she's going to cry. 'Why didn't you make up a sign that says, 'Last Date,' because I'm never going out with anyone again, not ever, if this is the way you're going to be.'

'Don't be so sensitive.' Mr Hudson starts filming from the top of Matthew's red hair to the bottom of his shoes.

Matthew's glad that he tied his shoes for a change.

'Matt doesn't mind, do you, Matt?' Mr Hudson puts the camera down and looks at him.

'He does mind. He minds being filmed like this. And he minds being called Matt. His name is Matthew. Look, Dad. We have to go now.'

'Wouldn't you like some milk and cookies first?' Mrs Hudson offers.

Cookies, Matthew thinks. What a great idea.

'No.' Jil! is emphatic. 'If we have milk and cookies, then you'll take pictures of us eating, and that will be so yucky. You always wait until there's milk drool down my chin or crumbs and icing on my nose.'

Matthew wonders what kind of cookies they are.

'Matt, I want to show you something.' Mr Hudson motions for him to follow.

'Dad, no.' Jil! follows, too, since it is obvious that her father will not take no for an answer, even if Matthew had said no.

They go into a room with a wide-screen TV, six feet by six feet.

'Wow,' Matthew says. 'That would make for a really intense Nintendo game.'

Lying on the couch is a boy of about six, who says, 'Are you Matthew? Are you the guy who I'm not supposed to bother, who I'm not supposed to tell things to about Jil!? Jil! bribed me to stay in here.'

'That's my brother, Jonathon. Ignore him.' Jil! makes a face.

Mr Hudson points to the wall opposite the television. 'Now, Matt. Wait until you see this.'

He opens some doors and shows that from floor to ceiling are shelves filled with videos. 'Many of these are family videos. We have almost everything on camera, all of life's most important moments.

'Dad,' Jil! pleads. 'We have to go. I promised to help Lisa set up for the party.'

Jonathon grins at Matthew, showing that his two front teeth are missing. 'You should see the bathtub videos of Jil! from when she was little.'

'Shut up.' Jil! glares at him. 'If you don't stop now, I won't give you the money I promised you.'

'Then I'll tell him about all of the potty-training videos.' Jonathon shrugs.

Matthew grins.

Listening to Jil! and Jonathon reminds him of the way he and Amanda fight.

Mr Hudson puts his hand on Matthew's shoulder. 'Matt, my boy, I've been taking videos since my in-laws gave us the camera when Mrs

Hudson and I got married.'

Jil! is mumbling about how she wishes the camera had never been invented. Mrs Hudson walks in, holding out a plate of sugar cookies. 'Are you sure that I can't interest you in any of these?'

Matthew's hand is halfway to the plate when he hears Jil! say, 'No. We really have to go.'

Matthew withdraws his hand, cookieless.

As much as he wants a cookie, he realizes that he's got to be loyal to Jil! right now.

That's when he realizes that he must really like Jil!.

Mr Hudson pats his wife lightly on the stomach and continues, 'For the new baby on the way, I've taken the hospital sonogram and spliced it to our tape. So our records will be even more complete.'

'I'm just mortified.' Jil! grabs Matthew's hand. 'Come on. We've got to get out of here.'

Matthew wants to ask Mr Hudson if they've ever considered filming from the *very* beginning, but knows that there is no way he's going to say that out loud.

It does, however, make him smile, which Jil! sees.

She punches Matthew on the arm, pulls him out of the room, and yells to her parents, 'We're going. Bye. See you later.'

'Wait. I want to film you as you go out the door and down the sidewalk.' Mr Hudson rushes after them.

'Let's make a run for it,' Jil! says.

'Do you think we could get away with mooning him?' Matthew whispers, thinking Jil! will say, 'Oh, Matthew. You're so silly . . . and gross.'

She shakes her head. 'I used to do that when I was little. Now when company comes over, he shows them those pictures. He calls it "Moon over Califon".'

As they rush out, they can hear Jonathon calling out, 'Don't forget. You owe me money. I didn't show him the one where you barfed on the roller coaster.'

'Race you to the end of the block.' Jil! runs faster than Matthew has ever seen her move in gym class.

Once they round the corner and are out of sight of her father and his video camera, Jil! stops, holds her stomach, and catches her breath. 'I am *mortified*. My family is just so embarrassing.'

Matthew grins. '*Your* family is so embarrassing? Let me tell you about mine. At this very moment my parents are probably on their way out for pizza. My mother will be dressed as a princess, my father a chauffeur. And you should see what my sister has done to her hair. And you think your family is embarrassing!'

Jil! looks at Matthew and grins. 'Maybe we should send my father over to your house to film it.'

'Let's not and say we did.' Matthew grins back.

'Maybe we should just go over to Lisa's house and get this party started.'

Chapter 10

'Lisa's cousin is so cute. So cute.' Lizzie Doran keeps staring across the room at Simon. 'I hope that I'm on his team.'

'What do you mean, team?' Matthew puts a potato crisp into his mouth.

'For the mystery-solving game that Lisa's parents planned,' Lizzie explains and then looks at Jil! 'Isn't he just the cutest? Lisa says he's in the eighth grade. Don't you think older men who live in New York City are just so sophisticated?'

Matthew is trying to balance a crisp on his nose.

'So sophisticated.' Lizzie sighs. 'Why didn't Lisa ever tell us that she has such a cute cousin?'

Jil! looks across the room at Simon, who she thinks looks okay but not as cute as Matthew. 'Lizzie, she did tell us that she had an older boy cousin. Remember when she couldn't go to Jessica's pyjama party because she had to go to Simon's bar mitzvah?'

'Oh, yeah, but she didn't say how cute he is . . . how cute and sophisticated . . . not like the boys in our class.' Lizzie looks over to a section of the room where some boys are trying to teach Lisa's parrot some new vocabulary words.

Looking over at the boys, Matthew thinks how it would be fun to be with them but he's not sure whether he should go since he and Jil! are dates.

'Maybe I should go over there and see what they are doing.' Matthew sees how much fun his friends are having and thinks about how boring it is listening to Lizzie talk about how immature the Califon boys are.

'Have another crisp.' Jil! shoves the bowl under his nose.

'Don't mind if I do.' Matthew grabs six crisps, stuffs them in his mouth, and tries to whistle.

'Want anything else?' Jil! grins. 'Like onion dip on your nose?'

Matthew grins back. 'How about a book about the rules and regulations of sixth-grade dating?'

'It was already checked out of the library when I looked for it,' Jil! kids.

Lisa claps her hands. 'Okay, everyone. First of all I want you to know that this mystery search for refreshments is not my idea. My parents have decided that we will all have a simply wonderful time solving "The Case of the Missing Soda." It is *not*, I repeat *not*, my idea – but they are my parents and they paid for this party and they are at this very moment sitting upstairs in the kitchen with my aunt and uncle, waiting for this thing to start.'

From across the room the bird squawks out one of the new words that it has just learned: 'Barfola.'

Lisa closes her eyes and says, 'I'm never going to have a party again. Not until I'm out on my own and can have my own apartment and plan my own party.'

'Relax,' Jil! says. 'We all have parents. At least your parents aren't using a video camera to record it.'

'My parents would probably be lying on the recreation-room floor pretending to be dead, spattered with fake blood, or they'd be dressed up as cat burglars.' Matthew thinks about how his parents love to get dressed up for things.

'It was a case of soda that was stolen, not a cat.' Zoe is confused.

Matthew decides not to explain.

'At least your parents both do stuff with you. My parents won't do anything together, unless their lawyers are with them.' Patrick Ryan thinks about the custody battle that has been going on, how his house is like an ecosystem . . . the Ryan ecosystem: The father leaves and it affects everything – the mother, the kids, the family budget, everyday routines. Sometimes Patrick feels like he's living in a rain forest with all the crying that's been going on.

Patrick makes a face, feeling a little weird that he's said anything. He thinks about how he always pretends that it doesn't bother him and how his parents have told him that it's no one else's business what happens in their family.

Sarah looks at him, wishing that she could say something to help him since she's been through a bad divorce, too, and knows that everyone survived.

But she feels shy.

Lisa calls out, 'First of all, we have to break into teams.'

'I'm on Tyler's team,' Zoe calls out.

'The lists are already made up,' Lisa explains. 'And yes, you and Tyler are on the same team.'

'I promise to eat green vegetables for a year if Lisa's cousin is on my team,' Lizzie whispers to Jil!

'You mean Allie?' Jil! teases, pointing to the third-grader who has been lurking near the boys who have been teaching the parrot new words.

'No! I don't mean Allie.' Lizzie shakes her head.

Lisa says, 'I'm going to call out the names right now and then each team will get a beginning clue. The clues for each team are different except for the last one. The team that finds the missing soda will receive free movie passes. And then we all get to drink the soda and eat the rest of the food. I am going to be on one of the teams because I don't want to hang around this house talking to my relatives while you're out looking for clues. Just know that I don't know where they hid the stupid soda. This is all my parents' idea and they set it up.'

Lizzie keeps crossing her fingers and toes, hoping that Simon is on her team.

Lisa continues, 'Team One will congregate by the television. Team Two by the tape deck. Now, here are the groups. It took me an hour to figure out these teams:

Group One	Group Two
Vanessa Singer	Matthew Martin
Zoe Alexander	Jil! Hudson
Tyler White	Joshua Jackson
Simon Bernstein	David Cohen
Billy Kellerman	Pablo Martinez
Brian Bruno	Cathy Atwood
Patrick Ryan	Jessica Weeks
Katie Delaney	Chloe Fulton
Ryma Brown	Mark Ellison
Sarah Montgomery	Lisa Levine
Lizzie Doran	Allie Bernstein

Nobody complains about their group. Certainly not Matthew, who is with Jil! and not with Vanessa, who is glad she and Matthew are on different teams. And very definitely there are no complaints from Lizzie Doran.

People go to their assigned areas.

The groups are handed Polaroid pictures of the missing case of soda as well as their first clues.

The groups sit around looking at the clues and figuring out where they should go.

Matthew is sitting quietly, writing something down.

'Any ideas?' Joshua asks him.

Matthew nods. 'I have an idea for the name of the group.'

'We're supposed to be solving a mystery, not giving ourselves a name,' Jil! reminds him.

He waves his hand. 'Pay no attention to that woman behind the curtain.'

'This is not *The Wizard of Oz*, you know.' Jil! shakes her head.

Matthew, who loves to quote or misquote from his favourite film, says, 'Well, DoDo. I guess we're not in Califon any more. We're in Mystery Land, and it's time to give the group a name, because all of my groups are G.E.T.T.H.E.M. Here it is: Group Eager to Triumph Handling Emerging Mysteries.'

'Not bad.' Pablo grins, thinking of Matthew's original group: Girls Easy to Torment Hopes Eager Matthew.

Once Group One hears that the other group has given themselves a name, they decide to use G.E.T.H.I.M. Originally Girls Eager to Halt Immature Matthew, it now becomes Geniuses Every Time Handle Important Mysteries.

And the mystery solving begins.

Chapter 11

```
┌─────────────────────────────────┐
│                                 │
│          Clue 1                 │
│                                 │
│   You don't have to look far    │
│     It's where we sometimes     │
│        put the car              │
│   Look for where to "pick" up   │
│       the next clue             │
│                                 │
└─────────────────────────────────┘
```

'The last line doesn't rhyme,' Matthew says.

'No kidding, Sherlock.' Mark makes a face.

'So where do we look? In the driveway? The garage? On the street? Those are the places your parents put the car,' Pablo, who lives across the street, says.

'I vote for the garage,' Lisa says.

'In New York City we park our car in a garage that is three blocks from where our apartment is,' Allie tells them.

No one says anything for a minute.

Allie continues, 'I know that no one wants me on your team because I'm only in third grade. But I couldn't be on the other team because that's where my brother is and he said that it was bad enough to have to be with "little sixth-graders" and he didn't want to have to be on a team with his "stupid kid sister". So here I am. I just want you to know that in my third-grade class at P.S. 87, I am very popular and people actually like to have me on their team.'

'Lighten up.' Lisa looks at her cousin.

'We don't mind having you on our team.' Cathy Atwood pats her on the head.

'I am not a dog.' Allie looks up at her and grins.

'Let's get started.' Joshua looks at his watch. 'We don't want G.E.T.H.I.M. to beat us. Let's solve this clue and find . . . the case of the missing soda.'

'The garage.' David starts running toward it.

Everyone follows.

The garage is filled with lots of stored things — deflated basketballs, boxes of old clothes that Mrs Levine is planning to donate to charity, unused bikes, garden tools, a guitar without strings, old tyres, and Mr Levine's model railway.

'Okay.' Lisa looks at everyone. 'Now you know

what secret slobs we are.'

'This looks neater than my room,' Chloe says.

'Don't you want this any more?' Allie holds up a Barbie cosmetic case.

'No.' Lisa blushes. 'You can have it.'

Matthew continues to look at the clue. 'The last line doesn't rhyme.'

'Tell me something new.' David starts searching in the railway carriages.

Matthew does not give up. *'Far . . . car . . . pick.'*

Jil! stands behind him, puts her chin on his shoulder, and looks at the clue. 'I don't get it.'

Looking around the room, Matthew finally says, 'Pick . . . you use a pick with a guitar. And *guitar* rhymes with *far* and *car* . . .GUITAR.'

Jil! and Matthew rush over to the guitar.

On the back is pinned a note.

'BINGO!' Jil! yells.

'Elementary, my dear Hudson.' Matthew thinks about all of the Sherlock Holmes films he and his father watch.

Lisa shakes her head. 'And my parents are such sickles.'

As G.E.T.T.H.E.M. rush out of the garage, they see G.E.T.H.I.M. heading in the opposite direction with their own clues.

'Let's make a run for it.' Matthew doesn't care as much about winning the movie tickets as just winning.

301

```
┌─────────────────────────────────────┐
│            Clue 2                    │
│      Go visit Mrs. Nichols.          │
│      She won't feed you              │
│          pickles.                    │
│      This will be a clue             │
│          that tickles.               │
└─────────────────────────────────────┘
```

The thought of Vanessa Singer having the chance to gloat is more than he can handle.

Arriving at Mrs Nichols's farmhouse, they ring the bell.

She is ready for them, holding out a feather. 'I understand you want something that tickles. Now, read the attached clue and I'll give you some chocolate chip cookies for the road.'

Lisa says, 'Thanks. Do you want to come over to our house later for cake? My mom said to let you know how much we'd all like that.'

Mrs Nichols looks at the group and smiles. 'No. Thank you. This is a party for "young folk" tonight. I'm just pleased to be part of the mystery hunt.'

'You can sit upstairs with the old folks,' Allie

offers. 'With my parents and my aunt and uncle.'

'No. Thank you.' Mrs Nichols holds out the plate. 'Please. Everyone have another cookie.'

Matthew has trouble staying patient. 'The clue. Let's read the clue.'

```
Clue 3
Now that you have the quil!
Walk up the hil!
Check under the windowsil!
```

'Look at the explanation marks,' Jil! calls out.

'Exclamation marks,' Lisa reminds her.

'Whatever.' Jil! shrugs. 'The next clue must be at my house on the top of the hill.'

'Bye,' Mrs Nichols calls out as everyone starts racing up the hill.

Matthew rushes down again and gives Mrs Nichols a hug.

'Bye.' He grins as Mrs Nichols hands him two more cookies.

Quickly he catches up.

'I'm going to be mortified again.' Jil! gasps from running and talking. 'I just know that my father is going to be there with his stupid video camera.'

G.E.T.T.H.E.M. arrives at the Hudson house.

Mr Hudson is there, holding the camera. 'Okay, kids. I want a group shot. Someone please stand in front holding this sign. How about you, the little one.'

Allie, who he has pointed to, runs up to get the sign, which says,

THE CASE OF THE MISSING SODA
JIL!'S TEAM

'Mortified' is all that Jil! keeps repeating.

'Please, sir. We have to do this fast or the other team will beat us,' Matthew tells him.

Once the pictures are taken, Mr Hudson points to a window with an attached flower box. Under that windowsill is the clue.

'My parents are such geeks.' Lisa shakes her head.

Everyone looks at Jessica, whose last name is Weeks.

'So that's why my folks kept looking at each other and smiling.' Jessica laughs. 'I thought something was going on, I just couldn't figure out what.'

'To the Weeks's house,' Matthew yells. 'And let's hurry. We don't want it to take months.'

```
┌─────────────────────────────────────┐
│            Clue 4                    │
│  Here's the final clue that          │
│    your group seeks.                 │
│  Let's hope that no soda             │
│    leaks.                            │
│  Go to the house that belongs        │
│    to the family named               │
│                                      │
│    ─  ─  ─  ─  ─                      │
└─────────────────────────────────────┘
```

The race is on.

G.E.T.T.H.E.M. knows where the soda is and hopes that G.E.T.H.I.M. doesn't.

Everyone races to the Weeks's house.

They get to the door just as they see the group from G.E.T.T.H.E.M. rushing down the hill.

Matthew rings the bell and yells, 'All ye. All ye. In Free.'

'This isn't tag, Bozo,' Vanessa Singer yells as she races down the hill.

Mr Weeks answers the doorbell and says, 'It's around the back.'

The group of G.E.T.T.H.E.M. gets to the soda first.

The case is sitting in a little red wagon, ready to be taken back to the Levine home.

Matthew grabs the handle and yells, 'We win.'

'Drats.' Tyler White sinks to the gound exhausted.

So does Zoe.

So does everyone else.

'That was fun,' Billy Kellerman says. 'I thought it was going to be doofy, but it was fun.'

Lisa agrees. 'It was. But don't tell my parents. They'll just say "I told you so" to me.'

Mr and Mrs Weeks come out to their back garden and look at the twenty-two people sprawled out on their lawn.

Mr Weeks announces, 'The Levines have one more rhyme for you and here it is:

> *'The first group will get movie passes*
> *But because we don't want any sad lads and*
> *   lasses*
> *So will the group in second place*
> *Because we don't want winners and losers in*
> *this race.'*

'Bad rhyme. Good idea,' David Cohen says.

'You know what this means.' Chloe jumps up. 'We can all go to the movies next week. Then we'll go to my house for ice cream sundaes.'

Everyone cheers and heads back to Lisa's to continue the party.

Chapter 12

'I'm so proud of you.' Mrs Stanton beams at her class.

'It's not always easy.' Zoe raises her hand. 'I tried to explain to my mother about how much water we could save if she didn't use the bathtub so much, if she took showers instead. But she didn't want to listen. She said that long baths are relaxation for her and she's not willing to give them up.'

Ryma turns to Zoe. 'Maybe you can get her to do some of the other things to save water. You could use less water in your toilet tank by putting in a plastic bottle filled with water and some stones. Doing this will also recycle small juice bottles or dishwashing soap bottles. You can save one to two gallons per flush.'

'If kings and queens did that with their toilets, it would be a Royal Flush,' David Cohen jokes.

Ryma ignores David. 'Zoe, ask your mother if she'd give up even one bath a week and take a shower instead.'

'I'll try.' Zoe sighs.

'My parents bought a special low-flow showerhead that uses much less water,' Vanessa informs everyone.

Matthew looks at Vanessa and wishes that she had taken a low-flow shower and gone down the drain to Siberia.

Matthew then looks at Jil! and smiles.

She is wearing a grey skirt, a pink shirt, a pair of pink socks over grey ones, and lots of rhinestone jewellery. Her shoes are tied with hot pink, sparkly laces. Her brown hair is held up with a rhinestone clip.

It's the first time Matthew even noticed a girl's clothes and cared.

Matthew thinks about Lisa's party and how his parents picked up him and Jil! afterwards to drive them home. He remembers how he walked Jil! up to the door and how they stood in the doorway in such a way that his parents couldn't see them from the car. He remembers how, just as he was going to give Jil! a kiss, his first kiss, her first kiss, their first kiss, the front door slowly opened and Mr Hudson walked out, pointing the camera at them.

Matthew looks at Jil! and wonders what it would be like if he had actually kissed her and whether his bubble gum would have ended up in her mouth.

Jil! is frantically waving her hand. 'Ow. Ow. Ow.'

'Jil!' Mrs Stanton calls on her.

'Even though my father usually totally embarrasses me, the other day he showed me a good way to check for water leaks. He said to put twelve drops of either red or blue food colouring into the toilet tank. So I put in red because with the water, it would dilute and become my favourite colour, pink. Then we waited fifteen minutes to see if there was any colour in the toilet. If there had been, then there would have been a leak.' She giggles. 'If any one wants to see it, you can. He took a video of it. In some houses they watch the Rose Bowl and the Orange Bowl. In our house we watch the Toilet Bowl.'

'Has anyone else noticed how much time we've spent talking about stuff like toilets and nappies and stuff?' Cathy scrunches her nose.

Mrs Stanton says, 'Do you think that all of this talk is a *waste*?'

Cathy shakes her head. 'No. But I would like to mention something that our group is going to do that does not deal with waste. We did a lot of research about wildlife, so we called a zoo, pooled our money, and joined their Adopt an Animal programme.'

'That's really terrific.' Mrs Stanton claps her hands.

Lisa said, 'Our group has a couple of wonderful ideas. We want to do some work on Mrs Nichols's property.'

'It's not just hers any more,' Mrs Stanton reminds them. 'We need to get permission from the conservancy. What do you want to do?'

Lisa counts on her fingers. 'One: We want to plant some trees. Two: We want to take some of the usable rubbish from the school cafeteria and use it to make a compost heap. Three: We want to plant things on the property that we can use in the cafeteria. We can use the compost to help make the things grow. If the school can't use the food because of rules or something, then we can give what we grow to some poor people who need it.'

'I'm very proud of you.' Mrs Stanton beams.

Mark Ellison raises his hand. 'Our group wants to try a one-day experiment. We want everyone in this class to give up using electrical things. No blow dryer –'

'No blow dryer!' Zoe yells. 'No way. I look terrible if I can't dry my hair.'

'You'll look fine,' Tyler says.

'My mother told me that no woman should ever be seen without makeup on and her hair neatly in place,' Zoe informs everyone.

'Aarg!' is Jil!'s comment.

Mark continues, 'No curling iron, no electric toothbrush, no can opener, no toaster, no electric juicer, no microwave, no TV.'

'No TV?' Joshua yells. 'Not fair.'

'No Nintendo.' Matthew pretends to be someone they studied about in history class. 'Give me Nintendo or give me death.'

'No electric Water Pik.' Mark looks at everyone. 'Come on. It's not forever. It's only for one day. It's to show us how much electricity we use on unnecessary things.'

'Nintendo is not unnecessary,' Matthew mumbles.

'Actually my dentist thinks that the tooth appliances are important, so maybe we should take that off the list,' Mrs Stanton tells them.

'Oh, okay,' Mark says. 'But I really think you could floss. One day. It's not going to kill you. Let's all take a vote. All in favour say, "Aye".'

There are several sighs.

Zoe can be heard softly saying, 'No blow dryer. Civilization will never be the same.'

'One day. Think of what it will mean to the environment,' Mark pleads. 'And we can ask other classes to do this too.'

There's silence for a minute and then Mark says, 'All in favour say, "Aye".'

Everyone says, 'Aye,' although it sounds like Zoe is saying, 'Aye-yaye-yaye.'

Mrs Stanton claps her hands once more. 'You are truly a terrific class. I'm very proud of you.'

Matthew grins. He's already given his report on precycling, talking about buying things that can be recycled or are already made from recycled materials. He's talked about buying toys that are not overly packaged or badly made.

The class voted and chose his computer design for the tote bag that they are planning to have made and sell to people to use and reuse, instead of plastic and paper bags. Profits would be donated to help save the rain forest.

Matthew's happy because Mrs Stanton has already said that he can go on the trip, that everyone can go.

There's only one problem that Matthew has had, and that was trying to convince everyone to use lunchboxes, Thermoses, and reusable storage containers instead of paper and plastic bags.

'Too doofy.' 'Only babies carry lunchboxes.' 'I'd die before anyone ever saw me carrying a lunchbox.' 'Get real, Matthew.' 'The seventh- and eighth-graders would make fun of us.' These were some of the responses.

Actually no one in the class would bring a lunchbox, even if they were hypnotized, not even Matthew.

The only person that he's convinced to use a lunchbox is his father, who now carries an ancient Howdy Doody one to work.

The bell rings, signalling the beginning of lunch.

Before Mrs Stanton dismisses them, she says, 'After lunch I'm going to announce where we will be going for our trip so that we can start to make arrangements.'

The trip.

Everyone's been guessing. Washington, D.C.,

Disney World, Paris, Action Park, the Califon Pond.

After lunch seems like such a long time.

It makes Matthew think of his favourite fourth-grade joke. Question: How do you keep a turkey in suspense? Answer: I'll tell you later.

'Can't you tell us now? Oh, please. Oh, please.' Jil! waves her hand.

Mrs Stanton shakes her head and grins. 'After lunch. Class dismissed.'

It's the first time all year that everyone in class can't wait for lunch to be over.

Chapter 13

'I hope it's Disney World,' Matthew thinks as the class sits down.

Everyone's excited.

Mrs Stanton sits on her desk.

Everyone waits quietly for her to speak.

'We're going to a very special programme run by the Franklin Institute in Philadelphia, Pennsylvania,' she tells them.

'I've been there,' several of her students say at the same time.

'I was hoping for Disney World.' Matthew is disappointed, even though he really knew that there was no real chance for that hope.

'Action Park. I wanted to go on all of the rides.' David makes a face. 'Drats.'

'This is special,' Mrs Stanton says. 'The programme is called Camp-In. We not only go to special programmes, we also get to spend the entire night in the museum. It's a terrific programme.'

'Do they have a room with beds?'

'Is it just us?'

'Do our parents have to chaperone? And if so, can they be banned from bringing video cameras?'

'What kind of food will they have for us to eat?'

'When are we going?'

Mrs Stanton holds up her hands. 'Enough questions for now. We'll be going in three weeks. It will be our last major activity before summer vacation.'

'Can I bring my hair dryer to Camp-In?' Zoe raises her hand. 'And where are we all going to sleep?'

Mrs Stanton informs her, 'No hair dryers allowed. Also no hair spray.'

'The aerosol ones are bad for the environment anyway.' Cathy Atwood has been doing her research.

As Mrs Stanton passes out permission slips, she says, 'You don't have to memorize all of what I am telling you, because the information is on the sheet of paper with the permission slip. I'm just going over all of this so that you will know the procedure. The week before we go I will remind you of everything.

'Now, here are some of the facts. On the Friday that we're going, the buses will pick us up after school right in front.

'Each of us is to bring a sleeping bag, a toothbrush, toothpaste, a flannel, and a plastic bag or duffle bag large enough for all of these items. If you use a plastic bag, don't forget to recycle it. Also you will bring a packed dinner, unless you want to buy something from the cafeteria there.'

'Do you think we could have pizzas delivered to the museum?' Matthew asks.

'Extra cheese and pepperoni on mine.' Joshua is practically drooling.

'No pizza delivery for students.' Mrs Stanton decides not to let them know that adults have a delivery made to their leaders' lounge. 'They will supply a snack to you at night and at breakfast.

'You must label the plastic bag with your name and the name of the school. You are not to bring pyjamas!!! We will be sleeping in the clothes that we wore that day.'

'And then we'll be wearing the same clothes the next day? Gross.' The girls make faces.

'What's the big deal?' Matthew asks.

'Will it be just our group in the museum?' Sarah asks.

'No,' Mrs Stanton says. 'There will be all sorts of groups there. School groups, Boy Scout and Girl Scout troupes, church youth fellowships.'

'Where are we going to sleep? Are we going to have our own room? Are we going to have to sleep in a room with strangers?' Sarah looks concerned.

'Several of the rooms in the museum are used for sleeping. Each group will be assigned to a room. There will be other groups in the room also, but we'll have our own section.' Mrs Stanton looks at everyone. 'Don't worry. This will be fun, sort of like a giant pyjama party, only no pyjamas.'

Someone starts to snigger.

'Enough.' Mrs Stanton frowns. 'You know what I mean. . . . A pyjama party with clothes *on*. . . . Look, this is going to be wonderful. Does anyone have any concerns?'

'What if someone snores all night and I can't sleep?' Vanessa is worried. 'What if someone has nightmares?'

'You are a nightmare,' Matthew wants to say, but doesn't.

'It's only one night,' Mrs Stanton explains. 'It will be all right.'

'Do parents have to chaperone?' Jil! can just imagine her father videotaping this one.

Mrs Stanton nods. 'There has to be an adult for every eight children.'

'I'm not a child. I'm a young adult.' Matthew tries to look mature.

'You're a child,' Vanessa wants to say, but doesn't.

'There are twenty students in this class and I'm bringing my own little girl, Marie. It would be a good idea to have three parents as chaperones. Ask your parents who would like to come. It does cost something for everyone, so be sure to bring in your money with the permission slip. If anyone has a problem about the money, be sure to speak to me privately. Everyone will be able to go on this trip.

Don't worry.'

'This is going to be so fun.' Jil! grins widely.

'A co-ed pyjama party. I'm not sure that my parents are going to approve.' Sarah looks worried.

'I'll talk to them,' Mrs Stanton says. 'I'll explain that it's a sleep-over in a museum with lectures, classes, and films — and a show at the planetarium.'

Ryma raises her hand. 'Over that weekend I'm supposed to go to my father's house. It's his joint-custody time.'

'Talk to him. See if he wants to be one of the chaperones.' Mrs Stanton stands up.

Ryma grins as she thinks of her father sleeping on the floor of a museum . . . her father, who once said that his idea of camping out was not staying at the Ritz Hotel.

'We were sort of hoping for Disney World or Paris,' Matthew tells her.

Mrs Stanton shakes her head and laughs. 'Maybe for your seventh-grade trip. You can ask Mr Arnold when you get to his class.'

'If we can't go to Disney World or Paris,' Matthew says, grinning, 'The Franklin Institute sounds great to me.'

Everyone agrees as Mrs Stanton starts to talk about all the things there: the Future Centre, the exhibits about the things that they have been studying, the Omniverse film, the gift shop.

'I just can't wait,' Jil! repeats.
Three weeks seems too far away.

Chapter 14

'Boy-Bonding Time.' Mr Martin stands at the bottom of the steps and calls upstairs. 'Let's get a move on.'

Matthew bounds downstairs, three steps at a time.

Mrs Martin comes into the living room. 'Are you two in training for the Olympic noise-making event?'

Both Martin males yell in unison, 'Boy-Bonding Time.'

Mrs Martin laughs. 'I get it. You're actually in training for the synchronized yelling competition, the one guaranteed to drive mothers and wives nuts.'

Mr Martin whispers something to Matthew.

Both of them pretend to do the backstroke, circling around Mrs Martin.

'Enough already,' she yells as they lie down on the floor, lifting their legs and pretending to be synchronized swimmers.

Matthew and his father look at each other and laugh.

Mrs Martin looks down at them and shakes her head.

The front door opens and Amanda walks in.

She looks down at her father and brother and gasps. 'Is everything all right?'

Her father jumps up. 'Everything's fine, honey. Don't worry. We're just fooling around.'

Matthew lies on the floor, continuing to kick his leg. 'And now it's time for the individual synchronized swimming. Although how can it be individual when it's supposed to be something that's done together?'

Mrs Martin looks at Amanda. 'Why do you have that scarf on your head when it's springtime? What do you have on your nose? Oh, Amanda . . . What have you done to yourself this time?'

Matthew jumps up and looks closely at his sister, who is wearing a nose ring. 'You got your nose pierced. Ow . . . how gross!'

Mrs Martin walks up to her daughter. 'Amanda, I want you to take off that scarf.'

Amanda puts her hands to her head. 'No. I don't have to.'

Mr and Mrs Martin exchange looks.

'Do what your mother says.' Mr Martin sounds stern.

Matthew looks up his sister's nose. 'What happens when you have to blow your nose? Does the snot get caught in the ring? Did it hurt to have your nose pierced? When you take the ring out, does the snot come out of the hole?'

'Matthew. Go upstairs. Right now.' His mother points to the staircase.

'Not fair,' Matthew yells. 'It's my house too. And I didn't do anything wrong.'

'Upstairs,' his father says softly.

'What happened to Boy-Bonding Time?' Matthew stamps his foot. 'How come she gets to ruin everything? And what do you care what she does to her hair this time? She's always dying it some stupid colour. This time she's probably done it black with a white stripe . . . so that she looks like the skunk that she is.'

'I did not.' Amanda interrupts. 'I didn't dye it this time.'

Everyone looks at Amanda, as she takes off the scarf.

She has shaved off her hair and is totally bald.

Mrs Martin gasps and starts to cry.

Mr Martin shuts his eyes.

For once Matthew does not make a remark.

Amanda looks at her family.

They look at the Amanda who used to have beautiful blonde hair . . . who used to have a nostril without a nose ring attached . . . who used to smile and laugh.

Now they see an Amanda who is totally bald, an Amanda who is wearing a nose ring, who is glaring at them.

'Honey, why?' Mrs Martin says softly, trying

not to cry.

'Because,' Amanda says.

'You can't go out looking like that.' Her mother shakes her head.

'Why not? It's my life. I can look any way I want to look.' Amanda stamps her foot.

'But you look terrible,' Mr Martin says softly. 'You used to be so pretty.'

Amanda starts to yell. 'It's my life. I can do what I want to do with it.'

Mr Martin yells back, 'You are thirteen years old. As long as you live in this house, you have to listen to us . . . I don't get it. We're good parents. We care about our children. We only want what is best for them. Why have you done this to us?'

Mrs Martin reaches out to touch Amanda's head. 'Honey.'

'Leave me alone,' Amanda yells.

'What's going on? What's wrong?' Mrs Martin is trying to be calm and understand what is going on in her daughter's head.

'I got tired of looking like everyone else. I want my life to be more exciting. On MTV I saw someone who looked really terrific with her head shaved, so I decided to try it.' Amanda takes a compact out of her backpack and looks in the mirror.

She starts to cry.

Her mother starts to hug her.

Amanda backs off. 'Stop being so understanding.

Why can't you just leave me alone?'

Mrs Martin backs off. 'Amanda, I don't know what to do. You get angry at me if you think I don't understand. You get angry at me if I am too understanding. I've tried so hard to be the kind of mother you can come to, to be a good mother. I've tried so hard not to make the same mistakes that my mother did with me. And nothing works. You're angry all the time. Nothing we do pleases you.'

Amanda stands quietly.

Matthew thinks about how he really wants to slug her.

Mr Martin softly says, 'Is there something we need to know? Can we help you? I have to ask you this: Are you taking drugs? Is there a problem with someone at school? What is going on?'

Amanda gasps. 'I don't take drugs. How can you think that about me? How stupid do you think I am?'

Stupid enough to shave all the hair off your head, Matthew thinks.

'I have to ask.' Mr Martin looks at his daughter. 'You must admit that you've been acting very different lately.'

Amanda stands there, looking in the mirror.

A tear trickles down her face.

This time Mrs Martin does go up to her daughter and hugs her, and this time Amanda does not push her away.

Amanda starts to cry.

Mrs Martin just holds her.

Mr Martin walks up to them and puts his arms around both of them.

Matthew's not sure whether or not he wants to murder Amanda for causing all this trouble, for getting all of this attention, for always messing up the time that he wants to spend with his father.

He's not sure if he wants to try to understand what Amanda is going through, if he can figure out some way to help his sister.

He's not sure if he should shave his own head to get some more attention.

Life in the Martin house is getting very confusing.

Amanda pulls away from her parents and looks at them. 'I just want things to be different, to not be so boring. I want to be more grown up and make my own decisions.'

Her parents stand quietly, letting her continue.

She touches the top of her head. 'I'm never going back to school again – not until my hair grows back.'

Mr Martin shakes his head. 'No way, kiddo. Hair or no hair, you have to go to school.'

Mrs Martin puts her hand on her husband's arm. 'Honey, why don't you and Matthew go out now? Amanda and I will do some talking and then she and I will go out shopping for a wig.'

Putting a paper bag over her head will be

cheaper, Matthew thinks.

Amanda continues to cry.

She keeps sniffling.

Mr Martin hands her a tissue.

Matthew checks to see if the nose ring catches what is coming out of her nose.

Amanda removes the nose ring.

Matthew sees that her nose isn't really pierced, that the nose ring just makes it look that way.

His parents notice that, too, and are very relieved.

They all look at her head, hoping that somehow it wasn't really shaved after all.

There are tiny hair bristles and nicks all over her head.

Mrs Martin puts her hand on her husband's arm again. 'Why don't you and Matthew go out now that things are under control?'

Mr Martin looks at his daughter, wondering if things are really under control, if they ever will be again.

Then he looks at Matthew, who is standing there, looking like he's landed on another planet.

Mr Martin goes up to Matthew and puts his arm around his shoulders. 'It's Boy-Bonding Time, son. Let's go.'

Chapter 15

'Fore,' Matthew yells, as his golf ball goes into the rabbit's mouth.

'Five,' Mr Martin yells, as his golf ball hits the rabbit on its forehead and falls back onto the imitation turf.

'I thought you were supposed to yell "Fore" when you hit the ball.' Matthew putts into the hole and marks down his score, 3.

Mr Martin picks up his golf ball, walks up to the rabbit's mouth, and throws the ball to the other side of miniature-golf-hole 6. 'I called out "Five" because you called out "four", and five comes after four. And anyway my score for this hole is five.'

Matthew shakes his head. 'No way, José. You hit that ball at least eight times . . . and I said "fore", not "four".'

'Duck,' Mr Martin yells.

Matthew looks at his father. 'Actually it's not duck, it's chicken. The next course has a chicken that you have to go through, so that it looks like the chicken is laying the golf ball like an egg.'

'No, I mean duck. I'm getting ready to hit this ball and I'm afraid that it's going to hit you. So, duck.' Mr Martin grins.

Matthew ducks.

Mr Martin's golf ball never leaves the ground, going straight into the hole.

'I ducked for nothing,' Matthew calls out.

Putting his arm around his son's shoulders, Mr Martin says, 'Remember the good old days . . . like last week, when we used to go to the carwash and duck when the machines went over the car.'

Matthew sighs. 'Yes. I remember the good old days.'

Both stand quietly for a minute remembering the fun at the carwash.

'Sometimes I wish that we'd never studied ecology.' Matthew shakes his head. 'Then I would never have learned how much water gets wasted in a carwash, how we're supposed to use a bucket and sponges instead.'

'It's not always easy to do the right thing when the other way is much less work and much more fun,' Mr Martin says. 'But look at the bright side . . . look at all the other things we can still do: miniature golf, batting practice, racing cars.'

Matthew hits his golf ball into the middle of a windmill. It goes through and rolls right up next to the hole. He goes up to his father and says, 'Slap me five.'

His father slaps palms with him and yells, 'Fore.'

At the last hole they try to get the ball into the clown's mouth for a free game.

Missing, they look at each other and shrug.

'On to the batting cage?' Mr Martin suggests.

Matthew nods. 'Let's use the major-league speed.'

Mr Martin nods back.

Matthew continues. 'And I'll pretend that the ball is my sister's bald head and I'll hit it as hard as I can.'

'A little angry, huh?' Mr Martin looks at his son. 'I think that we're going to have to talk about this, even though I wish we didn't have to because I'm not sure of what to say.'

'You're the grown-up.' Matthew looks at him.

Taking the golf club from his son and giving both clubs to the attendant, Mr Martin is silent for a minute. Then he turns to Matthew and says, 'How about getting some soft ice cream and sitting down and talking for a bit?'

'Chocolate-vanilla swirl with rainbow sprinkles?' Matthew asks.

'It's a deal.'

Once the ice cream is bought, Matthew and Mr Martin sit at a table under a huge sun umbrella.

Matthew uses his tongue to make paths in the ice cream.

Mr Martin stares at his cone for a minute. It's also a swirl but with chocolate sprinkles. 'I just have to check to make sure that none of these move, that none of these are ants. When I was little, my mother always used to tell me about the time my aunt saw some sprinkles in a dish, licked her finger, and stuck it into the dish. As she put her finger into her mouth, she saw something move in the plate. It was some ants that had got into the food.'

'Arg.' Matthew makes a face. 'An ant-eating aunt.'

Mr Martin continues checking. 'The coast is clear.'

He takes a bite of his cone.

Matthew starts to slurp his ice cream.

'About Amanda . . .' Mr Martin starts. 'I know that all of this fuss is not easy for you.'

Matthew shrugs. 'Who cares?'

'Obviously you do if you want to pretend the baseball is her head.'

'Her bald head,' Matthew reminds him.

'Don't remind me.' Mr Martin holds the ice cream away because it is starting to drip.

'Amanda is a pain,' Matthew informs his father.

'Amanda is going through a difficult time,' his father informs him.

'Amanda is a pain. And she is making my life a pain.' Matthew makes a face. 'It used to be so different in the house.'

'Amanda is going through a difficult time and as a result we are all going through a rough time.

Your mother and I have discussed it and we've decided to get some family counselling to try to help us. We would like you to get some counselling, too, since this also affects you.' Mr Martin looks at his son. 'How do you feel about that?'

'I don't need counselling.' Matthew glares at his father.

'I guess I wasn't very clear. We don't want you to get individual counselling, but we do want you to be there for family counselling.' Mr Martin shakes his head. 'Amanda's clearly not happy. Your mother and I are not sure how best to handle the situation. This is something we have to do as a family to help each other.'

'Oh, okay.' Matthew shrugs. 'I just want things to go back to the way they were.'

'Me too. But I don't think that's possible.' His father looks unhappy. 'We all have to work at making things better with the way that things really are, not the way we wish they were.'

'But it's not my fault.' Matthew looks angry. 'It's Amanda's problem and she's making it mine . . . ours.'

Mr Martin continues, 'It is our family's problem . . . Maybe there are some things that have caused Amanda to act this way. I don't know. What I do know is that we have a problem and we all have to work on it. And who knows, maybe soon Amanda will be able to work this all out of her system.'

'System . . . system . . . system . . .' Matthew thinks again about what he has been learning in school.

'So we all work together on this. It's a deal?' Mr Martin stares at his son.

'Deal.' Matthew starts to shake hands until he realizes that his hand is covered with ice cream.

Mr Martin grabs the hand and shakes it anyway.

Chapter 16

The bus pulls up and stops in front of the
Twentieth Street entrance of The Franklin Institute
at 6:00 P.M.

'Right on time.' Mrs Stanton stands up in the
front of the bus, right next to the driver's seat. 'I
have a few announcements to make before we get
off the bus.'

Mr Hudson starts filming her.

'Why couldn't he have stayed home?' Jil!
whispers to Matthew, who is sitting next to her on
the bus. 'Why couldn't my mother have stayed
home? She's three months pregnant. Doesn't the
baby need to sleep in a bed? Why did they have to
bring Jonathon? Why do they see the word
chaperone on the permission slip and think it
means the family of Jil! Hudson? Why doesn't that
camera break?'

Matthew is impatient to get off the bus. Several
hours on a bus is not his idea of a good time,
especially since Lizzie Doran sits behind them on
the bus.

It's a tradition that Lizzie gets bus-sick on every class trip.

This trip is no exception.

Her mother now packs barf bags, plastic bags to put the barf bags in (no recycling of those bags), and a nonaerosol deodorizing spray.

Matthew thinks that the entire bus smells like a combination of Lizzie barf and pine forest.

Mr Hudson calls out, 'Mrs Stanton. Look this way. Say cheese.'

Mrs Stanton does not say 'cheese'. In fact she does not look overjoyed at being filmed.

The clothes she has on are not her normal 'teacher clothes'. She is wearing jeans and a sweatshirt that says, 'Save the Whales.'

Her eight-year-old daughter, Marie, is wearing jeans and a T-shirt that says, 'Save the Humans.'

Mrs Stanton explains, 'When we get inside, everyone should stick together for a while. First I will register us and pick up our room assignment and schedule. Then we'll put our bags in the room, go see a film telling us about the institute, and have dinner. Remember, there will be no eating anywhere but in the designated areas.'

Ryma's father raises his hand. 'Is there a special area where adults can go to relax?'

Mrs Stanton nods. 'There is a leaders' lounge located in the employee lounge in the basement. Coffee and tea will be available. However, I do suggest that the chaperones see all of the exhibits and be available in case the students need them.'

Mr Browne says, 'Absolutely. I just need a few minutes to relax.'

Ryma calls out, 'Translate that into, He just needs a few minutes to have a cigarette, which he shouldn't have anyway.'

Several people on the bus hiss at the thought of cigarettes.

Mrs Stanton shakes her head. 'The museum has been designated a smoke-free environment.'

There is applause.

Mr Browne, however, does not look like a happy Camp-Iner.

Ryma looks up at her father and says softly, 'Daddy, don't get upset, but you know that smoking's bad for you. I just worry.'

Mr Browne looks down at his only child and gives her a hug.

Mrs Stanton continues, 'You can probably smoke outside the building.'

Mr Browne shakes his head. 'I'm going to try not to have a cigarette for the entire time we're here.'

The entire bus cheers.

Mr Browne looks down again at Ryma and says, 'Maybe I should have one last cigarette on the street before we go in . . . since I haven't had one since we got on the bus. I didn't give my system any warning and . . .'

'Oh, Daddy, please,' Ryma begs.

'Okay, I'll try,' Mr Browne promises.

'I've got that pledge on film.' Mr Hudson continues to point the camera at Mr Browne. 'How about if we have a shot of you handing your cigarettes to my wife for safekeeping?'

Mr Hudson gets the picture of the cigarettes being passed to Mrs Hudson, and one of the look of panic on Mr Browne's face.

Mrs Stanton says, 'When we get settled inside, we will see the film telling about the museum and the rules and regulations. Then we'll be able to explore. Have fun . . . this is a wonderful place with lots of terrific things to do. Now, everyone out of the bus.'

'Me first,' Mr Hudson yells. 'I want to film everyone as they get off the bus.'

'He filmed everyone as they got on the bus.' Jil! sighs. 'When will this ever end?'

People pile off the bus, carrying their plastic gear bags.

A group of the boys from Matthew's class gather by the door.

'Over here, Matthew,' Joshua yells.

Matthew heads over to join them, and then he remembers . . . Jil!.

Standing in the middle, he looks back and forth, not sure what to do.

Again he wishes that there was a manual published with the rules and regulations for stuff like this.

'Come on, Matthew. What are you waiting for?' Joshua calls out.

Jil! waits for a minute to see what his decision is.

When it becomes obvious that no decision is on its way, she decides to make it easy for him – and for her too.

'Matthew Martin.' She grins at him. 'We are not Superglued to each other.'

Matthew's feet finally become unglued from the sidewalk, and he rushes over to be with the other guys.

Zoe walks up to Jil! and says, 'My mother's the real expert, with all the dating and marriages that she's been through. And she says that it's best to keep your eyes on them.'

'Right now' – Jil! looks round – 'it's The Franklin Institute that I want to keep my eyes on. Let's go inside.'

Zoe heads off to where Tyler is waiting for her. 'Don't say I didn't warn you.'

Chapter 17

'Look at those little girls wearing feathers on their heads.' Matthew points. 'Maybe I should go over and tell them a couple of chicken jokes.'

'They're from a Y group, Indian Princesses. They meet each week with their fathers. I know because my little sister is one and when I was little, I was an Indian guide and my dad went with me,' Mark tells them. 'It's nice that he does that, since he's allergic to feathers.'

The downstairs is filling up as more and more people arrive. Some are dressed in Scout uniforms. One group is all wearing T-shirts that say 'Edgar School Is Best.' Almost everyone is wearing 'weekend clothes,' except for one father, who is wearing a three-piece suit and carrying a briefcase. He goes up to one of the people in charge and says, 'Has the group from Dover arrived yet?'

The woman handing out packets to group leaders checks her list and shakes her head.

'I just came from a business meeting in Philadelphia. Where is the men's room so that I can change?' He starts to loosen his tie. 'Please let them know that Bill O'Brien is here already.'

Matthew, who had been wondering if the man was planning on sleeping in the three-piece suit, says, 'I'm never going to have a job where I have to get dressed up like that all day.'

'What are you going to do?' Joshua starts to laugh. 'Get a job as a model for a nudist catalogue?'

Matthew punches his best friend on the arm. 'I said that I didn't want to dress like that. . . . I didn't say I didn't want to dress.'

'You could be a lifeguard . . . a garbage man . . . a cowboy . . . a basketball player,' are some of the suggestions that Matthew's friends make.

Basketball player is the suggestion that Matthew likes best, but he feels a little bad when he thinks about how he's not very tall.

He thinks about his family and how none of them are very tall either and he realizes that might not happen.

'You could always be a freelancer like my father,' Joshua says. 'He never gets dressed up.'

Matthew grins. He remembers when he was little, hearing that Mr Jackson was a freelancer. He didn't realize that meant he worked for himself. For a long time Matthew thought that Mr Jackson did the most wonderful thing in the world, that he was able to be a knight and carry a sword and go wherever he wanted to go and not charge anyone anything for the knightly things he did.

Matthew was a very disappointed second-grader when he discovered that Mr Jackson was a writer.

Mrs Stanton calls out, 'The Califon group over here, please.'

Everyone congregates around her. 'Here are your maps, schedules, and blue stickers. Notice that we are in the *blue* group. Wear the stickers to identify yourselves. Please note that we'll be sleeping in the Aviation Room. Let's go up there now and drop off our bags.'

As they follow Mrs Stanton up the winding steps, Matthew looks around.

Hundreds of people are carrying up their plastic bags.

'I thought we could only bring sleeping bags or pillows and blankets.' Matthew looks at a woman who is carrying up a patio chaise longue.

'Maybe older people have different rules,' Brian says.

'Maybe she has a bad back or something,' Mrs Stanton tells them, puffing a little as she goes up the steps.

'Let me help you with that,' Mr Browne says, taking Mrs Stanton's bag.

She smiles at him.

'Maybe they'll get married,' Zoe whispers loudly. 'Both of them are divorced.'

'My parents are separated, not divorced yet.' Ryma pokes Zoe on the arm, causing her to almost drop her bag.

Zoe grabs her bag more tightly and says, 'Dream on. They don't get back together. I know that.'

Patrick Ryan says nothing, but thinks about how bad it is between his parents.

Matthew thinks about how glad he is that his parents are happy with each other and wishes that Amanda would get a divorce from the Martin family. He thinks about the session with the family counsellor when Amanda said her family couldn't understand her and he said that they just couldn't stand her.

'Aviation Room. Here we are.' Mrs Stanton points to the room. 'Girls sleep in one place. Boys in another.'

Airplanes hang from the ceiling. There are exhibit cases all over. In the middle of the room is a loft area, with more exhibits.

Lizzie points up to the loft. 'Girls, let's sleep up there.'

Matthew wonders if Lizzie has ever been loft-sick and decides not to sleep in the area below the loft, just in case.

'Okay. I just don't want to sleep under the plane in case it decides to fall down.' Sarah bites her fingernail.

'It won't fall down, ditz-brain.' Billy shakes his head.

Sarah continues to stare up at the plane.

'Come on!' Jil! yells. 'Let's get the loft area before one of the other groups does.'

The Franklin Institute
Science Museum

1

1 Group Lunchroom
  & Orientation Center
2 William Penn Gallery
3 The Lunch Box
4 Communications
5 Discovery Store
6 Stearns Science Auditorium
7 Bicycles
8 Fels Planetarium
9 Railroad Hall

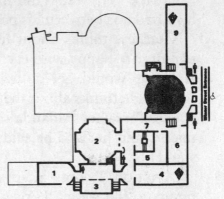

2

1 Ben's Restaurant
2 Benjamin Franklin National Memorial
3 The I.Q. Store
4 Bioscience / Heart
5 Preview Gallery
6 Electricity & Electronics
7 Aviation
8 Omni Cafe
9 Ticketing / Bartol Atrium
10 Future Store
11 Mandell Futures Center, Future Earth,
   Future Energy, Future Health,
   Future & You, Careers Center
12 Cutting Edge Gallery
13 Tuttleman Omniverse Theater
14 Science Garden (coming Spring 1991)

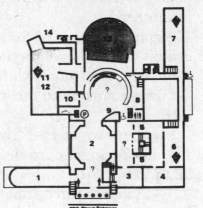

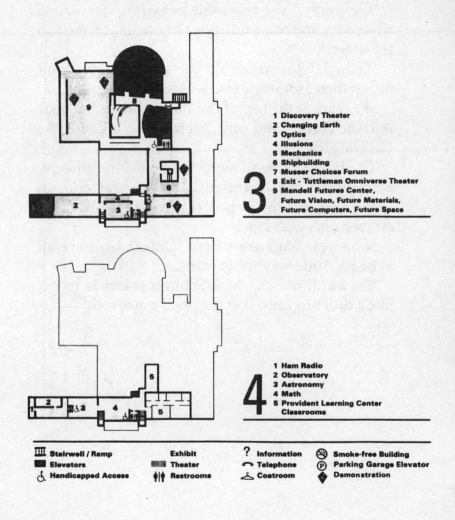

3

1 Discovery Theater
2 Changing Earth
3 Optics
4 Illusions
5 Mechanics
6 Shipbuilding
7 Musser Choices Forum
8 Exit - Tuttleman Omniverse Theater
9 Mandell Futures Center,
Future Vision, Future Materials,
Future Computers, Future Space

4

1 Ham Radio
2 Observatory
3 Astronomy
4 Math
5 Provident Learning Center
Classrooms

IIII Stairwell / Ramp	▓ Exhibit	? Information	⊘ Smoke-free Building
▓ Elevators	▓ Theater	⌒ Telephone	Ⓟ Parking Garage Elevator
♿ Handicapped Access	�restrooms Restrooms	⬠ Coatroom	◆ Demonstration

'Okay,' David Cohen teases.

'Girls only.' Vanessa folds her arms. 'You know what Mrs Stanton said: Boys in one place, girls in the other.'

'Enough.' Jil! rushes up the stairs. 'If we don't get up there, someone else will get it.'

She reaches the top of the stairs, throws her gear into the corner, and yells, 'I claim this area for the Califon girls.'

The boys decide to sleep by the exhibit directly across from where the girls are but far enough away so that if the girls decide to drop something on them, it won't reach.

Soon gear bags are stored. Dinner bags are all in hand. And everyone is ready.

'Forward, march.' Mrs Stanton pretends to act like a drill sergeant. 'Let the good times roll.'

Chapter 18

The Franklin Institute presents Camp-In

Evening Schedule

6:00 P.M.	ARRIVAL! Welcome to the programme. Follow your dinner schedule. Visit exhibits.
7:00–7:30	PRE-WORKSHOP DEMONSTRATIONS Papermaking – Communications, first floor Static Show – Electricity, second floor
7:45	Start moving to Science Auditorium, first floor.
7:55–8:30	EUREKA! Insight and Invention
8:30–8:45	FIRST GROUP MEETING, Science Auditorium

8:45–10:30	MUSEUM TIME
	Explore four floors of exhibit.
	Follow the museum map.

9:00–10:15	SPECIALS TONIGHT
	THE WONDERFUL WORLD OF
	WIND-UP
	Wind up a few friendly characters
	in this land of spring-powered toys.
	Bicycles – first floor

9:15–10:00	SNACKS
	Hungry? Come to LUNCHBOX
	for juice and crackers. No food
	beyond this point.

9:30–10:15	DISCO-MANIA
	Dance to your favourite songs in
	Express – first floor

| 10:15 | Start moving to the planetarium – |
| | first floor. |

| 10:30–11:05 | PLANETARIUM SHOW – first |
| | floor, Fels Planetarium |

| 11:05–11:15 | SECOND GROUP MEETING – |
| | planetarium |

| 11:15–11:45 | CAMPSITES – Get ready for bed. |

| 11:45 | QUIET HOURS begin. |
| | Shhhhhhhhhhhhhhhhhhh! |

12:00   LIGHTS OUT. Adults must accompany campers if they leave campsites. Nighty night!!

'Awesome. This place is absolutely awesome.' Matthew looks at the Shadow Freezer.

Joshua grins. 'This may be even better than going through the heart.'

The boys start to laugh when they think of how much fun it was going through the model of the heart, how they pretended to be corpuscles, how they hid inside and yelled 'Phlegm' at some girls entering the lungs.

'You've got to admit that my personal best time of twenty-three seconds running through the heart was unbeatable,' Joshua brags.

'I could have done better,' Matthew defends himself, 'if I hadn't got behind the lady who was yelling, "Get me out of here. I'm claustrophobic." Getting her out of there cost me a lot of time.'

Joshua laughs at the memory. 'She kept calling you a hero and saying that she practically had a heart attack in the heart.'

Matthew keeps looking at the Shadow Freezer. 'I wish those Indian Princesses and their feathers and their fathers would get out of there so we can go in.'

Billy, Brian, and Pablo join them.

'How does that thing work?' Brian asks.

'You push the button and then pose in front of

the screen until the lights flash. Then you step back and see your own shadow.' Matthew looks at a father holding an Indian Princess by her ankles and then setting her down so that they can watch their shadows. 'Awesome.'

The boys move closer to the Shadow Freezer area and start making loud hints.

'Boy. I sure would like to try that.'

'That looks like fun. I hope we get a chance soon.'

'What time is it?'

'I bet you Indian Princesses haven't seen the heart yet. You're really going to like it. And don't forget about the Physics Room, where you can do balancing things with weights.'

The Indian Princesses and their fathers finally move on, and the boys rush into the area.

All of them start grunting and doing karate moves.

'These shadows look awesome.' Billy poses like he's a muscle man.

Matthew looks to his left and sees Mr Hudson filming them.

'Pretty good, huh?' Matthew says, making hand-puppet motions.

Mrs Stanton comes up to the Shadow Freezer. She asks, 'Did you boys get to the Static Show?'

They shake their heads no.

'You missed something really terrific. The demonstrator made Vanessa's hair stand up on end by generating static.'

'He should have demonstrated the electric chair on Vanessa.' Matthew grins.

Mrs Stanton ignores his statement. 'They tried it with another girl, but she had too much mousse in her hair and it didn't work.'

Mr Browne joins them. He is biting a fingernail.

'How are you doing? Have you had a cigarette yet?' The boys want to know.

He shakes his head and smiles. 'Not yet. Not since four o'clock. That makes it five hours, fifteen minutes, and thirty seconds since I've had one.'

The boys cheer.

'How about letting someone else use this area?' Mrs Stanton suggests, looking around at the group that is waiting.

The boys finally allow others to use it.

Mrs Stanton says to them, 'Did you like the Eureka Show? Wasn't it great how they made it look like they'd brought Benjamin Franklin back from the past to talk about his inventions and about his life and how things in science work?'

'I especially liked how Joshua got chosen from the audience to help build something on the earthquake machine and how his team won.' Matthew grins and looks at his watch. 'You know what else I like? It's snack time.'

'A truly educational experience for you,' Mrs Stanton teases.

'Snack time. Great idea,' Billy says. 'We can get

something to eat and then go watch the girls act doofy. They said that they were going to the disco, and that's right next to the snack place.'

The boys rush down to the snack area.

Matthew has no idea that a very annoyed Jil! is looking for him.

Chapter 19

Matthew is drinking his fifth container of apple juice and eating his sixth helping of cheese and crackers.

He is considering buying candy and soda with some of the money that his parents gave him to spend at the gift shop.

Two of the Camp-In staff members walk by. One is using a walkie-talkie. The other is holding the hand of a little boy who has got lost.

Matthew thinks about how great all the people who work at Camp-In are, how a lot of them are only in high school and college, how he would like to work here someday.

'Jil! is looking for you,' Cathy Atwood says as she heads to the vending machine.

Joshua crosses his arms and sticks his hands behind his back. Pantomiming a couple kissing, he says, 'Oh, Jil!... Oh, Matthew... Oh, barf.'

'You can't do anything without Jil!,' Patrick taunts.

'Can too.' Matthew sticks another cracker in his mouth.

'Can not,' Joshua tells him. 'Every time I'm looking for you, you're with Jil!'

'Not true.' Matthew defends himself, thinking about how he spends a lot of time with the guys in his class.

Joshua, seeing how much Matthew is blushing, continues, 'You like Jil! even more than your computer . . . even more than Nintendo . . . even more than brownies and ice cream.'

Matthew is more used to teasing someone than being teased and isn't sure of what to say.

'Jil! is looking for you.' Her younger brother, Jonathon, comes running up to tell him. 'Am I glad I'm not you right now!'

'Jil! is looking for you,' Patrick mimics, using a whiny voice.

The boys start to laugh, all except Matthew.

Mr Hudson comes up, points the camera at everyone, and says, 'Smile. Hold up those juice cartons.'

Everyone but Matthew holds up the juice carton. Everyone but Matthew smiles.

Matthew gets up from the table. 'Bye.'

Matthew walks out the door.

'Jil! wants to see you,' Zoe and Tyler call out.

Matthew is getting very annoyed. 'No fooling. I never would have guessed.'

He heads into the room where the disco is taking place.

It's very dark.

Strobe lights are going.

There are a lot of people dancing. Girls and boys together. Girls with girls. Girls dancing alone. Boys dancing alone. Boys slamming into each other and throwing rubber lavalike rocks at each other.

Matthew watches as two grown-ups try to do the latest dance.

He is glad that they are not his parents and feels sorry for the kid whose parents they are.

'Jil!'s looking for you.' Lisa slows down her dancing long enough to call out to him.

'Duh,' Matthew mutters.

By the water fountain he finds Jil!.

'I've been looking for you,' she tells him.

Matthew, by this time, is sick of hearing about how she's looking for him. 'Well, you found me. What do you want?'

She shrugs. 'I just thought we could dance together. I haven't seen you all night.'

Several of their classmates come over and stand nearby so that they can hear the conversation.

Patrick says nothing but flaps his arms.

Joshua grins.

Softly Jil! says, 'Tyler dances with Zoe. You could dance with me.'

Everyone waits for Matthew's answer.

Instead of speaking, he grabs Jil! by the hand and takes her out to where people are dancing.

Looking over at the guys who have been teasing him, he starts to dance the way he thinks a chicken would.

Jil! looks at him and says, 'Matthew. Stop that. You're so embarrassing.'

Matthew looks at her and then looks at the guys and then looks back at Jil! and clucks.

She puts her hands on her hips. 'Matthew Martin. How can you do this to me? I hate you. I don't ever want to speak to you again.'

She turns around and walks away.

Just as Matthew decides to follow after her and explain that he was just joking around because he doesn't know how to dance and because all of his friends are teasing him, he feels someone punch him on the shoulder.

It's Joshua. 'Way to go! You really showed her.'

Patrick raises his hand and gives him a high five.

The lights come on in the disco, and one of the leaders announces that it is time to go to the planetarium.

As everyone heads to the second floor, Matthew looks for Jil!

Somehow he knows that they're not going to be sitting together for this show.

And he realizes that he's not very happy about that fact.

Chapter 20

'Lights out. Everyone to sleep.' The person from Camp-In switches off the lights in the Aviation Room.

Matthew gets hit on the head with a pillow.

It's Joshua.

Matthew hits Joshua back. 'Leave me alone, duh-brain.'

Joshua hits him again with a pillow and then hits Brian, who hits Tyler and Billy.

Soon all the boys from Califon are hitting each other with pillows.

Soon kids from other groups are hitting the kids from their own groups with pillows.

There's laughing and name-calling.

The lights go on and a man says, 'That's enough. I want you all to go to sleep. We have a busy day tomorrow.'

The lights go out again.

It's quiet.

Someone starts giggling in a corner and soon that whole corner is giggling.

One of the girls in that group has the kind of laugh that makes everyone start laughing.

The lights go on again. 'It's after midnight. I want to go to sleep.'

It quietens down and the lights go off again.

Some people actually manage to go to sleep.

One group is in a corner whispering the grossest jokes they know. An Indian Princess's father starts snoring – very loudly.

Matthew wonders what it's like for the people who are sleeping in the room with the heart, whether the heart keeps pumping all night.

He also wonders whether Jil! is ever going to talk to him, ever again.

She didn't stop when he tried to talk to her after the planetarium show.

She turned away when he tried to talk to her when they all got back into the Aviation Room, when he invited her to go sit up in the cockpit of the plane.

Matthew Martin is angry. He's angry at Jil! for ignoring him. He's angry at his friends for teasing him. He's angry at himself for acting so dumb when he doesn't know what to do.

Matthew listens to the snores of the Indian Princess's father and wonders about why everything is getting so complicated.

He listens to the laughter of the corner group and then thinks about how he isn't even a teenager yet, how he's only eleven, how everything around him is changing.

He wonders whether Califon School is part of an ecosystem of its own and whether what happens to each of the kids in his class affects the other kids.

He thinks maybe that's true because he knows that Joshua has been acting different since Jil! and Matthew started to 'go out'.

Thinking about the ecosystem makes Matthew think about food chains in nature. Thinking about food chains makes him think about McDonald's and makes him wish he'd eaten more at snack time.

He pokes Joshua on his side and whispers, 'Got anything to eat?'

Joshua rolls over and pulls something out of his sleeping bag. 'I've got some astronaut ice cream.'

'Where did you get it?' Matthew asks, taking a chunk of the freeze-dried ice cream.

'The gift shop,' Joshua says, eating some of it. 'Good, huh? Weird but good.'

All around the room Matthew can hear sounds.

Snoring.

One little girl is talking to the huge stuffed bear she brought in her gear bag.

Giggling.

Matthew can hear giggling from the loft area.

He wonders if all the girls are laughing at him.

He's always liked to make every one laugh, but not like this.

He wonders if Jil! is even thinking about him.

Matthew pokes Billy. 'Lend me the glow stick.'

Billy passes over the fluorescent light stick he bought at the gift shop.

Matthew uses it to look at his watch.

1:38 A.M.

And all is not well.

Chapter 21

A voice comes over the intercom. 'Attention K Mart shoppers. There's a special on dog food in Aisle 3. Limited supply available.'

Matthew sits up.

Someone has captured the intercom.

Someone else captures the kid who has captured the intercom and all is quiet again.

Looking at his watch, Matthew sees that it is 6:00 A.M.

He also sees that people are starting to wake up.

There are still people who are sound asleep.

The snoring Indian Princess's father continues to snore. He also grunts.

Matthew looks at his friends.

Pablo has totally covered himself with his sleeping bag.

Joshua has fallen asleep with his head on what was left of the astronaut ice cream, and there are freeze-dried ice cream crumbs on his face and in his hair.

Billy is sound asleep with his thumb in his mouth.

Matthew plans to remember that if Billy ever teases him about Jil!.

Matthew looks up to see Mr Hudson filming everyone start to wake up.

He sees that Jil! is walking across the room with her toothbrush in her hand.

Matthew jumps up.

Stepping over sleeping and waking-up bodies, he follows her out of the door.

'Wait up,' he calls out.

'Shhh.' Someone punches him on the ankle.

Hopping out of the door, he runs into Jil!, who stands there glaring at him. 'What do you want?'

'I want to talk to you,' he says.

'Shhhh,' is the sound from just inside the door.

'Please,' Matthew looks her in the eyes. 'I really want to talk to you.'

'I don't want to talk to you.' Jil! stamps her foot.

'And I don't want to hear either of you talking to each other at this hour.' An adult voice can be heard from just inside the door.

'Let's go over there.' Matthew points to a spot down the hallway.

Jil! looks at Matthew and shrugs.

He gets down on bended knee and begs, 'Oh, please.'

'Quieten down, out there.' The adult voice sounds more annoyed.

'Okay, Matthew Martin,' Jil! whispers. 'But just

for a minute so that I can tell you what I think of you.'

Matthew and Jil! go stand in a corner.

'You totally embarrassed me. All I wanted to do was spend some time with you and you acted like a real goof . . . showing off in front of everyone.' Jil! bites her lip to keep from crying.

Matthew nods. 'I know. But I was beginning to feel like I was number one of the Ten Most Wanted . . . like finding me was an unsolved mystery for everyone and their brother – actually everyone and your brother.'

Jil! nods back. 'I know. All the girls were teasing me and making me feel like we should be together even though I was having fun being with them. Zoe kept telling me that you had probably found someone from another school that you liked better.'

'That's dumb.' Matthew makes a face. 'I've only just started liking girls. And you're the one that I like, so why should I like someone else? Liking you is confusing enough.'

Jil! grins. 'I know what you mean. How come I can't just like you and you like me without everyone else treating us like we're a television show or something?'

'Like a Federation of Wrestling show?' Matthew starts to laugh. 'Or a cartoon show?'

Mr Hudson comes up to them and starts filming them.

361

Jil! looks at her father. 'Daddy. Would you please stop that? When are you going to realize that I'm growing up and I have my own life? When are you going to allow me some of the privacy that I need to become my own person?'

Mr Hudson puts down his camera and looks at his daughter, not sure of what to say.

'Oops.' He walks away to think about what his daughter has just told him.

'Wow.' Matthew looks at Jil! 'I can't believe that you said that.'

'I saw this show on *Oprah* that talked about parents and kids. I decided to try it out.' Jil! is feeling much better.

'Did *Oprah* have a show on the relationships of eleven-year-olds? If not, I think we should write to her and offer to be on the show,' Matthew laughs.

Jil! laughs too.

'Look. I'm sorry that I acted like a goofus,' Matthew tells her.

'Me too.' Jil! nods.

'So we can just be our age and like each other without it getting too mushy?' Matthew feels much better.

'Agreed.' Jil! reaches out to shake his hand.

Matthew shakes her hand and then starts to wrestle with it.

They both start to laugh.

Matthew leans over and gives her a little kiss on her cheek.

They stand there looking at each other for a minute.

'Maybe being a teenager won't be so bad,' Matthew says.

'Yeah.' Jil! agrees.

'Yeah. I can get my driver's licence then.' Matthew grins.

'Doofus.' Jil! gives his arm a little punch.

And so Day 2 at The Franklin Institute begins.

Chapter 22

Morning Schedule

6:30 A.M.	WAKE UP! Good morning. CLEAN AREA. Pick up gear. Follow directions by staff to storage area.
6:45–7:30	BREAKFAST. Go to Lunchbox Area.
7:45–11:30	VISIT THE FUTURES CENTRE. See the Nature Max film at the Omniverse Theatre. Visit exhibits. Attend workshops.
11:30	DEPARTURE BEGINS. All groups head towards the Science Auditorium to pick up gear. Use Winter Street doors to exit. Thanks for coming. See you next year.

'Breakfast.' Matthew races towards the eating area. 'It's my favourite meal of the morning and I don't want to miss it.'

'It's the only meal of the morning,' Jil! reminds him, as she races alongside him. 'Matthew, stop . . . look.'

Pointing to a green machine, Jil! says, 'It's called a medal maker. You know, one of those old things that stamps whatever you want to say on a round medal.'

'Breakfast.' Matthew holds his stomach.

'Please,' Jil! begs. 'I'll give you my doughnut if you wait just a few minutes.'

Matthew thinks about two doughnuts instead of one. Not only will he have more to eat but first he can hold one up to each eye, look through the hole, and yell, 'Glasses.' Then when he only has a little bit of doughnut left around the holes, he can hold them up to his eyes and yell, 'Contact lenses.'

'It's a deal.' He grins at Jil!, who is wearing an extra-large Futures Centre T-shirt as a dress. On her feet are pink sparkly socks and sandals.

She grins back at Matthew, who has on a Camp-In T-shirt. 'It'll be the souvenir of our visit.'

'Oh, okay,' Matthew says. 'What are we going to write on it?'

Jil! blushes. 'I kind of thought we could write our names on it and the date. The medal already says Franklin Institute.' Jil! takes a coin out of her belt pouch.

Digging into his pocket, Matthew says, 'I'll pay for it.'

The coin goes into the machine, and Matthew and Jil! imprint their names on the medal. Jil! adds the date.

Picking up the finished medal, Jil! says, 'This is great. I can put it on a chain and wear it as a necklace.'

'Does this mean we're engaged?' Matthew thinks about how the guys are going to react to the medal.

'No. It doesn't mean we're engaged.' Jil! looks at him. 'If you don't want me to wear it, I won't. In fact if you want me to, I can just throw it away and forget about it.'

Matthew can tell that Jil! will not just throw it away and forget about it.

He realizes that he probably is not handling this situation as well as he could, so he says, 'Don't get angry. I don't want us to be engaged and I don't want you to be enraged. And I think it will be nice for you to wear the medal. Now can we go to breakfast, please . . .?'

Jil! says, 'Don't you want a medal, too, as a souvenir?'

Shaking his head, Matthew says, 'No. Actually there's something in the store that I want as a souvenir. It's a basketball with a map of the world on it.'

How romantic, Jil! thinks.

'Breakfast.' Matthew starts to run. 'We better get going.'

Racing down the hall, Jil! holds the medal tightly in her hand.

Matthew thinks about how hungry he is.

'Slow down,' one of the teachers from another school calls out to them.

Matthew thinks about how 'Slow down' must be on a list of phrases that a teacher has to learn before getting in front of a class.

Arriving at the cafeteria, they get their breakfasts and sit down with some of the Califon group.

Jil! hands Matthew her chocolate-covered doughnut.

Matthew holds up both doughnuts and yells, 'Glasses.'

He then slurps down his juice.

Mrs Stanton hands him a spoon. 'I brought these from home. They asked that we all bring our own spoons that we can take home again so that they didn't have to use plastic utensils.'

Matthew quickly eats around the doughnuts, leaving a little cake around the holes.

Continuing, Mrs Stanton picks up her coffee cup, which says *Number 1 Teacher*. 'And I like the fact that they are using reusable and recyclable products whenever possible . . . and that they asked adults to bring their own mugs.'

'Why don't we have Mr Hudson take a picture

of you and your cup and then it would be a mug shot.' Mr Browne smiles and sits down next to Mrs Stanton.

Zoe looks at them and wonders, if her teacher and Ryma's father ever do date and marry, will they let her be a bridesmaid. She already has several dresses from her parents' weddings.

'How is it going? Be honest. Have you really not smoked yet?' Matthew asks.

Looking at his watch, Mr Browne says, 'Twenty-six hours, fifty-five minutes, and sixteen seconds. And how could I smoke? Every time I turned around, one of you was following me.'

'We took shifts. I organized it.'

'Thank you . . . I think.' Mr Browne smiles. 'It would have been nice, though, to have had a little more privacy in the bathroom.'

'I really did have to go,' Billy says, turning red.

'We had to check on you,' Vanessa tells Mr Browne. 'People going through withdrawal can *not* be trusted. I know . . . my mother gave up smoking seven times before she really quit.'

Matthew looks at Vanessa and thinks about how nice it was that she organized everything to help Mr Browne.

Then he remembers all of the anti-Matthew things she organizes and stops thinking positively about her.

Billy Kellerman is asleep with his head on the table.

Lisa Levine is pulling strands of his hair through Cheerios and then putting a little knot at the end.

'Disney World and Paris would have been wonderful.' Matthew turns to Mrs Stanton, who has just handed her doughnut to Mr Browne. 'But The Franklin Institute is great.'

Mrs Stanton looks at everyone at the table. 'Do you want to know the best thing?'

Everyone does.

'The best thing is that our visit isn't over, that we get to see the Futures Centre this morning.'

Matthew gets up with his tray. 'I'm ready for the twenty-first century. I hope it's ready for me.'

Jil! gets up also. 'I'm ready too.'

'I thought you were going to go to the Futures Centre with us.' Joshua looks at Matthew.

Patrick flaps his arms. 'Cluck. Cluck.'

Matthew looks at him. 'Wrong animal, Patrick. You ought to pretend to be the animal you're acting like, actually the part of the animal you're acting like. Say "Neigh" and turn around.'

Patrick stops clucking.

Matthew says, 'Jil! and I are going to the Futures Centre. Let's all go together.'

Joshua looks uncertain.

'Come on. I hear that there is a Jamming Room.'

'I thought they didn't allow food in the museum part.' Joshua looks confused.

Ryma giggles. 'The Jamming Room has a drum pad, marimba, and keyboard. It's to make music.'

'I knew that.' Joshua pretends that he really did know that.

Everyone gets up and heads off to the Centre, everyone, including Billy Kellerman, who has awakened and doesn't know that he has turned into a Cheeriohead.

Matthew makes a fast stop at the gift shop and picks up his globe basketball.

As everyone enters the door below a neon sign, Matthew walks backwards and says, 'Everyone do this with me . . . and it'll be *Back to the Future*.'

'Let's not and say we did,' Vanessa mumbles.

Everyone walks in . . . backwards or forwards.

And are in the middle of the twenty-first century.

Chapter 23

'Amazing. This place is absolutely amazing,' Jil! says, as everyone enters the Future Vision gateway exhibit.

Mrs Stanton looks at a map. 'There are eight main exhibits: Future Vision, Future Materials, Future Computers, Future Space, Future Energy, Future Earth, Future Health, and The Future and You.'

Everyone thinks about which place to go to first.

Mrs Stanton continues, 'Don't forget, I have the Unisys card and if you want any information from any of the computers, find me and we'll use the card and activate the printer.'

She holds up the bar-coded card, which gives her access to a computer information network in the museum, one that links the Futures and Science centres and can help plan specialized tours of the institute and get information. It will also help her get information and lessons to use later with the class.

'Lucky,' Matthew says. 'How come only leaders get those cards?'

'Because the machines would overload,' Mrs Stanton informs him. 'When you come back on your own, you'll be able to get one of these cards. Listen, there's so much to do and not a lot of time. You'd all better get going.'

Everyone rushes off to the exhibits.

As Jil! and Matthew stand by the large model of the earth, her father comes up to them.

He is still holding the camera.

Matthew wonders if the camera has become permanently attached to Mr Hudson's body.

Mr Hudson says, 'I would really like to take a picture of you in front of the globe.'

Jil! and Matthew look at each other.

'Oh, okay,' they both say.

Mr Hudson aims the camera. 'I want you both to stand in front of the globe. Matthew, I want you to hold your basketball in front of you.'

Matthew bounces the ball.

The teacher who earlier told them to stop running walks by and tells him to stop bouncing the ball.

Matthew twirls the ball on his finger.

Mr Hudson says, 'I want you both to smile.'

Jil! says, 'I want you to take this film so that we can see the museum before we have to go.'

'Get ready,' Mr Hudson calls out.

Matthew continues to twirl the basketball.

Jil! holds up the medal.

Mr Hudson films.

'It's a wrap,' Mr Hudson yells.

'My father really wanted to be a director.' Jil!

turns to Matthew.

Mr Hudson walks away, and Jil! and Matthew continue to explore the Futures Centres.

Chapter 24

'It's not fair.' Matthew looks around at the Future Earth Exhibit.

'What's not?' Jil! asks.

'I work out my problems. You're not mad at me. My other friends aren't mad at me, except for maybe Amanda and Vanessa, who hate every one of my guts and I don't care about them.' Matthew points to the twelve-foot model of the earth. 'Look at that. It shows what's happening to the planet . . . acid rain . . . the greenhouse effect . . . the ozone layer . . . It's so depressing.'

Jil! points to another area. 'But look. There's also an exhibit about how we can help.'

They walk over to it.

'There's so much to do and it isn't even my fault. I don't want to think about it, but I have to think about it.' Matthew walks over to an exhibit and starts to smile. 'Jil! Look. It's a miniature rain forest ecosystem . . . system . . . system . . .'

As they walk around the exhibits, Jil! says, 'I've been doing a lot of thinking. None of us can do all of the things that will save the planet but each of us can do some of them and all of that will add up and be better than nothing.'

'Boy, you guys are very serious,' Billy Kellerman says. 'Lighten up a little.'

'And you are being very cereal.' Matthew looks at Billy and laughs.

'I don't get it.' Billy looks puzzled.

Matthew points to one of the staff members who is wearing a shirt with EXPLAINER written on the back. 'Ask him.'

Billy shakes his head. Several of the Cheerios fall off.

'Dandruff alert!' Patrick yells.

Lizzie tries to look innocent.

Billy heads off to the Boys' Room, vowing never to trust his classmates again.

Matthew calls out to him, 'Some people get their hair corn-rowed. You got yours Oat Bran-rowed.'

Matthew has a great time as the group goes through the rest of the exhibits.

There is so much to do.

He finds out how much he weighs on Earth . . . Also on Mars, Jupiter, and Venus.

He calls Mrs Stanton over.

She refuses to weigh herself.

He and Jil! stand in front of a machine that shows their images on the wall and then lets them make patterns and colours on the images.

Matthew ends up red and striped.

Jil! becomes purple and polka-dotted.

Everyone in the class runs around trying out all the machines.

Matthew stands in front of a robot sensor and keeps jumping up and down while the sensor tries to measure his height.

The machine keeps telling him to stop squirming, to stay in one place. Finally Matthew stands still and the machine calls out his exact height.

An Indian Princess's father comes over and is measured at five feet eleven inches. He steps back and then returns, putting his arms above his head. The machine then tells him that he is six feet ten inches and must be eating his Wheaties.

Next comes the Space Tools Exhibit.

Jil! is chosen to demonstrate some of the wearable equipment and looks like a human robot.

Then a group of people look at the recyclable art.

A huge sculpture has been made out of all kinds of rubbish thrown together.

'That looks like my room,' Joshua laughs.

The tour continues.

Mr Hudson stands by the large picture of the astronaut uniform. In the middle of the helmet is a hole in which people put their heads and pretend to be astronauts.

As Califon students come by, Mr Hudson has each of them go behind the photo and use the steps to get up high enough to insert their heads in the hole.

'This will be filed under "Califon Sixth-graders – Space Cadets". ' Mr Hudson takes a picture of Billy Kellerman, who has removed most of the Cheerios from his head.

Jil!'s mother tries out a machine that shows what she will look like in twenty years.

'Yuck,' is her reaction.

'Look, Matthew.' Jil! points out several quotations on the wall. 'Look at that one from President John F. Kennedy:

> *Man is still the most extraordinary computer of all.'*

Matthew, who loves computers, smiles.
He likes being called a computer.
He also knows that he likes being a person.
Computers can't eat junk food.
Computers can't have friends.
Mrs Stanton stands next to her students. 'Look at the quote from Woody Allen:

> *It's clear the future holds great opportunities. It also holds pitfalls. The trick will be to avoid the pitfalls, seize the opportunities and get back home by six o'clock.'*

Looking at the Woody Allen quote on the wall,

Mrs Stanton says, 'That reminds me. We have to get ready to leave. Our time at Franklin Institute is over. It's almost eleven thirty.'

'Ratsafrats,' Jil! says. 'I feel like Cinderella.'

Everyone heads down to the area where the bags are stored.

Then everyone has to wait until Tyler and Zoe are located.

Outside the museum, Mr Hudson takes videos of the group.

Many of them are wearing the clothes that they have slept in.

Some have their new T-shirts on.

A few of them are having trouble staying awake.

Mrs Stanton and Mr Browne stand next to each other, smiling.

Mrs Stanton's daughter, Marie, and Ryma Browne look at each other trying to figure out what it would be like if they became sisters.

Matthew and Jil! stand next to each other.

He's making devil's horns behind her head.

'On the bus, everyone,' Mrs Stanton calls out.

People rush onto the bus, trying to get a seat that is not near Lizzie Doran.

Everyone gets on.

Matthew and Jil! sit together.

Joshua, sitting behind them, drops some astronaut ice cream on Matthew's head.

When Matthew turns around, he sees Ryma sitting next to Joshua.

Joshua flashes his best friend a look that says, 'You're dead meat if you open your mouth.'

Matthew hums a few bars of 'Here Comes the Bride' and sits down again.

Mrs Stanton counts heads.

The driver starts the bus.

It's back to Califon . . . before six o'clock.

Matthew thinks about how much has happened in sixth grade and wonders what it's going to be like when school is over.

Jil! raps him on his head with her knuckles. 'Earth to Matthew. Do you read me? Please make contact.'

Matthew pretends to pick up a phone. 'Matthew to earth. I read you loud and clear.'

Matthew feels as if he is on a spaceship, Spaceship Earth.

And he can't wait to see where it takes him next.

Not For A Billion
Gazillion Dollars

To Kevin Davis,
a truly great teacher and an even better friend

ACKNOWLEDGMENTS

Many thanks:
To my friends who listened to much of this manuscript
on the phone – Bruce Coville, Pam Swallow – and to
Ben Blair, kid consultant, and Craig Virden, for being
a very wonderful editor.

Chapter 1

"What do you think, Matthew, that money just grows on trees?" Mrs Martin stares at her son.

Matthew, who is on his knees with his hands in a praying position, debates saying to his mother, *If money doesn't grow on trees how come banks have branches?*

He decides against it. Instead, he begs, "Oh, please. Oh, please. Oh, please. It's the best computer program ever, the graphics, the capabilities. And it only costs a couple of hundred dollars."

"A couple of hundred dollars." Mr Martin leans back on the kitchen counter, pretending to faint and then revive. "If it's not a new game you want, it's a new computer program. If it's not that, it's a new bike. Or the latest shoes."

"I needed those shoes. They improved my basketball game," Matthew informs them.

Sighing, Mrs Martin says, "Practice improved your game, not a pair of shoes."

"This computer program does everything," Matthew continues to plead. "Please, Mom. Please, Dad."

He gives them his best look, the one that says, *I'm your only son. I get good marks. I don't cause any major trouble, at least not the way my older sister does. I have cute brown hair that gets very red in the sun and I know that you really love my freckles.*

His best look isn't working.

Matthew's parents just shake their heads.

"Why can't you just copy the program?" Mrs Martin asks.

"That's illegal." Matthew looks up at his father. "Dad, you're a lawyer. You know I shouldn't do that. Anyway, the company has it blocked so that no one can make a copy—and furthermore, buying the program also connects me through the modem with their special bulletin board."

Mrs Martin sighs again.

Not a good sign, Matthew thinks. So far his parents have sighed, frowned, and shaken their heads. Matthew's knees are beginning to hurt from kneeling. He doesn't want to give up, though.

This is all Amanda's fault, he thinks. Amanda, the sister from Hell. Life isn't fair. Amanda got born first and then she acted like a little angel for years so that he got into trouble for being the bad little brother. Then, zap, one day she stopped being a little angel and Mr and Mrs Martin decided to become much stricter parents. And now, Matthew is stuck trying to deal with all their new techniques.

"Don't you want me to get a good job someday? How am I going to become the best computer-game inventor if I don't have all the necessary materials? Do you want me to have no future? I'll end up jobless, with no self-esteem, with no place to go, not even a coin to phone home with to ask for help. Everyone will say, 'Those Martins. They let poor Matthew, the one with all that promise, fall by the wayside.' "

"I wish he would promise to stop nagging us." Mr Martin grins at his wife.

She grins back and then looks down again, at Matthew. "Get up, my son. You're wearing out the knees of the new jeans that you just couldn't live without."

Matthew clutches his heart and says, "My own parents."

Mrs Martin gestures for her son to rise.

Matthew gives it one last try, staying on his knees. "Please, I beseech you, oh, mighty parental units, who can afford to buy a brand-new deluxe estate car but can't afford to buy their only son a measly computer program."

Mrs Martin starts to get annoyed. "It's not a matter of what we can afford, it's a matter of how much we want to just give you. You have no appreciation of the value of money, of how hard we have to work for it. As for that estate car, I needed it for my business and what's more, I earned it."

She can feel her blood pressure rising.

Her son also rises.

Now it's his turn to sigh. "I'd earn my own money if I could. That's just a lot for someone my age to earn. By the time I saved up for that program, it would be out of date."

"Exactly. You're asking for something that won't be state of the art for very long. And it's not as if we haven't bought you excellent equipment."

"I know," Matthew acknowledges. "It's just that this is such a great program..."

His parents start taking out the ingredients to make milk shakes.

Mrs Martin takes out Tiger's Milk, wheat germ, protein powder, and oranges.

Mr Martin takes out milk, chocolate syrup, and ice cream.

They each use their own blenders.

Matthew gazes longingly at his father's blender.

"I'll share," his father offers.

Another sigh escapes the health-conscious Mrs Martin.

Matthew grins. "Thanks."

There's a pause as Matthew thinks, watching his father pour the mixture into glasses.

Matthew tries again. "You're sending Amanda to Camp Sarah Bernhardt. It's very expensive, right? It's an acting camp, right? I don't see why she gets to go to a camp to learn how to be an actress, which she will never earn any money doing, because she's a terrible actress. She can't even act like a human being most of the time. All I want is the money to buy a computer program, which will teach me skills that will help me earn lots of money when I grow up that will help me to support you in your old age. I bet that someday I'll even make enough to help support Amanda in her old age after she never gets a job as an actress."

"Matthew, your sister has known for a long time that she wants to be an actress. And even if she changes her mind, this camp is a good idea for her right now." His mother pours her health drink into a glass and then stirs it with a piece of celery. "And, for your information, your sister is paying part of the camp costs. She's using money from baby-sitting, birthday presents, and saved pocket money."

Thinking about how much trouble Amanda has caused, all the things that she's done in the past few months, Matthew wonders whether he should start doing some things, too, so that he can get what he wants. Maybe he should shave off all the hair on his head, pretend to get his nose pierced, spend a lot of time in his room crying the way his sister has been doing.

He decides that's not what he wants to do.

Instead he says, "I know. You love her more than you love me."

Arranging his face into a pout, lower lip slightly forward, trying hard to make the saddest face he knows how to make, Matthew waits for his parents' reaction.

Mr and Mrs Martin look at each other, shake their heads, and then look at their son.

Matthew tries to hold the look but starts to smile.

Handing his son a milk shake, Mr Martin says, "Enough already. You're not going to wear us down this time. Matthew, we're not going to spend hundreds of dollars on something that we're not even sure that you're going to use. We know that you like them, but you haven't been using the computer the way that you used to."

Now, Matthew feels really frustrated. "When I played computer games all the time, you told me to get out and be with my friends. Now I do that. But I still want to work with the computer, and this program is really the most advanced one ever."

"Matthew, over the years we've spent a lot of money on things that you just couldn't live without and then once we bought them, you lost interest." His father sounds very irritated.

His mother continues. "What about the remote-control car you *had* to have but never play with anymore? What about all of those computer games that you think are too easy now? What about the clothes you just had to have and won't wear anymore?"

Matthew tries to defend himself. "Mom, I'm too old for some of those things now. The games *are* too easy. *No one* plays with remote-control cars anymore. And what am I supposed to do, keep wearing my old Smurf clothes forever?"

"Matthew"—his mother starts to smile—"You know that I'm not talking about Smurf clothes."

Matthew's getting more and more frustrated.

Why can't his parents see that he's not a little kid anymore?

He takes a few minutes to think, slurping on his straw as he finishes his milk shake.

"I've got an idea," Matthew says. "What if I can earn half of the money—will you contribute the other half?"

His parents look at each other, doing their Martin parents' telepathic thing, and both nod yes at the same time.

"All right!" Matthew sticks his fist into the air.

Now all he's got to do is figure out how to earn the money—and show his parents that he really is growing up.

Chapter 2

ROOM TO RENT
NEED A PLACE TO STAY IN SCENIC CALIFON,
NEW JERSEY?

Room available for summer months in a really nice house, while sister is away at drama camp. During year it is used by a demented but neat thirteen-year-old. COST: Half the price of computer program that renter can't live without.

EXTRA ADDED ATTRACTIONS—Very healthy food served (especially if you like sprouty tofu—if not, my father and I will share our very excellent hidden supply of junk food). For a little bit more money you can wear previous occupant's weird clothes. (All different because she is "trying to find out who the real Amanda Martin is." I can tell you: She's a Barfburger.)

CONTACT MATTHEW MARTIN AT (908)555-1144

"What a doofus." Joshua Jackson stares at his best friend. "You can't rent out your sister's room."

"Give me one good reason." Matthew sits down on a picnic table at the recreation field. "Just give me one good reason."

Joshua starts counting on his fingers. "One, Amanda is still at home. She doesn't leave for camp for three more days. Two, your parents will never allow a stranger to stay in the house. Three, the neighbourhood isn't zoned for hotels. Four, your parents will not think that renting out a room in the house that *they* pay a mortgage on is what they meant when they said that you had to *work* for your half of the payment."

"I said, just give me *one* good reason." Matthew folds the ad for renting the room into a paper airplane.

"Five," Joshua continues, "you are really a doofoid if you think that Amanda won't kill you for renting out her room."

"I'm willing to share the profits with her." Matthew throws the paper plane at Joshua. "Ninety per cent for me, ten percent for her. Lately she's been threatening to move out on her own. This way she'll earn something without having to do anything. And this will give her some money to use at camp. And she won't even be around to have to deal with the stranger I rent her room to. *I'm* the one who will have to deal with the stranger."

"Stranger is what you get every day," Joshua kids. "You know that your family wouldn't go along with this scheme. Why don't you just buy a cheaper program? There are a lot of them you can get."

Matthew shakes his head. "Not one like this. With

this program I can make holograms, produce animated features, link up with a modem to a program with the best computer programmers on line."

"Okay, okay." Joshua stops him. "Enough already. I believe you. For someone who is always fooling around, you really do take this stuff seriously."

Wishing that his parents realized how serious he is about the program, Matthew nods and then gets hit on the head by a basketball.

Tyler White rushes over. "I'm sorry. Are you all right?"

Feeling his head for bumps and blood, Matthew says, "I think so."

Billy Kellerman also rushes over. "Let me help. Do you have a concussion? A subdermal hematoma?"

"I'm fine." Matthew does not want Billy to do anything.

Billy comes closer, touching Matthew on the head. "I'm going to be a doctor, remember? I'm a doctor's son. Let me help you."

"Checking for head lice?" Vanessa Singer stops by the table and makes a face at Matthew.

Matthew looks at her and snarls. "If he was looking for lice, or more likely, a louse—he would have come straight to you."

"Maybe Billy's going to become a psychiatrist. That's why he's examining your head." Vanessa laughs at her own joke.

Matthew stares at the person with whom he has a mutual torment society and says, "If he's a headshrinker, he certainly would have no reason to check you out—pea brain."

"He's got you." Joshua licks his finger and acts like he's keeping score on an air scoreboard.

Rubbing his sore head, Matthew looks at Vanessa and says, "Why don't you just mind your own business? Why did you come over here? I wasn't bothering you."

"Not this time." Vanessa gets ready to list all of the times that Matthew has bothered her.

Matthew cuts her off by saying, "Look if you've come over here because you want to play doctor with Billy, why don't you just say so?"

Billy pretends to take a stethoscope out of an imaginary medical bag.

Blushing, Vanessa says, "You boys are such pigs."

As she leaves, the boys start to oink and snort.

"You're so mean to her." Jil! Hudson walks up to them. "She'll never forget this moment of torment as long as she lives. When she comes back to the fiftieth reunion of our graduation from sixth grade, she'll still remember how you all oinked and snorted at her."

The boys all stare at Jil!, whose high sense of drama caused her to change the second *l* in her name to an exclamation mark and who, her parents tell her, "makes mountains out of molehills."

"They don't have reunions for sixth-grade graduations," Matthew reminds her. "And she started it."

"She did." Joshua sticks up for his friend.

Tyler grabs his basketball, makes sure that there's

no blood on it and that Matthew has not dented it, and heads back to the basketball court.

Billy and Joshua follow him, leaving Jil! and Matthew alone at the table. Jil! sits down and looks at the field by the school. "Just think. By this time next week the summer recreation programme will be here and I'll be stuck up at the lake, watching my bratty little brother and waiting for my mother to give birth to another future person that I will have to baby-sit."

"Are they going to pay you?" Matthew asks.

Jil! nods. "Yeah. But not enough for all that I have to do, especially now."

"Can I borrow the money that you make? There's this really great computer program that I have to have and my parents won't—"

Jil! lightly slugs him on the arm. "Matthew Martin. You already owe me money for the last movie that we went to. I don't mind paying for myself, although I have heard rumours that in some cultures boys actually sometimes pay for their date's tickets. And anyway, I want to use that money to buy myself some clothes for seventh grade so that my mother can't always tell me what to wear."

"But it's a great program. I'll even let you use it." Matthew puts his hand on the hand that has just lightly slugged him on the arm.

Jil!, knowing how much computers mean to Matthew, realizes that he has just paid her a great compliment. She also likes having his hand on hers, but she is not going to give in. "No, Matthew. I'm not going to

loan you the money. You know that you owe half the
kids in sixth grade money and that you never pay it back."

Matthew nods, knowing that she's not going to give in,
knowing also that it's not half the class that he owes
money to, but three quarters of it.

Jil! changes the subject. "Are you going to miss me
when I go away? After all, I'm going to be gone most of
the summer."

Matthew continues to think about how he's going to
get the money that he needs for the program.

Jil! takes his hand off her hand and sticks out her
lower lip. "Answer. Aren't you going to miss me?"

Matthew looks at Jil!, remembering how just a few
months ago, he thought that all girls were slug slime
and how different it's been now that he likes her. He
also thinks about how he's been discovering how
much more fun it is to kiss a girl than kiss a relative
and how until just recently he and Jil! have talked
about spending the summer learning to become really
good kissers by practising a lot.

But her parents have decided that renting a cabin at
the lake will be restful for Mrs Hudson, who is very
pregnant and "wants to just stick her feet in the water."

It doesn't seem fair to Matthew that Mr and Mrs
Hudson have ruined Jil! and Matthew's kissing plan
when they have obviously been doing some kissing of
their own.

Matthew, even though he is not absolutely positive
of all of the steps that caused the future Baby Hudson,

knows that his and Jil!'s plans don't go that far. In fact, they secretly call the plan "Elementary Lips."

Matthew wishes that Mrs Hudson would just stick her feet in the home bathtub instead of having to go to the lake.

"Are you going to miss me?" Jil! repeats.

Matthew, realising that he really *is* going to miss her, nods and thinks about how quickly some things change when you're growing up.

And then he thinks about how slowly other things change, about how hard it is to convince his parents that he really is growing up, and how it's sometimes hard for him to think about growing up, and how Elementary Lips was doomed before it even started.

He stops thinking when Jil! leans over and gives him a quick kiss, when no one on the playground is watching.

Suddenly summer seems a long, long time.

Chapter 3

"Why do I have to lay the table?" Amanda slams the dishes down. "How come that little turd-le brain never has to do anything?"

"I laid the table last night. And anyway, they like me better than they likc you." Matthew informs her, and then turns to his parents, who are preparing two kinds of salad dressing, cucumber yogurt and Russian. "Did you hear what she called me — turd?"

"I said tuRTle." Amanda looks smug.

"Whose idea was it to have children anyway?" Mr Martin mixes the mayonnaise with ketchup. "Honey, would you please refresh my memory?"

Mrs Martin adds caraway seeds to her dressing. "I think it was my mother's idea. She kept clutching her heart and saying, 'When will I have grandchildren? What if I die before I hear some sweet little voice saying, "Grammy, I love you."?' So we decided to do it for her and then she moved to Florida. Now our children call her and say, 'Thanks for the cheque,' and 'Grammy, I love you,' and then we have them the rest of the time."

"We should have got a parrot instead. Over the phone she would never have known the difference." Mr Martin adds more mayonnaise to his dressing.

"You two think you are so funny." Amanda slams another dish down on the table. "You're always telling us how much you wanted to have us and now you're making up this dumb story just to be funny. Why does everything always have to be a joke with you? I can't wait to get to drama camp, where all I have to do is study acting and not be treated like a waitress and not always have you kidding around."

Mr Martin taste-tests his dressing and adds a little more mayonnaise to it. "Someday you're going to thank us for making you lay the table. Most people who want to be actresses end up waiting on tables at some point in their careers."

Amanda sticks her nose up in the air.

Matthew thinks about lobbing a spoonful of mayonnaise onto it.

"Let's all sit down and have a peaceful dinner," Mrs Martin pleads. "Tonight is Amanda's last night with us and I want it to go well."

Amanda looks at her watch and says, "I'm going out to meet some friends after dinner."

"Be home by ten," Mrs Martin tells her. "You've got to finish packing and you're going to have to get up very early tomorrow."

Amanda sighs but nods yes.

"So what's new?" Mr Martin asks, once everyone is seated and has started to eat.

"New York . . . New Jersey . . . New Hampshire . . . New Monia," Matthew answers.

"Can't you tell him not to be such a dork?" Amanda looks at her parents.

"I said New York, not New Dork." Matthew takes a forkful of mashed potatoes.

Mr Martin decides to change the subject. "Do you know yet what plays they will be doing at camp?"

Shaking her head, Amanda watches as Matthew puts the mashed potatoes into his mouth and tries to blow a bubble with them.

Choosing to ignore him, she continues. "They don't announce it ahead of time any more because some of the kids used to come to camp with the parts that they wanted totally memorized. Some of them even worked with their own drama coaches before they got there, and that wasn't fair to the other kids."

"Are you nervous?" Mrs Martin says softly.

Suddenly Amanda doesn't seem so angry. She nods, quietly.

"It'll work out okay." Mrs Martin pats her daughter's hand and remembers how hard it was growing up.

"I really want to go, get away from here," Amanda says.

"Are we that terrible as parents?" Mr Martin says, thinking about all of the family counselling sessions they have attended.

"No," Amanda says softly. "It's just everything. Nothing's gone right this year. I don't know who I am. I don't know why Danny broke up with me. I don't know why everything seems so hard all of a sudden. No. You're not *that* terrible as parents."

Matthew asks, "Am I that terrible as a younger brother?"

She nods and grins.

Matthew grins back. "Good. I do my best."

"If you want to come home from camp, don't be afraid to tell us. You can come home any time," Mr Martin says.

There goes the chance to rent out her room, Matthew thinks.

"But don't give up too easily, either, honey. I bet that this is going to be a great summer for you," Mrs Martin reassures her.

"I hope so." Amanda finishes eating and looks at her watch. "Is it okay if I go now so that I can see my friends and be back by ten?"

Mrs Martin is unsure. "The person who lays the table is supposed to clean up also."

Matthew volunteers. "I'll do it."

Everyone looks at him unbelievingly.

"I've been possessed by a demon," he kids. "To-morrow we can call an exorcist. Tonight I'll clean up."

"Are you going to try to make me pay for this?" Amanda wants to know.

Matthew shakes his head.

Mrs Martin looks on in disbelief.

Mr Martin, who loves an old television show called *Leave It to Beaver*, picks up his plate and says, "Well, Beav, you certainly are being nice to your sibling. Let me help you clear this table."

As the Martin men clean up, they hum the theme music to *Leave It to Beaver*.

Amanda leaves, mumbling, "This is some kind of plot to make me miss them, to make me be homesick, to not let me try to separate and become my own person. It's not going to work."

Drying the dishes, Matthew thinks about how, in less than twenty-four hours, he's practically going to be an only child, about how his first and only sort of girlfriend is going away for the summer, and about how he's already had enough advances on his pocket money to keep him broke until school starts in September.

And the summer is just beginning.

Chapter 4

"Well, here we are. Another summer at the recreation programme. New grounds, new equipment, same old stuff for the little kids to make." Matthew sits down on a table and picks up some of the pot holders left behind by some of the six to eight-year-old campers. "Do you think I could pay those kids twenty five cents for each of these and then sell them for fifty cents?"

"Not another money-making scheme." Billy pretends to yawn. "That's all we've heard about lately."

Holding up a fluorescent pot holder, Matthew says, "I bet someone would pay fifty cents for this. My mother always paid that for mine."

Lisa takes the pot holder from his hand. "She bought it because she's your mother and it's a parent thing to do, to buy misshapen, loosely looped, and miswoven pot holders from their kids. But no one, except for a relative or a neighbour of the kid who made the stupid pot holder, will *buy* the stupid pot holder."

Matthew tries to think of other ways to earn money.

Lisa looks around the table at everyone who has gathered. "So where are all of the soon-to-be seventh graders?" she asks. "Inquiring minds want to know."

Zoe Alexander tosses her blond hair. "I know. I know."

"Zoe spends half her life on the telephone." Tyler White puts his arm around Zoe's waist.

"But the other half I devote to you." Zoe puts her head on his shoulder. "I have since we first started to go together."

Oh, puke, Matthew thinks.

Zoe begins her list of classmate whereabouts. "Jil!, as Matthew knows so well, has just left for the lake."

"She'd rather jump in the lake than be around him for the summer." Vanessa looks up from the lanyard she is making.

"I hope that's a noose you're working on, one for *your* neck." Matthew glares at her.

"Lighten up, you guys. All of this fighting is getting very boring." Billy pretends to yawn.

"She started it," Matthew says, thinking about how many times he has used that phrase, first about his sister Amanda and now about Vanessa.

Zoe ignores them, continuing her report. "Lizzie's spending the summer with her father and his family in Montana. Jessica and her family are going driving cross-country, camping out."

Matthew thinks about how much he likes teasing Jessica and her family about their last name, which is

Weeks, and says, "As soon as they left town, the summer in Califon got shorter, since four Weeks are now gone."

People groan and Vanessa says, "That is just so lame."

"Sarah and her horse have gone off to riding camp. Katie and her bike are part of a tour around the Grand Canyon. I spoke to her last week and the blisters on her feet have blisters." Zoe giggles.

"Your phone bill must be so gigantic." Ryma Browne shakes her head.

"It's part of the divorce settlement. My mother's lawyer negotiated it so that I could make all the phone calls I wanted and my father would pay them," Zoe explains. "To continue, although I have not heard directly from the boys, since most of them hate to use the phone, I can only give you some information: David Cohen has gone to space camp and then his parents are driving cross-country. He'll be back soon. Patrick's parents' divorce went through and his mom is making him move away to where she's going. Pablo is going to Puerto Rico to spend the summer with his grandparents."

"And I'm looking after his snakes." Mark Ellison walks up to the table. "And here they are, Boa'd With School and Vindscreen Viper."

Most of the girls scream and run off, except for Vanessa, who mumbles, "How immature," Cathy Atwood, who likes snakes, and Zoe, who goes "Eek! Eek!" and falls into Tyler's arms.

"I'm taking them for a walk," Mark informs all of

those who are left.

"Don't you mean 'taking them for a slither'?" Matthew grins. "Where are their collars? Do they have a new leash on life?"

"That was a very dumb joke, very dumb." Vanessa makes a thumbs-down gesture.

"For once I agree." Joshua holds his nose. "That joke stinks."

Zoe moves out of Tyler's embrace and he puts his arm around her waist. "And our next-door neighbour, Daniella, told me that her niece, Lacey, and nephew, Jimmy, will be visiting her for the summer, while their parents are building houses for some group."

"How old are her niece and nephew? Are they old enough to be on our baseball team?" Tyler is always trying to get the best team together.

"The girl is our age. And the boy, I think, is a little younger."

Tyler takes his arm away from Zoe's waist and swings an imaginary baseball bat. "I hope that they're good. I want our recreation team to be the best."

"I'll be the best cheerleader." Zoe tilts her head and places Tyler's arm back around her waist.

"I know just what the cheer should be." Matthew gets up from the table and pretends that he is holding on to pom-poms. "Give me a *B*...an *A*...an *R*...an *F*...What do they spell...?"

"I shudder to think about what he's going to be like with Jil! away. She was such a good influence." Zoe looks at Matthew, who has just fallen in the dirt trying to do a cartwheel.

Matthew gets up, wipes off the dust, and thinks about how boring it gets during the summer when there's no place to go and not much to do. *Someone*, he thinks, *has got to make things exciting.*

And then he thinks, *That someone is me. This is going to be a Matthew Martin summer production....Tune in tomorrow.*

Chapter 5

"All right, you guys. You think that this is your turf? Well, I'm here to tell you it's not. Your days are numbered." Matthew tries to sound like the hero of every action movie he has ever seen. "I'm the one who's gonna cut you down to size."

There's not a sound from his opposition.

Matthew continues. "You think you can just sprout up where you want and exhibit your blades and that everyone will just let you grow freely, run wild over this land? Well, I'm the man who's gonna mow you down."

There's still not a sound from his opposition.

"Scared, huh?" Matthew speaks menacingly. "Well, you should be. I'm gonna run circles around you and cut you down in your prime."

Matthew finishes mowing his initials into the grass and then continues work on Mrs Levy's lawn. "This is so boring. It takes a lot to make it interesting." He thinks about how many neighbourhood lawns he's mowed lately and about how it's taking so long to earn the money he needs. Then he accidentally runs the mower into a cow lawn-ornament, one of those fuzzy cloth things that look like there's a midget bovine munching on the grass.

"Sorry. You should have mooooooooooooooooooved over." Matthew starts to laugh.

He looks up at the house to make sure that Mrs Levy, the "Cow Collector of Califon," hasn't seen him almost run over the large ornament.

It's a shame we don't live in Cowlifon, Matthew thinks.

"Matthew," Mrs Levy calls from the house.

Oh no, he thinks, she's seen me. *It's an udder disaster.*

"Matthew." Mrs Levy repeats her call.

Turning off the lawn mower, Matthew heads up the hill to her house. As he walks past the cow mailbox, he thinks about how he's almost done with the mowing and now he's going to have to use the money that he's earned to pay for repairing the cow.

Mrs Levy's looking a little frantic.

Matthew thinks of what his father always says — "Don't have a cow over this" — and hopes that Mrs Levy doesn't have one because he ran the "lawn mooer" over her yard ornament.

Mrs Levy is very nervous. "Matthew, I've just had a call from my friend who lives a few blocks away. She's had an accident carving up a turkey and wants me to come over immediately. Theo and the baby are taking a nap, and I think it would be easier and faster if I left them here for the few minutes I will be gone. Would you mind baby-sitting for them until I get back? I'll only be gone a few minutes."

A few minutes — easy, a piece of cake, Matthew thinks, and says, "Sure."

Mrs Levy doesn't look very confident. "Matthew, are you certain you can handle this?"

Matthew gives her what he hopes is his most competent look. "Yes, I can."

"The baby is very young, only two months old. Maybe I should take her with me, but I hope I'll be back before she even wakes up. It's just around the corner. I've written down the number and put it next to the phone with all of the other emergency numbers."

The phone rings.

Mrs Levy picks it up. "I'm on my way. Don't panic. I'll be right there."

Putting down the phone, Mrs Levy looks at Matthew and says, "Are you sure you can handle this?"

Matthew nods. "I can always call my mother if there's a problem."

"Promise?" Mrs Levy keeps walking to the door and back again.

"I promise." Matthew opens the kitchen door. "It'll be all right. I'm very mature for my age."

At least I'm very mature for my age right this second, Matthew almost adds, but realizes that a joke at this time is a very bad idea.

Mrs Levy says, "Look, Matthew. My friend is a bit of a hypochondriac. She's a big worrier. So all this is going to take, I hope, is my going over there, looking at the cut, telling her that she's going to live, and then coming right back here. This is not the first time something like this has happened."

"I'll be glad to help out," Matthew says, thinking, *What can go wrong?*

Mrs Levy stands there for a minute and then makes a decision and leaves, telling Matthew that she'll be back in just a few minutes. Matthew is left alone in the house with two children, who he hopes stay asleep until their mother returns. He decides to check out what kind of junk food is in the refrigerator. Just as he gets to the refrigerator door, he stops and thinks about how he wants his parents to see him as grown up and responsible.

Going straight to the refrigerator does not seem the best way to prove it, so he goes to the phone to call his mother. Matthew wants to let his mother know that Mrs Levy thinks that he is grown up enough to handle an emergency. He also wants to make sure that his mother is on alert in case he needs to call her for help.

Matthew picks up the phone, which is shaped like a cow lying in a pasture. Picking up the top part, he holds it up to his ear.

It feels weird, as if any minute the cow is going to start leaking milk into his ear. *Oh, well*, he thinks, *I guess it's time to cowll my mother and tell her what's happening.*

He dials, the phone rings, and his mother answers. "Martin's Missives. May I help you?"

"Mom, it's me." Matthew can feel the cow-tail yarn tickle his chin. "Don't worry. It's no gigantic emergency. I just have to tell you something."

"Are you sure that everything's okay? I have a customer on the other line, but I'll ask her to wait if it's an emergency."

"I can wait," Matthew informs her.

Mrs Martin switches back to her other phone call, putting Matthew on hold. Being on hold means having to listen to a taped message about his mother's company. Matthew listens to how a person can hire a person dressed in a costume to deliver a gift or message.

He wonders if anyone has ever sent Mrs Levy a messenger dressed as a cow. He debates sending her someone in a boy cow costume, along with a message saying, "Your collection is really a lot of bull," but decides that wouldn't be very good for his own business and he really does want the new computer software.

Mrs Martin gets back on the phone. "Okay, honey. What's happening?"

Matthew explains about Mrs Levy's emergency and how he's looking after her two still-sleeping children.

"Honey, you've never been around a baby for any amount of time. Do you know what to do?"

"It's not hard. I watched Jil! practise on an old doll, so I can feed the kid and burp it." Matthew takes the cow tail on the end of the phone and puts it on his upper lip, pretending it's a moustache. That makes him feel older and much more competent.

Mrs Martin sighs. "I wish that I could come over and help, but I've got to watch the store and answer the phone. If this is an emergency, I will close down and come over."

"Mom. This is *not* an emergency. What do you think I am? A baby?" Matthew feels that, once again, he isn't given enough credit.

"Okay." Mrs Martin decides to let Matthew handle the situation, although she's nervous.

She spends the next five minutes telling him how to hold the baby, what to do if the baby starts to cry, how to change the nappy, and how to warm up formula.

Suddenly a telephone operator comes in on the call and explains that Mrs Levy wants to talk to him.

Matthew says good-bye to his mother and hello to Mrs Levy, who is frantic because the telephone line has been busy for so long.

"Matthew, is everything all right? Please. I don't want you to stay on the phone talking to your friends." She sounds upset. "Are the children all right?"

Matthew starts to get annoyed and then remembers that he mowed into her cow, and if she knows about that, she probably thinks that he's going to do that to her kids.

He explains that he was talking to his mother, getting instructions on the care, feeding, and nappy-changing of babies.

"And, Mrs Levy," he informs her, "Mom says if there is a big problem, she'll close the store and come over here immediately."

There's a huge sigh of relief from the other side of the phone.

Mrs Levy explains that her friend has cut herself very badly and they are rushing to the hospital. Then she gives him the number of the casualty ward and makes him promise to take good care of her children.

Matthew promises.

After the phone call is over, Matthew goes into the baby's room and looks at the sleeping two-month-old.

Putting his finger in front of her nose, Matthew checks to make sure that she is breathing.

She is.

He walks into Theo's room. Theo is awake and jumping up and down on his bed.

Matthew thinks about how much fun it would be to join him, but then remembers that he is now in charge and that would probably not be such a good idea.

Theo stops jumping and asks for his mother.

Matthew explains that she's gone out for a few minutes and Theo starts to cry.

Matthew tells him not to worry. Theo continues to cry.

"Want to read a book? Watch television? Play baseball?"

More crying from Theo. "I want my mommy."

There's a moment when Matthew thinks about how he wants his mommy, too, to help him out of his dilemma, but then he starts offering more choices.

"How about playing a game? Doing a puzzle? Looking

under the sofa cushions for loose change?"

Theo is still crying.

"How about looking in the refrigerator for something good to eat?" Matthew suggests.

Theo stops yelling, "Mommy. Mommy. Mommy," and says, "Ice cream."

"If it's in the freezer, it's ours." Matthew smiles.

The boys head into the kitchen, look in the refrigerator, and discover a carton of cherry swirl ice cream.

In three minutes they are eating the ice cream and quietly watching television.

Matthew is sitting there, proud that he has handled the situation so well, even though he knows that neither of the moms will be overjoyed by the consumption of junk food.

He thinks about how easy this is going to be.

The phone rings.

It's Mrs Levy again, checking to make sure that her children are all right.

The phone wakes up the baby.

And the crying really starts.

Chapter 6

Matthew and Theo stare down at the screaming baby.

"I guess she won't shut up if I give her some cherry swirl," Matthew says.

"My mother usually breast-feeds her when she wakes up," Theo tells him.

"No way." Matthew shakes his head.

Theo giggles.

"How old are you?" Matthew asks him.

Theo holds up one hand. "This many." He has four fingers raised.

"Well, you remember this better than I do. It was done to you more recently. What did your mother do to stop you from crying?"

"I already told you." Theo sticks his thumb into his mouth.

"The formula," Matthew remembers.

He heads to the refrigerator and takes out a bottle, trying to remember about warming it up. Matthew holds the bottle in his hands, staring at it with all sorts of questions in his head. *How hot do I make it? How*

*do I warm it up? Can it be nuked? What happened to
the nipple on the bottle?*

In the background he can hear the baby screaming.

Theo stands in front of him. "More ice cream."

"Not now," Matthew tells him.

Theo starts to cry.

"Not now," Matthew pleads.

"Now." Theo stamps his foot.

"No ice cream now. No crying now," Matthew demands.

Theo drops to the floor and starts pounding on it. In the
background the baby seems to be screaming even louder.
Matthew rushes into the living room, where he remembers having seen a portable non-cow phone and
quickly calls his mother.

"Martin's Missives."

"Mom. I need help. Everyone's crying except me...so
far," he tells her. "Theo is throwing a temper tantrum
because I said he couldn't have any more ice cream."

"*You* said no more ice cream?" she exclaims. "Let me
mark this date on my calendar."

"Mom, this is no time for sarcasm. I'm having a major
problem here." Matthew moves towards the baby's room,
holding on to the cold bottle of formula.

Reaching the cot, he says to his mother, "Here. I want
you to listen to this." He holds the phone next to the
screaming baby.

Then he gets back on the phone. "Mom, why is she
crying like that? She's been doing that since she woke
up."

"Remember what I told you earlier? Did you pick her up? Give her warm milk? Check to see if her nappy needs changing?" Mrs Martin asks.

"No, I didn't do any of those things," he says.

"Put down the phone for a minute and pick her up carefully. I'll wait to see what happens."

Matthew puts down the phone and carefully lifts up the baby, who continues to cry. He lays her down and picks up the phone again. "I guess she doesn't find me charming."

"Look in her nappy. See if she's wet or something."

"Do I have to?" Matthew starts to whine.

"Yes."

Matthew checks. "She's wet *and* something."

His mother chuckles.

"This is not funny. This is gross. Couldn't they have house-trained her?"

This is so disgusting, Matthew thinks as he looks at the contents of the nappy he's just changed. *What have they been feeding this kid? Cream of baked beans?*

Matthew finishes the job, leaving the dirty Pamper in the cot. He wipes the baby ointment off his hands onto his jeans and gets back on the phone.

"Mission accomplished."

"Put the nappy in the garbage," his mother tells him.

Matthew can't figure out how she knows things she cannot see. Mrs Martin then reminds Matthew how to warm up the bottle, how to feed and burp the baby.

417

"Call me once everything is done and let me know how it's going," she says.

"If nothing works, would you please come over here?" he begs.

"Yes. But I have faith in you that you can handle this," she informs him, and then hangs up. She worries again but decides to wait and see.

Over at the Levy house Matthew feels like his only line to the outside world is gone and he's caught in Baby-sitter Hell.

The baby continues to cry and Theo is running around the room pretending to be an airplane.

Matthew picks the baby up and sings every song he knows to her. Finally, the fifth time he has hummed the theme song from *Leave It to Beaver* to her, she quiets down and starts looking at her fingernails.

Theo leaves the room, yelling, "I'm going to land now and refuel."

Matthew looks at the baby's fingernails and wonders how anything can be that small and ponders when those hands will be old enough to change someone else's nappies on her own.

He puts her back into the cot and goes back into the kitchen.

Theo is sitting at the kitchen table, eating ice cream straight out of the container.

Matthew wonders if he should get a spoon and join him.

Theo looks up at him and then spits into the carton. "All mine."

Matthew, at first is disgusted, and then marvels at
Theo's way of getting all the ice cream. He wonders
why he never thought of doing that so that Amanda
would not want the ice cream.

Still angry at Matthew for having said no, Theo is
making up a song about how he's going to chop Matthew up and feed him to the cows. Ignoring Theo,
Matthew tries to remember everything his mother told
him. First warm up water in a pan. Then fix the bottle
so that the nipple is outside. Then put the bottle into
the pan, making sure that it is no longer heating up.
When it seems ready, sprinkle a little of the formula on
the wrist to make sure that it isn't too hot or too cold,
that it's just right.

While he's waiting, Matthew looks around the
kitchen. There are cow salt and pepper shakers, cow
napkin rings, a cow creamer.

Matthew thinks about that. If the manufacturers
were being accurate, the milk should not be coming out
of the cow's mouth.

Matthew continues to look around. Cow mugs. Cow
prints on the wall. A cow butter dish. A cow calendar.
Cow egg cups.

Since when do cows come from eggs? Matthew wonders.

The milk is ready.

Matthew is not sure that he is ready to feed the baby,
but he goes back into her bedroom.

She's still there.

Theo walks in and watches as Matthew puts down the

bottle, picks up the baby, sits down in the chair, and realizes that he can't reach the bottle.

"Theo, please hand me the bottle," Matthew asks.

Theo looks at him. "I'll give it to you if you promise to buy me snot bubble gum."

"What?" Matthew yells.

The baby starts to cry. Matthew looks down, rocks her a little, and then looks back at Theo. "Snot bubble gum?"

"Yeah. My mommy said it was a waste of money and disgusting and I want it. It's a nose and you pull back this thing and snot bubble gum comes through the holes in the nose," Theo explains.

Matthew wonders why he's missed out on this nifty item. "Okay. Hand me the bottle and I'll get one for each of us."

Theo hands him the bottle, which Matthew then puts in the baby's mouth.

"It's not doing anything. Nothing's coming out." Matthew is feeling frustrated.

The baby starts to cry.

He takes the bottle out of the baby's mouth and holding it up to his face to look at it, he squeezes the nipple.

Milk squirts into his eye.

"Here goes." Blinking, Matthew puts the bottle back in the baby's mouth. "Yo, ho, ho and a bottle of formula. Drink up or ye'll have to walk the plank."

Pirate movies are another of his favourites.

The milk goes into the baby.

Matthew can also feel the milk come out of the baby.

It's streaming out of the nappy leg that he didn't make tight enough.

Matthew's lap is wet.

He sits there thinking about how he hopes that no one sees him going home.

Matthew remembers that he's got to burp the baby.

Carefully picking the baby up, he puts her on his shoulder, forgetting to place a cloth on his shoulder.

Patting her softly on her back, he starts to sing to her. "The worms go in, the worms go out, the worms play pinochle on your snout."

Theo listens, learning the words, and then joins in.

Matthew keeps patting the baby on the back.

The baby makes a little popping sound from her mouth.

"Mission accomplished." Matthew feels proud of himself until he feels a little stream of warm liquid running down his neck and into his T-shirt.

Picking the baby up, he puts her back into the cot and goes into the bathroom to take a look.

As he walks, he can feel the liquid trickling down his shoulder and onto his chest.

He can also hear the baby start to cry.

Matthew walks into the bathroom, takes off his shirt, and tries to clean it off by wetting a piece of toilet paper and rubbing it across the shirt. Soon there are wet, linty pieces of paper attached to it.

Taking more toilet paper, he wets it and wipes the liquid off his body.

Just as he is putting on his wet, linty shirt, Theo walks

in.

"Come play trucks with me." Theo tugs at Matthew's shirt and then wrinkles his nose. "Oh, you smell."

"Thank you for sharing that with me." Matthew glares down at him.

Theo says, "My daddy puts something on to make him smell good."

He points to a bottle on the shelf. Matthew realizes that it is the same stuff that his father uses and debates whether there is a rule about baby-sitters being able to use cologne.

He decides that if there is a rule, it should be yes, the baby-sitter may use the cologne if the baby-sitter smells like baby poop and puke. and didn't come into the house smelling like that.

Matthew uses the cologne, putting some on his shoulder, his chest, his neck, any place that he thinks may have been touched by baby puke, and then, as a final touch, puts some under his armpits.

"Me too." Theo grabs Matthew's knee.

The baby is still crying in the background, so Matthew quickly puts some on Theo.

They go back into the baby's room.

This time Matthew puts a cloth on his shoulder, picks up the baby, and sits down. The baby sticks her fingers in his eye.

Matthew manages not to say the bad word that is in his brain.

He's got to bribe Theo with another snot bubble gum to get him to bring over the bottle.

Soon, everything is quiet.

The baby is again drinking from the bottle.

Theo's on the floor, playing with his entire collection of trucks. "Vroom. Vroom. Vroom. Vroom."

Also on the floor is a tiny metal herd of cattle.

"Vroom. Vroom. Vroom. You cows stop having babies." Theo drives a dump truck into the herd.

Matthew talks to the baby. Not sure of what her interests are, he teaches her soccer rules and regulations, using a silly voice.

The baby laughs and laughs.

"What's your sister's name?" he asks Theo.

"Spot the Dog" is the answer.

"Theo, be serious." Matthew grins, remembering how he likes to call his own sister Godzilla.

"Her name is Cleo." Mrs Levy walks into the room and looks very relieved that her children are alive and well.

She picks Cleo up.

"Watch out. She's leaking," Matthew tells her.

"She does that." Mrs Levy smiles at him.

"Actually, she seems to leak from a lot of places." Matthew is relieved that Mrs Levy is back and that her children are alive and well.

"I know." Mrs Levy nods. "How did it go?"

"Okay, I guess," Matthew tells her. "It got easier after a while."

"Anything I should know?"

Matthew decides to tell her. "I put the nappy in the little rubbish bin. All of your ice cream is gone. And if it isn't, I don't think it's a good idea for the rest of the family to eat it."

"It was an accidental spit." Theo looks at the floor.

Mrs Levy looks at Matthew. "That's a new trick he's learned in nursery school. Something tells me that Theo is not totally happy not being an only child."

"I can understand that," Matthew says.

"Do you spit in the food too?" Theo asks.

"Big boys don't spit in their food," Matthew informs him.

Theo stares up at Matthew as if he's a hero. "Well, I won't either anymore."

"Thank you. Thank you. Thank you," Mrs Levy whispers to Matthew.

Suddenly Matthew feels very grown up.

"How's your friend?" he asks.

Mrs Levy says, "She's going to be all right. It was very messy and scary for a few minutes. The cut was very deep and took several stitches to close. No more electric carving knives for her."

Theo points to his mother's clothes and says, "Boo-boo."

Matthew notices that there is some blood on Mrs Levy's clothes.

Patting Theo on the head, Mrs Levy says, "Don't worry. It's not Mommy's boo-boo. I'm not hurt."

Mrs Levy speaks to Matthew again. "I'm very glad that I didn't take the children with me. It was not an easy situation."

Matthew tries to imagine what it was like.

Theo tugs on Matthew's leg. "Don't tell her about what you promised me."

Mrs Levy says, "What?"

"Not snot bubble gum," Theo tells her.

"Is it? Did you?" Mrs Levy asks.

Matthew does not like having to tell on Theo.

Mrs Levy lets him off the hook "You've done a good job. It's all right. Don't worry. I'll get him one the next time we go to the store."

"Two. He promised me two noses." Theo holds up two fingers.

Mrs Levy sighs but nods.

Matthew decides to confess about a few things. "I accidentally ran into the cow on your front lawn with the mower. It's okay, just a little bald in one spot. I'll pay for the damage."

"Don't worry. My husband actually ran over it once with the mower, so it already was damaged. He appears to be getting a little tired of my cow obsession."

"I can't understand why." Matthew tries to look serious and then he starts to laugh.

Mrs Levy laughs too. "Anything else I should know?"

"That's about it." Matthew tries to remember if there's anything else. "Oh, and I had to use some of your husband's cologne."

"I noticed." Mrs Levy smiles. "Let me guess. Cleo threw up on you."

Matthew nods. "And leaked."

Mrs Levy smiles and then takes out her wallet, which is make-believe cow hair, but not real cowhide. "Let me pay you now."

"Okay." Matthew is glad that she isn't making him pay for the cow or the cologne.

She hands him money for the mowing and then money for baby-sitting.

Matthew looks at it and then makes a decision. "Take back the money for baby-sitting. That was an emergency and I wanted to help out."

Mrs Levy gives him a great big smile and shakes her head. "Thank you. You're very nice. You worked hard. So I want to pay you."

Matthew smiles back and thinks about how good it was to make the offer and that it's also nice to still get the money.

He realizes that even if she had taken the baby-sitting money back, it would have been okay.

Leaving the house, he can hear Theo singing, "The worms crawl in, the worms crawl out," and he can hear Mrs Levy saying, "Who taught you that?"

Matthew also realizes that as much as he needs money, baby-sitting is not going to be the way he's going to earn it.

Chapter 7

Matthew Martin, Computer Genius, Matthew thinks as
he sits in front of the terminal creating a card for Jil!.

The person who I miss is Jil!
I would fone but I'm afraid of the bil!,
I like her better than pickles, sweet or dil!,
My heart, with major like, she does fil!,
If I were a fish, instead of my heart it would be my
gil!,
It's really Matthew and Jil!, who went up the hil!,
Thinking of how far away you are makes me il!,
I'm tired of having so much time to kil!,
I'm so glad that your name is not Lil!,
I can't think of a sentence for mil!,
I'm not sure if you spell this word nil!,
Vanessa Singer is still acting like a pil!,
And I want to jab her with a quil!,
I wish that you were in Califon stil!,
(the still like in "still here" not the still that makes
illegal alcohol where people pay and put money in
the til!)

If your parents let you come back soon, I will remember them in my wil!

Matthew pushes the print button and the card comes
out.

Pleased with it, he only wishes that he already had
the new program. Then he could create something
really special.

There's a knock on the bedroom door, actually five
knocks, followed by two more — *dum, dum, di, dum,
dum . . . dum dum* — followed by Joshua calling out,
"Ready or not, here I come."

The door opens.

Joshua jumps in, pretends to trip, and crumples to
the floor, calling out, "I've fallen and I can't get up."

Matthew looks at his best friend and says, "You've
been watching too much television."

Joshua continues to lie on the floor.

Every few minutes he attempts to rise and then slumps
down again, saying, in an ever-weakening voice, "I've
fallen and I can't get up."

Matthew steps over his friend and says, "Let's get
going. We've got work to do."

Joshua crawls over to the computer area to see
Matthew's latest project.

Jumping up, he grabs the card that is lying on the
table.

Matthew rushes over to stop him but it is too late.

Joshua starts reading it aloud and laughing.

"Come on. Stop that." Matthew tries to get the card

out of Joshua's hands but can't get to him because
Joshua keeps jumping away from him, like a kangaroo.

"Why don't you just fall down again and not be
able to get up?" Matthew tries to trip him.

Joshua jumps over Matthew's foot and exclaims,
"Jil!iet, oh, Jil!iet, where fort art thou?"

"That's 'forth', as in 'Where forth are you?' And it
was Romeo, not Juliet. And that's 'forth', like 'You're
acting like a forth grader.' F-O-R-T-H." Matthew
laughs. "Don't you remember anything about Shakespeare's plays after the unit Mrs Stanton taught us?"

It's Joshua's turn to laugh. "The grade is F-O-U-R-
T-H. You are the worst speller in the world."

"Thank you. Thank you." Matthew bows and then
grabs the card from Joshua.

"Whatever happened to the Matthew who hated
girls, who wanted nothing to do with them?" Joshua
teases. "The Matthew who started G.E.T.T.H.E.M.—
Girls Easy to Torment Hopes Eager Matthew?"

Matthew shrugs.

He's not sure he can explain it. He's not sure he
even understands it.

Joshua continues. "Matthew, who got girls so angry
that they started a group called G.E.T.H.I.M., Girls
Eager to Halt Immature Matthew? And now girls like
him, not just Jil! either? That new girl, Lacey, the one
who is just visiting her aunt for the summer, keeps
hanging around you. Do you like her?"

"Yeah. She's nice." Matthew shrugs.

"I mean, do you really like her?" Joshua looks

embarrassed.

"No, not like Jil!, if that's what you mean." Matthew shakes his head. "Lacey's okay. We're just becoming friends. She just likes to talk to me."

"Yeah. Sure." Joshua doesn't look pleased.

"Look, Lacey just came to the recreation centre two days ago." Matthew decides to tell Joshua what Lacey has been saying, even though he promised her that he wouldn't.

"Actually, the only reason that she talks to me is because you're my best friend and she wants to find out all about you."

"No." Joshua stares at Matthew. "Are you kidding me?"

Matthew raises his hand. "I swear. She's always talking about you, asking me questions like do you have a girlfriend?, do you like blondes?, what are your hobbies?"

"Really?" Joshua tries to act nonchalant. "And what did you tell her?"

"I told her that you hate most girls, think that blondes are the most disgusting people in the world, and that your hobbies are taking pictures of warts and counting people's nose hairs."

Joshua bangs his head against the wall.

"Just joking." Matthew stands next to him. "I told her that at the moment you don't have a girlfriend. I didn't tell her the truth that at no moment ever have you ever had a girlfriend. I told her that you liked girls with blond hair and that I can tell that you like her."

"How can you tell?" Joshua challenges his friend.

Matthew laughs. "I can tell because you punch her on the arm and yesterday you went up to her and showed her your special talent, how you can take your tongue and stick it all the way up your nose."

Joshua bangs his head on the wall again. "I can't believe I did that. It was so dumb. I just wanted to walk up to her and ask her if she was going on the ten-pin bowling trip, and instead I showed her that dumb trick."

Matthew pulls Joshua away from the wall. "It could have been worse. You could have stuck your tongue up *her* nose."

Joshua starts laughing. "That's so gross."

"I know. Thank you. Thank you. Thank you." Matthew bows as if he has just received the highest compliment in the world.

Joshua decides that it's time to change the subject before Matthew really decides to start teasing him about Lacey.

He picks up the computer card that Matthew has made for Jil! and waves it in front of his friend, teasing before he can be teased. "Jil!iet, oh, Jil!iet, Where fort art thou?"

Matthew tries to grab it and trips Joshua, who, falling to the floor, grabs Matthew's leg, pulling him down.

The boys jump up and run around again.

Mrs Martin walks into the room, her hands on her hips. "What do you think, that we live in a gymnasium?"

Joshua and Matthew pretend to be sumo wrestlers.

Mrs Martin looks at the two boys and thinks about how the summer is just beginning and she says, "I want the two of you to go outside and play."

"We're practically seventh graders." Matthew stands up next to his mother and realizes that he's almost taller than she is. "Seventh graders don't play. We just hang out."

Joshua gets up too. "Play? We have other plans."

Matthew and Joshua exchange looks.

They've almost forgotten.

Work.

They have figured out a way to earn money.

Joshua wants a new skateboard.

Matthew wants his program.

Now if only their plan works. Only time will tell. And no one, they hope, will tell their parents.

Chapter 8

"Hey, mister, do you want your windscreen wiped?" Matthew goes up to a car waiting at the traffic light.

The man smiles and says, "Sure."

Matthew uses a squeegee to get the window clean and then asks the man if he wants to also buy an air freshener, lemon, cherry, or pine scented, to hang from his inside car mirror.

He wants a pine-scented one.

Pocketing the money, Matthew thinks about the number of people who pay them something for doing their windows and about how he and Joshua sold some old comic books and bought a whole box of air fresheners to hang in cars and how they are selling them for about double what they paid for them.

The light changes.

Matthew and Joshua go to the other part of the intersection, where there are cars waiting for the light to turn green. The first car that Matthew walks up to is driven by a man who obviously is not interested. He has turned on the windscreen wipers, motioning with his hands to not go near the car and saying, "I have

433

to deal with this every day when I commute into New York. I don't expect to have to do this in Califon, New Jersey. I moved out here to get away from all of that."

The light changes again and it's back to the other side. Matthew and Joshua keep working, making money and thinking about their future purchases.

Matthew starts to think about how maybe they can start selling franchises, having other kids all over the country doing this and selling a special kind of air freshener, a product, using both of their last names, called Martin Jackson. The scents could be odours like popcorn, favourite ice cream flavours, and chocolate brownie mix as it bakes. For people like his mother they could be granola and bean sprout scented.

A car pulls up.

It's Mrs Stanton, his favourite teacher ever.

She pulls her car over to the side of the road and gets out.

Matthew rushes over.

So does Joshua.

While they are standing on the sidewalk, cars whiz by.

Matthew looks at them and thinks about how much money they are losing, but then thinks about how good it is to see Mrs Stanton again, even though school has just ended.

Matthew gets right to the point and asks the question that many of their classmates want to ask. "Are you going out with Ryma's father? Are you going to marry him?"

Mrs Stanton looks at him. "Matthew Martin. Do I ask you personal questions like that?"

"Ask him if he's going to marry Jil!," Joshua suggests.

"Ask Joshua if he's going to marry Lacey." Matthew steps on Joshua's foot and then says, "I just think that it's a good idea. Mr Browne is really nice, and so are you. And your daughter, Marie, and Ryma are really nice. And Ryma is not in your classroom anymore, so it wouldn't be what my dad calls a 'conflict of interests'. And some of my mom's friends, who aren't married, are always saying stuff like 'There just aren't a lot of good men around.' And Mr Browne is a good man, right? And as my grandmother says about people, 'You're not getting any younger.' So I think you ought to marry him. And when I see him, I could tell him the same thing, because he's not getting any younger either."

"Matthew . . ." is all that Mrs Stanton manages to say before Matthew starts talking again.

"And I think it would be nice for Ryma and Marie to be sisters, since they are 'only children'. It's nice to have other kids in the family except in my case, where my sister is a dirt ball."

"Matthew"—Mrs Stanton stops him—"Enough. I know you care about me, but my relationship with Mr Browne is really something that I don't care to discuss."

Matthew looks confused. "Did I say anything bad?"

She smiles at him. "Not bad. Maybe a little nosy, but not bad."

He grins at her. "Well, if you do get married, can I have a piece of the wedding cake?"

She sighs and nods. "Look, boys, I didn't pull off the road to discuss my social life. I did it because I'm very concerned about what you are doing. Even though Califon is a very safe place, it's not a good idea to be going up to all of these cars and talking to strangers, walking around in the middle of traffic that may suddenly start moving, and smelling petrol fumes."

"We won't get into any cars," Joshua says. "And we're strong. No one can hurt us."

Mrs Stanton shakes her head. "You know, a lot of kids think that nothing can hurt them, that nothing can happen to them. You have to be careful. I don't want to scare you from having adventures, from trying out new things, but you have to use your common sense. It's really not a smart idea to be doing this."

"But we're making money. I need it to buy a computer program. You know how you're always saying that we should learn new things," Matthew defends himself, and watches as cars filled with potential buyers of air fresheners whiz by.

She continues. "There are lots of other things that you can do to earn money."

Remembering baby-sitting for the Levy kids, Matthew says, "But this one is so easy. And really, nothing bad has happened."

"I'm only telling you this for your own good." Mrs

436

Stanton looks at both of the boys. "I don't want to lecture you, but I really care and don't want to see anything happen to you. I want you to understand. I want you to be responsible and careful."

Matthew hates it when grown-ups say they're only telling him something for his own good, especially when he realizes that maybe they are right.

Looking at the cars, totalling up in his head how much more he can make in a couple of hours, and figuring out how much he and Joshua spent on the box of air fresheners, he makes a decision. "We'll just finish doing this today, and then we'll find another way to make money. Please, promise that you won't tell on us to our parents."

Mrs Stanton sighs again. She thinks about how much easier it would have been for her if she hadn't decided to go shopping that afternoon, if she taught in a town where she didn't live.

"Please. Don't tell them." Matthew puts his palms together and begs her.

Before she has a chance to answer, another car pulls up behind hers.

It's Mr Jackson, who has just been called by a neighbour who saw the boys doing windows.

Mr Jackson does not look very happy.

Chapter 9

I'm in deep doo-doo. Very deep doo-doo, Matthew thinks as he sits down on the living-room couch.

His father is sitting on the recliner to the right of the couch.

His mother is sitting on the rocker to the left of the couch.

Looking from right to left, from left to right, Matthew thinks, *Oh, great. This is going to be in stereo . . . a parent on each side yelling at me.*

From the frowns on their faces, their eyes narrowed to tiny slits, and their arms crossed in front of them, Matthew realizes that his parents are not going to go easy on him.

One of the things that is really making him nervous is that his parents hardly ever yell at him, hardly ever punish him, and have never believed in spanking. He's not sure what they are going to do in this situation.

Another thing that is making him nervous is that his father is a lawyer and is really good at handling criminals, although Matthew is not quite sure of how big a "crime" they think he's committed.

He also feels bad because he has been trying so hard to be more grown up, to make them see that he is no longer a child.

"Matthew," his father says in his deep, serious voice, "we want to give you a few minutes to think about why we are here having this discussion, about what you have done that concerns us."

For a minute Matthew considers saying, *We're here because it's more comfortable for discussions and family meetings than, say, the bathroom.*

He decides not to open his mouth.

Mrs Martin frowns. "We want you to think about this seriously, not try to get out of it by making jokes, trying to be cute."

Rats, Matthew thinks. *Cute is usually the thing that works best on her.*

"Think, Matthew, think. And then be prepared to discuss this." Mr Martin has the recliner straight up, a sure sign that there is not going to be any relaxation for a while.

His parents say nothing for a few minutes and then start giving all the reasons why they are upset by what he has done.

Matthew has heard the same things from Mrs Stanton, Mr Jackson, and now his parents.

Matthew, who has perfected the art of looking at people as if he is paying perfect attention, stares intently at his parents and starts to think about other things. *This is all Amanda's fault. If she hadn't gone away to camp, they would be spending all of their time*

*worrying about her, disciplining her. This is all Josh-
ua's fault. If he didn't have a father who was a free-
lance writer, no one would have been home to get the
call from the busybody who told on us. This is all the
computer company's fault. If they didn't charge so
much, I wouldn't have had to try so hard to earn the
money. This is all my parents' fault. They make
money. They should be willing to share it with their
kids.*

Matthew thinks about how it's not fair to torture a kid
like this — to keep lecturing him when all he tried to do
was earn some money for an educational and fun computer program.

He recalls how Mr Jackson yelled at them and, when
he dropped Matthew off at his house, ordered him in the
name of his parents to go directly to his room. He made
Matthew promise to stay there until his parents came
home, not to use his computer, not to watch television, not
to use the phone, except to call his parents, whom Mr
Jackson had spoken to from his car phone.

It was torture for Matthew to wait, to not know what
his parents were going to say.

It was such torture, so nerve-racking, so boring just
waiting, that he actually cleaned up his room, an act
that he hoped would make his parents less angry at
him. An act that also yielded four quarters, two dimes,
seventeen nickels, one hundred and thirty-two pennies —
three dollars and thirty-seven cents towards his program.

But Matthew can't stand it much longer.

He can't stand thinking about what he did, what's going

440

to happen next. Wishing that it was already a half an hour in the future, he bites his bottom lip and speaks up as soon as his parents finish with their concerns. "Look. I didn't mean to do anything wrong. You knew that I was going to try to earn some money, and I did. I didn't do anything illegal. Don't you believe in free enterprise?"

"Bad argument," Matthew's father says.

So I want to be a computer programmer, not a lawyer, Matthew thinks, getting a little angry but afraid to say it out loud.

His father continues, "If you thought that it was all right to do this, why didn't you tell us?"

"We didn't think it was going to be such a big deal, honest." Matthew looks first at his father, then at his mother. "It was just a way to earn money."

"You should have told us," Mrs Martin says.

Matthew decides to try to make his parents feel as guilty as they're making him feel. "I would have, but you are always at work, always too busy."

There's a gasp from his mother. "Matthew Martin. I didn't go into work until late today. Someone else was watching the store. We had time enough to discuss Shakespeare's plays this morning. We would have had time enough to talk about your business idea."

Matthew's not ready to give up trying to make his parents feel guilty. "If you had just bought the program for me, this would have never happened."

His parents exchange looks.

Mr Martin speaks. "Matthew, you and Josh could have been hurt . . . or worse. That's the issue here. Didn't you boys think about the risk?"

"No." Matthew is adamant. "We didn't. Joshua and I were watching television and we saw a show where people did it and we thought we should try. We really, honestly, truly, just thought that it was a good way to earn money. And it was."

His parents exchange looks again.

"Okay, Matthew. We're willing to believe you, but can you see why we're so concerned?" His mother rocks back and forth on her chair.

Matthew thinks about it. All of the stuff that Mrs Stanton said, all the reasons Mr Jackson gave, his parents' concerns.

He thinks. It was really easy money. It also was a little dangerous. The petrol fumes made him cough. Joshua really had to jump once to get out of the way of a car that was trying to run the light. Matthew decides to give in on this one but hopes that he can come up with another way to make money.

He gives in, not happily, but he does relent. "Okay. So it was dumb. I'm sorry. I won't do it again."

"Good. And you'll talk to us before you do something to earn money," his mother continues.

Matthew nods again. "Okay. Is there a time limit on this rule, though? Is there ever going to be a time I'm old enough to pick my own job?"

"Don't get smart, young man." His father shakes his finger. "You're only eleven years old and we want to help you to do the best."

"I'm going to be twelve soon," Matthew reminds

them.

"When you're twelve, we're still going to be offering advice and, at times, telling you what you have to do," his father informs him.

"Matthew, when you are forty one, almost forty two, we'll probably still be offering advice, trying to guide you," his mother tells him.

"Am I going to be punished?" Matthew can't stand the suspense anymore.

"Do you think you should be?" his father asks.

Matthew shakes his head. "No. Absolutely, positively not. I think that this is what you call a 'learning experience' and I've learned and shouldn't have to be punished."

There's silence, and then . . .

"We agree," his mother says.

"Whew," Matthew takes a deep breath.

"There is something that we want you to know." His father leans forward. "We've talked with Joshua's parents and we don't want you boys to keep the money that you've earned."

"Oh, no," Matthew sinks back into the sofa cushions and lets what his parents have just told him sink into his brain. "Not a cent?"

"Not a cent," they repeat.

If this isn't a punishment, Matthew is not sure what it is.

"Can't we even get back the money that Joshua and I paid for the box of air fresheners?" Matthew begs.

"You can get that back, but the profits you boys will give to charity."

Matthew scrunches his nose. "How about fifty percent to charity and fifty percent to us?"

"Not negotiable," his father says. "You and Joshua will pick out a charity and donate the money to it."

Defeated, Matthew thinks about which charity to choose.

He decides. "I know. We'll give the money to the charity that helps out the homeless in New York, especially the people who wash windscreens."

"Good." His mother comes over to the sofa, sits down, and hugs him.

Matthew debates telling her that he is getting too old for hugs, at least ones from his mother, but decides not to, since he really likes the hug, especially now.

His father says, "We have another matter we want to discuss with you."

Matthew goes through a list of things in his head that his parents might want to lecture him about . . . his normally cluttered room, the chocolate bars that he keeps hidden in his underwear drawer, his new interest in girls. He decides that's it. They are going to give him the big talk, the one about birds and bees. The one about S-E-X.

Mrs Martin stops hugging him and puts her hands on his shoulders. "Your father and I have decided to tell you something very important and very personal."

This is it, Matthew guesses.

And he waits expectantly for the Big Talk to begin.

Chapter 10

Mrs Martin speaks first. "You may have wondered why your father and I aren't buying you the computer program. We want to explain."

Matthew's a little confused. *Is there*, he wonders, a *computer program for sale that teaches people about the facts of life?* He thinks about how that really gives new meaning to the term *user friendly*. He wonders if the person operates a keyboard or mouse to get all the answers, to get all the information shown on the computer. Matthew wonders what the graphics would be like for that program.

"Matthew, back to earth. This is important," his father says. "Your mother and I want to explain to you why we want you to earn part of the money for the computer program, the one that we've agreed to share the cost of."

Oops, not the S-E-X lecture, Matthew figures out. He is very disappointed, and at the same time a little relieved.

Mrs Martin looks at her son. "When your father and I first got married . . ."

Well, maybe, he thinks.

She continues, "We were just starting out and didn't have very much money, so we got into very bad habits. We borrowed money against our future earnings. We charged far too much on credit cards. We spent more than we made."

Matthew starts thinking about what his parents are really talking about and he starts to get very worried. "You don't do that now, do you?"

"No." Mr Martin takes over. "We don't. We cut up all of our credit cards, except for the ones we use for business. We worked out a repayment schedule and a budget. It took a long time but everything got straightened out."

Mrs Martin holds on to her son's hand. "Matthew, honey, Dad just made it sound very easy . . . but it wasn't. There were times when we were afraid to pick up the phone, that there would be yet another creditor on the line."

"It was like a juggling act — rent, phone, food, clothes, charge cards, paying back loans from our parents, college loans." Mr Martin has a very pained look on his face.

Mrs Martin looks very sad.

Mr Martin gets up and joins his wife and son on the couch. "We were young, just out of college. It was the first time that we had our own money — two salaries, no kids — and we bought all sorts of things. A car . . . new furniture. We went for immediate gratification, meaning if we saw it and wanted it, we bought it, even if we didn't have the money saved. Lots of companies gave us credit and we used it. And then, it just got to the point where we were totally out of control."

Matthew is amazed. He's always thought that his parents could handle just about anything, that they never had any problems. He hardly ever thinks about the fact that they even had a life before he was born.

"It was a terrible time. We had to go to a special agency that helps out people who are in that kind of trouble. They made us cut up our cards. They contacted all of creditors, got them to accept less money over a longer period of time. We had to live on a very strict budget."

"We used to have pasta almost every night because it was so cheap." His father wipes the tears off his wife's face with a handkerchief.

She begins to smile, remembering. "The only good thing was that we couldn't afford to buy junk food."

"That was one of the really bad things," his father remembers.

Mrs Martin shakes her head quickly, as if trying to toss all the bad memories out. "So you see why we worry about you. You're doing some of the same things that we did. When you want something, you have to have it immediately, even if you can't afford it. You never plan ahead, never save any money. You get advances on your pocket money that you never manage to pay back. You owe money to a lot of people. It makes us very nervous. We know that sometimes we confuse you because we buy a lot for you and your sister. But we want you to know that there are limits. So now you know, and we want all of us to work on this problem before it overwhelms you."

Matthew feels overwhelmed by what they have just told him. "Maybe someday I can win the lottery. Then I won't have to worry about all of this. I'll win so much that I can have whatever I want."

"This is not going to be easy." Mrs Martin sighs, then continues, "Look, Matthew, we *earn* our money. We don't expect a magical solution."

Rats. Matthew thinks.

Mrs Martin says, "We have savings and no longer overspend. We're able to meet our needs and buy some luxuries. But we do know what really counts. And we consider ourselves very lucky. Look at all the people in the world who don't even have the basic necessities."

Matthew is getting a headache, hearing more than he wants to hear. His parents have made major mistakes. He has yet another possible growing-up problem. His very own parents sometimes had trouble handling grown-up things when they were grown-ups. Clearly this having to handle money in an adult way is not a one-shot deal.

He wishes he never had to deal with all of this stuff, and he begins to realize that he's not even going to have a choice about whether or not he can deal with this issue. He's going to have to do it no matter what.

"Rats," he says. "Now I really understand why Peter Pan never wanted to grow up."

His father nods. "Once I tried calling up AAA, The

American Automobile Association, the group that helps members plan trips — and asked them for the road map to Never-Never Land."

Matthew laughs.

"It's true. He really did it," his mother informs him.

"And?" Matthew wants the details. "Let me guess what they told you, that there was no way to get there from here."

"And," his father says, "They told me that there was no way to get there from here."

Matthew knows that he doesn't want to deal with all of this money stuff — not even for a billion gazillion dollars. He also knows that he has no choice.

Chapter 11

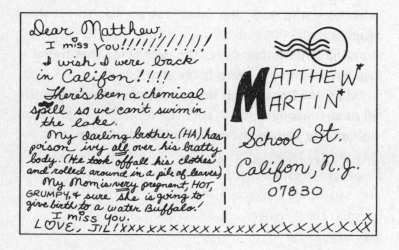

Dear Matthew,
    I miss you!!!!!/!/!!!
    I wish I were back
in Califon!!!!
    There's been a chemical
spill so we can't swim in
the lake.
    My darling brother (HA) has
poison ivy all over his bratty
body. (He took off all his clothes
and rolled around in a pile of leaves)
    My Mom is very pregnant, HOT,
GRUMPY, & sure she is going to
give birth to a water Buffalo!
    I miss you.
LOVE, JIL! xxxxxxxxxxxxxxxxxxxxxxx

MATTHEW
MARTIN
School St.
Califon, N.J.
07830

Matthew puts the postcard back in his pocket and
thinks about how much he misses Jil!, how he doesn't
really understand this whole boyfriend-girlfriend
thing, but he knows that he really likes her a lot.

If Jil! were here, he could talk to her about all the
stuff that's going on . . . how his parents made him
write down a list of everyone to whom he owed money
. . . how they loaned him the money to pay off his
debts, and how he now has to pay them back by getting
only fifty percent of his pocket money until the debt

clears. If Jil! were here, he would have someone to hang out with who really liked his sense of humour, someone who thought he was really special.

If Jil! were here, he would have to pay her the money that he owes her, money that he forgot to put on the list.

But Jil!'s not here, he thinks, and walks over to the recreation field. As he walks past the stands, he can see a high school couple, who are not part of the town recreational programme, kissing. Matthew guesses that they have their own recreational programme.

Eddie, the head counsellor, goes over to the stands to tell them to stop.

Matthew thinks about Jil! and wonders whether they would be kissing on the stands if she hadn't gone away. He decides that they probably wouldn't, that they would be hanging out with the rest of their friends. He thinks much more about kissing than actually doing it.

Looking around, Matthew can see that the recreation field is filled. The nine to ten-year-old group is lined up by the pool, getting partners, having their names put up on the buddy board to be sure that they all stay safe and accounted for.

Walter Carlson is swatting girls' rear ends with his towel.

Anita Mastripoli gives Walter a karate chop.

Their counsellors separate them.

Playing dodge ball, the five and six-year-olds are screaming loudly as they either try to duck from or hit each other with a huge foam ball.

One of the little boys is hiding out behind a rubbish bin, trying not to get hit and picking his nose.

It reminds Matthew of one of his favourite jokes:

Q. What's the difference between snot and broccoli?

A. Kids won't eat broccoli.

Matthew continues walking across the playground, passing by the group of seven and eight-year-olds, on the equipment that the people of the town designed and built.

Matthew finds his group in the arts-and-crafts building.

As he enters, he notices that Joshua is standing next to the bench where Lacey is decorating a sweatshirt with puff paints and glitter.

Matthew debates asking Joshua since when has he become so interested in the puff paint and glitter movement in American art but decides not to embarrass him, at least not in front of everyone else.

Vanessa Singer holds her nose and says, "Fe, fi, fo, fum, I smell the smell of a dum-dum."

Matthew turns to her. "You wouldn't if you learned to use deodorant."

"A point for Matthew." Joshua licks his finger and keeps score on the air.

"Unnecessary. This squabbling is so unnecessary." Susie Gifford, the arts-and-crafts counsellor, looks up from the T-shirt she is helping Cathy Atwood fix after an unfortunate spill of puff paint and glitter.

"It is so necessary," Matthew explains. "Squabbling with Vanessa is my hobby."

Vanessa glares at Matthew. "Two years ago I made a

452

list of rotten things to say to Matthew, and I'm only halfway through them."

"Susie, just give up any thoughts of them getting along." Lisa scratches a mosquito bite and leaves a patch of pink puff paint and glitter on her face. "We're all used to it. If someone ever wrote a story about those two, it would end, AND THEY FOUGHT HAPPILY EVER AFTER."

"I'm studying psychology at college. They could be my case study." Susie tries to wipe the mess off Lisa's face.

"No problem," Vanessa explains. "We just don't like each other. We abhor each other, detest each other."

"We have allergic reactions to each other, have contempt for each other," Matthew elaborates.

Susie thinks about studying something else, like forestry.

Lisa decides to change the subject. "Who's going on the ten-pin bowling trip?"

Most of the kids look at each other to make sure that others look like they're going before raising their hands.

Tyler and Zoe are the first to raise their hand — actually hands — but since they are always holding each other's, it looks like one hand.

Everyone else raises his or her hand, except for Matthew, who with his reduced pocket money has to figure out if he's going on the trip or going to the movies this week.

Finally, he raises his hand.

"Rats," Vanessa says.

"Why are you calling for your family?" Matthew asks, and then turns to the rest of the group, ignoring Vanessa. "So what are we making in here?"

"Glitter T-shirts." Ryma holds hers up. On the left side she has drawn a glitter pink puffed heart.

"What are the guys doing?" Matthew has no desire to work with glitter and puff paint.

"Watching the girls make these dorky things and hanging out talking to them," Billy Kellerman informs him. "The counsellors won't let us use the basketball courts now because the little kids are using them, and they say we pick on them and don't give them a chance to play."

"Us?" Matthew laughs. "Would we do a thing like that?"

All of the boys think about how when they were little, the big guys did that to them and now it is their turn — not to torment the younger kids, but just to let them know who's boss.

Matthew and Joshua go over to the side of the room and sit alone at a table.

"Did your parents yell a lot?" Matthew asks.

Joshua shakes his head. "No. They just said that they, and your parents, decided that we had to give the money we *earned* to charity."

"Bummer." Matthew pulls at a splinter on the table. "I really could have used the money."

"Me too." Joshua envisions the skateboard that he

454

would have bought.

"What are we going to do with the rest of the air fresheners?" Matthew makes a face. "We're stuck with a lot of those suckers."

"At least our parents let us keep the money we spent on them," Josh reminds him. He takes off his baseball cap and puts it on backwards. "So even though we're stuck with them, we didn't lose the money, since we sold enough of them at double what they cost us."

"Maybe we should sell them door to door." Matthew has visions of being ninety years old before he gets the computer program.

"Fat chance." Joshua punches him on the arm. "You doofus, do you really think that our parents will let us do that? They'll say that we could get killed by an axe murderer."

"But we know practically everyone in our neighbourhood," Matthew argues.

"I know our parents," Joshua says. "They'll say that we could be killed by a *visiting* axe murderer."

Matthew shrugs. "Well, I'm going to ask my parents if it's okay. If it's not, maybe we can sell the air fresheners for kids to put on their bikes or sell a pair as earrings. . ."

Joshua looks at Matthew as if he's gone off the deep end.

Even Matthew realizes how silly it sounds, but he really wants to buy the program.

Zoe walks up. "I spoke to Jil! last night. She really

liked the card you sent her. I think the things that you wrote are really sweet."

Blushing, Matthew can't believe that Jil! read it to Zoe, Califon's own answer to the Pony Express Information Service.

"She said that it arrived a little rumpled," Zoe informs him. "She said it looked like someone had been using it in a game of keep-away."

Matthew and Joshua look at each other and think about how the game was more like "Where Fort Art Thou".

Zoe continues speaking, putting her head on Tyler's shoulder. "Even though my Tyler is a practically perfect boyfriend, I wish that he would send me a card like that. Jil! is sooooo lucky."

Matthew blushes again.

"What does the card say?" Billy Kellerman jumps into the conversation, hoping to find out something to tease Matthew about.

Zoe shrugs. "I'm not sure I remember. After all, it wasn't about me. But I remember thinking that I wished Tyler would do something like that for me, using *my* name."

Getting up to go to the girls' room, one of the few places that she doesn't go with Tyler, Zoe repeats, "It would be so wonderful if my Tyler did that for me."

Zoe goes out of the room.

Once everyone is sure that she is out of hearing range, the comments start.

"Oh, Tylerpoo, please write something for me!" Billy

uses a high-pitched voice.

"Well, Tyler, if you want her still to think you're perfect you'd better write a card just as wonderful as Matthew's. You know Zoe when she decides she wants something." Cathy puts a rhinestone on her creation.

Matthew thinks about how hard it would be to do a poem that rhymed with Zoe—Zoe E. He decides that the only way to make it work would be to make believe that every rhyme ended with *O E*.

Thinking for a minute, he finally says:

"There once was a girl named Zoe,
Who in a blender stuck her Toe,
She cried out E I E I O E,
Tyler came along and pulled it out with a Hoe,
Now she's out of Woe,
And glad that she goes out with Tyler instead of some guy named Joey."

"That is so lame." Brian laughs.

"I like it," Tyler says, flexing his muscles. "It shows what a hero I am."

Someone at the girls' table starts making retching sounds.

"Would you make up a computer card for me?" Tyler turns to Matthew. "You know, write it up, adding pictures like you always do."

Matthew thinks about how much time it will take.

Joshua steps up to Tyler. "How much are you

willing to pay him? I'm his business manager."
Matthew looks at his friend and realizes once more
why he is glad that Joshua Jackson is his best friend.

"You can do it yourself. It's a piece of cake,"
Vanessa tells Tyler.

Matthew looks at her and realizes once more why
Vanessa Singer is his worst enemy.

"Not as well as Matthew can," Tyler decides.

The boys settle on a price for the card before Zoe
returns.

Matthew and Joshua exchange glances.

A new business is about to start, one that won't
upset their parents.

Matthew Martin is one happy person.

He can't imagine what else could happen to make
the day any better.

Chapter 12

Everyone starts talking at once.

Everyone, except for Matthew, who sits there very quietly, very glad to see Jil!, but not very sure of how to react in front of everyone else, not very sure of how to act to Jil!

The questions come all at once.

"When did you get back?"

"How long are you staying?"

"Where did you get that outfit? Can I borrow it sometime?"

"Are you going on the bowling trip later this week?"

"Is something the matter? Is your Mom okay?"

"How come you didn't tell me when we talked on the phone that you were coming back so soon?" Zoe has walked back into the arts-and-crafts room. "Did you miss Matthew so much that you ran away from the lake and returned here to be with him?"

Everyone looks at Zoe and starts to laugh.

She is offended by their reactions. "Well, it could happen. Something like that just happened on my favourite soap opera—and anyway, something like that happened with my mother and one of her husbands."

People stop laughing, because they know that Zoe's life is so much like a soap opera, with her parents' many marriages and divorces, that she expects just about anything to be possible.

Jil! starts answering the questions. "We got back about an hour ago. Actually, we weren't expecting to come back at all, but my mother said she couldn't stand seeing my father only weekends. He couldn't commute to work from the lake, and we couldn't use it because it was polluted by some dumb factory. It was so depressing watching all the dead fish floating on top of the water. And then my stupid little brother got poison ivy all over his stupid little body, and spent the entire time sitting nude in the house, covered with calamine lotion, whimpering in his stupid little voice. And although I did try to be a saint about the whole situation, I guess I did complain just a little bit about how much I missed all of you, about how much I missed being in Califon, how there was no one at the lake to hang out with, about how my stupid little brother and his stupid little whining was driving me crazy. So my mother, who, as you all know, is going to give birth sometime in September, decided to return to Califon."

"Boy. She's only been gone a week and I forgot how dramatic she is." Billy strikes a pose. "Ask her a question and you get a three-act play."

Jil! slugs him in the arm.

And then she looks at Matthew.

He looks back, feeling a little shy in front of all their friends.

"So is that a new outfit?" Cathy asks. "It sure would look good on me."

"Why don't you try it on right now?" David asks. "You could change right here right now."

Cathy picks up the jar of glitter and sprinkles some of it on his head.

"You have to excuse him," Joshua laughs. "He's been like this since his brothers started sharing their copies of *Playboy* with him."

"There is no excuse for him." Cathy pours a different colour glitter on him, glad that the counsellor has stepped out for a break so that she isn't there to yell at her for wasting materials.

Matthew thinks about how one of David's older brothers used to go out with his sister, Amanda. He's sure that Danny didn't go out with Amanda because she looks like a *Playboy* centrefold. The only resemblance, he thinks, is that the paper it's printed on is flat and so is Amanda.

He wonders for a minute how Amanda is doing at camp and he thinks about how quiet it is in the house without her.

He looks at Jil!, who is looking at him.

Wondering if he is supposed to say something to David because of his comments, he decides not to.

Instead, he stands up and says, "I'm thirsty and am going to the fountain for some water. Want to come

461

with me, Jil!?"

" Ooooow . . ."

"How can she ever turn down a offer like that?"

"How romantic."

Jil! stands up and curtsies. "Why, sir, I thought you'd never ask."

As they walk out of the arts-and-crafts area, they can hear some of the boys making kissing sounds on their hands and some of the girls saying, "You are soooooooooooooo immature."

Matthew looks at Jil!

Jil! looks at Matthew.

Neither is sure of what to say or do. But they are very glad to see each other. As they walk past the nine to ten-year-old group, they can hear them singing,

"Everyone's doing it . . .

Doing it . . .

Picking their nose and chewing it,

Chewing it,

They think it's candy . . .

But it's . . . snot."

Jil! looks at Matthew. "That song is so disgusting."

Matthew, who really likes the song, just smiles.

Reaching the water fountain, Matthew, still not at all sure of how to act when you have a girlfriend, lets Jil! get the first drink of water and resists the temptation while she is sipping to push her head into the fountain, which is what he would have done a few months earlier.

It's his turn and he bends down to sip the water. Jil!

pushes his head into the fountain.

Lifting his dripping wet head, Matthew looks at Jil! and says, "Welcome back."

Chapter 13

"This meeting is now called to order." Matthew raps on the desk in his father's study. Since he does not have a gavel, he uses the four-foot-tall purple crayon that usually leans against the wall.

"Order. I'll order a hot pastrami sandwich on rye bread." Joshua raises his hand. "And a root-beer float."

That reminds Matthew. "Did you bring any junk food from your houses?"

"Chocolate brownies that my dad baked." Joshua holds up a bag.

Jil! also holds up a bag. "I got M & M's, Mallomars, and chocolate-covered prunes."

"Ugh" is the response from the boys about her third offering.

"Chocolate-covered prunes. You don't even want to know the disgusting things I'm thinking about that." Matthew grimaces. "Where did they come from?"

"From chocolate-covered plums." Joshua laughs.

Jil! shrugs. "My mother has these strange cravings

when she's pregnant."

Matthew, a person who will eat almost anything that has chocolate, realizes that he has finally found something he will not taste.

He raps on the table again. "I move that we eat the Mallomars now and then discuss our company. All in favour, say aye. All opposed, give their cookies to me."

There are three ayes.

Eating the cookies, the three friends start discussing the company they are starting.

Everyone will be equal, get an equal share of the profits.

Matthew will be in charge of developing, designing, and producing the products that come out of the computer.

Joshua will be the publicity and promotion person, the one who oversees getting business, advertising, and the distribution of the finished products.

Jil! will be in charge of keeping track of the finance — what is spent, how much goes back into the company, and how much they get. She will also help Matthew with his spelling.

"So here are the items on the agenda." Matthew licks the chocolate off the top of the Mallomar. "What are we going to name our company? What exactly are we able to do? What do we charge? And how many snack breaks do we get?"

Since there are three members of the company, the name choices start out by centring on that fact: The

Three Musketeers. The Three Stooges. The Three Bears, The Three Bares (that from Joshua, who has been looking at David's copies of *Playboy.*). The Three Little Kittens . . .

"Forget it." Matthew picks up another Mallomar. "How about Mart in Cards? You know, like Mart, selling . . . like Martin, my last name. I love puns, don't you?"

"Not as much as you do." Joshua grabs two Mallomars, afraid that if he doesn't get his share right away, Matthew will vacuum the rest of the cookies into his body. "Look, we're all part of the company. We could take part of each of our names and make it Martin, Jackson, and Hudson . . . two sons and a daughter."

"Not enough pizzazz." Jil! tries one of the chocolate-covered prunes and immediately spits it into her hand. "Aarg."

"Aarg is a dumb name for the company," Matthew informs her.

A quick trip to the bathroom to throw out the chocolate mess and a fast wash of her hands, and Jil! is back. "I have it. Let's use none of our own names. Let's just make up a name. That's what all the big companies do. I bet there is no Betty Crocker, no Aunt Jemima."

"No Mac Kintosh," Matthew adds. "You know, like the guy who invented the computers."

"That's Macintosh, like the Apple, doofus." Joshua sighs.

Matthew grins.

Jil! continues. "So here's my idea. Let's call the company Ima Card, Inc. We'll leave out the skiggly line between I and m and act like Ima is the person's first name and Card is her last. And the Inc. is for Incorporated. That's all of us."

"The skiggly line is an apostrophe," Joshua informs her.

"Whatever." Jil! shrugs. "It's summer. I don't have to remember school stuff now."

Matthew runs over to the computer and types something into it. Then he puts rainbow-coloured paper into the printer and pushes a button.

A banner is made — IMA CARD, INK.

Joshua and Jil! applaud and then look at the banner carefully.

"Matthew, you spell Inc. I-N-C." Joshua shakes his head.

"I like it." Jil! giggles. "It looks like we did it intentionally, since we're going to be printing things up."

The three friends stare at the banner.

Matthew thinks of a phrase he has heard his father use when he talks about things going really well.

He picks up the sign and hands one end of it to Joshua.

The middle section goes to Jil! and he holds the other end.

"This is," Matthew says, "going to be a banner year for our company."

And so the business begins.

467

Chapter 14

IMA CARD, INK.

DO YOU NEED:

★ specialized cards ★★ signs ★★ banners ★
★★ letterheads ★★ certificates ★★ invitations
★★ menus ★★ address books ★★ personalized
calendars (you'll never forget an important date)
★★ book markers ★★ book covers ★★ board
games ★★ wallpaper ★★ wrapping paper ★★
your own comic books ★★★★★★★★you name it
— we'll do it (keep it clean, etc.)

Contact:
Matthew Martin
Jil! Hudson   } phone # 555-9763
Joshua Jackson

Matthew Martin	5|4 — 9	9|/ — 27	8|1 — 36	7|2 — 45					
Jill	5|4 — 9	28	8|1 — 37	9|/					
Tod	3|2 — 5	5|1 — 11	8|- — 19	5|1 — 25					
Tyler	9|/ — 20	X — 40	4|/ — 59	9|/					
Joshua	6|3 — 9	5|2 — 16	8|/ — 33	7|1 — 41					
Lacey	3|5 — 8	6|/ — 27	9|-	X					

"Mister, is it all right for me to put this sign up on your bulletin board? Please." Matthew hands one of the Ima Card, Ink, signs to the man behind the desk.

"Just a minute, sonny," the man says. "I have to give these two little girls their bowling shoes and then I'll be right with you. It'll just take a minute."

"Don't you have any with sparkly laces?" one of the eight-year-old girls asks.

"This is a bowling alley, not a shoe store," the man says for the eleventh time that morning, for the one thousand five hundred and forty-second time since he bought the business.

"Do I have to wear a pair of shoes with the size printed on the back? When I wear them, my brother

says that four and a half is my IQ, not my shoe size."
The other girl puts her elbows up on the counter.

Matthew thinks that her older brother is probably
being generous in thinking that her IQ is that high.

He is anxious, since it is almost his turn to bowl.

Shaking his head, the man says, "These are our
rental shoes. Take them or leave them. Take them and
you can bowl. Leave them, and unless you have your
own regulation bowling shoes, you can sit on the
sidelines and watch your friends bowl. It's your
choice."

Looking toward the lane where his friends are
bowling, Matthew hopes the girls make a decision
quickly.

Finally, they decide.

The bowling shoes go on their feet and they leave.

Matthew turns back to the man. "So would it be all
right to put this up on the bulletin board?"

After the owner looks at the sign, he asks, "Is this
your business?"

"Mine and two friends," Matthew informs him.
"We're just a couple of kids trying to earn some
money, keep ourselves out of trouble by printing up
things that people can use." Matthew is impressed
with his own explanation and hopes that the man is,
also.

"So, if I let you put this up on my bulletin board,
what's in it for me?" The man smiles at him.

Matthew thinks fast and smiles back. "What's in it
for you, you ask? I'll tell you — our undying gratitude

and we'll make up a couple of signs for you to put up on your counter. One will be THIS IS NOT A SHOE STORE. IT'S A BOWLING ALLEY. The second one will be, YOU'LL NEVER STRIKE OUT AT THE CALIFON BOWL . . . WE HAVE BOWLING BALLS TO SPARE."

"Matthew, it's your turn," Jil! yells.

"In a second," he yells back.

He stares at the man and says, "Oh, please.... say yes. My friends are always telling me that I won't take care of the business stuff, that I just want to create. This will help get them off my back."

"Matthew." Joshua cups his hands and yells.

The owner says, "I'll get the two signs? Right?"

Matthew nods.

"You can put your sign up and I'll leave it there for the month." The man turns to get shoes for new customers.

"Thank you." Matthew tacks the sign on the bulletin board and returns to his friends

He looks at the scores.

Tyler is ahead, but that's no surprise.

Tyler is always ahead in anything sportslike.

Zoe is losing because she can't manage to concentrate on anything that's not facing in the general direction of Tyler.

Matthew looks at his own score. He's not going to win, but he's not embarrassing himself either.

Just as Matthew is ready to bowl, the little boy in the right alley drops his ball. It comes rolling over and hits Matthew's foot.

It's gutter-ball time for Matthew Martin.

Limping slightly and dramatically, Matthew moves to throw the second ball.

This time a little girl on the left alley rolls her ball and herself down the lane.

Matthew loses concentration and only gets five pins down.

As Matthew sits down on the bench, Joshua says, "Tough luck."

Matthew watches as Joshua tries to find a way to put his arm around Lacey's shoulder. Matthew sees Joshua's arm rise slightly, then fall back, and then watches as Joshua tries to nonchalantly place his arm on the back of Lacey's seat.

Just as Joshua's arm is close to Lacey's shoulders, she gets up to bowl.

Matthew remembers how he used to be that way with Jil!

Joshua decides to get his mind off the arm-around-the-shoulders problem and asks, "Do you think we'll get more work soon?"

"I just got a job from that kid over there." Matthew points to a six-year-old who is tripping over his shoelaces as he bowls.

"Probably not one of our bigger jobs," Joshua guesses. "We're not going to get rich from that one."

Matthew laughs. "Actually, he wants a card made for his older sister, one of Amanda's friends. He wants it to say EAT POOP AND DIE."

"Matthew." Jil! makes a face.

"I told him we would do it for ten cents. That's all he could afford. I figure younger brothers have to stick up for each other against older sisters."

"I'm an older sister with a younger brother," Jil! reminds him.

Matthew chooses to ignore her statement. "Every penny adds up."

"It will cost more than ten cents to make." Jil! sighs and then says, "Oh, well."

Lacey returns and sits down.

Joshua manages to put his arm around her shoulder.

"Your turn, Joshua," Tyler calls out.

As Joshua gets up, he moves his arm, catching his wristwatch in Lacey's hair. Both of them look like they are going to die, especially since everyone else starts laughing.

Finally Jil! helps liberate the watch.

As Josh goes up to bowl, he can be heard mumbling, "Okay, Earth. Just swallow me up right now. Do your worst."

"He's just so cute." Lacey pats her hair back into place.

Joshua bowls a strike and comes back to sit down feeling a million times better.

Jil! says, "Business meeting in four days. On Friday."

"So soon?" Matthew hates business meetings because Jil! always wants to talk about things like budgets, costs, and effective use of time.

"So soon." Jil! hands him a piece of her candy bar.

"Oh, okay. Until then we can just have fun?" Matthew pops the piece of candy into his mouth, quickly swallows it, and then sticks a chocolate tongue out at her.

"Until then we can just have fun." She relents.

Matthew grins at her and hopes that by Friday she will forget about the meeting. Somehow he knows that isn't going to happen.

Chapter 15

"Matthew Martin. Joshua Jackson." Jil! stamps her foot. "I want the two of you to stop playing that computer game right now."

Staring intently at the screen, Matthew says, "Just a few more minutes."

"You said that a half an hour ago." Jil! holds up some papers. "We have to hold a business meeting and discuss what we've done, what we still have to do, and how to get more business."

Matthew, who likes the creating part of the business but hates the details, keeps staring at the screen. "Rats. You made me miss."

"Finally." Joshua takes over the controls. "I thought I was never going to get another turn."

"Rats. You made me miss," Matthew repeats. "And I was sooo close to beating my own record."

"What a pity," Jil! says sarcastically. "Just because you've made almost enough to reach your goal doesn't mean that it's time to quit. We still have a lot of orders to fill and I think we should get more business. Just think of all the things we can buy and not have to beg our parents for money . . . and anyway, I think doing this has been very exciting."

"Kaboom," Joshua yells. ''I just got blown away."

"My turn." Matthew takes over the controls again.

Jil! stares at the two boys and then starts mumbling, "I'm so glad that we had this little conversation. It's such a joy to be in charge of the organizational part of our business, especially when there is so much co-operation. Well, never mind about me. I'll just go sit in the other room and see what is on television and maybe bite my nails down to nothingness, while I await your presence at the meeting. Or maybe I should just sit and listen to my ulcer develop when I think of how I'm going to have to explain to our customers why their orders are not ready."

Matthew and Joshua continue to play the computer game as Jil! goes into the living room.

Finding the remote-control device, she throws herself down on the sofa and aims the control at the TV. "Zap. Take that."

The TV switches on to the station that Mr and Mrs Martin watch the most, the public television channel.

Jil! gets ready to change it until she notices a little girl on it, one with blond braids and blue eyes, who looks just like her cousin.

Looking closely, she quickly realizes that it is not her cousin but stays tuned anyway.

The announcer is talking about how the little girl's family lives at the poverty level.

Jil! is positive that she's not her cousin, since her

aunt and uncle have a lot of money.

Matthew walks in and sits down next to Jil!. "I quit the game. I wasn't even losing. I'm sorry that I was such a doofus. I know we should be working. Joshua is still playing the game, but only until we make up and then he'll come in and join us."

"Shhhhh." Jil! puts her hand on his arm. "I want to listen to this show. It's so sad."

Matthew keeps quiet, knowing how Jil! is always interested in sad things. He remembers how every book report she did in fifth grade was about someone who was sick, dying, or dead. He remembers how in sixth grade she would get really upset when Mrs Stanton would talk to them about some of the problems in the world.

Sometimes it amazes him that someone who is as "up" as Jil! usually is can also get so "down".

Rather than get Jil! mad at him again, he sits quietly, listening to the show.

The interviewer is talking to the little girl's mother, who is crying as she explains how hard it is to have a two-year-old and to run out of milk four days before she has enough money to buy more, about how hard it is to explain to the older children that they have to ration food.

"Is this some other country?" Matthew whispers to Jil!

She shakes her head no.

Matthew thinks about the cartons of milk in his refrigerator and wishes that there were a way to mail some of them to the family.

Jil! starts to make little sniffling sounds.

Matthew puts his arm around her.

Jil! puts her head on his shoulder.

For a minute Matthew thinks about Elementary Lips but realizes that this would be really the wrong time.

Just sitting that way with Jil! makes him feel a little better, even though he still feels very bad about what is being said on television.

The interviewer is now talking to the family's doctor, who says, "When I think about poverty, it has a face. I think of this little girl and of all the people who go to bed hungry and often without shelter."

The show ends.

Matthew takes the remote control out of Jil!'s hand and turns off the television.

They just sit there quietly, staring at the television screen, even though the set has been turned off.

Kissing the hair on the top of Jil!'s head, Matthew says, "I wish we hadn't watched that."

She sighs. "Even if we hadn't watched it, she still wouldn't have enough food."

Joshua can be heard yelling out in the hall. "Okay, you guys. I'm getting ready to join you in the TV room. I'll be there in just a minute. Okay, you guys."

Loud clomping sounds can be heard in the hallway.

"I'm almost there," Joshua yells. "I'm going to count to one hundred and then I'm coming into the room."

Jil! looks at Matthew. "Exactly what does he think we're doing in here?"

"I told him that I was just coming in here to talk to you, to apologize." Matthew grins at her.

From the hallway Joshua can be heard. "Eighty-seven, eighty-six, eighty-five, eighty-four . . ."

Looking at each other, Jil! and Matthew start to laugh.

"Since he and Lacey have started going out," Matthew explains, "Joshua has developed a very active imagination."

"Seventy-nine, seventy-eight, seventy-seven . . ."

More sounds of clomping right outside the door can be heard.

"Should we just put him out of his misery, tell him to come right in and start the meeting?" Jil! wipes the tears off her face and looks at Matthew.

"Sixty-five, sixty-four, sixty-three and a half . . sixty-two . . ."

"We have a whole minute left." Matthew whispers something in Jil!'s ear.

"Sixty, fifty, forty, thirty, twenty . . . It's getting very boring waiting out here. Get ready," Joshua yells out.

"Ready or not here I come."

As Joshua walks into the TV room, a sofa cushion held by Matthew attacks him on the left.

A sofa cushion held by Jil! hits him on the right.

Within a few seconds it is Elementary Pillow Fight.

And everyone is getting an A+.

Chapter 16

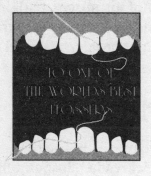

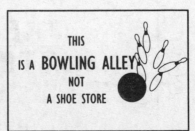

PET  WALKING

CALL: PABLO MARTINEZ 908 555-7643

BRIAN BRUNO'S ROOM

KEEP OUT

(THIS MEANS YOU ESPECIALLY FRITZI!!!!!!)

SORRY YOUR
FAVORITE SOAP OPERA CHARACTER
DIED

SO... YOU'VE FINALLY LEARNED TO PROGRAM YOUR V.C.R...

WELCOME HOME

IMA CARD, INK!

JIL! HUDSON
555-9763
LETTERHEADS, CARDS, SIGNS, BANNERS, MENUS
INVITATIONS

DEAR FAMILY :
☐ I LOVE CAMP.
☐ THE FOOD IS GREAT.
☐ THE FOOD IS VOMITUS.
☐ I LOVE MY BROTHER.
☐ SEND MONEY.
☐ I'M GOING TO BECOME A STAR.
☐ I PROMISE TO WRITE MORE OFTEN.
☐ I MISS MY FAMILY.
☐ I'M BEING GOOD.
☐ I'M BEING BAD.

Love,
Amanda

CALIFON
THE BOARD GAME

"Ima Card, Ink is doing very well," Jil! reports. "Let's go over each of these items individually so that we can learn from what we've done."

Looking at each other, Matthew and Joshua think about how they were hoping that Jil! would just split the profits three ways.

"Dr Warren really liked his flossing cards." Jil! pastes the card into their business scrapbook. "He didn't order a lot of them because he says that there are so few good flossers in the world. I suggested that he order cards that say WORK HARD ON BEING A GOOD FLOSSER. That way he'll need a lot more cards."

Matthew raises his hand.

"It's summer. You don't have to do that," Joshua reminds him.

"I have an idea." Jumping up and down, Matthew continues to wave his hand. "How about cards that say MY FLOSSOPHY OF LIFE IS TO TAKE CARE OF MY TEETH."

Joshua groans, but says, "Good idea."

Jil! agrees, writing it down in a special notebook. "Mrs Levy really liked her business card. And that's no bull."

Matthew just grins.

"Mr Allen was very pleased with the card for his wife. I don't think that it's a design we'll be able to use much. After all, how many people in Califon go on *Wheel of Fortune*?" Jil! pastes the next card into the scrapbook.

484

"And come in second?" Matthew sticks a cupcake into his mouth.

Jil! holds up the FREE KITTENS banner. "We have to discuss this item. It seemed pretty clear to me what it meant and we printed it the way that Mrs Axelrod asked us to do. I don't think we should be blamed for what happened."

Matthew speaks with cupcake in his mouth. "How were we to know that Fritzi Bruno would take the kittens out of the box and set them loose around the neighbourhood? That she thought that 'Free Kittens' meant 'let them loose'?"

Joshua takes a cupcake and balances it on his nose. "It's a good thing that we found them all and put them back in the box before they got hurt."

"Brian was so embarrassed." Matthew laughs, spraying cupcake crumbs. "Can you imagine having a sister like Fritzi? She probably thinks SAVE THE WHALES means putting them in a bank."

"If she lived in England," Jil!, who loves to read about royalty, adds, "and if spelled the way that you do, Matthew, she'd probably think that it was SAVE THE WALES and decide it had something to do with the royal family."

"Just how dumb do you think I am?" Matthew pretends to pull a knife out of his heart. "How come you're always picking on me? My spelling has improved."

"Is that why you messed up Pablo's pet-walking sign, spelling *gerbils* with an *e*?"

"There *is* an *e* in gerbils." Matthew pretends to wipe the blood off the imaginary knife.

"One *e*, not two." Jil! holds her hand out to take away the imaginary knife.

Matthew carefully hands it to her. "So no one is perfect."

Jil! locks the imaginary knife in an imaginary safe.

"You two are crazy. You two deserve each other." Joshua laughs.

Jil! continues, "That job cost us money. We had to reprint them for no extra charge. Matthew, just let me check the work before you do it. You know that's the arrangement we worked out."

"It seemed so easy and you had to spend the day baby-sitting for your little brother and helping your mother out. So I thought I could handle it myself. I showed it to him before I printed it up, so it's not totally my fault. And anyway, maybe Pablo wants to walk gerbels, not gerbils." Matthew shrugs. "Or maybe Mrs Levy has gerBULLS for him to walk."

"I think that you've got to give in on this one," Joshua tells his best friend.

Matthew sighs, but relents. "Oh, okay."

"Now, the rest of the cards and banners went well. No problem with them," Jil! continues. "I can't believe Mrs Arden made that VCR card for her husband because it took him four years to learn to record programmes."

"My mother's never learned. No matter what station and time she puts in, she ends up recording the four A.M. show on channel seven," Joshua tells them.

"My parents were really happy with the cards we made to send Amanda to fill in, since she's written only one letter since she's left for camp. They didn't love all of my additions but said that since we didn't charge them for that work or the stuff for Mom's store, they wouldn't charge us for the use of the machine or their supplies that we've used."

"A good deal." Jil! nods.

"And the Califon Conservancy members like our board game. They're going to sell it at Christmastime and use the money to continue to help pay off the debt for the recreation land." Jil! holds up the game. "So we didn't make a profit on it but we do have our name on the acknowledgments page."

"That's really going to help me pay for my skateboard and my big date with Lacey." Joshua makes a face.

"Where are you planning to take her? To Hawaii?" Matthew does the hula.

"There's this concert we want to go to at Garden State Centre before Lacey has to go back home, My parents say we can go only if we go with my sister and her boyfriend, and my sister and her boyfriend say they'll take us only if I buy their tickets. That's four tickets." Joshua takes a bite out of a cupcake. "It's not fair, but we really want to go to the concert and Lacey doesn't want to ask her aunt for any more money."

"Bummer." Matthew licks the icing off his third cupcake.

Jil! looks into the book where she keeps track of the

money. "With the way profits are going and with the jobs that we've got planned, you should have enough money for the concert in the next two weeks."

Matthew does some figuring in his head, using brain cells that he'd planned to rest over the summer vacation.

He realizes that with the money he's earning from Ima Card, Ink, the small amount of money he has managed to save from his reduced pocket money, and the money he has earned from odd jobs, he should be able to buy the computer program in two weeks.

Fourteen days — and computer store . . . here comes Matthew Martin.

Chapter 17

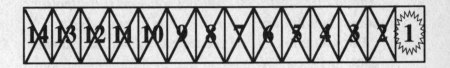

Today's the day, Matthew thinks, crossing off the last number.

Sitting on his bed, he puts the final change into coin roll packets. He counts it all up and looks on his bed at the bills, some wrinkled, some perfectly smooth, new and crisp. There are rolls of coins, all neatly sorted out — pennies, nickels, dimes, quarters — and they add up to enough money to buy the computer program, finally.

Matthew thinks about how long it took to get the money, about how many lawns were mowed, how many errands run, about the time he baby-sat for the Levys and about all of the computer work that was done.

"Way to go!" Matthew says to himself, realizing that he has enough money left over to pay back his debt to his parents and can go back to getting his normal pocket money.

There's a knock on the door and his father walks into the room. "Ready, son?"

Matthew points to all of the money on the bed. "Ready. There's enough here for the program and what I owe you."

Mr Martin smiles. "I can feel a *Leave It to Beaver* moment coming on."

Matthew thinks of all the repeats of the old shows that he has seen. "You mean one of the times when Ward Cleaver, the father, says to Beaver Cleaver, the son, 'Boy, I'm proud of you'?"

Nodding, Mr Martin comes over and sits on the bed next to Matthew. "Yes. One of those moments."

Father and son smile at each other for a few minutes without saying a word, and then Mr Martin speaks. "Let's make this a Martin family moment. Matthew — seriously, your mother and I are very proud of you. You worked hard. We've noticed that you're not wasting money the way you used to . . . although I have noticed that you haven't turned into a miser."

"I really needed to own this year's anthology of award-winning science fiction" — Matthew continues to smile — "even though it was kind of expensive."

"Your mother and I don't think of book buying as a luxury, but as a living expense. So that was fine, especially if you let me borrow it after you're done."

For a second Matthew thinks about charging him
rent for the book but decides against it. "Sure. I'll loan
it to you."

Mr Martin ruffles his son's hair.

"Please don't do that." Matthew pats his hair back
down again. "That drives me crazy. By the way, I also
spent some money on junk food."

"Oh, please. Oh, please." Mr Martin puts his hands
together in a begging gesture.

"Oh, please. Oh, please, oh, what?" Matthew is
very sure of what his father is going to ask for.

"Oh, please. Oh, please. Can't I ruffle your hair one
more time?"

That's not what Matthew thought his father was
begging for.

"And, oh, please. Oh, please. Share the junk food
with your dear old dad." Mr Martin looks like a
puppy begging for a treat.

Matthew stares at his father, laughs, and lowers his
head for one more hair rumpling. "Oh, okay. We have
Oreo cookies and Circus peanuts."

"Those Circus peanuts are disgusting." Mr Martin
licks his lips. "I love them."

Matthew goes over to his closet and pulls out the
hidden stash of junk food, bringing it over to the bed.

As they alternate between mushing up the marshmallow Circus peanuts with their fingers and then
eating them and pulling apart the Oreo cookies, eating
the cream first and then the chocolate wafers, Matthew
and his father collect all of the money and put it into a

bag that Mr Martin will take to the bank tomorrow.

"Are you guys ready?" Mrs Martin calls from downstairs.

"In a minute," they yell in unison.

Matthew hides the junk food back in the closet while his father puts the cash away.

Meeting in the hall in a few minutes, they vow not to tell Mrs Martin about their junk food consumption.

Trying to look totally innocent, they go downstairs.

Mrs Martin is waiting for them in the hallway.

She takes one look at their faces, which have remnants of cookie crumbs on them, and sighs.

Mr Martin puts his arm around her waist and starts to kiss her.

She backs away and wags her finger at him. "Lips that . . ."

All three say at the same time, ". . . touch sugar will never touch mine."

Mr and Mrs Martin then kiss each other.

Matthew watches and says, "Is this the way to be a proper role model for your favourite son? Saying one thing and doing another?"

"Forgiveness is a good trait to learn." Mr Martin grins.

"Did you also eat Circus peanuts?" Mrs Martin makes a face, wiping her mouth.

Both of the Martin males hang their heads in mock shame.

"You two are impossible." Mrs Martin looks at them. "Oh, well, let's get going."

They all pile into the family estate car.

Matthew and Mr Martin sing the theme songs from every television show that they remember.

By the time they get to the store, Mrs Martin is complaining of a gigantic headache because of the singing.

Matthew and Mr Martin know that she's kidding and sing her every aspirin commercial song that they can think of.

"I only hope that you two can behave yourselves," Mrs Martin says as they walk into the store.

They go up to the counter.

Mr Martin takes out his chequebook, having decided earlier not to make the sales clerk deal with all of the change and bills that Matthew has earned.

Matthew tells the sales clerk the name of the program that he wants.

The sales clerk pulls one off the shelf and tells them the price.

The program has gone on sale and is eighty dollars less than the original price.

"If only I'd known," Matthew says, ''we could have already been using the program to make some of the stuff."

The salesman says, "Why don't you buy another piece of computer equipment or another program with your savings? We have other great bargains."

Matthew looks around.

There are so many things he would like to have.

All of this extra money . . . what he earned . . . the money his parents promised him.

He looks over at the television section and sees that one of the sets is playing a repeat of the public television program that he and Jil! had seen. He can see the same little girl, the one who has to go without milk.

Matthew turns to his parents. "Look. I want to donate the rest of the money to charity, to help other kids."

"You don't want another computer program?" the sales clerk asks.

Matthew looks over at him and wants to say, *Doofus, of course I want another computer program. I just want to do this more.*

Instead he repeats, "I want to donate the money."

Both of the Martin parents smile at their son.

While Mr Martin writes the cheque Mrs Martin comes over to Matthew and says, "Matthew, sometimes, once in a while, I can see the kind of man you are growing into—and I know that I'm going to love that grown-up very much. I want you to know how much I love the boy that you now are. I'm very proud of you."

Mr Martin walks over, carrying the package.

"And I am too."

Matthew is very happy that his parents are starting to see that he's growing up, that they are accepting that fact. He's also very happy they are in such a good mood, because there's something that he wants to discuss with them. "Can we go to the ice cream store and try out three of their new flavours?"

He gives them his you-just-said-I'm-wonderful look

followed by the now-how-about-a-little-reward look.

"Some things never change," says Mrs Martin with a sigh as they walk out.

"And some do." Matthew takes the package containing the computer program he has earned. "And some do."

Heading to the ice-cream store, he feels like a pioneer, going in a new direction.

"Wagons ho!" he yells.

And Matthew Martin leads the way.